StarFire

MIKE LEE

BREAKWATER HARBOR BOOKS, INC.

Scott J. Toney and Cara Goldthorpe, Founders
www.breakwaterharborbooks.weebly.com

Cover Art by Angelina Onofrio. Special thanks to her for her fine work. Angelina is a true pleasure to work with, and I recommend her to all my author friends for cover art (and other art, as well.) She can be contacted at artbyangelina.onofrio@gmail.com.

Book file and cover produced by Jeff Ludwig | Editing, Writing. Special thanks also to him for his fine work in the production process. I highly recommend him for services ranging from production to formatting to editing. He can be reached at jeffrey.ludwig76@gmail.com or at http://jeffludwig.wordpress.com.

Special thanks to Gerry RingErickson for his help with corrections to the final copy of the manuscript.

With great thanks to Phil Trimble and John Trimble, whose patient endurance of my worst ideas, and generous contributions of their good ideas, thoughts, and observations, not to mention encouragement, are appreciated beyond expression. Without them, nothing I write would turn out as good, or be as fun to produce.

THANKS, BROTHERS.

StarFire

PROLOGUE

I have always found ships to be majestic things. As a boy, while my father moved us around the galaxy, I would marvel at the most modest of the spacefaring ships, whatever I could see from any window lining the dock concourses of any port we were on. I suppose it has been much the same way with boys and ships, even from the time ships were sail-driven across the oceans of Old Earth. Then-- as now, I'm sure-- the boys who grew up in awe of ships became the men who sailed on them to new worlds. But the men who built those ships to cross oceans could never have imagined what I had seen, that day, standing at the docks of my duty station.

I watched, completely dumbstruck, as Alliance Military Ship *StarFire* came in, a truly awesome thing to behold. In just volume and mass, she more than equaled any fabricated space station I had ever visited. She carried a battle complement in excess of 3,000 sailors and marines. Fully 2,100 of those were combat-skill personnel, with weapons and combat-related primary posts. More than a battleship, she was a planet-killer and a fleet-destroyer, without equal in the known universe. The pride of the Alliance Fleet, and the first of three Star-class battleships already contracted for, she showed us the future, the direction the Alliance Navy had chosen. And this base, my duty station, became her first port of call outside the Galactic Core. A lot of us had turned out to watch her come in.

In space there's often not a lot to lend perspective to what you see. *StarFire* actually maintained a very high approach velocity, but her size made her appear to be much closer than she actually was. As a result, she seemed to move at a snail's pace. Most of us watched her all the way in, anyway. That sort of spectacle gave a man a sense of pride, of belonging to something big, something significant. As she came closer, that feeling grew as the perception of her size grew, until she approached close enough that the true scope of her mass dwarfed everything else in sight. It felt like watching a moon drifting slowly in on a collision course.

Amazed, and exhilarated, and finally humbled, I asked myself, who knew we could even build such a thing? Who could conceive of a ship like this? What could stand against a weapon of this magnitude? I couldn't have imagined her, before that day when I first saw her, coming in to dock at the space defense station, and she stood as a testament to the things we, as a race, were beginning to comprehend we could do.

I shook my head, sitting on the edge of my bunk. It was a nice memory, but that's all it was. *StarFire* had come to represent something entirely different, in retrospect. Just a few weeks after that first sight of her, it seemed she had changed the course of my career, and consequently my whole life. Now, if I couldn't be with my men, doing my job, I just wished I could be out at the docks, watching the ships come in and go out. But that wasn't in the cards. Not for me. I couldn't even leave this room; the guards standing outside the door wouldn't allow it. So I gave up that line of thought, and turned my mind instead, to the events just after the ship's brief visit, the circumstances that tied my own future to the fate of AMS *StarFire*.

CHAPTER 1

Defense Space Station G-13, 246.163.12

After Action

My new room sat far from the bustle of station business, and remote from the workshops and power plant. Entirely empty, with no one yet assigned to this block of Navy officer's quarters, there was no traffic in this wing of rooms, except what was necessary to deal with me, and there was little enough of that. The result was dead silence in there, most of the time. But just now, I could hear the tramp of feet, still distant, but coming down the long corridor. Since I had been confined to quarters, with two men posted outside, my habit was to leave the door fully open all the time, even when I slept. It was symbolic defiance, like saying, "It's just convention that keeps me here; you two sentries don't matter in the slightest. I don't even notice you." And, I suppose, it was true enough. I wouldn't have ventured out, anyway. Given orders to stay confined, I was my own jailer. Much more so than those two outside were, anyway. Likewise, I refused to give any indication that the activity outside my room interested me. I sat in my only chair, and had been reading, before the noise distracted me. Now, without shifting my position in the least, my attention followed the sound of the steps approaching.

I immediately realized there were more feet than the usual changing of the guard, the times when a fresh pair of sentries came to relieve the two jailers outside already. Now, as the sound of steps came closer, I picked out a different pitch and rhythm belonging to one of those pairs of feet. It was the click-click of smaller, dressier shoes, instead of the tramping of duty boots, and a faster rhythm, denoting shorter steps. That was interesting, and my eyes flicked up from my reading almost of their own accord, though I prevented my head from popping up, at least. I had a good view of the corridor, from where I sat, just by raising my eyes minimally.

I could see four men, two of them carrying objects, and they were accompanied by a woman. She was someone new, and I looked her over at some thirty yards distance, the length of my room (less than ten feet) plus the length of the hallway (probably a bit less than thirty yards.) Tallish, I thought, though it was hard to say, as she was walking next to sizeable men escorting her. They were large enough that, her business-like stride notwithstanding, she still took three steps to their two. As insulting as it was to have guards, I took it as a compliment that they always assigned big men to watch me, though it probably had less to do with me, personally, than with the reputation G-Marines in general enjoyed. I brought my attention back to the woman.

I took in her uniform at a glance, while they were still some way down the hall, looking for an indication as to her purpose here. Service uniforms varied slightly, according to rank and duties. This woman was in Alliance Navy office whites, the style marking her as an officer. She had a briefcase and no sidearm in evidence, which told me she wasn't from Military Police, but nothing else. A clerk, perhaps, come to fit me for a prison uniform? Or a mental health worker, assigned to assess me for any tendency towards suicide? I couldn't guess, so I gave up trying and waited, still looking her over.

She looked to be attractive, as she got closer. A slender, athletic figure, and dark hair piled up on her head, it was nice contrast with the whites she wore, in the glare of the harsh station lighting. I noted that she moved gracefully, with unconscious, feminine ease, but her expression and manner said, "All business." I wondered again what she wanted, as her shoes tap-tapped on the floor, towards my door. I forced myself back to my reading, part of my image of sanguine confidence, and my pretense that if the military wanted to give me some time off, I would happily use it for rest and recuperation. I would not give her, whoever she was, the satisfaction of staring at her all the way down the hall as she approached.

When they arrived, my guards exchanged places with their replacements, and my female visitor rapped on the door jam, inviting me to recognize that I had company. I couldn't reasonably pretend I hadn't noticed her any longer, and I looked back up at her.

"Captain Vince Lombard?" From long habit, I glanced immediately at her collar insignia, determining her rank, and then ignored her question. This block of officer's quarters was entirely empty, except for me. It wasn't like she had to pick me out of a lineup, and therefore, it wasn't really a question. At least, not a sensible question. And I knew I wouldn't need to come to attention if she barked at me, because I outranked her slightly, so I just waited. Anyway, she didn't bark, and I didn't move, and in a moment, she went on.

"I'm Lieutenant Linda Tillman." That was a touch informal, so she wasn't reporting to me, just introducing herself before getting on with whatever job they had sent her to do. She was a naval lieutenant, junior grade, equal to a Marine Corps first lieutenant. Just one rank below my own. Close up, I could see she was indeed a looker, the kind that worked pretty hard to minimize their appearance, at least on duty, or they would never get anything done for all the interruptions any men in the vicinity would be making, trying their luck with her. A dark brunette, with big brown eyes, and skin hinting just enough olive tone to show that, on a beach, she probably tanned before she burned. And the kind of figure that probably made even hydrophobic men want to visit a beach she might be vacationing on.

She had not entered my room yet, but still stood in the doorway. And she hadn't asked me a question, so I held my peace and continued to look at her, just composing my expression as best I could to suggest I was indifferently silent, as opposed to resentfully silent. It was a little petty, perhaps, but Navy was responsible for putting me here, and I wasn't feeling particularly friendly towards any of them, at the moment. So I tried to look calm, instead of sullen, and waited for her to get uncomfortable enough to speak again. It didn't take long.

"I'm here to interview you about your recent mission."

I considered revising my earlier estimate of "all business" to "slow learner," since she still hadn't said anything that actually required a response from me. I suppose she expected me to make some gesture to make her feel welcome, since that's what most men probably did. I went this far: I raised my left eyebrow a millimeter, just to show I was listening. A moment passed before she caught on that that was all she was getting.

"Well, then." She turned and gestured to the pair of men carrying what turned out to be furniture; a simple folding chair, and a small folding desk, like a school desk. They stepped in and set up the furniture quickly, efficiently, each of them keeping one wary eye on me as best they could, and then they stepped back out into the hallway. After that, my previous guards and the two men carrying the furniture left, while my replacement guards took up their posts outside the doorway.

These quarters were actually much nicer than my own, and larger. Because I was being held on Navy orders, in the as-yet still empty section of the Naval Officer's block, I suspected someone had screwed up and assigned me quarters as if my captain's rank was Naval, as well. That would be the equivalent of a colonel, in the Marines. In my own regular quarters, over in the G-Marine Corps sector of the base, I would have had to join her outside my room in the hallway to have a business-like conversation. Here, there was room for the extra furniture, but not much more. The desk had to be set up facing the wall, and Lt. Tillman had to sit so that if she was using the desk she was sideways to me, but if she turned to face me we were almost knee-to-knee. As she sat down, a trace of her fragrance wafted over to me, and I allowed myself a moment to enjoy all the smells she had brought with her: soap, women's shampoo, a touch of perfume and, I'm sure, the unconscious awareness of female pheromones her athletic body and woman's skin were producing, because in spite of myself I found I was looking at her as a woman, rather than as the enemy she surely represented. I actually wished she had been the mental health worker, now that I knew what she was here for. But she clarified that for me, in case I didn't already get it.

"Captain, I'm an investigator, and I've been assigned to depose you prior to the inquiry into the loss of the *StarFire,* and incidents leading up to that-"

I interrupted her right there. "So, they've decided on a formal inquiry, then?"

She didn't look at me as she spoke, keeping her eyes on the desk where she was organizing her things. "That is my understanding, yes. I'm looking forward to gaining a full understanding of the situation, and making a full and fair report." Now she met my gaze, and tried a polite little smile, a sort of, "Come on, I'm just here to help you," kind of smile. I didn't smile back, but I didn't snarl, either. I didn't need another Navy stiff after my scalp, so I tried to decline, politely.

"Lieutenant, I've made my report, in full, and in writing. Two days ago. I have nothing to add."

Her coy smile faded to match my impersonal, poker face.

"Yes, I've read that report, Captain. It starts with you receiving orders to proceed to sector G-14, after you were already shipped-out, and moving in that direction. We both know the story begins somewhere before that." She paused there, reading my resistance. "Captain, a Board of Inquiry has already been formed. We have very little time until that board is formally convened. This incident you were involved in involves the loss of a major military asset, and whatever happens, you won't avoid that inquiry. If the board goes badly for you, you face a full court-martial. I've seen the paperwork, and I can tell you, a charge of treason has been mentioned, and I think it's very possible the prosecution will pursue that charge." She paused, taking my measure again, and then took another run at me.

"This is your chance to get anything else into the record, anything not in your previous report, anything that might justify your actions. You can bring up whatever you like in this interview, make explanations, give full and complete answers to questions without being cut off in mid-answer. Everything you say to me will go into the official record, and all the officers on the board will have it before them. But it won't be like that when you are before the board, yourself. There, you will only give direct answers to questions, and only to the extent that you are instructed. Your answers will be limited to exactly whatever questions are asked of you." Now she cocked her head, like a teacher leading a particularly slow student through a difficult lesson. "I'm not the bad guy, here, Captain. I'm just an investigator, and my job is to get a complete picture of what happened. A smart man might cooperate, and make the best of it. Don't you think?"

I took a deep breath, let it out as a sigh, and settled into my chair a little.

"Alright, Ms. Tillman. What would you like to ask me?" Using "Ms." instead of "Lieutenant" was a way of keeping things businesslike, a slight touch more formal than the way this lieutenant was speaking to me. The last thing I needed was to let my guard down for this, I was sure. But she was right, I needed to make the best of this opportunity to put my story on the record in full, and address anything my written report left open for interpretation. I wanted her to drive the conversation, though. I thought her questions might let me in, a little, on what the brass was thinking. She was Navy, and her bosses, who sent her, were Navy. She could, and almost certainly would, be telling me quite a bit, if I paid attention, just by nature of the questions she thought were important.

"For starters, Captain Lombard, perhaps you will tell me why you were picked for this assignment."

I looked away from her for just a moment, thinking back to the days before it all started. But I looked back and made eye-contact before I made my answer.

"Oh, I think it was just routine procedure. Luck of the draw, really. Could have been anybody, but my company was available." That wasn't, strictly speaking, the whole truth, but it would serve. I knew exactly why the assignment had fallen to me, but I couldn't think of anything I could gain by telling that part of the story.

It didn't matter. I didn't fool her.

"Come, now, Captain. I've reviewed your records. You've shown a particular talent for boarding actions, haven't you?"

I realized then that this would be more than just going over my report, fleshing out my statement. Lt. Tillman had an agenda.

CHAPTER 2

Military Transport/Lander 246.163.12-08

Prior to Action

A combat boarding action against a hostile spacecraft in motion is a complicated maneuver. There are maybe a couple thousand variables that all have to be accounted for when the order to board comes over the coms. Fortunately, flight computers take care of maybe half of those. High Command decisions and combat doctrine, combined with rigorous training, take up the slack on a few hundred more. Subordinates and specialists share the load, too, lightening the remaining burden, but I figure the commanding officer on the scene is left with a few dozen critical decisions, which doesn't sound so bad—until you're the commanding officer in question, the one making those decisions. That was my job.

The Corps had a specialized craft for boarding actions, called a "transport/lander." These small vessels, fast and handy for all their ungainly appearance, served the purpose of ferrying Marines into battle in any circumstance, landing them on planets, asteroids, space stations, and on hostile spacecraft, whether stationary or in motion. Transport/landers were boxy-looking craft, with a small forward cockpit ahead of a larger main cabin where the troops were contained, one full platoon of fifty men, and a couple of officers or senior sergeants, plus a detachable equipment and supplies container to the rear of the main cabin, snugged in between the main thrusters.

Obviously, enemies are generally unlikely to open the main hatch and let hostile Marines inside, so the preferred method of effecting entry to a hostile ship involves using the primary thrusters of the transport/lander to burn a hole in the hull of the target while on approach. That necessitates approaching a hostile ship backwards: butt-first, so to speak. Once the transport/lander is locked-down on her hull, the men on board exit through the equipment container at the rear. They enter the container by means of the cabin-side hatch, and exit through the aft exterior hatch, literally jumping straight out of one ship and into the other, through the hole that the thrusters put in the target's hull. If necessary, those two hatches and the space between them can function as an airlock, though in a combat boarding action the main cabin is always simply depressurized. Assault teams generally don't take time for niceties like conserving air by cycling through a lock.

The transport/lander I currently occupied, with one of the platoons from the company I commanded, settled in on a rapid approach vector, streaking towards a large alien-manufactured ship, which also moved at a substantial fraction of light speed. Our craft moved a little faster, naturally, but speed--especially in space--is relative. Without the bothersome effects of atmospheric resistance, our handful of percentage point's advantage in speed might as well have been a bit better than a brisk walking pace, for all we could tell as we edged up on the target. The target ship herself appeared motionless to us, as long as she didn't change trajectory. But I could see we were closing, and I figured soon the pilot, who was calculating our intercept point, would start reporting the estimated time to contact over the com at regular intervals.

I took a quick glance around at the men. Some of them were glued to observation portals, a couple more were bent over, grabbing at their bellies, or covering their mouths, trying to hold down the motion sickness. That always seemed curious to me; we couldn't feel the motion unless we changed course or velocity. But somehow, their stomachs knew better, or their inner ears, or something. Well, the human body is amazingly adaptable, and those were all new guys. They would get used to it. My veteran marines lounged in their acceleration couches, and a couple of them seemed to be dozing.

"Four minutes to contact." The announcement over the internal com speaker didn't faze the vets, but the newbs all started looking around, and grabbing at their gear, inventorying it as if there was anything they could do about it now if they had forgotten something. They didn't know it yet, but four minutes is an eternity in this kind of operation. Still, better to get everything ready sooner than later. I turned to one of my non-coms, seated near me.

"Go ahead and open the storage access, 'Toon Simpkins."

"Yes, sir." Platoon Sergeant Steve Simpkins pulled his bulk up and out of his seat and shambled to the rear of the cabin, where he grabbed a couple privates, one veteran and one cherry, and set them to opening the cabin's rear access hatch. That's good, I thought to myself, the vet will show the cherry how to do it, and we, as a unit, will be one more infinitesimal step toward greater readiness, with another troop who knows that procedure for the next boarding action. Platoon Sgt. Simpkins will oversee and ensure they do it properly.

Now I looked over at the warrant officer seated at the weapons console. His bent over posture put his eyes almost right on top of his screens, and I couldn't see his face. He was 'lander crew, not one of my men, and since I couldn't remember his name, I leaned over and nudged him. He didn't even notice the first time, intently monitoring his screen.

"What do we know?" I asked him, when I finally got his attention.

"No pivot guns on the hull. But no specs on internal conditions. I've never seen this model before, and the database they gave me doesn't list it, so we got nothing on layout, either. We can get you on her easy enough, but after that, you're on your own."

"Okay. Give me a look at the outside."

The warrant officer brought up an image of the target ship, and I looked her over. Aliens built ships all kinds of crazy ways, and I was looking for clues as to what I might expect inside. The ship had bilateral symmetry, not radial, so I thought artificial gravity was likely. Radial ships often rotated, meaning centrifugal force instead of artificial gravity, and a radial ship not rotating usually meant a zero gravity assault. But artificial gravity could be turned on and off, and there was no guessing what conditions we would find, once we got in, with this kind. Could be nothing, could be up to three gee, in there. There were no ports, either, and no obvious seams from large access hatches, like for a cargo bay, nothing to give us a clue regarding the internal design of the ship.

Looking closely, I could just make out the outside edge of a massive hull-patch, just at the top of the image, along with a few other combat scars hastily repaired over the years. That large patch looked like someone had accessed the ship in that spot, sometime previously.

"Sergeant Alvin, what do you make of that patch-work, on top?"

Company Master Sergeant Alvin T. Alvin, a large black man with years of experience in all G-Marine Corps evolutions, and my right-hand man, always stayed close by my side in action. He also stayed ready to cut to the core of whatever issue came up, if I asked his opinion. He took a quick look at the screen, and then minced no words.

"Beats me, but I'd avoid it, Cap. We shouldn't have any trouble getting in through the regular hull. Who knows what that patch is made of?"

"Yeah, okay. Me, too," I agreed. I keyed the internal com to the cockpit. "Let's come in below that old patch, if you can do it, Pilot." The double-click response told me the pilot had his hands full right now, but he would get us in under the patch. A moment later, though, either he or his copilot came on the com again.

"Three minutes to touchdown."

Now the vets began to stir, and I began to give out some operational information, as each man stood at his seat, ensuring that his gear wasn't hung up on anything, then turned to the man on his left, to double-check gear for each other.

"Men, listen up. We have no internal specs at this time, on atmosphere, gravity or crew. We observe no pivot guns on the hull, so that's a plus. Stay in your squads, complete your assignments. Let's do it by the numbers, men. Sgt. Alvin, the men have their assignments?"

"Yes, sir," Alvin spoke loud enough for everyone to hear him. Of course the assignments were already made, and the men briefed; we were just reminding them to be focused on carrying those assignments out. As was customary in my company, Alvin went on to recite them. "Squad One, boarding operation security. Squad Two, secure hatches and access points to boarding zone. Squads Three and Four, deploy and prepare to advance on command, Squad Five, transport/lander security. Squads One and Two, form up to follow on, as Squads Three and Four advance. Close-combat tactics until the target is secure. Squad Four, you are first-response on casualties. This is a boarding operation, so first-aid on site, wherever they go down. Peel off two men for security, and the rest follow on. Squad Five will recover casualties after the target is secured."

I waited just a beat, to let the men concentrate on repeating their assignments to themselves one last time, and then nodded at Sgt. Alvin, and turned back to face the men. "Seal up; lock and load."

By the time I finished speaking, everybody had checked their gear, and now they started putting up their "hats," the helmet integral to the vacuum suits, and then checked their suits' seals. Then, each one turned to his left again and checked that Marine's seals. Then they all turned to the right, and did it again. Each suit had been checked by its owner and two other men before the two-minute warning. If anyone did have a seal problem, they had two minutes to get to the cockpit, which would stay pressurized when the main cabin was vented, but no one reported a problem. We were one-hundred percent go.

Now, as the two-minute mark passed, each man checked his weapon. These were standard issue sidearms only, essentially very large beam pistols, with a variety of settings regarding rate of fire, and energy level. Optically sighted, and equipped with a detachable and/or collapsible shoulder stock, they were suitable for a variety of uses. We had other weapons available, of course, for different kinds of assault actions, but the Convertible Automatic Beam Carbine was standard for boarding actions. Projectile weapons rarely see use in this sort of scenario. The steel and durasteel construction of spacecraft make ricochets problematic. And no heavy weapons, either, in the tight confines of a ship, although one man in each squad did carry a series of breaching explosives for use inside the target ship. It wouldn't do to go to all this trouble just to find ourselves thwarted by a quickly sealed internal hatch.

Those breaching charges were handy, well-engineered little devices. About the size of a golf ball, each was a half-sphere of an explosive compound, a shaped charge with enough plasticity to adhere well to any irregular surface, and a small dimple in the center of the flat side, which tended to act as a suction cup for stable attachment to any smooth surface, even something wet, or slick with an oil film. Each charge also sported its own detonator mechanism, an electro-mechanical system which allowed for time-detonation, or instant detonation by means of a twenty-foot lanyard, spooled up on the device itself. Further, they could be linked with little trouble, so multiple charges could be detonated simultaneously, using those lanyards as electrical conduit. They were an excellent example of military ingenuity and design.

Four squads would deploy forward, so four men loaded with that gear meant a lot of charges. At least three times more than we would ever possibly need for this kind of target, whatever we found inside. In my company, each platoon carried a couple other non-regulation goodies, as well.

"One minute to contact," came the pilot's voice over the com. "Thrusters off, rotating now."

The transport/lander cut thrust, and a moment later vector jets fired. The ship began to turn on her beam, and in a few moments we were hurtling along bass-ackwards on the same course we had held a moment ago, closing on the target. Artificial gravity prevented us from feeling the maneuver, except for the lack of thrust when engines were cut, but a few of the new guys made the mistake of looking out the ports while the rotation took place, with predictable results.

Sergeant Alvin and I were checking our own gear, but over my vacuum suit's com I heard a couple of the cherries finally lose whatever they had in their stomachs during the maneuver, and a few of the vets commented, "At least they held it until they had their hats on." Marines aren't much on empathy. It had to be unpleasant for those men, but the helmets would vacuum away the waste and keep the suits functional, if a little less pleasant than they were a few moments ago.

"Can that chatter!" Sgt. Alvin barked over the coms, and immediately, all we heard was the final retching sounds of the cherries. "Exterior hatch detail, to your posts. Make ready to blow the aft hatch," the sergeant continued. The two-man details for both interior and exterior hatches were drawn from Squad Five, the security squad assigned to guard the transport lander. They would be the last four men off, sealing the hatches again behind them. Two men hustled through the storage compartment, out of our sight, to the exterior hatch and reported ready, while the other two, the men Simpkins had earlier set to opening the interior hatch, held posts there.

"Thirty seconds to contact," the pilot announced, sounding louder now that we heard him over suit coms, instead of the cabin speakers, and then, "Firing thrusters in . . . ten seconds. Nine . . ." As he counted down, men stepped from their seats into the aisles in between them, but braced themselves by grabbing handholds on the acceleration couches with their right hands, and put their left hands on the shoulder of the man in front of them, grabbing a loop in the suits, put there like epaulets, just for this purpose.

"Make ready for deceleration . . . Now, firing thrusters." The main thrusters rumbled, and the men, with this warning, braced themselves for some harsh deceleration. They all kept their feet, but there was a lot of bumping and staggering for a moment. Then the thrusters stopped firing, and a moment later the harsh clang and thump, signaling contact; a soft landing, by boarding standards, and no one fell down. I looked to the chief warrant officer, who had the duty of calling the doors. He studied his screen intently.

"Contact. Magnetically mated." He pinged the hull of the target ship from his control panel, as he continued reciting the checklist for boarding actions. "No return on ping- open space below us. Venting main cabin . . . Mechanical mating complete, we are locked down . . . Main cabin venting complete, opening aft hatch," he chanted. Without atmosphere the sounds of the rear hatch opening carried through the coms, and that only because one of the men stationed at the aft hatch put his helmet against the interior wall next to the hatch, because if the hatch didn't open, one of the men on the detail would have blown it open with a small charge. It wouldn't matter much; the aft hatch was actually a part of the storage compartment, and therefore replaceable, and the cabin could be re-pressurized as soon as the interior hatch was closed and sealed. But having to blow the hatch would have reflected badly on the transport/lander crew, since their job included making sure the craft was fully functional and suitable for deployment. A last "clang" indicated the hatch had fully opened.

The chief gave his final instruction, then. "Calling the doors: Aft hatch is open. Boots down, board, board, board. Thank you for flying with the Galactic Marine Corps. We hope you enjoyed your flight, and have a nice day." His wit got lost in the bustle as my men surged forward in pairs, and jumped through the rear hatch, through the hole our thrusters had burned into the target ship's hull, and into that ship itself.

* * *

Afterwards, our training report looked very good. The ship's defenders were all projected, and there were no actual personnel on board, of course. There were a few surprises, a couple of simulated booby-traps, and one of the cherries got a "kill" on a projected "enemy," which is always good for a new man's confidence. Computer projections allowed realistic, but entirely holographic defenders to pop up according to a pre-programmed pattern, to be fired upon, and even to simulate return fire. If the computer calculates a kill to the enemy, the projection slumps over and "dies," sometimes very graphically, since projections allow for as much blood and guts as is deemed useful in training. If a hit on a boarder is calculated, the computer cuts power to the man's suit, except for life support. He's electronically blind, his weapon stops firing, and he has no communication unless he overrides, say, in an actual emergency. I had heard stories that the projectors used to simulate gruesome injuries on our own soldiers, once they were deemed hit, but that some of the ranks started showing signs of post-traumatic stress after a few training missions. Eventually they discontinued that practice. Now days, orders are to lie down in place if you go blind, to simulate the kill. The computer marked us down for six casualties due to "enemy fire" before we had the ship cleared, and one more due to "friendly fire," when a cherry accidentally discharged his training weapon on a teammate after I had ordered weapons secure. That would hurt our score, and cost that man a week of some suitably onerous extra duty, a much better way to learn the lesson than dealing with the aftermath of a real friendly-fire KIA in combat. There would be enough of those, anyway, when we were really in action.

As a training exercise, it had gone well. Top marks again, in spite of the friendly-fire kill. In fact, we were doing well enough as a unit that I rapidly began to become unpopular with my fellow company commanders. At the debriefing, a few hours later, I took some good-natured ribbing from some of my colleagues, and some less than good-natured resentment from some others.

We were bunking on a transport carrier, a medium-sized ship designed to carry up to a dozen 'landers, and up to six companies, but providing supplies, repair facilities for the smaller craft, and more comfortable quarters for the men. These ships normally ferried 'landers close to the actual site of battle, especially when extended transportation times were expected, and then launched them all in one large wave when we engaged any enemy. The carrier also contained a large mess hall, a recreation and exercise deck, and a decent sized conference room, which is where I was headed now, to discuss the exercise with my peers and commanding officer. I walked through the gleaming white-painted corridor, and into the conference room. Glancing around, I saw I was the last to arrive, but that was okay, since mine had been the most recent mission. Other company commanders, as well as our own commanding officer and his staff, had all seated themselves around a large conference table. An enlisted man was pouring water into tumblers around the table, and it looked like they had been waiting a few minutes for my arrival.

"Lombard, you have a larger percentage of veterans than any other company. It's time to spread that experience around a little. Half of my men were recruits just eight weeks ago!" That remark came from Captain Ben Bowman, the company commander who had consistently earned the poorest scores on the exercises so far.

"That's enough, Captain Bowman." Colonel Rick Parsons, the base C/O, intervened. "Captain Lombard has the highest percentage of veterans because his men re-up at a higher rate than yours do. I'm not going to take his men away after he managed to retain so many of them. Turning recruits into seasoned Marines is your job, Bowman."

Colonel Parsons was the kind of C/O I liked to work for. There were no politics in his command, and he rated officers by how well they did the job, nothing else. Even more importantly, he kept Navy Fleet Command out of our hair, for the most part. He went on speaking.

"Captain Lombard, why does your team always turn in the best times? We even threw you a curve on that last exercise, and deleted the target data from the database before we tossed you in there. So, why do you still have the best times? You have an inside track on target information?"

"No sir."

"Well, what is it? Your men clear ships faster than any other company, and if it's more than just experienced Marines and non-coms, I want to know how you do it."

"Sir, it's just . . ." This was going to be difficult, but Parsons wasn't a man you screwed around with. ". . . one of my sergeants spotted it when we watched the video after the first two exercises. Look, you have the same guys programming the projected defenders for every exercise. And they're lazy, sir. They program the same kind of resistance, over and over. After the first couple, it was pretty easy to predict how they would behave, and we planned for it on subsequent exercises."

A thoughtful silence followed for a moment.

"Okay. Tell me what that program looks like."

"Yes sir. Well . . . right off, when the first projected defender pops up, if he's in a vacuum suit, then they all will be. If he's not, none of them will be. So, if that's the case, then all you have to do is breach each compartment, wait a couple of minutes, and the computer scores the defenders inside as KIA, due to vacuum. Because the pattern is, when they aren't in vacuum suits, they won't be aggressive. We don't have to clear those compartments, just have somebody stick his head in long enough to make sure the programmers haven't changed their pattern.

"Second, the programmers always concentrate the resistance around the bridge. Once we know where that is, nobody approaches it until we've organized everything else, and can make a full, planned attack. There's no benefit to hurrying, since the defenders already have their defense mapped out by the programmers, regardless of how fast we get there. That way, we start the assault with the full complement of men, and it goes faster in the end because there's always covering fire for men moving in on the objective. And, it keeps casualties down. Look at the records, and you'll see that almost all my casualties come from the final assault on the bridge in each scenario, because I haven't lost anybody clearing non-essential compartments. I'm going into the bridge-assault phase with maybe ten percent more guns on the targets than the other officers are, because of the breaching tactics we use. In a platoon-size action, that's about five more guns."

"But we've had a few runs where the defenders are very aggressive, Captain Lombard. Sounds like you are getting different exercises than we are," another company commander objected.

"Yeah, well, when the projected defenders are suited for vacuum, which they usually would be in real combat conditions, they are aggressive, every time. So, we figured out that once you breach the compartment, they're usually programmed to attack through the breach. After we see the vacsuits, we know they will come for us as soon as we breach, and we don't enter those compartments at all. We wait in the corridors and play defense, ourselves. We pop them as they come through the breach. That takes longer, but we just drop two guys behind, to pop the enemy coming out through the breach, and the others move on to the next hatch. We still get to the final shootout with more guns, and that means less time spent actually taking the bridge. You guys are getting bogged down on the bridge assault, because you have lost too many men clearing compartments. The key is when you find out if the defenders are suited or not."

Colonel Parsons looked over to one of his staff, then, and raised an eyebrow, waiting for a response. The lieutenant spoke up.

"Sir, the captain is telling you what we picked up on a week ago. So we did change up the programming, and had the projected defenders in vacuum suits, but hanging back in defensive posture on a few of the exercises. We thought it would slow them down, requiring his men to clear each compartment. After the first one, Captain Lombard still had the best time on those scenarios, too. And he averaged only three casualties on each one. That's even better than his over-all average, so we quit running that one."

"Well, yeah," I responded. "That was the easiest one. Once we saw that they were all staying put, we stopped breaching compartments, and instead just sealed the hatches. Sergeant Alvin came up with that one, making sure that our demolitions guys carried some welding tape, as well as explosives. That's the only use we have found for it, so far, but it sure is handy."

I took a breath before going on, addressing the colonel again. "Look, the point is, your programmers are lazy. Instead of programming individual defenders, they program them all the same. They are all aggressive, or they are all defensive. Once we know what we have, we adjust for it. In real combat, you would have some aggressive, some defensive, some leaders and some cowards. That's real, and you would have to find out what you are up against, one group, or even one combatant at a time. In that situation, we would have to go compartment-by-compartment and see what we have in each one. But your programmers are making it easy, because they want to save some time in programming."

I turned back to the lieutenant, then. "You want to make it a challenge? Put Sergeant Alvin in charge of your programmers for a couple of rounds. Let him tell the programmers what a crew really does when they are being boarded." I stopped and glanced around the room, noticing the sudden and complete stillness.

Four company commanders were glaring at me. I realized then that I had just suggested pitting them head-to-head against my sergeant, and that was a no-win proposition for them. If they won with good scores, big deal. They were captains, against a sergeant. But if they lost, or scored poorly . . . oh, that would chap their butts, losing to a sergeant. Which, as I thought about it, was a real possibility, putting them up against Sgt. Alvin. The colonel leaned back in his chair, considering what I had said.

"Captain Lombard, you are suggesting that Sergeant Alvin knows more about programming projection exercises than my staff does?"

"No, sir," I hedged, "I doubt Sgt. Alvin knows anything about programming in general. I'm suggesting he knows a lot about how real boarding actions go, and he knows this as a result of being involved in quite a few of them personally. Sir, Sgt. Alvin can make all of these exercises more realistic, and therefore more challenging, than a bunch of programming techs who have never seen a real boarding action. The truth is, sir, most of my good scores come from suggestions Sgt. Alvin has made, and those suggestions come from his observations about how the simulations fail to represent real crews of real ships. He's . . ." I was making too many suggestions to a superior officer, so I toned it down and fell back on formal speech. "Sgt. Alvin is a resource we should more fully exploit. Sir."

I hadn't made any friends with that idea. I mentally shrugged, a moment later, though, while the colonel thought the idea over. I didn't join up to make friends, and if Bowman or a couple of the others couldn't handle Sgt. Alvin, maybe they didn't deserve to be company commanders. Then I started wondering if I could beat the vaunted Sgt. Alvin myself.

CHAPTER 3

Defense Space Station G-13, 246.163.12

After Action

"So, I'm to understand that Sgt. Alvin was the reason for your success? He was your 'ace in the hole,' and it was his ideas that made your high scores, is that right?" Lt. Tillman was scribbling away, actually making notes on a pad, with a pen, not just typing into her com. That was why her goons had to bring a desk for her.

"Absolutely. The colonel was going to put him in charge of developing the next series of exercises, consulting with the programmers to make them more realistic, but we were recalled the next morning, before that went into effect. And my company finished the maneuvers with the best scores." I stopped talking while she caught her notes up. I wondered if she was using shorthand to write down everything I said, and wondered why she bothered to take notes, since all of this was undoubtedly being recorded anyway.

"Moving on, then . . ." Tillman looked at me for a moment, squinting her eyes as she thought through some of what I had just said, and looked for the right question to ask. "What about the last couple of days before you deployed?"

I shrugged. "What about them? We came back a little early, had some time to catch up some things, and went about our business."

Lt. Tillman dropped her gaze back to her pad, saying, "Oh, so, you had no reason to think anything unusual was going on?"

Now it was my turn to think about what I had just said, because there was something going on here. Tillman had presented me with an open expression of interest, making eye-contact, and using facial expressions that revealed her engagement in my story. That quick disengagement, looking back at her pad, and pretending to write down my non-answer, that wasn't congruent. I had a quick flashback of Sgt. Alvin, teaching me to read people at the poker table.

"There are as many ways to bluff as there are people who play poker, Cap. And any emotion or expression can be a tell, something that lets you know when a player is bluffing. The guy to watch out for is the guy who shows you the absolute least behavior at all, because the more you can see, the more likely you are to spot the tell." Lt. Tillman didn't know it, but she had been showing me too much encouragement, to get me to talk openly with her. I had been watching, and saw all I needed to. I had learned something of her style, and now I spotted the change, immediately.

"Well, Lieutenant, I didn't say that. I said we went about our business. Of course, there were rumors. And Colonel Parsons made it more clear than usual that he wanted my men ready to deploy, if necessary." I had to gauge this carefully. The message I got was that Lt. Tillman was uncomfortable because I was leaving something out, something she already knew. And if I left it out of my statement, it might be construed as evidence I was covering something up, something illegitimate. But if I was reading her right, she would open up again when I addressed that detail, whatever it was. "So, in the interests of combat-readiness, we put the men to catching up on their duties, and I put Sgt. Alvin to looking into the status of the 'landers on base and feeling out the pilots. If we were called on to deploy, I wanted to know which pilots were reliable, which were bold, and which were skittish." I watched her, but got no reaction from any of this. I took a breath and went on. "I also discussed communications with Sgt. Alvin. He had some ideas about how our own systems could be vulnerable in a way an enemy might exploit." Lt. Tillman looked up, an expression of unguarded interest plain on her face. I thought, so that's it, that's what she thinks she knows. What I couldn't figure out, though, was what she thought it meant. And that was going to be important to me, I realized, as I tried to decide what to tell her.

CHAPTER 4

Defense Space Station G-13, 246.163.12

Prior to Action

The combat-boarding exercises had taken place in a little bit of space just, by galactic standards, a short distance from our home base, Defense Station G-13, 263.143.12. The "12" designated our base as the twelfth defense station in the system located at coordinates 263.143, sector G-13. It also happened to be the last and largest defense station built in that system. Since G-13, or Gamma-13, became the most recently opened sector for exploration, this resource-rich system was slated for what the government calls, "private industrial exploitation." Planet-side development hadn't started yet because corporations are loath to invest the massive expenses necessary to begin operations until the system defenses are in place and running, but it would start soon. The military was getting comfortable, having had all the stations and systems up and running for nearly a standard year now. Soon, the Navy would move in fleet support personnel, and everything would be up to spec. No doubt, the first corporate ships were already in-bound.

Station 12 fit into the category known as, "asteroid-based" defense stations. That meant that, in addition to large guns and a lot of armor, an extra several hundred meters of rock and raw metal existed between the surface installations and the core of the asteroid, where defense headquarters were located, along with hangers for a few dozen Navy and Marine Corps craft, in areas cut out of the asteroid's belly. A fair squadron of small craft resided there, which could combine with the other larger Navy ships at the surface docks, and in space nearby. While not exactly an armada, the combined resources could be substantial.

When we got back home to the station, it didn't take long to catch the buzz going on. In no time at all, several different people sidled up to me, dishing up the most recent scuttlebutt. Rumors that *StarFire* had fallen out of contact just a few days after leaving the station were making quite a stir. Nobody knew what to make of this, but everybody knew that Fleet Command seemed very worked-up over it, and the gossip mill was working overtime.

System 264.143 sat close to the border between sectors G-13 and G-14. G-14 had not yet been explored, except for what could be seen with long-range scanning from posts already established in G-13. Vast reaches of space over there had never been looked at, or even listened to with radio telescopes. And that was where they sent *StarFire*, the first vessel to venture in more than just along the edges of G-14.

There could be any number of explanations for her silence. All kinds of weird anomalies cropped up in space, periodically, and the astrophysicists occasionally observed variations of them, often with unique and unexpected characteristics. It could be something simply interfering with communications. The quantum physics that allowed for faster-than-light communications required that how far a message had to go determined how long it took to generate the message signal. Several libraries of data could be sent in no more time than it takes to send a postcard's worth of information, so long as both messages had to travel the same distance. A message from G-14 probably took something between six and twelve hours to generate, just to reach this space station, and it didn't matter whether it was a complete report or a single word. If the ship was experiencing power fluctuations that required system shutdowns every five hours, that alone would prevent any faster-than-light signal from ever reaching us.

That sort of thing might explain *StarFire's* silence. But it could also be she had tripped over an alien race that we had not previously encountered, and perhaps even been attacked by them. It could even be she fell into a black-hole, or any of a hundred other things. Or, it could just be that a stray micro-meteor swarm took off her exterior com gear, and she couldn't talk again until she made repairs. No one knew.

And that was the crux of it. No one, including Feet Command, knew why she was silent. You might think that at interstellar distances, a day or two of no communication with a capital ship wouldn't be that big a deal, but you would think wrong. It's like this: Marines are basically "fire and forget" weapons. Command can send a unit of Marines on a mission, whether it's a squad, a company, or a whole division, and as soon as they do, there are a bunch of people working around the clock to get that mission accomplished. Under the ultimate direction of Alliance Naval Fleet Command, the Corps is essentially used to accomplish whatever jobs the Navy can't reach, isn't suited for, or doesn't want to commit a ship for.

There's a lot of that last category, because Marines are cheap, compared to the funding investment a big ship requires. The way it works out is, when a bunch of Marines are sent somewhere, they are told what to accomplish, and the means are pretty much left up to them. If they fail, or are lost in action, another bunch, or maybe two, can be sent to try again. And if we start to run low on Marines, the next batch is only a year away, because that's about how long it takes to train up a new recruit. As long as there is a plentiful population of young, healthy people to recruit from, we are never more than a year away from the next batch of Marines.

But battleships are something else entirely. They are the very definition of a finite resource. It takes about a generation just to build one, not counting the design and appropriations phases. If a battleship is sent to one place, and that turns out to be the wrong place, there may not be another battleship handy to send to the right place. Communications are critical to get that ship turned around and hustling into the proper position. There is always a certain amount of tension even in tasking a battleship to do something in peacetime, because if she is needed, she is likely to be needed in a hurry. Most of the really big ships are held in a constant state of reserve, in case they are needed worse for the next emergency than they are for whatever the current emergency is. *StarFire* had probably only been tasked on her current mission because of the need to put her out on a shakedown cruise, to familiarize the crew with the ship, and work out any bugs in the numerous new systems she came equipped with.

So, naturally, *StarFire*'s reticence, whether intentional or involuntary, had Navy apoplectic. She wasn't even just a battleship. She was the pride of the fleet, a new class of battleship, and the most significant weapon in our mobile arsenal. All that combined to make *StarFire* going silent officially a Big Deal.

* * *

Since the orders to return to base came unexpectedly, my company had nothing on its agenda immediately when we got back on the Defense Station. We had tentative orders to make ready for deployment, but that was standard stuff. It only meant that our status on the duty rosters could be listed as "deployable," whereas, while we were detached on exercises, we were listed as "not deployable." In fact, we were ready for deployment within about an hour after arriving back home.

There would necessarily be a slight gap between returning to base and the sergeants finding something for the men to do, so my Marines used up the unassigned time to see to personal equipment issues, recreation, and generally loafing around their quarters. In my book, giving the men an unexpected break now and then qualifies as a good thing, so long as it doesn't happen too often. Myself, I sat down in the company equipment hanger to play cards with my lieutenants and a couple of sergeants. Sergeant Alvin wasted no time sitting down himself, to take us to school, again, today.

Sergeant Alvin T. Alvin was the kind of man who made on impression on folks. A few years older than me, he had been a sergeant for longer than I had been in the Corps. In a service known for its rough humor and abrasive edges, he never got ribbed about his unusual name. He had the uncanny ability to communicate the dead certainty that any amount of laughter you got from broaching that particular peculiarity would not be worth the pain that came with it. Not that I had ever heard him say such a thing. So far as I knew, Sgt. Alvin had never had to actually speak to make that point clear. My explanation for that was simple: Sgt. Alvin took the talent for intimidation to a whole new level.

For all his nonverbal communication skills, I found it very difficult to read him, right then, at the card table. Sergeant Alvin had just raised my last bet substantially, and I needed to decide if he was bluffing, or really holding something in his cards. I watched his expression carefully. Sergeant Alvin just looked back at me, his impassive face exuding the same confidence it always did. I folded.

In the middle of calculating how much longer my finances could take this beating, my personal com chimed, alerting me to a message. It was a summons to the colonel's office. The message read that I should present myself there, "As soon as is convenient," which is Marine Corps code for "Why are you still reading this message instead of moving your ass?" I'm pretty sure I heard one of my lieutenants breathe a sigh of relief as I got up from the table. He must have been getting cleaned out even worse than I was, and with me gone, he wouldn't have to sit and let Sgt. Alvin take his money any longer, either. The game started breaking up. I already said Alvin had been sergeanting longer than I had been in the Corps, but I suspected he had been playing cards long before he became a sergeant. I had never seen him lose money on the card table. I headed for the colonel's office.

* * *

When I got there, I was met by a grizzled old non-com, a master sergeant who had been with the colonel for a very long time. Command Master Sergeant Bart Hastings currently served as the colonel's secretary. The colonel could have had a lieutenant for that post, and it said something about both of them that he chose to keep his old non-com buddy next to him, instead.

"Captain Lombard. Please have a seat, sir. The colonel is meeting with some naval officers, just now, but I expect he'll be free momentarily." About the time I got sat down, the office door opened and two Navy captains shuffled out. I jumped to my feet, since Navy captains are good couple of rungs higher up on the ladder from Marine Corps captains. They ignored me, and likely didn't even notice me. Colonel Parsons, though, right behind them, did.

"Captain Lombard, please come in." He turned around and went back into his office, and I followed.

Colonel Richard "Ric" Parsons, was a Marine's Marine, with close-cropped, grey hair, and his uniform fresh and crisp, even this late in the normal workday. "Have a seat, captain," he tossed over his shoulder, as he maneuvered towards his liquor cabinet. "I'm having a drink. Can I pour you one?"

This was unexpected. The last thing I wanted, at least until I knew what the colonel had summoned me for, was to dull my senses with alcohol, and especially as I met with the one man in the galaxy best positioned to crush my career with a stroke of his pen. I made the appropriate response.

"Ah . . . yes, sir. Certainly . . . whatever you are having, sir. Thank you."

I didn't want the drink, but captains don't turn colonels down. Then I remembered, the colonel had also invited me to have a seat, so I picked out a chair and sat down, both feet squarely on the floor, and my back ramrod straight, a couple inches from the back of the chair. Colonel Parsons handed me a tumbler with a couple inches of whiskey in it, and set his own down on the corner of his desk. And then, instead of moving behind the desk, as I expected, he took off his jacket and hung it up in the corner of his office. It surprised me to see he wore non-regulation suspenders under his jacket . . . which I realized, upon reflection, likely meant that I had never seen him in uniform with his jacket off before.

"Vince, this meeting is off the books, so I think we can be a little informal."

"Yes sir." It meant he could be informal, that much was clear to me.

"I suppose you have heard that *StarFire* is out of contact?"

"Yes sir. I've heard the rumors."

"Of course. Well, in the best of circumstances, that would cause some problems for us. And these aren't likely to be of best circumstances." I spent just a moment wondering just what the "best" circumstances for losing track of a battleship actually were.

"Yes sir." I wasn't contributing much to the conversation, and we had a little silence after that before the colonel went on.

"Vince, Fleet Command has sent out a couple of sloops to look for *StarFire*. Those were the captains you saw leaving a moment ago. They came to make a courtesy call, to let me know what their orders were. The orders from Fleet went directly to them through Navy channels." He meant they had bypassed him. That was a bit of a slap to Colonel Parsons. He commanded this base, and those sloops were technically under his command as long as they were stationed here. He didn't dwell on that aspect, though.

"So, Fleet is taking the most conservative approach they can . . . and I'm concerned that may leave our butts hanging out in the wind, if something bigger is going on. If something serious has happened to *StarFire*, we need to know exactly what the problem is."

"Yes sir. In case something has happened . . . like . . . ?"

"Like anything other than a simple communications problem, or an accident."

"Yes sir." Another pause ensued. Unsure what the colonel had in mind, I filled it with one of the things a Marine can always say without fear of going far wrong. "Well, we'll be ready if you call on us, sir. For anything you require."

The pause resumed, then, but the colonel didn't dismiss me, and I settled in to wait it out. It was obviously going to be more than just, "Have your men ready, we may have a job for you." He let out a long breath, then, and finally began coming to the point.

"The way I see it, there are two possibilities here. The first, obvious one, is that *StarFire* has come into contact with something bigger, something sufficiently overpowering that it handled her decisively. I don't need to tell you that anything that could handle *StarFire* so easily will be a big problem, if it comes this way. If that's the case, we need to know it, as soon as possible."

"Yes, sir. I can see that." A beat went by. "You mentioned two possibilities, sir?"

"Vince, this may be the kind of situation which ultimately hurts everyone that comes close to it. I feel we have to consider something else, too. In the absence of any other information, we have to at least consider the possibility that *StarFire* is simply choosing not to respond to Fleet communications."

I blinked at that for a moment, confused until the import of his words sunk in enough for me to make sense of them. "You mean . . . mutiny? You think-"

The colonel cut me off right there, raising his hand to stop my train of thought before I could even express it fully. "I don't think anything, yet, Vince, except that we have to be prepared for any and all possibilities. And I don't expect to hear that you have spoken that word aloud outside of this office, either."

"Yes sir."

"The point is, Vince, either of those scenarios is very dangerous for this station, and for the whole of system defense, here. *StarFire* herself is more than enough ship to chop up our defenses. Anything that could have taken her out is even worse. So, either way . . . a hostile *StarFire*, or an unknown enemy, it looks like bad news if it happens here next. I can't rely on Navy to give me a heads up about what's really going on. Not that they know either, yet, but they may have information they haven't given me. If they do, I have no confidence that they will be letting me in on it, even though it's my men and resources they are already sending out to address the issue. And that's unacceptable to me. I have a responsibility to Fleet Command, but I also have a responsibility to the men, here, on this base, and to the rest of this system."

Colonel Parsons did have a problem. The defense of this system fell to him, and in the Corps, there are no excuses. Not that he would have made any, in any event, but his concern that they were about to order him to handle something, or even worse, something might show up here that he had to handle, without the benefit of the fullest intelligence on the problem, was very real. Beginning to get the picture, finally, I took a guess.

"You want me on one of those sloops, as an observer, sir?"

Parsons waved that off. "No. I thought of sending someone, but those captains are good men. If I put an observer on board, they would have to advise Fleet Command, and who knows what Fleet would do then. That's not the answer."

"Yes sir. Then, what do you have in mind, sir?"

"Just this, Vince: If we don't have this solved fast, and I mean immediately, as soon as those sloops get on station at *StarFire*'s last known position, I'm going to need someone out there having a look. Someone I trust, and to me, that means a Marine. But I wanted to give you the heads up that there are some possibilities that could turn out to make this a very dicey mission to be associated with."

I understood now what Colonel Parsons was trying to say to me. If *StarFire* had been destroyed, by accident or design, well then, the chips had fallen where they fell, and all that remained would be simply preparing a response to whatever caused the loss of the ship. But if she had been captured, or even worse, taken over by a mutinous crew, then whatever the final outcome, it would be bad. Any actual combat with an Alliance military ship meant that losses would be real, and victories unheralded. There would be no heroes recognized for action against Alliance Navy ships, whether captured, mutinous, or whatever. It looked a lot like a no-win situation. If *StarFire* still existed, and the trouble turned out to be anything other than a space anomaly, only more trouble would come of it. I finished the drink the colonel had fixed for me, suddenly grateful to have it. But I still wasn't sure of one thing. Why had Colonel Parsons called me in for this discussion? I asked him that.

"Vince, if those sloops can't resolve whatever is going on with *StarFire*, or find out what happened to her, it's going to take someone who thinks outside the box to handle this. The kind of thing you showed me over the last week of exercises. Add that to the fact that I can afford to send a company of Marines." That made sense. If the station were attacked, the infantry Marines on this station would have essentially nothing to do until and unless the enemy actually invaded, assuming any Marines survived the bombardment that preceded it. And, as I already said, Marines are cheap, compared to any other option. Parsons went on, "I'm doing what I can to be ready for any eventuality, but timely intelligence is critical. I'm also talking to Fleet about getting some bigger ships out here, but unless they get us some support fast, you know that even if we threw everything we have here on station against *StarFire*, she would hardly feel threatened. Something big enough to take *StarFire* out probably wouldn't even notice what we could attack with, as things stand right now." Colonel Parsons leaned back in his chair. "And, I don't mind telling you, Fleet isn't too happy with my requests, either. They don't want to think about all the possibilities. They're just counting on finding *StarFire* disabled from random events, or something similar." Now he leaned forward again.

"Vince, this is the kind of situation that men lose their careers over, and the staff over at Fleet Command are staying as far away from it as possible. They'll stay away until it's resolved one way or another, and then coming rushing in with sharp knives, looking for a scapegoat, if it goes sideways.

"Now, look: I picked you to give a heads-up to on this. But if we need you, it will be a thankless job, any way you look at it. If you want to decline, speak now, and I'll call in another company commander. But you're my first choice, if you're up for it. Think it over for a minute."

Colonel Parsons stood and refreshed his drink, and then waved the bottle at me, asking if I wanted another. I declined with a gesture, thinking about what the colonel had said. Though still young for a captain, my service jacket looked good. I would be due for promotion inside of a year, and would very likely make major on my first review. So long as I continued to do my job, and didn't ruffle too many feathers, anyway. I'd been lucky, in my career. I had taken every assignment they gave me, and either worked it out, or found men in my command who could work it out. I'd never complained about an assignment, or failed on one I'd been given. But I hadn't ever been given a job like this. Before, I had always drawn straightforward, non-political, and within standard Galactic Marine Corps doctrine assignments. I stood up.

"Thank you sir, but . . . Colonel, if you call, we'll be ready. My company will accomplish whatever orders you cut for us. Will that be all, sir?"

Colonel Parsons smiled wistfully at me. "I was pretty sure of you before I called you in, Vince. But thanks. Think about what the mission might look like, if we need you. If I do call on you, you might not have a lot of lead time. Try to anticipate anything you will want or need, and let's be ready, if we have to send you. Who knows? In a couple of days, we may hear back from those Navy sloops, and find out we can forget this whole conversation. Let's hope, eh? And if that happens, I won't forget your answer, today." He offered his hand, instead of waiting for my salute, and after shaking it, I took my leave.

* * *

Back at the hanger, I saw with some little relief that the game had stayed broken up, and everybody had found some of the dozens of little jobs awaiting their attention. They were still at loose ends, with no orders and no pending exercises or projects. Free time was scarce, in this military, and they were making the most of it, catching up on things they had been putting off. That made it easier to pull one of them aside, without the others wondering what was up. I sauntered over to where Company Master Sergeant Alvin stood going over an equipment maintenance list, and gave him a quick jerk of my head that meant, "Follow me." Then I stalked off towards my office. Alvin gave me a minute's head start, understanding that I didn't want an audience for this conversation, before joining me.

"What's up, Cap?"

"Alvin, I just got word that we may be called on for a mission."

"Somebody's cat stuck in a tree, again? Maybe we got another pirate crew working one of the space lanes?"

I just looked at him, and he caught on. "Or . . . something bigger?"

"You heard StarFire is missing?"

"Yeah . . . But that's Navy's problem, Cap. What do they think we can . . . Oh. Oh, no. What do they want us for? A boarding crew?" He started shaking his head. "No, sir. That ship carries three thousand, Cap. One third of those will be G-Marines. That's five companies. Even if they send us all, we only have four companies on this station. That's eight hundred marines, and we don't have sixteen transport/landers. We have eight, and two of those are down, last I heard. Six 'landers operational, that's three hundred men, Cap. They can't mean it."

"Relax. We don't have the call, yet, Alvin. And they're talking about a recon, not a boarding action. But if the call does come, we're going. It's just intelligence, and one company is overkill for something like that. They're going to want us to find StarFire and see what's going on with her."

"That's what frigates are for, Cap . . . fast, with long range scanning, and low sensor profiles . . . I don't get why they're looking at us for it. They should send a frigate."

"Well, first, there isn't a frigate assigned to this station."

"They can just un-assign one somewhere else, then. A fast frigate could be here in a week from almost anywhere in the sector, sir!"

"And second, the colonel wants Marines on this, Sergeant." By switching to calling him sergeant, I let Alvin know that the discussion about whether our orders were reasonable was about over. He made the proper inference.

"Yeah, well, that part makes sense, I guess. Whenever Navy has their butt in a sling, it's G-Marines who bail them out. So . . ." he took a breath, "What do you need me to do?"

And that brought up another sticky detail, right there. What could I tell Sgt. Alvin? How do I give him a direction to work in without violating the colonel's instructions to keep things quiet?

"Well . . . we should figure out the smartest way to go about this, Alvin. Try to be ready for a wide variety of possibilities. Like, finding out anything we can about StarFire. See if there's anybody on station that knows more about the StarFire than we do, which will be anybody that knows anything at all. You know the drill. But, Alvin, you have to do this all quietly. I don't think Parsons is ready to advertise that he already thinks StarFire is in real trouble. Fleet wants to believe it's just a com problem."

"Yeah, well, Fleet can kiss my . . ."

I walked away while Alvin was still finishing that thought.

* * *

About twelve hours later, I met with the sergeant again. I'd spent some time thinking about the mission, and then slept for about six hours, but Alvin looked like he hadn't stopped moving since our last meeting.

"I found a few guys who came in on *StarFire*, sir. Here's a list of names, replacements who were mostly transported out from the Core, and a couple more, picked up on the way. Mostly cherries who won't know up from down, but there's a couple of older hands among them, who could be worth talking to. And I was thinking that if we go, you will want to hand-pick our pilots, so I also got a list of four transport/lander pilots who came highly recommended by guys that should know. Gives you a starting place, anyway.

"As for spacecraft, the word is, except for two down for scheduled maintenance, there's only one transport/lander you want to avoid. It's got a glitchy electronics problem, intermittent, so it's hard to track down. That leaves five in good shape, and we only need four, if you're right and they only send our company.

"As to intel on the ship, it's all locked down tight. If you want schematics, they will have to come from Fleet. Looks like even the *StarFire*'s engineers had trouble getting all the systems diagrams."

"Okay, Alvin, good work." I was looking at the list of pilot's names. "Have you met any of these guys yourself?"

"Just one, Duvall. Met him in a card game in the pilot's quarters a couple months ago. He's the guy I asked for recommendations from. He put his name on the list first."

"You like him for this? Feel good about relying him in a pinch?"

Alvin just shrugged. "The man pays his bets. That's a good start, anyway."

"See if you can drop by and see him, get a better impression of him. Don't tell him what's up, just feel him out. Maybe ask him who he would recommend for a ticklish job. See if he's the kind that likes a challenge, or wants his steak cut into bite-sized pieces for him."

Alvin made a note for himself before going on. "So, about load-out and weapons . . ."

"Yeah, Alvin, listen, I need to fill you in on another detail." I had made a decision, somewhere along the way, to trust Alvin with the colonel's concerns. He would be in a much better position to make recommendations to me, that way.

"What's that?"

"Just . . . The colonel went out of his way to make sure I considered the possibility that maybe nothing happened to *StarFire*. Maybe . . . maybe she just isn't taking orders from Fleet anymore."

"Oh, yeah, I thought of that."

"You did?"

"Yeah, of course. I mean, I don't like the idea, but it's an obvious possibility we should consider." It hadn't been obvious to me, but I let that go.

"Okay, so . . . does that change our plans?"

"Yeah, well, some. I mean, here's the thing: If all we do is grab a look and then head on back home, it won't matter what we take with us. And we aren't going to go stirring things up by ourselves if we find some new race out there, spoiling for a fight. But we can't really load out for a straight up fight with something like *StarFire*, either. I mean, not and think that what we're doing makes any sense. We'd be dealing with an Alliance ship, and up to one thousand G-Marines. The most we can transport is maybe two-fifty, in one wave, even if we took all four companies. A full-on assault isn't really an option, so load-out isn't the issue."

"Okay. So, what are you thinking of? What do we need to be thinking of?"

"Well, Cap, I think maybe we want to go stealthy. Rig the transport/landers for long range, and skip the carrier delivery. And maybe we want to pay special attention to our coms."

"Okay . . . Keep talking, I'm listening."

"Yeah, that's sort of my point. Anybody else on that ship who wants to will be listening, too. Navy ships use the same gear our transport/landers do. They will hear us, and see our location pings on their screens every time we use the coms. They'll have every transport/lander pinpointed from the second we are in range, if we rely on standard coms and gear. Hell, that ship's bridge has a whole deck designed to track Alliance G-Marines on missions, and that includes while we're on transport/landers."

"Oh . . . yeah, you're right." That hadn't even crossed my mind, and it would have been a disaster. "You're exactly right, Sergeant. So, you have a suggestion?" I prompted.

Alvin shrugged. "Hey, I'm not a tech type. I just think we need to get one of those boys in communications thinking about it, maybe figuring up a work-around."

"Okay." He was on target, and I knew it. "I'll handle that. What else?"

"That's not enough, Cap? Hey, we get all this squared away, we already got a leg up on this mission from where we started. I'll get back to you when something else crosses my mind, okay?"

"Yeah, okay, Alvin. Good work. Go see Captain Duvall, see what he has to say."

"On the way, sir." Alvin saluted and left. For all his familiarity, I appreciated Sgt. Alvin as the excellent non-com he was. The best I knew of, actually. And I knew he respected me. It was just his way of getting the job done to shelve the formalities while the real work got handled. I headed over to the communications shop.

* * *

Communications is a specialized field, and not everyone is well suited for it. Anybody can work on a radio, and have a fairly good chance of plugging in new parts until it works. But real com specialists are men who write the programs that keep the communications for a thousand men, or a hundred thousand men, on one network, plus command, plus transport, all sorted out. Clear for the home team, and encrypted for anybody else listening. Computers do the work, sure, but somebody has to figure out what the computer is going to do before it can do it. It's not the kind of work the average combat infantryman is suited for.

When I got to the com center, the first guy I saw looked like a caricature of the type I was expecting. Tall, and so skinny he seemed to swim in his Galactic Marine Corps fatigues. A shock of orange-red hair, freckles, and a scattering of post-adolescent acne across his face. If I hadn't known better, I would have picked him for a couple years too young to have joined up. When he spotted an officer coming, he at least had the decency to come to his feet, but his poor posture left me unsure if he was actually attempting to come to attention or not. Never mind, I told myself, this isn't the time to focus on troop discipline, just when I need to ask for a favor, "off the books." I read his name tag as I introduced myself.

"I'm Lombard, company commander. Nice to meet you, ah, Technician Duggard."

"Yes sir . . . what do you need, Captain?"

"Duggard, I have a theoretical question for you . . ." It took a minute, but I explained, in broad terms, what I needed. I framed it as a suspicion that one of the other company commanders might be cheating, using the communications gear to track the maneuvers of the opposition team during exercises. "So, what I need is something nobody else can hear, nobody can pick up on the position graphics, but I can still talk to my team mates. Could you do that?"

Duggard stood still while I talked, slouching a little more as I went on, and then seemed to be preoccupied with other thoughts, as I waited for an answer. Eventually, just as I began to wonder if he understood I had asked a question, he responded.

"Well, yeah, man. I mean . . . well, we can't make something no one can hear, but we can make it impossible to understand, and we can even bury the position codes. So . . . I could do it, if you want, sure." His reluctance appeared evident. He meant he could do it, but it would be a lot of work, I thought. And I didn't miss the lack of a "sir" on the end of his answer. I just decided to ignore it for the time being.

"That's great, Duggard. What would you need?"

"Well . . . nothing, really. I mean, just some time for writing some code, I guess."

He had sort of trailed off, but it felt like there was more. I raised an eyebrow, waiting him out. He struggled with himself for a moment, like he had something to say, but didn't want to talk himself into even more work than what I had already outlined. After an uncomfortable moment, he gave in and expressed himself.

"Well, I mean . . . what a dirtbag. Cheating and all that, you know? So . . . like, I wouldn't just want to keep him out of the coms. I would want to . . . like, spoof him."

I began to suspect that after that first "sir" I had gotten when I first walked up, I had likely exhausted Duggard's discipline quotient for the day. But what he said intrigued me, so I asked him to explain it.

"Well, see, it's one thing if he doesn't know where you are, or what you are saying. But he's using our own equipment, so . . . we could make him see whatever we wanted, you know? So, if you wanted him to see, like, a false position on a couple of transport/landers, moving one way, when they're really somewhere else, moving another way . . . well, we would just have to send the right signals to his computer, you know? I mean, the computer doesn't really know where the signals come from. We use techniques like variable signal cancelation and redundant wave spawning to prevent ordinary location methods like triangulation. Quantum communications made all that possible when we developed FTL coms. We know where our own guys are because our signals have encrypted location codes embedded in them. So, we could send the right codes with the wrong coordinates. Even if we wanted to, like, just make up a bunch of ships, who aren't really even in the area, we just have to make the signatures of the false signals match outfits that he thinks might be there, so he doesn't think twice about who these new guys are, you know? If it's smooth, he'll never spot the spoof, until somebody shows up where his computer screen says they aren't."

Already intrigued by the possibilities, I asked, "Really? What prevents an actual enemy from doing the same thing, then?"

"It's the hardware. That's where the secrets are, and unless you had the same hardware, you couldn't pull this kind of thing off. The transmitting hardware encrypts the message, and the receiving hardware decrypts it. But really, it's more than that. With the quantum communications we use, what we're really talking about is encrypting the actual physics of the signal. You can't just write a software program to decode it. Someone with different hardware might not even realize a signal is being sent, much less ever sort out the message. But, you're talking about our own guys, so," he shrugged, "same hardware."

"Duggard, you put that together for me, and I'll find a way to put you planet-side somewhere nice for a weekend of leave. Or maybe on a casino station, at least. Okay?"

For the first time, Duggard smiled at me. "Really, man? That would be outstanding! Yeah, let me see what I can do." I saw that I had finally motivated him.

"Perfect, Duggard. But listen, I don't want anyone hearing about this and letting the other team know we're on to them, you know? So, I would need you to work on this alone, and keep it to yourself. Can you do it without asking anybody else for help, or input?" Parsons had asked me to keep what he discussed with me quiet, for now. I couldn't have my request getting out on the rumor circuit, and some clever tech-type with too much time on his hands putting the pieces together.

Duggard gazed at me for a moment, as if weighing my question, or possibly assessing my sincerity in asking, before he answered, "Man, I'm not just a technician. I'm a G-Marine technician." It was a recruitment advertisement, and a little sarcastic. But it was a real answer. For a guy like Duggard to make the G-Marines, he had to offer something special. I got my straight answer a moment later. "Easy-peasy, man. Think of something harder, so I can earn a whole week's leave, would you? Now leave me alone, I got work to do. I assume you want this done before I plan my vacation, right? Cuz it's going to take a while to figure the angles and write some code." Duggard made up in confidence what he lacked in discipline, but I still doubted.

"Duggard, how can it be that easy? I mean, it just seems like a real weakness in the system, if it's that easy."

"Sure, man. But, like I said, that's the thing. The safeguards are in the hardware, and we're all using the same hardware. Nobody protects us from ourselves, man. And since the safeguards are in the hardware, and I'll be working with the software, that'll make updating your own team's spacecraft a snap. We don't want your own team buying the spoof, too. Now give me five or six hours, and I should have it all figured out. A day or two to write the code . . . Maybe a couple more days to tweak the changes into a loadable program you can send out on coms. Then you can turn it on and off, and come back with your systems back in government-issue spec." And then, I'm pretty sure Duggard winked at me. It took me a minute to figure out that he was sort of reveling in being the unseen hand of justice, returning the dirty trick one officer was playing on another with a somewhat better and dirtier trick. I happily let him believe it. It kept him just a bit further from the truth. But either way, I could see I had managed to get him enthusiastic about the project. Or excited to spend a weekend on a casino station, at least.

I just nodded, and went on to my next task, which was tracking down and interviewing the list of personnel Alvin had gotten me, people who had transported out on *StarFire*.

CHAPTER 5

Defense Space Station G-13, 246.163.12

After Action

"So, I checked it out with a tech guy, named Duggard. He confirmed that our coms were secure, unless someone had the same hardware we had, but that there might be a hole if someone had captured equipment, and knew the methods we used. That sort of thing wasn't really within my expertise, so I filed it in my memory, and then forgot all about it. I mean, until we got the call to go out looking for the missing ships. And then, well, it was just obvious, I thought. I was looking for ships with our same hardware, it seemed sensible to take a com tech. I chose Duggard to take with me, because I had met him. He seemed competent. I thought maybe he could tell me what our vulnerabilities might be, as the tactical situation developed, if there was one. And maybe even figure a work-around for vulnerabilities, if we wound up broadcasting to the ships we located. That's all." There was no reason I could think of to throw Duggard under a bus. The deal he thought he was making with me, to jimmy the coms for an exercise, would very likely result in disciplinary action, at the very least. I could be pretty sure he wasn't telling that story, and nobody else knew it. Most likely, he would simply assert that after being called upon to accompany me on my mission, I asked him to work out the software. And if he did that, he would be alright, no matter what happened to me. And Tillman seemed to be buying it.

After listening to my story, she nodded, and turned to reviewing what was now many pages of notes. I took advantage of the opportunity to study her profile. She had a gently rounded forehead, no bangs left out to cover it, after her hair was put up. With longish eyelashes, she seemed doe-eyed from this perspective. Her nose ran straight and narrow, but not delicate, just . . . maybe "minimalist" would be the right word. Her jawline turned in a mild curve under her high cheekbones, leading to a slender, almost pointed chin. I was just getting to her lips when she spoke again.

"Well, Captain Lombard. That brings us to the important part doesn't it?"

"Excuse me?"

"The mission, captain. I think it's time to talk about your orders."

"I was ordered to reconnoiter the area where we lost contact with the battleship, as well as the two sloops sent out on the previous mission. I was given wide discretion in choosing equipment and personnel, and I was told that the mission priority was to get a report back home."

Tillman turned to face me again, and crossed her legs while she cocked her head to one side. It was the perfect pose of a woman who, having just been asked out, is going to say yes, but she's going to make you work for it a little before she does. I wondered how much of what she did was actually training, and how much was just intuition, because it was a slam-dunk image of skeptical encouragement. A woman saying, "Maybe you can talk me into that . . . give it a try, and we'll see. But you better step up your game, because I'm not falling for any crappy pick-up lines." What she said was right in line with that.

"I've read the written orders, Captain. They are exactly as you describe them. But you and I both know that Colonel Parsons discussed this mission with you before he wrote those orders, and that discussion was where the real priorities were laid out. Yours, and his."

It wasn't so much a question as it was a dare. She was letting me know she thought there was more to this whole thing, and daring me to persuade her I was being open and honest in my account of it all. It was like I had been walking along for a while now, fat, dumb and happy, and suddenly realized I was treading in a minefield, with no idea how long I had been stepping in lucky places, and no idea how long my luck was likely to last.

CHAPTER 6

Defense Space Station G-13, 246.163.12

Prior to Action

After my chat with Duggard, I spent the rest of that day, and half of the next, talking to everybody on the station who had ever set foot on *StarFire*. I learned that the crew seemed competent, nobody had any impression of morale problems, and during transport, they had largely been restricted to their quarters and a couple of common areas, including the mess and the entertainment deck. Nobody had seen much of the ship outside of those areas. Nobody had noticed anything that seemed unusual or troubling. Nobody had anything useful to tell me.

* * *

Later, I was at mess when Parsons' sergeant found me again. I had just finished eating dinner and was sipping coffee, figuring I had another three or four hours of detail work I could get done today. I had been neglecting routine company business, researching the *StarFire*, and thinking about how I might go about the mission I might get.

"Captain Lombard, the colonel would like to see you in his office." I looked up at Sgt. Hastings, suddenly very relieved I had gotten Sergeant Alvin right on the project. I figured the colonel wanted to know how we were progressing, just in case he decided to send us out, and I would have something to tell him. But I was wrong. I should have caught on when the colonel sent his sergeant, instead of just messaging me on my com unit, but the thought slipped by me, and I just went to report in. When I got to the colonel's office he looked haggard, and got straight to the point.

"Vince, *Elysium* and *Archer* have both gone silent. They're six hours overdue to report." These were the sloops Fleet Command had sent out on *StarFire*'s projected path, looking for the silent battleship. *Elysium* was a communications ship, small and fast, and crammed with sophisticated, state-of-the-art com gear. Nothing should have been able to block her signals. Even more to the point, her sophisticated gear should have generated a quantum signal powerful enough to be heard here in just a couple of hours. So, if she wasn't getting through, something that took less than a couple of hours to happen had already happened to her. I registered the bad news, and waited for Parsons to go on.

"We will be talking with Fleet immediately, of course, but I can tell you right now, they won't give us any directive for another twelve to twenty-four hours. They don't move fast, and, frankly, I think most decisions are made by committee, these days, over there. Nobody wants the responsibility, and they'll talk it to death before deciding anything. When they do make a decision, it will be a compromise. I'm guessing they will ask for a four or six-ship mission, along the same parameters as what we sent the last two on. And, right now, I think that'll just serve to deplete our available forces by four or six more assets.

"So, we have a window of opportunity to get something else going now. Those sloops are Navy, and went out on Fleet orders, but they are my assets. I'm justified in trying to take care of my own assets. But if I mobilize any other Navy ships, Fleet can override my orders in no time if they don't like them. And they won't like them. They'll want to debate any ideas for a good while before anything else is done."

I got the direction of his thoughts. "Sir, you want to send Corps assets?"

"Yes. That limits your options, I know, but it will be much harder for Fleet to interfere. A recall order would have to work its way down through the Corps command structure, and I can probably count on them to run a little interference for me. And, when I do talk to Fleet, I can tell them I happened to have you in the neighborhood, and that I sent you to have a look around as soon as I heard we had lost contact, again."

It didn't just limit my options, it more or less eliminated them. But it was right in line with what I was already thinking, for the most part. The only Corps assets we had were transport/landers, a few fighters, and a transport carrier, which was simply a large ship designed to get transport/landers close to an operational area before deployment. Transport carriers are lightly armed, with defensive, close-range guns only. They were fast, though, and had good sensor range. Parsons went on talking, and I pulled my attention back to what he was saying.

"My sergeant will have a complete list of operational equipment that can be ready in twelve hours or less. Get your men lined up. Report back to me in no more than eight hours, with an idea of how you want your orders to read. You can do this any way you want, Vince, but I need to know what's happening out there. You have to get me some intelligence. Whatever happened to *StarFire* just happened to two more ships, and I want to know what it is before it comes here and happens to this station, and the rest of this system."

I saluted, and left.

* * *

After picking up the equipment list, I hustled over to the company quarters and grabbed the first sergeant I saw. I told him to muster the men, and send Sgt. Alvin to my office. I had twelve hours before the colonel thought Fleet would act, so I wanted to be on the way out in well under that. It was really plenty of time for a G-Marine company. I did some quick calculations, and decided to target a six-hour departure time.

Sergeant Alvin, sitting across from my desk, took the news with characteristic aplomb. "So, Navy needs their ass pulled out of the sling again. Welcome to the Marine Corps. And they aren't even going to help, we have to do this whole thing with our own assets. Lovely."

"Sergeant, I'm thinking that's not so bad. I mean, what could they do? Provide us with a couple of gunboats, or a Solaris-class destroyer? That would just put us under some Navy puke's command, and light up a radioactive beacon on our backsides, saying, 'Here we come!' The fact is, even Navy doesn't have the assets out here to take on *StarFire*, if they threw everything in this sector at her. But Corps assets are small, fast, and low-profile. Alvin, I'm thinking of taking just one 'lander."

Gazing at me like he was waiting for the punch line to a good joke, it was a long beat before Sergeant Alvin responded to that.

"Well, it's bound to get the painful part over with quicker, Cap." Alvin was drier than desert sand. But this time, I wasn't really looking for input, I was marshaling my thoughts before I presented them to the colonel. Alvin was just my practice audience.

"Alvin, have you ever hunted big, dangerous game? Other than combat, I mean?" He sat there, looking at me, again waiting for my point. "The thing is, if you have a big enough hunting party to be safe, your real safety winds up lying in the fact that you will never get close enough to the game to be in danger. It will just hear you coming, and stay out of your way. If you want to bag the trophy, you have to take the chance that, in the crunch, you can handle yourself well enough to get the job done on your own. Make the good shot, finish it off without giving it a chance to hurt you."

"Yeah, I get you, Cap. So, if you bag *StarFire*, where the hell are you gonna find a wall big enough to hang her on?"

"Hey, this is an intelligence mission. We just have to bag the answers to some questions. And if we're bird-dogging for a bigger force, we will have to stay around and help out, if things get hostile. This way, we can bug out any time, once we have what we need and feel the urge to go."

We hashed out a few more points, pro and con, but I could see Alvin was coming around to my way of thinking. Either that, or he was just too good a non-com to argue with me after he could see I had made up my mind. Either way, we cobbled together a plan, of sorts.

Alvin had identified the best of the transport/lander jockeys, according to his acquaintance pilot, Duvall. No surprise, Duvall said he was the best. I could have predicted that; I mean, pilots, right? But Alvin

surprised me, there. "I think he really is the best, Cap. I mean, his
assessment of the other pilots was pretty spot-on, and when I talked to the
other guys he recommended, they all said he was top-drawer."

"Okay. Sneak over and fill him in, quietly, alone. See if he wants to
go. I won't be taking anybody who isn't behind the idea. If he doesn't want
it, ask him who is most likely to. When you get a flier, let him pick the
transport/lander craft himself. They'll know which ones are most reliable,
regardless of what the paperwork says. Then get the company sorted out.
Pick a platoon. I think First Platoon would be my choice, but you know the
men better. Get them geared-up and ready to embark. Plan for departure
in six hours . . . twelve is our absolute limit, but I don't see any reason to
wait that long, if Parsons will clear us earlier. So, six hours. We go then,
have the men ready. Oh, and talk to the pilot. We'll be going to G-14, but I
don't know how far, or what part. See if he wants a carrier to ferry us out,
but suggest I would rather do it on long-range fuel cells." There were a few
more details to work out, but that covered the critical aspects, except one.

"I'll be at Parsons' office, going over our op-orders, if you need
me." I was scribbling a note on a piece of stationary while I spoke.
"Meanwhile, get someone to take this over to Communications. Tell him to
find out which officer a tech named Duggard is assigned to. When he
knows, have him deliver this note to that officer personally. Then you
collect Duggard yourself, tell him to bag up whatever he needs to finish the
job I asked him to do, and hot-foot it back here with Duggard in tow. The
message to Duggard is, we're lifting off in six hours, less if we can. He's
working on something for me, and if he's not done by then, he goes with
us. You'll have to make a decision about whether to spend the last hour
letting Duggard work, or outfitting him with a vacsuit and a sidearm."

* * *

Colonel Parsons saw me immediately. I went over my thoughts,
and Sergeant Alvin's input. I told him I wanted Duggard detailed to me for
the mission, and Duvall to pilot, if he was willing, and suggested we
needed some details at this point, such as a target destination point to start
the search. This was data nobody could clear me for except the colonel.
He lost no time thinking it over, just gave me what I asked for. Then we
went on to other things.

"Captain Lombard, I understand your operational decisions. You
are thinking small, fast, and low-profile. But, one transport/lander? You
have to take some kind of minimal firepower. And I want multiple platforms,
anyway. Somebody has to get a report off, or bring one back, and I don't
want one lucky shot to screw that for us. You will take three independent
vessels, minimum. That's not negotiable . . . but you pick what you want to
make up the other two, besides your transport/landor."

I noticed that when he was talking to me in theory, it was "Vince,"
but now that a mission was being put up on the boards, it was back to

"Captain Lombard." That was fine, just as it should be. This was not a favor he was asking, but a mission he was assigning, at this point.

"Sir, the sloops you sent are about as small as ships go. And whatever happened to them, if it was hostile action, it seems likely to me that someone noticed them and disposed of them, right away, before they could get a report off. So I think if Duvall wants it, we could use a transport carrier, but if we can get by without it, I would rather leave it at home. If it goes with us, I will have to leave it behind, anyway, when we approach the operational area. That's the whole point of going small."

"True, Captain. But a transport/lander only has one gun, and frankly, you couldn't even burn an antenna off the *StarFire* with it, until you spent about an hour inside her guns' range. You'll need something else."

I considered this for a few moments before speaking.

"Well, that brings up another point. This isn't a 'seek and destroy' mission. This is intelligence gathering. The crucial thing at this point is to get a report back home. So, if you are going to send anything with us, it should be something faster than we are. As it is now, we can outrun *StarFire*, if we have to, but not if we get within sensor range of her. She will see us coming a lot further out than we can see her, and by the time we get our sensors on her, we'll be in range of her guns. So, what's faster than a transport/lander, and has long-range sensors?"

He knew what I was getting at. Nodding, he said, "You want some long-range fighters. That fits the mission you are describing to me. But, they'll be in the same boat you are; fine for ducking and running, but a hit from any one gun on *StarFire* will likely destroy any fighter we have."

"Sir, that's almost true of anything we have at all, fighters and ships. There's nothing here that could trade punches with *StarFire* for more than a few seconds. So why give them a bigger target? It only makes us more visible, and easier to hit."

Parsons didn't really like it, but it came down to this: Was he serious when he said I could do it any way I wanted, or was he going to renege and micromanage the operation? We negotiated a little then, and when I agreed to accept two fighters, he acquiesced to the mission as I had outlined it.

* * *

Sergeant Alvin had picked the platoon, and the lieutenant was very disappointed when I told him I was taking command. A young guy, named Caruthers, he was even less happy when I told him he wasn't going at all. He thought it was because he had no combat experience, but Caruthers was a good officer, and I remembered what the colonel had told me about the career risks if anything went bad. I figured that young lieutenant was better off at home. Anyway, the colonel had asked me to go, and two officers to handle fifty men was just overkill. If anything happened to me,

Sgt. Alvin was well equipped to take over and handle the men, while Duvall completed the mission.

A few hours later we were in space. In the end, it was one transport/lander, flown by Captain James (Jimmy) Duvall, his copilot and two warrant officers, as cabin crew, and two long-range fighters, with pilots picked by Duvall, both of them briefed in and volunteers. Oh, and fifty G-Marines, suited-up and geared-out, plus one communications tech, looking like a teenager who has just found out that he has to go to summer school. Duggard hadn't been able to finish his project before we left.

CHAPTER 7

Defense Space Station G-13, 246.163.12

After Action

"So, your mission brief did not include any provision for an attack on *StarFire*? It wasn't even brought up?" Linda Tillman was driving nails in my report, pinning down every detail she could, in no uncertain terms. I knew what that was about. It was what a good investigator did when the job wasn't really to find out what happened, but rather to tie the witness down to testimony which would be very difficult to change later. It was to prevent prosecutors from having to ask questions they didn't already know the answers to, or to allow them to trip up defendants and witnesses in contradictions, so as to impeach their testimony. I didn't answer, right away. I didn't want to believe she was doing it deliberately, and sort of hoped it was habit, or actually just clarification. But we don't always get what we hope for, and she just waited me out.

"It was only brought up in terms of vulnerability; in other words, if we found ourselves in a hostile situation—with anyone—we didn't have much to work with, except speed. That's why I wanted nothing slower than our 'lander, and why the colonel agreed to the fighters. For speed. For evasion. Not for an attack mission."

"So, when did you make your attack plans? On the way out?"

I had been looking up, at the ceiling, while we talked, but now I glanced sharply at her. I had let my mind wander, just a little, in my memories, and let my guard down for a moment. I hadn't seen the tell, and I didn't know if this was just a question, or another tripwire. I had been playing poker with Sgt. Alvin for several years, and I knew how to keep my mind on the table, but I was having trouble doing it now. I redoubled my resolve to keep my head in the game. But a moment later, I realized, on this question it didn't matter. The simple truth would serve better than anything else could, on this point.

"We not only didn't make any plans to attack, we never discussed the possibility of it. Well, except Sgt. Alvin, when he thought the entire complement of Marines on the base would deploy with us. He was worried that six working 'landers wouldn't be enough, because they could only ferry us in groups of three hundred at a time, two-fifty, if the glitchy 'lander was down. And he thought that would be insane, even with four companies. So that was the sum of our offensive discussion. It would be crazy."

Tillman looked at me; guileless, Bambi-eyes steady on mine, and she leaned forward, towards me, all earnest attention. "Then, what was your plan? You had to have something in mind. With two days of transport time on the way out, you had time to think of lots of things . . . what did you intend to do?"

I leaned forward, myself, until our noses were a good bit less than six inches apart, mocking her pose and her intensity. I spoke softly, as if telling her a secret, like maybe I was hoping the recording wouldn't pick up what I was going to say.

"Well, Linda . . ." I looked over my shoulder, as if to see if the guards were listening. "I thought we were going to look for some lost Navy ships. And then go back home and tell my boss where they were. Those were the only plans I made."

CHAPTER 8

Military Transport/Lander G-13, 246.163.12-02

Prior to Action

Most of the details came to us over the coms from base, after we had departed. We took off with little more than a general vector, to get us into the right area, and I suspected that was so none of the Navy-types back at base could get wind of the job, and send a little bird flying back to Fleet with the information that we were headed to G-14. Whatever, it worked. We were away, and four hours later, nobody had called us back, so it looked like the mission was a go. We had a couple of days travel time ahead of us, and I determined to make the best of it.

I very shortly found that I liked our pilot, Duvall. He was the kind of pilot that gave straight answers, and didn't butt into operational issues that didn't require his input. A Marine pilot, he was my equal in rank, but I was operational commander, and that put me in charge, overall. He did tell me one thing that helped a lot.

"Captain Lombard, those two fighter-jocks we're flying with are a couple of sharp operators. Smithson and Harley, you can count on both of them. If I was in charge, I would be letting them know the whole score, because you can figure they'll have some input that might come in handy, sooner or later."

"Thanks. And call me Vince, if you like."

"Sure thing, Vince. I'm Jimmy. My co-pilot here is just a lieutenant, so I'm going to make him call you captain, but his name is Mark Goddard."

I shook his hand, saying, "Nice to meet you, Mark. Your boss tell you what we're up to out here?"

Mark gave me a firm handshake, saying, "No sir, he didn't. But I'm used to that. He just brings me along to polish the windshield from time to time," he lamented. "Never tells me anything." It sounded like a long standing joke between the two of them, which Duvall confirmed for me when he leaned forward in his seat just then, pulling a rag out of his utility pocket, and proceeding to rub at the cockpit duraglass.

"That's right. And I won't give you any more responsibility until you learn to do that much properly, Lieutenant." Duval caught my eye in the reflection on the duraglass, and gave me a quick wink. He was letting me know that Goddard was a fine pilot in his own right, and not to take any of this game seriously. But I already knew that. Duvall wouldn't have been horsing around with a substandard pilot. He would have been demanding improved performance, with no hint of a joke about it.

The cockpit area wasn't very big, and I had to squeeze up about three quarters of the way in between them, in the tight area between the seats. It was pretty uncomfortable, so I got to the point.

"So, guys, the thing is, we're scouting for *StarFire*, and we don't really have any idea what to expect. We're not looking for trouble, just want to get a picture of what's happening. Once we know that, we can talk about rendering aid, if it seems appropriate, or we can bug the hell out. Mission priority is to get a report back to Colonel Parsons, whatever else happens, and whatever we find. Jimmy, maybe you'll pass that info on to your fighter-pilot friends?"

"Sure thing, Vince."

"Good. Then, when you guys get the course laid out, maybe pass me the word when we can expect to be at our initial destination, ready to commence a search. We've got some time, so I'll come back after you guys have everything sorted out for getting us on-station, and then maybe we can have a conference with our fighter contingent. We'll see if you pilot-types can think of anything we need to be ready for when we get there." I returned to the main cabin then.

My men were comfortable, sitting in small groups, talking and otherwise killing time, or napping in their acceleration couches. The man at the weapons station was a warrant officer, part of Duvall's crew, and the chief warrant officer sat right there, beside him. They kept to themselves, paying attention to the screens at their station, and I assumed they were augmenting the pilot's sensor scans, watching for any problems or signs of trouble. That was their job.

Sgt. Alvin was busy lining up a card game, and he had kept a seat for me. I was pretty distracted, trying to think ahead of the mission parameters. I sat down anyway, and then gave up my seat after about forty minutes, having no focus to spare for cards at the time. There wasn't any shortage of men ready to take my place, though. Boredom had already set in, with nothing for the men to do except pass time. They were pretty clear that there was no reason for them to think they were going to be engaged, even when we got to our destination. I was the only one playing "what-if" in my head, so far as I could see. It was the burden of responsibility. For the first time, it crossed my mind that for this mission, I could have left the whole platoon home, and just come myself, with the pilots and crew, and the two fighters accompanying us.

After a while, the co-pilot, Mark, came back and tapped me on the shoulder, telling me what our scheduled arrival time on-station was going to be. Checking the time, I got up and went back up front with him, entering the cockpit after Mark was back in his seat, and Duvall set up a three-way open com with the fighter pilots. That was what I had come up front for, and we spent a lot of time hashing out different scenarios over the next couple of hours. It wasn't like we thought we could guess what was going to happen, but we tossed around different possibilities, and got to know each other a little. As Duvall pointed out, it was the next best thing to actually having a history of combat together. We started to get a feel for how each officer was prone to think. I was impressed with all three of them, actually, but I was a little out of my depth, since what they were mostly talking about was spacecraft deployment and maneuvers. Things like proper dispersal, so a stray round fired at one craft, and missing, wouldn't coincidentally hit another one, close by.

We stayed at it until I was tired enough to think of catching a little sleep, and then I excused myself. On my way out, I heard the two fighter jocks talking about taking turns setting their autopilots on "follow the leader" mode, so they could catch some sleep, too. I stopped and asked Duvall about that, suddenly wondering if I should have requisitioned the carrier, so my fighter pilots would be fresh. They were single-seat fighters, and there were no co-pilots to spell them.

"Oh, don't worry about them, Vince. Those fighter pilots, and me and Mark, too, have much better acceleration couches than you boys in the back. We'll be fine. Hell, I don't know a pilot that wouldn't rather sleep in his cockpit than in his quarters back on base. Well, except Mark, here. He says he keeps having nightmares, sleeping on the transport. He keeps dreaming that I'm ordering him outside to clean the windshield while we're at full throttle."

"Now, tell the whole story, Captain." Lt. Goddard spoke up. "I said, 'While we're at full throttle, and under fire.'"

"See what I mean?" Duvall asked me, in mock exasperation. "These kids, they all signed up to be pilots because it's supposed to be a 'safer' job than lugging a beam rifle. I keep telling him he needs to resign and work for a cruise line if he wants 'safe.'" I left them trading friendly insults, and went back to check up on my men.

Everything was in order in the main cabin. Maybe half the men were sleeping, and the other half were talking, or otherwise passing time. One guy was off by himself, hunched over something in his lap, and I went over to check on him. It was Duggard. I had forgotten about him.

"Technician Duggard. Sorry to have pulled you along with us so abruptly."

"Oh, uh . . . Captain . . ." Duggard was flustered, his lap covered with papers he had been scribbling on, along with his com unit, and a large, flat display pad. A couple of reference books lay on the floor beside his seat, opened, and face-down. He was trying to gather his stuff up, so he could stand up, perhaps to salute me.

"As you were, Technician." He stopped struggling, then, and I sat down next to him. "So, what do you have for me?"

"Uh . . . Well, Captain, I- that is, the sergeant sort of told me, it's not really like . . . well, you said it was for another company commander, but it's not . . ."

"Yeah, I know, Duggard. I didn't give you the real story. But the principles are the same, right? I mean, my concern is still that somebody might have the same hardware we do. How do we keep them out of our com net, so they aren't listening and getting position pings every time one of the fighters signals our pilot, and our pilot signals them?"

"Okay, so . . . yeah, it still works the same way. We just have to tweak the software in the com gear on our transport/lander and those fighters, so that when we send an executable file in, the computer onboard accepts the override."

"Override?"

"Well, yeah. Our computers will have an override that tells them to ignore certain data. The other guys, whoever we're looking for, they won't have that. Their coms will read that data and display it. The problem we have is we can't prevent them from seeing the real signals . . . I mean, I could have done that if we had, like, another week to work with, but we don't. So, the best we can do is to put in some ghost signals, but tell our computer to ignore them, see?"

"Okay. That might work, if they can't tell the difference between ghost signals and the real signal. So, what's the problem?"

"Well, the only real problem is that our software is protected against those kinds of commands. What you're asking for is essentially a virus, you know? And it's against regulations to open up the software and make it vulnerable to a virus. I mean, think what an enemy could do with that. I've figured out how to do it, but you need to understand, it's absolutely against regulations just to design a way to do it."

"Duggard, that's good work. You get the virus, or whatever, ready. I'll worry about the regulations. Fair enough?" He nodded at me. "And when it's ready, how do we get it installed on the fighters, too?"

"If they're on the same com net we are, we send it to them over the com."

"Okay . . . but wouldn't anybody else in range be able to pick it up at the same time?"

"Yeah, that's how it works . . . will work, I mean. But if we can give the pilots a code ahead of time, one that we won't be sending over the nets where anybody can pick it up, we can key the program to activate when that code is entered. Will that do?"

"That will do indeed, Duggard." I clapped him on the shoulder and stood up. "Stay at it, Marine. I want it ready to go if I call for it. Once you have it all figured out, see if you can't educate our pilots on the capabilities of what you have done, okay?"

"Sure . . . I mean, yes, sir." Duggard's discipline seemed to have grown a little since he found himself shanghaied for this little venture. I'd seen it before. The potential for being shot at has a wonderful focusing effect on many men. I left him then, with a pat on the shoulder. It was time for a little sleep, and then I would be checking in with the fighter pilots and Duvall again. I found my way forward to my own acceleration couch.

* * *

Arriving at our destination was a little anticlimactic. Tension had been building for the last couple of hours as we neared the last known position of the sloops, *Elysium* and *Archer*. But as we got closer, and the fighters reported nothing on sensors, first the tension started to melt away, and then the restless boredom started to set in again. It proved to be short-lived, though.

The system was pretty spread-out, with a middling central sun, and four planets in orbit. Between the third and fourth planets was a dense asteroid belt that covered a lot of space. This system was the last known point of contact with *StarFire*, and it was the destination of *Elysium* and *Archer* when they had been sent out. But we weren't sure that any of them had actually reached this location. Doctrine was to progress slowly, completing a thorough scan upon entering an unknown system, especially with the threat of something hostile in the area. Duvall argued against that.

"We aren't here to map the system, and we should keep some decent speed on. Speed is our only defense, and same for the fighters. The slow and steady entry strategy was written for capital ships, Vince, which need to watch out for mines or other surprises. But we can be pretty sure that all three of the other, much bigger ships came in that way, and something happened to them. I think we should come in fast, and keep our speed up all the way through our first pass. We can slow down once we're sure we're alone." The fighter pilots concurred with him, over the coms, and I deferred to their experience. Consequently, when we arrived we were hurtling in from the outer edge of the system at perhaps eighty percent of maximum velocity.

Both of the fighter pilots were running ahead of us, one off to each side. I was concerned that they would try to stay too close to us, and wanted them well spread out, in case somebody got into trouble. I had to be sure at least one of the spacecraft we brought made it back with the report. But they were busy scanning the area with long-range sensors, and, as it turned out, the search pattern kept us all at moderate distances from each other. We were still clipping along when one of the fighters called out an anomaly after a little while.

"There's some debris that doesn't look like it belongs to that asteroid belt up ahead . . . Nothing very big, not like anything we're looking for, but I should run over and take a closer look. It's reading as high metal content, like a lot of the asteroids, but the drift trajectory is all wrong." It was Smithson, and he veered over to get a better reading. It took him a few minutes, but no one spoke while we waited for more information. When he got closer, he could tell right away it was something out of the ordinary.

"Yup, it's foreign, and it's pretty tightly clustered. It hasn't been drifting long." Foreign to this system is what he meant, and that shot the interest value way up, under current circumstances.

Duvall spoke up then. "Yeah, I just got it on my sensors now." He was talking to me, not the fighter pilot. He tapped on one of his screens in front of his seat. "I don't like this much, Vince. I can't read the makeup from here, but the spread and momentum is all wrong. Somebody dumped that stuff here, or something got smashed up right here, and in the last few days." Now he switched to coms. "Harley, you go with Smithson, but not too close. We'll be alright, here, until you boys can get back."

"Roger that, Jimmy. We'll be back pronto. Can I pick you up anything while were gone?"

"Good idea. If you make any stops, pick up some more glass cleaner for Mark." That's what pilots do to show nothing rattles them, I think. They make jokes of everything, like a contest to see who can be the most calm, whatever's going on. But I didn't say anything. I could tell that these guys were worried about what that debris might turn out to be.

A couple of minutes later, the answer came over the coms.

"Jimmy, I'm looking at the remains of *Archer*, here. And there's not much of that." It was Harley. And a moment later, Smithson confirmed the rest.

"Yup. *Elysium*, too. She's been smashed into rubble. That's why we couldn't pick up the reading until we got so close. There's not a single piece of her here bigger than maybe five or ten kilograms."

I was still absorbing that information, but Duvall was way ahead of me. "Boys, I'm slapping the throttles up right now." He was, literally, slapping the throttles wide open. "Form up on me, as fast as you can get here." Then he looked at me, switching the coms off. "Vince, pick a direction. I want to put on all the speed I've got from here on out. When something sees us, I want every advantage I can get, and speed is the first one."

"Okay . . . um . . . which way is that debris field moving?"

He checked, quickly. "Sunward, Vince. Almost directly. Chances are, that's the direction they were moving when they got hit, and most of the mass is still headed that way." That was the same vector we were on, just a little ways off to the side. I didn't know if that meant anything or not. I needed more input to make a decision.

"Jimmy, you're the pilot. Do we want to go where they were headed? Or somewhere else?"

Duvall shrugged. "We don't know what they were headed for. Without another destination, the default is usually sunward, for an initial pass through. But their scrap metal is all bunched up together. I mean, both ships, all together like that . . . They got hit before they knew they were in trouble, and it was all over before they could even maneuver much."

"Then, we don't go where they were headed. But . . . damn, Jimmy, this isn't my specialty."

"Okay, what would you do if we were on the ground somewhere?"

"I'd look for cover, and hole-up while we sorted things out."

Duvall looked at me for a moment, and then nodded, glancing at his screens. "I think that's an excellent suggestion." He keyed the coms. "Boys, I think our buddy Captain Lombard has come up with a great idea. We're going to duck down into that asteroid belt for cover, and settle in for a little discussion, assuming we get there without spooking up anything unpleasant. I'm going silent on coms. When I've picked out a place to park, follow me down. I'll contact you on tight-beam after we're down. Everybody switch to passive sensors only. If they're here, they might know we are too, by now. Let's get down without painting a target on our asses."

The fighters acknowledged, though the other pilots sounded a little less enthusiastic about the idea than Duvall was. That was their training, I figured. A fighter pilot wants to be in a ship, in space, and moving fast when something hits the fan. I already knew Duvall had the same instincts, so I was surprised when he locked-on to my remark the way he did. But maybe that was because his craft wasn't well enough armed to be anything but a target, if we got spotted by anything that didn't like us.

* * *

About an hour and a half later I met our fighter pilots in person. Duvall had picked out a good sized asteroid with a high metal content, which made for good camouflage. The others landed very close by, with not more than a hundred meters separating all three craft. With one tight-beam communication, he instructed the fighter pilots to power down their craft and walk over, and we cycled them in through the aft hatch, using the storage area as an airlock, as it was designed.

I shook hands with each pilot as introductions were made. Lt. Robert Smithson was tall for a pilot, and athletically slender, like a swimmer. His blond, curly hair and quick smile lent him a youthful appearance, and I wondered if this might be his first deployment. But I wasn't going to ask; Duvall had said he was a sharp operator, and that was good enough for me. Lt. John Harley was the opposite, and more the stereotype of a Galactic Marine Corps fighter pilot. Short in stature, he was a bundle of wiry muscle and energy, and while he was also younger than either myself or Duvall, he was the type of guy that nobody ever asked about how much experience he had. It just wasn't something that crossed your mind, when talking business with a guy like John Harley.

The four of us sat down in a corner of the main cabin. Mark was up front, keeping an eye on passive scans, while my men occupied themselves as best they could. Some of them sat at the ports, looking at space outside, while others talked and joked among themselves. Alvin, of course, was playing cards, or maybe giving lessons, which is what he did when nobody had any money left to lose to him. Duggard, off in a corner by himself, still, seemed to be grinding way on his project. I made a mental note to check in with him, later, and see how he was progressing.

Duvall started our discussion. "Bob, John, sorry to pull you out of your craft. I know you fighter jocks hate to be away from your weapons. I just wanted the lowest signature possible until we come up with a plan of action, and I wanted your input, without any risk of signal scatter." Smithson deflected the apology with a wave, and Harley dismissed it altogether by turning immediately to the business at hand. Pulling out his personal com unit, he selected a file and asked our com codes. Then he sent it to each of us. When I realized what he was doing, I shot a look at Duvall, who understood my concern immediately.

"No problem, Vince. Transport/Landers are among the best-shielded vehicles in the fleet, because coms are necessary to talk to the troops, after decompressing for deployment, and these things are often at the spear-head of any attack. Nothing leaks from inside here."

Our coms chimed to say they had received files, and we opened them up. It was a graphical analysis of the debris field we had found, and Harley explained what we were seeing.

"The mass is maybe sixty percent of the two ships' total weight. They're both here, and this is all that's left. Depending on how they were hit, and how they broke-up, some of the mass would have been sent off in random trajectories at high speed. The rest was probably lost reacting with the energy that took them apart. Without a detailed scanning search of the whole area, there's no way to know how much mass was lost to either effect, but sixty percent is a pretty low number for residual mass. I've been wondering why, so I started looking this over on the way here.

"The trajectory of the remains of those two ships varies a little across the debris field, and as a result it's spreading out pretty fast, as you would expect after explosive decompression and break-up. But what nags at me is, I think it's spreading out too fast. There's a lot of velocity variance, like a lot of that debris field has been maybe hit, or moved, even after breaking up. I think that's why there are no large pieces; whoever slagged these ships kept firing at the largest remains until they were all broken up into stuff the size we saw out there. That would also help explain the low remaining mass, as lots of extra shots were put into the debris."

"What does that suggest to you?" I asked him. I had the feeling everybody else was drawing conclusions I couldn't quite feel my way around to yet, no doubt because they were combat pilots, and were used to looking at things differently than I was.

Bob Smithson answered me. "It means that after they took out the sloops, they stayed around and took some target practice. Like they didn't have any place else they needed to be in a hurry. And maybe they wanted to disperse the debris, so it would be hardor to detect sooner. Or maybe they just didn't want any bigger pieces left for some other reason. Either way, if they were bugging-out, why would they care what was left in this system?"

"So . . . that's what makes you think maybe they're still here? But wouldn't your long range sensors have found some trace of them?"

"Maybe . . ." He nodded, weighing out his answer. "Probably. Unless they were trying to stay undetected. They could slip in behind a moon somewhere, if they knew the direction we would approach from. And we did come in from approximately the same approach that the sloops did, so they could maybe have predicted that. Or, they could be behind any of the larger asteroids in this belt. Or they could be on the far side of the system, on the other side of that star, just by chance. Any of those would give them plenty of cover. If they kept their emissions down, they could be much closer than that. Even if they knew where we would come from, they wouldn't know exactly when, so they could even be hanging out almost anywhere, and just taking a peek now and then to see who comes calling."

"Wouldn't they have seen us? If they were watching from anywhere in the neighborhood, this side of the star?"

"We're small, and we came in very fast. We weren't out in the open long, and came pretty well straight into cover . . . here, let me have a look . . ." Bob fiddled with his com, and after a couple of minutes, he sent us all another file. It was a graphical presentation. "Look here . . . if they were close enough to the star to use the interference to mask their emissions signature, they would lose a lot of ability to observe the system effectively. This asteroid belt would provide pretty good cover for a good slice of the system, from there. We should be okay, if that's where they were, because it would only work to hide them if they stuck to passive scanning." He frowned, thinking it through. "It's not what I would have done, though."

"What would you have done?" I asked him.

With a shrug, Bob just replied, "I wouldn't have been shooting at Alliance Navy ships, so who knows what's on their minds? It depends on what their mission parameters are. And what their equipment is. But, assuming they're big enough to take out *Elysium* and *Archer* at the same time, they're bigger than anything that's going to come looking, so I don't know why they aren't out in the open, just daring somebody to come over and check them out. But if they're on passive scanning only, they could be anywhere in this asteroid belt. We wouldn't see them easily, and they would have missed us unless they were very close by this section when we entered the system. We came in very fast, and then got down pretty fast, too, you know? So, without knowing what their equipment is, I would say if they have some real size, they have to be gone, or far enough away that they had a low probability of spotting us."

Duvall spoke up, then. "I think we know what their equipment is. We're talking about *StarFire* here, for sure."

"How do you figure that, Jimmy?" I asked. If it was obvious, I wasn't getting it. "Just because someone fired on Alliance ships out here, that doesn't mean it was *StarFire*, does it?"

"Vince, there's no sign of debris from anything but the sloops. Whatever took them out has massive firepower, and great range, because they were toast before they even got a report off. Well, that's not so hard to do with something the size of a sloop, but if there is something else hostile out here, and *StarFire* was also destroyed, it had to be big enough to take out *StarFire* the same way it took out the sloops. That's a much taller order. How big would that have to be? And how hard would it be to hide? And where's the debris from that battle?"

"Okay, but why does it have to be the same thing that took out these sloops? If there's no debris from *StarFire*, maybe she moved through this system, and got hit or ran into trouble somewhere else."

"It's Occam's Razor. What are the chances there are two behemoth ships out here, *StarFire*, and something else big enough to handle her? And our first three ships in the sector ran into that unknown mother of all starships, one right after the other? I don't buy it. Too much coincidence. Anyway-" He was interrupted by Mark's voice, coming over the cabin com speaker.

"Captain Duvall, you want to have a look outside, to starboard. Right now."

We all got up, but the starboard-side ports were already crowded with bodies, all craning for a look at something. Sgt. Alvin, always alert when I was moving around, saw the problem immediately, and bawled out, "Fall in!" Bodies started jumping and bumping into each other as Marine Corps conditioning kicked in, and the men lined up at attention in ranks. Then the pilots and I stepped through the ranks to the now-empty ports.

And there we saw a distant ship, drifting through our sky, left to right, at about eleven o'clock. There weren't any lights we could make out, no surprise at this distance, and Duvall quickly ask Mark, over the coms, what he could pick up from her. "Nothing," was the reply. "No emissions at all, and certainly no identification codes," he reported. But I knew what she was. I had watched her come into dock at Defense Station 12, just a few weeks ago. We were looking at *StarFire*. We stood there and watched her sail right past, until she was out of our view.

* * *

My first thought was that she was a dead ship, and maybe had been from the first missed report that had gotten Fleet so stirred up. I was still running that through my head when I heard Duvall urgently ordering Mark to stay only on passive sensors, while Mark was sending files from his sensor screens to Duvall's com unit, internally. When I heard Duvall ordering Mark to tag the ship as a target, and track her, I came back to the issue at hand. Our first objective was now successfully completed: We had found *StarFire*. What remained was to assess the situation and get a report back to Colonel Parsons.

When *StarFire* had passed out of sight, the pilots and I sat back down, while the troops on board returned to talking among themselves. But nobody was talking about anything other than *StarFire*. Lt. Harley pulled up the files the copilot had sent to Duvall, and started analyzing them. His first comment corrected my previous impression.

"She's not a dead ship. Look at the trajectories." He drew a line following the course of the ship back, and then superimposed the drift of the asteroids over it. It didn't take long to find where there would have been an intersection, had the *StarFire* been floating dead, on a straight-line. "If Mark can keep her on the passive sensors long enough, we'll see her fire up soon, to avoid another asteroid . . . somewhere about . . . here." He marked the place on the charts we were all following on our com units. "If I were flying her, I would say maybe six more minutes, give or take, until she fires her thrusters." It actually took a little over seven, and even then, she fired only the bare minimum to scrape by the rock.

Duvall said it. "She's here, and she's not dead, but she has almost everything shut down. She's hiding, or hunting. So, what do we need to do? I say, what we have seen already makes it almost a certainty that she fired on *Elysium* and *Archer*. If it wasn't her, then she should have come to the defense of those sloops. But look here, at the video Mark took. I don't see a mark on her, even at maximum magnification."

"Could she have been taken by hostiles before the sloops arrived?" Lt. Smithson asked. Finally, I had something to add to the conversation.

"Not the way we take ships. No way was she boarded and not a mark left on her. For starters, sealing entry hatches is one of the easiest things to do. Hatches are strong, stronger than the main parts of the hull. And harder to repair, afterwards, too. Anybody boarding that ship would have done what we do, and burned a hole in the hull for entry. And the fire fight while they got close enough should have marked her up, even more. Even if she didn't detect them coming until they were close alongside, there should be evidence of some damage . . . and if she was boarded on the other side, the side we didn't get a look at, there should still be some evidence of a fire fight on the near side. I would say she has not been fired on."

The conversation went on like that for a while, but eventually, we came back to the question we started with. We found her . . . Now what?

The mission parameters were still the same. Find *StarFire*. Determine her status. Get a report home. We had done the first, but I wasn't sure we really knew the answer to the second yet. Duvall disagreed, saying, "What else could have happened? You think she watched those two sloops be destroyed and didn't lift a finger? Just hid out in these rocks? No, *StarFire* hid in this belt until the sloops were close enough that she could take them both with one salvo, and then she fired. And now she's doing the same thing. If we had showed up when she was closer to this part of the belt, we wouldn't be having this conversation. Or any others, for that matter." He made sense.

"I think you're right, Jimmy," I acknowledged. "But what I think doesn't matter. We are going to have to give Colonel Parsons some real evidence, other than our personal assessment. Look, the good news is, there's not another race out here with something big enough to take on *StarFire*. The bad news is, *StarFire* is still too big for anything in Sector 13, and probably too big for everything in Sector 13. We don't have another Star-class ship due to launch for a few years, at best. Parsons is going to need proof that *StarFire* is hostile, just to get Fleet's attention."

After a quiet moment, Lt. Harley was the one who said it, out loud, in the end. "Vince, the only way we get that proof is if *StarFire* attacks us. And that's going to happen anyway, if she finds us. Look, we don't know where she is just now. She's powered-down, and our passive sensors can't pick her up very far away in that condition. We also know she's using passive sensors, or we would hear her pinging away out there. But as soon as we go to main power on any of our craft, she will pick us up, unless she has left the system by then, or worked her way back around the belt a good ways away. We were damn lucky we landed here before she spotted us. If we try to send a report, she will pick us up before we get the signal off. If we try to lift off and run while she's close, she will pick us up. And while any of our craft can outrun her, unless we know where she is there's a good chance we will be well inside her gun range when she spots us. She has incredible range. Once we clear the belt, we won't have any cover, and a hit from any one of her guns will destroy any one of us." Harley slowed down to take a breath before he went on.

"So, we're in a pickle here, guys. The only way we get out without a shooting fight is if we sit right here until something else comes along to distract her, and we get a fix on her position. Even that might not help, if we fix her position anywhere too close. Then we still can't run, and she shuts down again, and we are back where we started. And if we don't get into a shooting fight, all we can tell Colonel Parsons is where we saw her. That's not the mission."

I considered that for just a moment. "Well, we aren't sitting still while someone else flies into this situation, and gets hammered while we try to run. Parsons might send something bigger next time, and we would be buying our fifty-some lives with maybe hundreds of others, say, if he sends a cruiser or a destroyer. Hell, Navy could send a whole squadron, not knowing the situation here." And as I spoke, I was thinking, and I realized something else, just then. "That's what she's doing. It's a deadfall trap. She doesn't know what might be coming, so she's hiding in the belt, firing when something gets close enough that she can be sure of stopping it. But why? She might not know exactly what we have in G-13, but she sure as hell should know there's nothing in known space she needs to be afraid of." Nobody knew the answer to that, but Smithson was willing to speculate.

"Maybe it means she doesn't have anywhere else to go. She doesn't have a mission or destination, so she's still here, while whoever is in command works it out."

"Or," Harley suggested, "she's training a new crew. Or working out automated systems to fly and fight her with a partial crew."

"Okay, either of those makes sense. But I guess it doesn't matter right now," I responded. "Our mission is the same. We have to engage her, prove that she's hostile, and get out. Somebody has to last long enough to send a report, and ideally, somebody has to get home, too." We got down to the brass tacks of operations, then. It was a long discussion, and at one point I excused myself, to check in with Duggard. His project would have greatly simplified things for us, but he was nowhere near done. I returned and talked it over with the pilots, who all agreed we probably shouldn't wait for him. We came up with something else.

* * *

Later, after we had made some decisions and settled on a plan of action, the fighter pilots returned to their craft, and spun up their longer-range sensors, keeping them in passive mode. When they got no reading, they took a chance, and fired up their steerage engines long enough to move slowly. In the low gravity of the belt, it didn't take much, and they were able to keep their signatures very low. It was still a tense hour, until we were sure StarFire wasn't vectoring in on them. Then we all sat back to wait.

We figured StarFire had hung around this long, she wasn't likely to leave yet. Which meant she would be passing by us again, sooner or later. We also calculated that, at her rate of drift, she wasn't orbiting the sun, moving the whole length of the belt. More likely she was loitering in the part of the belt closest to the area Elysium and Archer had come from. But we didn't know how far in either direction she was going. Far enough that she hadn't detected us immediately when we arrived, but that didn't tell us a whole lot. We were left watching, guessing and hoping . . . but in the end, she did come back, and from the direction she had gone in, as we had guessed she would.

StarFire came into sensor range slowly, and as before, we could have missed her entirely if one of the men hadn't physically seen her through the porthole. But this time we had a previous record to compare. No doubt the fighters picked her up first, but they couldn't alert us. We had to stay on a strict com silence between the craft, because even a little laser-splash or tight-beam leakage could give the game away.

We had separated the three craft trying to ensure that one of us would be pretty close to the StarFire's path, and at least one of us fairly far away. The plan, such as it was, called for whoever was closest, when StarFire came back, to pop-up suddenly and try to lead the StarFire on a little chase away from the others. We all knew that someone would have to engage *StarFire* if we were going to prove she was hostile. But it was going to be a very dangerous job, and one vessel would be enough to risk. Both Smithson and Harley, to their credit, tried to assume that the decoy would be one of the two fighters, arguing that the fighters each held just one man, while the transport/lander held fifty, plus the crew. Duvall, when he heard this argument, just looked at me and waited to hear my position. It was my mission, and my men, after all, but I could tell he didn't like it. He figured we should all be willing to take the tough job, even odds all around. I agreed, and we deployed accordingly.

Whichever craft wound up drawing the short straw, the remaining two could then record what *StarFire*'s reaction was and, if she was drawn off sufficiently far enough, giving chase to that one, the others could both risk breaking cover and make a run for it. The theory was that when *StarFire* engaged the first one, she would go active on sensors. With her pinging active sensors, the others could track her exact position, and know when it was safe to pop up and run. But there was also the chance that *StarFire* would slag the first craft up before moving far enough away from the others. In that scenario, we presumed she would then revert to passive scanning, and disappear from our screens, leaving no one sure of her exact position. We would be back where we right now, but one spacecraft lighter. To prevent that, if the first one took a hit too soon, we agreed, the next closest craft would light up, and continue to engage, in the hope of getting the third one a clear chance to run. I made it clear: Under no circumstances would the third craft engage. The orders were that the third craft would take their best chance of leaving the system unharmed, regardless of whatever else happened. The mission was the same. Get a report home.

* * *

Eventually, slowly, we could make out that the big ship was drifting back towards our vicinity. She was silent, and seemed dead again. Sensors couldn't pick her out from the asteroids, except that she showed up as movement against the momentum of background drift of the asteroid belt. As soon as we had calculated a vector for *StarFire*, I knew who the first rabbit would be. Lt. Robert "Bob" Smithson had deployed to our starboard, and *StarFire* was set to pass us to that side, between Bob's fighter and our transport/lander, but closer to Bob than to us. My jaw ached from clenching it too long, as we watched her coming in, and I thought about the risk Bob was about to take. Added to the fact that he would soon have *StarFire*'s whole attention, the first ship up had to do something else, too. It had to come up as a "friendly." That meant IFF (Identify Friend or Foe) beacons had to be lit, and he would be transmitting ID codes, non-stop, at least until *StarFire* started shooting. We simply had to know that any action *StarFire* took against the fighter was not an accident, even though the beacons would make him a very clear target. The pilots had all played down the risk aspect, but I had very little hope that Lt. Smithson would survive the tactic, if we were right, and *StarFire* started shooting.

Maybe because *StarFire* was between his position and the transport/lander, Smithson might have jumped the gun a little bit, coming up sooner than I anticipated, and making sure we didn't decide to beat him to it. Or maybe he just took careful note of *StarFire*'s position and the available asteroid cover, and picked his moment, but he popped up just as we had discussed, lit up a like a Christmas tree, with beacons and codes blaring. I was jammed up in between the cockpit seats again, watching the whole thing play out on the screens over the copilot's shoulder.

StarFire reacted sluggishly, like she was asleep. Just for a moment, hope flared that we had guessed wrong, and she wasn't hostile at all, or even that nobody was actually onboard, and she was flying autonomously. But then two shots snapped off from her bow batteries. Even so, they were poorly aimed, and Smithson had the advantage of being a very fast moving target, close-in by battleship standards. And he had one other thing going for him: This belt we were in was one big field of giant boulders offering pretty good cover. He lost no time ducking down low, following the curve of the rock he had jumped off.

But now *StarFire* was awake, and on the screens I could see her coming to life and bringing her systems on-line. Her main thrusters flared, and she started putting on speed to give pursuit. Smithson's job was to stay alive as long as he could, while drawing her out along the asteroid belt, giving Harley and Duvall the best opportunity he could manage. If he stayed alive long enough, both the other craft might make it away. In a perfect universe, Smithson would duck and dodge through the asteroids until he had gained enough of a lead to try to escape, himself. But while I watched Smithson hugging the side of an asteroid he had picked out for cover, *StarFire* let go an entire volley. Half of the salvo she fired tore into the asteroid itself, so close was Smithson flying to the surface of the thing, trying to turn the corner and get behind it. In a moment, our passive sensors were overwhelmed with the debris of dust and rocks flying up from the asteroid. The computer would sort it out in a few minutes or so, as the debris cloud thinned and cleared, but for now, we were blind to Smithson's position and status.

I watched as Duvall started punching buttons on his display, setting the sensors to follow *StarFire*'s plotted trajectory, because she would be in the dust and debris herself, in another minute. It was an automatic response on Duvall's part, ingrained from long training and habit. *StarFire* was a hostile target, and transport/landers were tasked to track all hostile targets. The massive battleship was now designated on the computer screen as target A-1, and Duvall clicked another couple of buttons. A moment later, the computer flashed a solution on the screen, and Duvall reported, pro-forma, "Intercept to target A-1 plotted. Estimated time to intercept: three minutes, forty seconds." It was just standard procedure, the same as plotting missile trajectories or anything else.

Duvall was busy tracking *StarFire*, and plotting intercepts, but Mark was free to replay all the data we had collected through the sensors up to that last salvo by *StarFire*, and he did so. It wasn't good news. He was able to determine that *StarFire* had connected with her main guns on Lt. Smithson's little fighter. It wasn't the devastating hit that we had all dreaded, but it appeared to be enough to slag the directional dampers on one of his main thrusters. Mark caught the exhaust flare on-screen just before Bob's fighter disappeared behind the dust storm. Energy readings indicated that Smithson's engine efficiency had gone from very high, above ninety-eight percent, down to something much, much lower, immediately after the hit. Mark informed us that it was very likely that Smithson could no longer outrun *StarFire*.

I ran through the data in my mind. Smithson was alive, for the moment, but it was clear that he would not last long enough. *StarFire* was still too close, and that lucky shot on his dampers would mean a short chase. We were next in line, according to the plan we had all worked out a few hours ago. If Smithson had drawn her off far enough, both of the other ships would have run. But with her this close in, it became our duty to play the rabbit, to increase Harley's chances.

It was such a bitter outcome, I could almost taste it, and for the second time I cursed my decision to bring a platoon with me. Knowing what I knew now, the cost of this mission was always going to be at least one spacecraft. Now, due to a bad break, it would be two. But it could have been a half-dozen lives, instead of fifty-plus. My Marines would die without ever firing a shot, wooden ducks in an arcade shooting gallery. I had lost men before, but suddenly, and for the first time, I found myself guilty of the most heinous crime a loyal officer can commit, by my personal code: I had been careless with the lives of my men.

While this was working its way through my head, something else happened. *StarFire* slowed down, and started rotating, end for end. It was exactly the correct decision by the pilots flying her. Nobody went nose-first into a debris field like the one in front her now, if they could help it. At the speed that ship was moving, the material that made up the debris cloud would punish the front bow surfaces, and cause significant damage. Nothing catastrophic, but serious damage it would take weeks to repair fully, in space. In any other situation, a ship would simply go around the debris field, and avoid a situation like that. But in an emergency, or in combat, she would enter backwards, relying on her momentum to carry her through, and using her thrusters, at very much reduced power levels, to clear a path. The exhaust from those thrusters would do to the debris from the asteroid exactly the same thing our thrusters did to the metal hulls of ships: Burn it, melt it, turn it to plasma. And since Smithson's fighter was much slower now, they could finish him off in a leisurely fashion, using the lighter aft batteries. When that was done, she would increase power, and already be very nearly exactly on her old trajectory, if she cared to resume it. I watched her as she completed her rotation, and now *StarFire*, still moving towards Smithson's cloud of asteroid dust, was already running slower, and backwards. The solution numbers changed on Duvall's screen, and he repeated them as they came up.

"New intercept plotted, target A-1. Time to intercept: two minutes, nineteen seconds, and dropping." But this time, he looked at me when he said it.

The plan I had discussed with Duvall and the fighter jocks called for a quick lift off, and evasive maneuvers. But the plan had just gone to hell, and Duvall and I both knew it. If *StarFire* didn't keep a good head of steam on, she would remain closer, and react that much faster to anything else that popped up close by. And by turning her aft batteries on Smithson's craft, she was turning her main batteries towards us. That was a much more dense salvo than the aft batteries we had counted on facing if we had to lift off after the first craft drew her away. In another few moments, we would face coming up directly in the line of fire for her main, forward batteries. We, in the transport/lander, suddenly didn't have a snowball's chance of evading *StarFire*. And very little chance of distracting her long enough to make Harley safe, either. We would go down as fast as Smithson had, or faster, since his fighter was even more nimble than our 'lander. All this, and more, was running through my head when *StarFire* disappeared, drifting into the dust cloud. We couldn't see her anymore, and passive sensors couldn't pick her up through the interference. Likewise, *StarFire* herself, still operating on passive sensors, was blind in our direction . . . and would be until she cleared the debris field kicked up off the asteroid by her guns.

It was one of those decisions you don't make consciously; you just act, and if you live through it, look it over hard later to see if it was justified. I ran the information I had through my head, and then reached forward and keyed the com, so my men would hear me in the back while I put my orders on record. "Captain Duvall, execute intercept on target A-1 for boarding, based on projected data from last sensor tracking."

The co-pilot, Mark, turned to face me, his eyes open as wide as his mouth. Duvall simply said, "Yes, sir, intercepting target A-1. Estimated time to intercept, two minutes, three seconds. Lifting off now." And damned if the men in the back didn't start cheering, as the thrusters rumbled to life.

There are maybe a couple thousand variables that have to be accounted for in order to board a hostile ship in space. But the first one is always the same: Someone has to make the decision to attack. That was my job, today. We weren't going to go down as a running decoy. We were going to fight.

CHAPTER 9

Defense Space Station G-13, 246.163.12

After Action

I was tired. Telling this story took more out of me than I expected, and I supposed it was due to the emotions involved. Writing it the first time, in my after-action report, hadn't been this bad, but written reports tended towards a certain style of sterile language. Telling the story to another person, though, out loud, brought back the memory of every feeling and emotion. I wrapped it up, suddenly exhausted.

"When I made the decision, the only things in my mind were the mission priorities, and the knowledge that my men would go out fighting as G-Marines, the way they had always thought they would. Not as random debris, blown out of the tin-can target they happened to be sitting in. I gave them a mission: To fight long enough and hard enough to get Lt. Harley a chance of survival. I counted them all as lost, before we even started, but I also gave them a chance at victory. If Harley got away because of their sacrifice, that would be their victory."

Lt. Tillman sat quiet for a time, then. We were still sitting almost knee-to-knee, and I had a good, close-up view of her face. I thought something in the story had touched her, because I could see her controlling herself, tamping her display of emotion down. Or maybe that was just me, projecting, because I was sure enough trying to tamp down my emotions. After a minute, suddenly, she straightened.

"Captain, I think we need a break. This has been good work on your part, so far. I'm getting a far better picture of how things evolved out there. But we have a long way to go, I'm afraid. I'll go eat something, and I recommend you have something brought here to you, as well. We'll resume in, say, an hour and a half?"

I hadn't moved since I stopped speaking. And now I still didn't, except to wave my acquiescence to her suggestion. Lt. Linda Tillman rose and gathered up her things. Then, without another word, and without another look, she left the room, her no-nonsense shoes clicking their way back down the hall, alone this time.

I sat for another minute, reflecting on what I had told Lt. Tillman. Most of the truth, holding back only what I felt was necessary to keep anybody else out of the crosshairs that had settled on my back over this whole thing. It wasn't my job to protect Colonel Parsons, but it wasn't my nature to shift responsibility, either. On the other hand, it was my job to protect the men serving with me, under my command, so long as they did their best, followed orders, and didn't violate the code of conduct in their methods. They had all done exactly as they were ordered, and more. I had no complaints about any of them, and no one else had a right to complain, after the fact, either. I needed to do a better job of it, when Tillman came back, if I was going to protect my men without throwing myself down on the sacrificial alter.

Tillman had given me an hour and half for lunch. I didn't doubt that she would use the time to make preliminary report to her superiors, and prepare for a long second session, after soliciting the guidance of those superiors on what they wanted her to accomplish in that session. I decided right then, I would use that time to prepare myself, as well. Starting with getting a little blood flowing, and clearing my head.

I rose and went to the door, to speak to my jailers for the first time since I had been confined to quarters. I sized them up, and spoke to the one I figured was slightly older than the other, on the chance that he might more likely be in charge.

"Hey, regulations say that prisoners get exercise. An hour a day." I hadn't brought this up before, but now I was thinking a half-hour of sweat, and a light lunch while I thought about what I would say this afternoon would be about right. Because if I was going to persuade anyone that I had only done what was necessary, it wouldn't be with what we had talked about already. It would be in what would come this afternoon. I knew that, even if Ms. Tillman didn't. Yet.

CHAPTER 10

Military Transport/Lander 246.163.12-02

Action

Duvall was a good pilot, I'll give him that. Within moments of my order he had that transport/lander streaking towards the *StarFire*'s projected position, though not directly. He took an angle maybe fifteen or twenty degrees to port of a direct heading towards the other ship, and glanced at me over his shoulder as we got moving, while he answered my unasked question

"If we rotate, and go through the center of that cloud butt-first, like *StarFire* did, we lose a lot of speed, and come out right in front of her. But we don't have to do it that way, and speed is our friend. *StarFire*'s trajectory, if she doesn't change it, crosses starboard to port, in front of us. That will let us skirt along the outside edges of that cloud, in our proper orientation. We keep our velocity, and come out of the cloud much closer to her, with this little detour. Plus, we come out off to her side, instead of head-on. It's a little chancy, but we can accelerate all the way, and I like that better than facing that main battery, anyway. If her course is stable, we'll come out damn close up, and it will put us outside of the zone her main guns can be trained on immediately." He glanced back at me, as if to make sure I was following what he was saying. "If I'm right, the velocity we keep will gain us time, even though we're going the long way around." I didn't even answer him. I just clapped him on the shoulder, to let him know I was good with his decisions, and then left the cockpit. Piloting was his worry. I had problems of my own to solve, and not much time to do it.

Stepping back into the main cabin, I saw my non-coms pulling the men together. Everyone was checking their load-out, making sure they had gathered up anything they had set down on the journey up to this point. I was busily trying to cobble together a strategy for the boarding action, myself.

StarFire was too big to capture; that was obvious. But fifty G-Marines can do one hell of a lot of damage in a very short period of time, and I was shuffling options in my head, trying to pick out a course of action that made sense. If we could interrupt any one of several systems onboard *StarFire*, we could give Lt. Harley a much greater chance of getting away.

If we could do severe damage to multiple systems, we might even be able to make a run for home ourselves.

What it came down to was a simple bit of prioritization. The best chance, I figured, would be weapons control and targeting systems. Maybe sensor systems would do the trick, too. Then, as far as saving any of my own men, the best option for that might be attacking the engines. So, tactically speaking, it was a question of setting priorities for systems we would attack, if we could find them, and trying to guess how much damage was enough before we could make our own break. It was unbridled optimism, even bothering to calculate for our own retreat, but Marines are trained for survival, not suicide missions. It was my duty to make some sort of plan for the possibility of completing the mission, and withdrawing the survivors.

Frankly, I didn't see any way we were coming out of this, ourselves. Any one operational gun, from any battery on the ship, could take us out with one shot. And a withdrawal would start from right on top of *StarFire*'s own skin, with a long run before we were out of range. It wouldn't even take a particularly lucky shot, unless we pulled the whole targeting system completely down. I pushed that thought aside. The job was, get Lt. Harley a running chance, and this was the only way to do it. Getting back off ourselves would be a question of timing, and the right time wouldn't even come up unless we were unnaturally lucky. I figured I would know the moment when it came. If it came.

On that score, I was determined that if we did manage to get locked down on *StarFire*'s hull, it was going to cost them. We were little more than a flea about to bite an elephant's butt, but we were going to make it a bite that hurt.

* * *

Out in the main cabin, I saw my men making ready to deploy. Squad sergeants were counting heads and checking load-outs on individual troops, while Platoon Sergeant Simpkins told off Squad Five as 'lander defense, and went over hatch details with four of them. I was looking for my company sergeant, Alvin, and finally spotted him, over towards the back, checking the seals and rigging on a troop's vacsuit. I didn't know why, since that was the responsibility of that man's squad sergeant, and I headed over to speak with Alvin. As I got closer, I saw the trooper in question was Duggard, and he didn't belong to a squad. As usual, Alvin was on top of things, taking responsibility for anything that might otherwise fall through the cracks. Duggard was a tech, but he was a G-Marine first, and Alvin saw him as another gun available for the assault. Therefore, he was preparing him for deployment. But I had a different idea.

"Alvin, Duggard won't deploy with us, so if he doesn't get his seals checked, he can post up in the cockpit when we depressurize." I turned to the other man. "Duggard, I need some help here. We talked about ship-to-ship coms, but what about our boarding party's coms? When we board that ship, are they going to be in our com net? Our internal company net, I mean?"

Duggard was on the ball, and grasped the question immediately. Even better, he knew what I was really asking, and gave me the whole answer, instead of me having to pull it out of him piecemeal.

"Yeah, they'll be in the net, if they want to be, and the system will update your locations on the ship every time you use the coms. But if you use secure communications, they won't understand what you are saying. Not for a while, anyway. If they want to, they will catch the signals you send to each other, and know where on the ship you are, but to get voice signals in clear, they'll have to work out which algorithm you're using, and that takes time."

"How much time?"

Duggard shook his head. "It doesn't matter, we can counter that. The answer you want involves setting up a schedule of automatic code changes. Each suit com processor gets a schedule of codes, and instructions to implement it at a certain time. We'll have time to send out the schedule before they get the algorithm sorted out. After that, they'll never catch up, and your coms will be secure, except for location beacons."

"Duggard, I want you running the com net, from here, on the 'lander. Work up the solution you just described to me, and implement it. You track the action, and if they get into our nets, figure it out and sort out a solution for that. Can you do that?"

"Yeah. In my sleep. I can send out the schedule once, and after that, it will all be automatic. It won't take fifteen minutes to set up. I can even put in a little secure routine that will let me update and change the program, in case a suit com gets captured. Just tell your men it's a sign/countersign routine. Got a sign/countersign all your men already know?"

Alvin answered this one. "Use names from company personnel. The query should be the last name, the countersign, the first name." He turned to me. "Someone in each squad will know the first name of anyone we use for this."

"Okay, Duggard. Get on it. Set it up." I turned to point to Squad Five, staying back for 'lander security. "They can give you the names. I'll tell the squad sergeants, they'll tell the men. Be sure you use the names the men are used to. Like, Vince, not Vincent. I don't want men locked out of the nets because some lieutenant's legal name is different from what everybody is used to hearing."

I turned to Alvin. "Alvin, you get to each sergeant, and let him know that every time the coms are used, it will send a signal with their location which can be read on the bridge of our target ship. They can only use the coms when the enemy already knows their location, like in a firefight that lasts longer than a few seconds, or right before they are moving out to a new location. Explain it, and tell them to let their men know." Alvin nodded, and went off to find sergeants.

"Duggard, let's gather up your stuff. I'm putting you in the cockpit."

"Better to leave me here, sir. My seals are fine. I went through the training, like all these other guys. Let me just move a little out of the way, and get to work. We're going to be pressed for time." I just nodded, and went on with my job.

* * *

I knew we had entered the edges of the debris cloud, because the smooth, seemingly motionless ride suddenly turned into a bucking, stuttering cacophony, as the little ship struck small bits of debris at very high velocity. It was dangerous, because something the size of a plum could hole the ship from end to end, and anything it struck inside, as it passed through the ship, for that matter. Including any of us. What was causing the turbulence was little more than dense pockets of dust. But there was nothing for it now, and I had to trust to Duvall's skill and instincts as a pilot.

And then, as suddenly as it started, it was over, and everything smoothed out. We were out of the cloud. I stepped back into the cockpit, for an update.

Duvall had been right. We came out of the cloud with a great deal of velocity on, and very near the *StarFire*, off to one side, and slightly above her. We were far enough back to be safe from the forward guns and, at worst, at the very periphery of the aft battery's field of fire. More importantly, *StarFire* did not appear to have seen us coming, because she wasn't maneuvering at all. She was still just coasting, backwards, and tossing off shots at Smithson's fighter. I wanted to watch, to pull for Smithson to keep evading that fire, but I had other priorities, just now.

Duvall heard me come in, and glanced around, quickly, before speaking.

"Vince, I'll be coming in as hot as I dare. Could be a rough touchdown. Got any preference as to where I should put you?"

"Not unless you see something that looks critical, or easy," I responded. "Maybe best to just to set down as fast as you can, or else put her down somewhere that could give us an advantage later, if we get a chance to cut and run."

"Okay. I can put her down further forward, so if we take off again we'll have a little room to build speed, running down her hull before we clear the ship and wind up with a battery facing us."

"Fair enough, Jimmy. Listen, I'm leaving a com tech on board to handle our com net. Don't let your warrant officers kick him off as a coward or anything."

Duvall chuckled at that. Marine Corps conditioning made it virtually impossible for a man to hang back at the outset of an attack. "We'll take care of him, Vince. Now, unless there's something really important to talk about, you should get yourself in back. We're touching down in a little over a minute."

I left the cockpit.

CHAPTER 11

Defense Space Station G-13, 246.163.12

After Action

Lt. Tillman returned exactly ninety minutes after she had left. Alone, this time, I knew the sound of her shoes as soon as she turned the corner, entering the long hallway leading to my quarters. I had spent the time, as I had planned, getting a little exercise and eating a light meal, and then I sat down and called up my copy of my after-action report, the same report I had written and turned in two days ago. I reviewed it, carefully, for about twenty minutes, awaiting the arrival of my investigator.

I was looking for anything that someone could misinterpret, or read something into, anything that would give someone a different view than what I had intended when I wrote the thing. But if it was there, I couldn't see it. Sterile, unemotional language relating chronologically every order I had given, and every action taken, by myself and my men, relating to those orders. What I left out was only my own thoughts, and some of the conversations I had with various men on the mission.

After my review, I still found myself left with a question: What was Tillman looking for? What did she, or her superiors, think there was to find? I couldn't see anything, and listening to her steps clicking down the hall again, I was out of time. I gave up, cleared the report off my com screen, and waited.

She knocked on the doorjamb again, when she arrived, even though I was sitting there, looking right at her, this time.

"Captain Lombard. Ready to start in again?"

"How was your lunch?" I asked her, deflecting her question.

She flashed a smile, the kind that started and stopped with teeth, and never made it to her eyes, and looked away, casually, at nothing, and too quickly to be genuine.

"Fine. Really good. How was yours?" So, she hadn't had a chance to eat, I thought, observing that Lt. (JG) Linda Tillman was an uncomfortable liar, perhaps not the most useful trait to have as an interrogator. But she doesn't want to broach the topic of what she was doing instead, I observed, silently. I rose to my feet, and gestured for her to enter the room. If Lt. Tillman was an uncomfortable liar, I was going to do everything I could to make it harder for her, starting by being more of a gentleman than I had been previously.

"My lunch was fine. Ms. Tillman, I'm afraid I haven't been as friendly as I could be. I apologize for that. It's all just very stressful, for me right now, I'm afraid."

She waved that off, as she crossed the tiny space to her chair.

"No problem." She settled into the folding seat, and put a fresh pad out on the desk. "So, shall we pick up with the actual boarding of *StarFire*? I think that's where we left off."

"No problem," I echoed her.

CHAPTER 12

Alliance Military Ship StarFire

Action

The approach was rapid, and Duvall didn't rotate the craft until the last second. Well inside the minimum angle *StarFire*'s guns could be trained to reach, there was no hostile fire, but Duvall understood that getting down and onboard before the target was able to muster her defenses for repelling boarders was critical, and he bent himself to that task. Likewise, when we touched down, his warrant officers went through the deployment drill as if someone was holding a stopwatch, and they were trying to set a record. From the jarring "BANG" of contact to the moment the Chief called the doors couldn't have been more than half a minute, barely enough time for my men to get back to their feet, after half or more of them stumbled on touch-down. But the men were ready just in time, and as soon as the Chief announced the aft hatch open for disembarking, G-Marines were jumping in pairs, out of the 'lander and into a combat environment. Alvin and I were the last pair, except for the four men detailed to handle the hatches, and in our turn we approached together, building a little momentum, and then, with our carbines held at port-arms, we dove headfirst, through the open hatch.

It can be tricky, moving from one gravity field to another. Sometimes there's an orientation shift that can cause problems. Without knowing the layout of the target, it could be difficult to predict the direction of gravity onboard. What's directly "down" on the 'lander might be "up" or "sideways" on the target ship. That invariably resulted in a percentage of the men falling awkwardly, and the occasional sprained ankle or worse, over the course of fifty men suddenly finding themselves falling in a new and unexpected direction, as they crossed the threshold from one gravity field to the next. But we were lucky, or else Duvall was just that good, as he had put us down so that gravity at our invasion point was oriented in the same direction as the field we were leaving; in layman's terms, we had burned through a wall, not a ceiling or a deck. In the end, it was about the equivalent of diving straight through a window, set six feet or so off the ground outside; nothing a fit, athletic man couldn't handle, and more so after being trained for it. Most of the men simply executed a shoulder roll, and stood up.

After my own jump and tumble, I came to my feet without injury, and fully oriented, both to my position, and to where my men were. I looked around, hastily, to ensure the men had met no resistance upon entering the compartment. Breaching this compartment for entry had released the atmosphere to space, and in vacuum there would be no sounds of combat to alert me; instead, I had to look around for the blue flashes of beam weapons in order to determine if any actual fighting was taking place. I saw none of that. Either we had come aboard in a compartment with no enemy personnel present, or the first pairs through the breach had handled any resistance before I got here. But that reminded me that we still didn't actually know what we were up against, so I looked around more carefully, to see if there were any bodies. There weren't.

Next, I looked at the room itself. It was large enough to have held two or three times as many Marines as the fifty, plus two, that I had available to put in it, but there were large stacks of crates and boxes, strapped and anchored down, scattered across the room. Enough of them that lanes of visibility were somewhat limited by the cargo, and I could see many more boxes of supplies occupied shelving which lined each of the four walls around us. This compartment was a storage hold, which wasn't an unusual purpose for compartments around the periphery of a ship's body. Storage holds can be left with hatches sealed, most of the time, to provide a margin of safety for a combat vessel, which might experience sudden decompression of the outlying compartments frequently during battle. Using those outside layers as a buffer was good defense, adding a layer of security between enemy guns and critical areas onboard. I grabbed Alvin, next to me, and pulled him close enough to lay my helmet against his.

"Detail a man to have a look at this stuff. See what kind of material this is." Alvin could hear me well enough without using the coms, so long as our helmets were touching. I watched him grab the closest guy next to him, and press his helmet against that man's, passing on the order. It was important information to have, because the type of stores held here might indicate what sorts of systems and equipment were housed nearby. Replacement parts for large-bore guns would suggest gun batteries close by, while food stores would make it likely we were near the mess hall, and therefore, probably close to the off-duty quarters for the crew.

While Alvin's man was checking the stores, I looked the men over. They were forming up. Squad Five, assigned to 'lander security, and still short the four men who were securing the hatches on the 'lander, took defensive positions around the room, using the stacks of crates and whatnot for cover. One man tethered himself with a safety line and was boosted by his mates back up to the surface of the ship's hull, where he would watch for any attempt to storm the 'lander from the outside, across the hull of the ship.

The other squads formed up in ranks, and hunched down in low-profile positions, on one knee, or crouching. Each of them cradled a beam carbine in one arm, and used the other arm to link up with their mates, grabbing shoulder loops or linking arms. They were getting ready for another round of what the ship's personnel would call "catastrophic decompression." That was because Platoon Sergeant Simpkins was preparing to blow the entry hatch to this compartment.

This first hatch had to be handled a little differently from others we would encounter later, because we wanted to be able to put it back in place in a few minutes, with the use of sealing compounds. Sealing gel is a viscous, goopy substance which, when a little catalyst is sprayed onto it, hardens almost instantly into a crystalline matrix. It has great adhesion properties and pretty significant structural strength. It's brittle, but strong enough to fill in gaps of almost an inch width without support, even between pressures of one atmosphere and complete vacuum, and substantially larger gaps if any sort of supporting material is laid over it. Usually we used small metal plates for this. I had never seen it done, but I figured someday, a hatch blown out of a wall would be lost completely, and some enterprising G-Marine would just seal the whole breach with a little sealing gel and a hodge-podge of metal plating.

Generally, blowing hatches meant opening them, and not caring if they would ever close again. Easy enough to do, just by blowing the latching mechanism. But we wanted this hatch to function properly when we put it back in place, and that meant that instead of using one charge to blow the mechanical latch, 'Toon Simpkins would use four charges, and try to blow the whole hatch assembly right out of the wall. It was a slightly dicey evolution, and sometimes it didn't work, but it was worth the effort. Walls were easy to repair, being relatively flat surfaces, while a breeching charge could easily mangle a curved hatch-cover beyond use, leaving it bent and creased so severely it could never be straightened sufficiently to function properly again, and provide a reliable seal.

The immediate concern for the men was that as soon as the wall which the hatch was set in was breached, a rush of atmosphere through this compartment would follow. Since we didn't know what was behind that wall, it could be a relatively small venting, or a really massive event, literally tons of air trying to sweep us all out into space. That was why the men hooked arms, and those sitting next to stacks of supplies hooked onto the straps holding them in place.

When everything was ready, all four charges placed, and detonators linked together for simultaneous activation, 'Toon Simpkins gathered the lanyard of the closest charge into his meaty hand, moved well to the side of projected blast radius, and then turned to face me, waiting for me to signal him to proceed. We were still on com-silence, although I was confident that warning lights were flashing on several instrument panels all over the bridge, telling our enemies exactly which compartment was now in hard vacuum, thereby effectively giving the enemy our exact location.

I scanned the men quickly, noting that all of them were watching me closely. They saw me give Simpkins the signal, and fifty men tensed and put their helmeted heads down, while the sergeant gave a single, sharp yank on the lanyard, detonating his charges.

Without atmosphere, the explosion created no noise; just a bright flash, and a sudden, strong vibration through the deck spoke of the violence of the blast. But a moment later, a rush of air through the compartment buffeted everyone there, and for a few seconds we could all hear the sound of wind streaming past our helmets. The hatch itself blew out of the wall and into the room we occupied, but the men had been careful to be out of the way of its path, and almost as soon as it went by, the forward men rushed out into the corridor beyond the wall, which now sported a gaping hole instead of the hatch and its mounting frame. I couldn't see my men after they turned the corner, but again, no one broke radio silence, and I didn't see any beam fire flash past the gaping opening, so I assumed they had encountered little or no resistance. As the men flooded out, I noted that the corridor wall past the opening was close, allowing room for perhaps two men to walk comfortably, shoulder to shoulder. That suggested a small and therefore perhaps remote secondary passageway, away from the main areas of activity onboard the ship. That was to our benefit, so long as we got out and got moving rapidly, but would work against us if we got hung up here for more than a few minutes.

Alvin appeared next to me, putting his helmet on mine to make a report.

"The stores are general electrical replacement parts. Nothing to indicate special systems or weapons." I just nodded to him. Landing at a random location, it was too much to hope for that we would stroll right into one of the critical systems we needed to disable. I waived Alvin forward, and we exited the cargo hold, into the corridor, outside.

The corridor was narrow, as I had thought, suggesting it was a minor tributary to the larger corridors we would find as we moved closer to the center of the ship, but it was long, running in both directions, as we stepped out of the compartment. Fortunately, along with the hatch accesses to a number of compartments running along the path of the corridor, there were also hatches placed to isolate areas of the corridor intermittently along its length. That would be important to us.

The men formed up, down the length of the corridor, and at each end, three men squeezed into the available space and lay prone. Behind them, three more men kneeled, and they were in turn just in front of three men standing. All of them with their weapons trained down the length of the hallway. In this way, we presented nine guns, ready to fire, when we could reasonably expect to face only two, or at most four at a time, wielded by any mobile group coming to repel us, from either direction. But with maybe a thousand G-Marines on board, it was a measure which, as Sgt. Alvin would have put it, would simply prolong the inevitable if we got caught here. We were still in the most vulnerable moments of the assault.

Bunched up, with little idea of where on the ship we were, and no room behind us to run, a single enemy with even a middling explosive weapon could have turned the corner at any moment and taken most of us down in one fell swoop. We planned to get out into the ship and spread out a little before that could happen. The deeper into the ship we got before encountering substantial resistance, the harder it would be to pin us down for a protracted fire-fight, and the less bunched up we would be, lowering our vulnerability to a single large weapon.

But we had another issue we had to address, as well, and it would work to our advantage to get it done first. While any competent enemy would already know where we were coming aboard, we were still operating under radio silence. Any use of our coms would have started augmenting the intelligence of our adversaries, assuming they knew how to use the equipment. It would have shown them that we moved from the lander out into this corridor, instead of, for example, blowing our way straight into the compartment below the one we entered through, and moving out from there, the kind of trick that was pretty popular with G-Marine boarding crews. So, with coms limited to critical use, we needed to be able to talk, without the necessity of pressing helmets together and passing orders one man at a time.

In order to get ordinary verbal communication back we needed to re-pressurize the environment. To that end, 'Toon Simpkins already had men wrestling the blown hatch from our previous compartment back into place, slathering sealing gel liberally along the seams where the hatch would fit back into the wall. More sealing gel and small filler panels served to stop any gaps that remained, until the repair was air-tight. At the same time, other men were moving to place small breaching charges on the walls next to each sealed hatch in the immediate vicinity. And finally, the prone men at the vanguard of each end of our column rose to a crouch, and moved forward to the closest bisecting hatch in the corridor, which they manually closed and dogged tight.

In just a couple of minutes, Platoon Sgt. Simpkins was looking to me again, for the go-ahead signal. The hatch we had just come through was in place, and we were ready to proceed. Simpkins stood, one hand raised above his head, in a fist, the sign for "ready." I looked over the men, and saw they were all set, then raised my own hand above my head, in a fist. When I pulled it down directly to shoulder level, and pumped it up and down twice more, that was the command, "proceed."

A string of small explosions, right down the corridor in both directions, followed a second later; flashes of bright light, and slow drum beat of vibration in the walls and the deck below our feet. Even before the explosions stopped, the sound of rushing air took over, as atmosphere from each newly breached compartment rushed to fill the void of vacuum in the corridor, but this time, due to the replacement of the hatch to the compartment we came through, the air didn't rush out into space. Instead, it was held in the corridor we occupied.

It would require venting quite a few more compartments before the pressure started to equal one atmosphere, but we were making progress, and the men got ready to move on. There was one more thing to do, though, before we advanced. Men moved to open the hatches on every compartment that had just been vented, and once open, they moved inside to inspect the rooms. It wasn't long before they found what they were looking for.

A couple of the compartments were occupied. Personnel, who had been attending to duties; taking inventory, fetching replacement parts, whatever, were inside when the charges went off. These men were disoriented, first by the explosions that breached the compartments they were in, and second by the rapid decompression of the atmosphere in that compartment. Almost immediately, the reports came back with each pair of my Marines who entered those areas, and dragged bodies back for my inspection. We were gaining some useful information, now, and it wasn't good.

First, my men reported that, although they were unarmed, each and every survivor they encountered, even wounded ones, resisted until they were killed. To a man, they simply attacked, barehanded, as soon as they saw the boarding team, and kept attacking until finally my men shot them with beam carbines. It was noteworthy, especially since those men should have been bordering on unconscious by the time my men got to them, both from the shock of the blast, and from oxygen deprivation. But more important than what my men reported was what I could see for myself.

The bodies were all uniformed, in standard Alliance Navy-issue fatigues. This ship hadn't been taken by hostile aliens, or pirates, or anything else. We were fighting the crew of AMS *StarFire*.

CHAPTER 13

Defense Space Station G-13, 246.163.12

After Action

"So, now we knew. It wasn't some alien race that we hadn't come across before. The crew of *StarFire* was in control of the ship, they had fired on Smithson's fighter, and presumably on *Archer* and *Elysium* before that. It was the best answer we could hope for, in terms of human-kind avoiding another war, but it was the worst possible answer to that particular question for us, fighting that battle. And it changed things." I was lost in my thoughts, again, remembering that moment when I had recognized the uniforms on the first bodies, and known we were up against our own. But, suddenly remembering myself, I came back to the present quickly, and studied my attractive interrogator closely, as she scribbled my last words down in her pad.

When she had caught up, Linda Tillman looked at me, waiting. When I didn't go on, she dropped a little encouraging question, I assume just to try to keep me talking.

"What did it change?"

The question surprised me, or at least her tone, in asking, did. It seemed . . . experiential, not evidentiary, as though she was actually interested in the humanity of the experience, and I thought a moment before answering.

"Mostly, it changed us. That ship was crewed by over three thousand. With Alvin and me, we were fifty-two." I took a deep breath, let it out as a sigh, and looked away as I tried to answer her in a way that conveyed the significance of those uniforms. "The news that we were up against regular crew had a lot of ramifications. It meant that we no longer had any reasonable hope that we might be facing a smaller group, the survivors of a capturing raid who had taken the ship, or even a prize-crew, trying to learn to operate it long enough to get it home. We had no reason to hope that the ship was being handled by someone who didn't know her well, both the ship layout and the systems on board. So, there was suddenly a lot less hope that we might pull off the raid and get a chance to run for home. If we had any idea that we were trying to do a hit-and-run raid, it died right then, for most of us. Every man who saw those uniforms immediately came to the same conclusion. Sooner or later, the five complete companies of G-Marines who belonged to that ship were going to find us, and roll over us like a rising tide. We could fight like hell, and maybe get Lt. Harley away safe, but . . . that's all we had, at that point."

I glanced over at Linda again. She was writing, not looking at me, now. Her eyebrows were drawn down, and her lips pursed, as if she was concentrating, trying to accomplish some delicate task, which would go wrong with the slightest error. And maybe it was a difficult task. Not so much taking down my words, like dictation, but at the same time, focusing on my testimony, and how best to frame her questions to move me towards the goals her superiors had set for drawing me out. Whatever it was, it seemed to be taking a toll on her, hunched over her little desk. Even her writing hand seemed tense and cramped, her fingertips white where they grasped her pen tightly.

I just waited for her to catch up again, knowing she would push me towards the testimony she wanted—again—and hoping I could glean a clue from that as to what her masters were looking for. But when she looked up, she didn't steer me towards anything.

"It must have been a terrible moment," she said, not unkindly.

I nodded, and mumbled, "Yeah, it was. And it only got worse from there." I was thinking of the events that followed, the parts of the story I hadn't told yet, and which weren't really emphasized in my after-action report, because there's no room for emotion and speculation in a written military report. So many of my memories of the next phase were foggy, from the fatigue and confusion of battle, but some few were so crystal clear in my mind, I could see them as if I were still standing there, in the moments after they happened.

"Worse? How did it get worse?" She sounded like she couldn't think of anything worse, and I would have agreed with her, if I didn't know better.

"How did it get worse? Linda, I suppose the real answer to that is, 'A little at a time.' We didn't notice anything, right away. It's normal to see strange things in combat situations, people behaving in ways that don't really make sense. But after a while, it started to add up, and at some point, looking at lots of little things in aggregate . . . well, it was very strange. And, eventually, it was worse. We didn't know what we were up against, yet. I still don't."

CHAPTER 14

Alliance Military Ship StarFire

Action

After taking in the uniforms, and all that told us, it finally registered on me that they were in uniform, yes . . . but they were not wearing vacuum suits. Donning vacuum suits was standard procedure in Alliance military ships going into combat. It is among the very first things new recruits are taught. How to put on a vacsuit. Then, how to put one on in a hurry, or in total darkness, in zero-gravity or high-gravity, and so on. Whenever, however, in whatever circumstances, Alliance sailors and Marines learn to put on the suit. Then, when they have learned that, the very next thing they learn is WHEN to put on a vacsuit, and the answer to that is simple: At the first sign of trouble. Always, immediately, and most certainly under any kind of attack, donning the vacsuit is the first response because, while the risk of sudden decompression isn't high in normal space travel, in combat the odds are stratospheric that the hull integrity will be breached, sooner or later. "Sooner" is the assumption the military trains us to work under. The actual purpose of virtually every ship-to-ship weapon, including boarding crews, is essentially the breaching of the target ship's hull integrity. Even ships which are victorious in small actions routinely experience breaches. Calling hands to battle stations invariably starts with everybody grabbing their vacsuits, and extra suits were stored in various parts of all Alliance military ships, so that anyone caught away from their quarters or duty station can still suit up, before combat is initiated, or at the first sign of trouble.

Standing there looking at those plain Navy uniforms, I mused that some cocky bastard on the bridge hadn't thought that Smithson's little fighter was enough of a threat to justify even a "battle stations" alert, and they either hadn't seen us, approaching in the 'lander, or they saw us too late, and hadn't had time yet to sound the boarding alarm. Whichever it was, I decided immediately to capitalize on that, and make sure the error cost them.

I looked around and found the squad sergeant for Squad Four. I had to push by a couple of troops to get to him, but when I did, I put my helmet on his, and issued some quick orders. He then tapped his men on the arms and shoulders, and gave them a quick sign for "follow me," and led them to the other end of the corridor we were standing in, where he started passing on his own orders. In the meantime, I signaled Sgt. Alvin to get the main body moving as well, in the other direction.

On both ends of the corridor, men pried open the sealing hatches, and we lost most of what atmosphere we had gained from the breaching of the various compartments here, as it rushed to fill the hard vacuum in the longer length of corridor which had been vented earlier. No problem, we would be moving into areas still pressurized as we moved into the ship further, but regaining atmosphere was still a priority. I wasn't ready for our enemy to begin to track our movements through our location pings on the coms, but this other idea, that I had sent Squad Four to put into action, took priority even over that.

Alvin and I moved aft, with the larger body of men. The squad I had detailed off in the other direction had orders to move as rapidly as possible, venting more compartments as fast as they could find them. Since the crew hadn't donned vacsuits already, I suspected that we had a short window of time to cause further casualties, simply by depriving any crew located close by of enough air to breath. It wouldn't last long, but you know what they say: Make hay while the sun shines. Well, maybe that's not the best metaphor to use for killing people, but the point is the same. We had an opportunity, and we would exploit it. The larger body of my Marines hustled down the corridor, aft, while the smaller group started identifying hatches to blow, and setting charges. The tactic had another benefit, besides causing casualties, in that it would rapidly set off a dozen or more vacuum warning lights on the bridge, showing an attack moving forward, towards the prow of the ship, and suggesting that we were moving in that direction. Meanwhile, three fourths of my men actually moved in the opposite direction. With luck, we might be quite a ways off before we had to fight, revealing our real position in that way. All this time, the smaller group would raise havoc venting compartments, right up until the ship's marines managed to catch up with them. It would draw the bulk of the enemy in that direction, forward. Or so I hoped.

Then, when they finally caught up with Squad Four, those men would have to execute a retreat, or perhaps a running action, trying to evade the superior force *StarFire* would inevitably bring to bear on them eventually, but with a little luck, they could do that for quite a while, if they were diligent, and didn't get bottled up somewhere without an exit. I had ordered them to break com-silence and let me know when that started, as the enemy would have them located at that point, anyway. And I warned them I would not be able to respond to their report, if we were not yet engaged ourselves. It was too great an advantage to toss away lightly, giving away our position just to let someone know I had heard them.

* * *

Our group moved off fast, intermittently feeling the shockwaves of each charge the other group set off, though they were rapidly fading in severity, as we moved farther apart. The air around us was thin enough that what we did feel of the small explosions came through the deck, anyway. Before too long, we came to a sealed hatch. We didn't want to simply open it, and let atmosphere from the ship rush in to equalize pressure with the whole length of corridor we had just come through, though. For one thing, the drastic pressure change would notify the ship's bridge that someone was moving in this direction, something I hoped they were not yet aware of. But also, it would render the breaching of compartments that Squad Four was doing moot, as soon as the length of this corridor was re-pressurized. We needed to isolate this end section of the corridor before we allowed atmosphere back in here. When we realized we had gone as far as we could, I had the forward men hold up, while a pair ran back to the last previous hatch bisecting the corridor, and sealed it behind us. Now, I hoped, opening the next hatch ahead of us would create only a slight change in pressure, something easily overlooked on the bridge. When we were ready, my men pried the hatch in front of us open, and we all felt the pressure equalize, outside our suits.

One of the men took a pressure reading, and then, rather than trying to signal to all of us, he simply opened his helmet, letting it fold back behind his head. That told us all that the atmosphere was normal, or close enough to normal, at this point. We all dropped our helmets back, and finally, we could talk just using our normal voices. I took immediately advantage.

"Men, we don't know if they will have noticed that pressure change on the bridge or not, so let's keep moving," I called out to my troops. "Stay alert, close combat drill; be ready to return fire at all times." I glanced towards Alvin, and lowered my voice. "Take over, here. Get them moving out, keep them ready for surprises. But let's get this show on the road, while we can, and hope we find what we need to before they get us pinned down in a large fire-fight we can't win."

Sgt. Alvin, never one to hesitate when action is called for, started barking orders, and the men, already formed up to advance, readied their carbines and closed their ranks slightly. Close-combat doctrine dictated operating in four-man fire teams, two men with weapons on rapid, full automatic fire, for suppressing enemy fire and mobility, and the other two set up for single-shot, precision fire. These teams were already set up, and each team had been drilling together for some time. All Sgt. Alvin was doing was making deployment decisions based on math; the geometry of the terrain, the size of forces we were likely to encounter, things like that. And to cope with those things, he was deciding details like how many teams would deploy forward, and how far back the security elements should be, covering our backside against being surprised from the rear. In addition, Sgt. Alvin designated placement for the support teams, which were fast mobile fire teams whose job was to run to the sound of action,

ahead or behind, and offer supporting fire to any group which was
engaged.

     Hallowed G-Marine doctrine was that, in most situations, the side
who got the most guns on the enemy fastest usually won the engagement.
That's what shaped our tactics. With a couple of fire teams out front, only
four to eight men could be taken out rapidly by any enemy ambush or
tactic. Whenever the enemy engaged, support team training indicated a
rapid, but sensible approach, with the goal of putting more fire power on
the enemy as quickly as possible. Other techniques, such as enfilading
fire, were useful in a variety of situations such as planetary surface
combat, but on ships, in boarding actions, it generally came down to this
simple equation: More firepower kills more enemies. Flanking and other
basic infantry maneuvers, while desirable, were often impractical in this
kind of environment, and typically were only applied as ways of executing
the tactic of bringing more guns to bear by the fastest means possible, or
in the odd situation when the enemy actually was firing from a good cover
position. On a ship assault, that was the exception, rather than the rule.

     In practice, it was simple. Outside of rear-security elements,
everyone else's job was to get to the fight, start shooting, and overwhelm
the enemy as rapidly as possible. It was great doctrine when fifty men
attacked a ship with a complement of fifty to a hundred crewmembers. To
my knowledge, it had never been tried with fifty men attacking a total crew
of over three thousand. We would need to resolve contact as fast as
possible any time we engaged the enemy. It would be critical to win every
fight fast, before the enemy could mass to respond, and they would try to
delay us while they brought in replacements and reinforcements. With that
in mind, Alvin started the forward teams moving out, and put follow up
teams quite close behind them. Support very close behind the forward
teams put more men at greater risk of falling into an ambush, or getting
pinned down all together, but it would also allow us to push the response
time down, and work to resolve conflict faster. On balance, it was good
tactical decision making.

     So, formed up tightly, we were moving through the last hatch we
had opened, and it turned out to lead to a much wider hallway, which
suggested we had finally found our way into a main thoroughfare inside the
ship. That was good; it was likely to lead to areas more critical than spare
parts storage. I stayed in the middle of the men and watched them, much
more than I kept on eye on our surroundings. They moved well, some men
advancing while others took whatever minimal cover offered, or crouched
in defensive positions that offered smaller targets, covering whoever was
moving at the time. In a moment I had caught up to Sgt. Alvin, who had
gone forward with the first teams out. Alvin, seeing me, passed tactical
control back to the platoon sergeant, Steve Simpkins. The big man
acknowledged the order, and moved on, while Alvin stuck with me. When I
was close enough for conversation without raising my voice, I let Alvin
know what was on my mind.

"Alvin, it's been, what, almost fifteen minutes since we took that storage hold? Where's the resistance?"

"Don't know, Cap. Chasing those guys you set to blowing up hatches, I hope."

"They haven't reported on the coms, Alvin. That should mean they haven't been in contact with the enemy, shouldn't it? They understood, once they were located, they should report, right?"

"Yeah, they understand, Cap. But they're moving fast. Could be they're staying ahead of the defense."

"You think you could take fifteen minutes to make contact, if you were in charge of the defense, Alvin?"

He just shrugged. "It's a big ship, Cap. And maybe they were all on the entertainment deck when we breached the hull, had to go back to their quarters for their gear. Hell, maybe the officers were all in the head when the alarm went off, and it's taking them fifteen minutes to get their pants back up. Who knows?" Alvin was sanguine. He didn't care why we hadn't met any resistance; he just hoped it would last. But it bothered me. It didn't make sense. Just as our goal was to engage with massive firepower as quickly as possible, ship defenders should have been trying to slow us down, limit our progress, and harass us by any means possible. Even one or two troops with beam weapons could slow our advance significantly, tossing random shots our way, as they fired and retreated. It would reduce our rate of progress dramatically, each time we had to take cover and deal with them. Early defenders should have been taking pot-shots at us, by now, firing and retreating, while they called in our position to the bridge, and officers there directed more defenders to the point of contact.

"It's not right, Alvin. No marines harassing us, none of those first bodies we found suited for vacuum . . ." I looked over at him, as we moved further down the corridor. "I don't think the alarm has been given at all."

Alvin disagreed, immediately. "No way the bridge doesn't know we're here, Cap. They're just reacting slowly. It's a new crew, new command, and an unfamiliar ship. They're still trying to figure it all out."

I shook my head. "No. I mean, yes, that's all true, to some extent. But something else is going on here. The crew of *StarFire* went through the same training as we did, but they aren't acting like it. We need to figure out what's going on. Be ready to counter it, if it's tactics, and see if we can exploit it, if it's error."

"Looks to me like we're exploiting it just fine right now, Cap. We're moving through the ship, not taking losses. If this keeps up, the only thing better would be if we had free beer on the way."

Well, I didn't disagree. I just think we both knew that it couldn't keep going the way it was, even without the free beer. We fell silent, moving along with the men, while I tried to think things through and get an angle on the whole thing. But before I could make any progress putting it together, we heard something that put all other considerations aside, for the moment. It was gunfire.

Alvin and I shared a look at the first sounds, like each of us was just about to say to the other, "Does that sound like gunfire to you?" But before either of us spoke, the continuation of what we were hearing rendered the question moot. There just isn't a lot else that sounds like beam weapons fire, especially onboard a spacecraft.

Unlike projectile weapons, there isn't any big "bang" of exploding propellant when a beam weapon is discharged. There isn't even a "ping" when the bullet strikes a metal bulkhead, because beam weapons don't throw projectiles. Beam weapons do have a unique sound, unlike anything else. It's a static tearing sound, like a huge zipper being run up and down, really fast. Or like a hundred or a thousand ordinary-sized zippers, I suppose. Pops and crackles of electricity accompanied the tearing sound, but all of this is really pretty modest, in terms of volume. What really makes the noise in an environment like this one is when the beam contacts the target. A beam hit on flesh sounds like dropping a red-hot kitchen pan in water, or a juicy steak on a very hot grill. It's all sizzle and boil, a sound followed quickly by the smell of burning meat. That's if you hit a person with a beam carbine. But if you miss, it is something altogether different. On a spacecraft, a miss with a beam weapon tends to result in the beam striking something else, usually whatever is directly behind the body you are aiming at, and that is almost invariably a metal bulkhead. When that happens, the beam superheats a small area of the metal in an instant, causing rapid heat expansion in the metal at the point of contact. At the same time, in a few milliseconds the surface of the metal actually begins to melt. The now-fatigued metal, expanding rapidly with the heat where the beam is touching it, but not expanding at all over a broader area, where a beam is not touching it, almost always buckles right at the point of impact, and it makes a "bang" sound, in the moment of buckling. It sounds like a hammer blow on the side of an iron bathtub.

That was the sound we heard, like someone swinging away on an old piece of iron. But very quickly, that single hammer became a rapid cacophony of noise, as more shots were fired, and more misses struck the bulkhead behind the target. It went from one hammer on a bathtub to a dozen or so steam hammers in an old boiler factory, in less time that it takes to tell it.

It was a constant and rippling wave of sound, happening close by, which drowned out everything else. But having heard it plenty of times before, I could still tell that it wasn't a direct sound, coming from straight down the corridor. It had a hollow ring, a very slight echo. This noise was indirect, coming from around a corner, or even several corners, somewhere.

Alvin and I raced ahead, along with a couple of the support fire teams, who were close by us, and reacted at the same time we did. But small actions on ships tend to start quickly, and be over just as quickly, and as suddenly as it had started, the noise of beam fire stopped, just as we were approaching an intersection in the corridor. We already knew as we arrived that we were at the right place, because we saw burn mars blazed into the previously perfect paint on the walls of two corners in this intersection. I started slowing, as we approached the corner on the side away from the scorch marks, and Alvin slid in front of me.

It was part of Alvin's job to keep me out of harm's way, but that didn't make it more comfortable when he pulled up, peeking around the corner, suddenly putting one hand out in front of my chest like a traffic cop signaling "stop," to prevent me from exposing myself to weapons fire before he had scoped the scene around that corner. It felt like walking into a wall, more than walking into his hand.

But a moment later, Alvin dropped that hand and stepped out, lowering his beam weapon at the same time. That was enough of an "all clear" for me, and I followed right behind him.

What we found was one of our fire teams, one man down with a significant, but not crippling, burn wound to his thigh, and four bodies sprawled out, a little way past him. The bodies were in G-Marine uniforms, and they weren't suited for vacuum. They were *StarFire*'s marines, I concluded, and they were the first armed crewmembers we had seen. I looked for more, based on the volume of fire we had heard, but this was all there was.

* * *

While I was taking all this in, Sgt. Alvin, as usual, was taking care of business. He picked out the ranking member of this group, a corporal, and asked for his report. The corporal drew himself to attention, and gave us his account of the events.

"Private Butcher was on point when he spotted them—the enemy, I mean—coming down this side hallway. But I guess they saw him at the same time, because they opened up about the same time he did. He got off a couple shots, but he was wounded pretty quickly, and went down. Probably saved his life, though, because there was a lot of beam fire coming this way, right about then, and if he was still on his feet then, I think he would be toast, now. I thought there had to be ten or more enemy combatants, from the weapons-fire I saw, from back here in the main corridor.

"Anyway, the other point man, Johnston, he took cover at the corner before engaging, and then he started tossing some automatic fire their way about the time Butcher went down. He was attempting to suppress the enemy fire, while me and another team mate got into position to support. I took the near corner, standing over Johnston, while Peterson managed to get across the hall to the other corner." He paused a moment, then, either searching his memory for anything else significant, or deciding how to phrase what he said next. "We, uh, put them down pretty quick, then, without taking any other injuries."

It was a good report, succinct and informative, and it suggested these men were following their training. Well, except Butcher, who should have peeked around the corner before stepping out into the open, and then should have given priority to taking cover, since he was outnumbered, four to two, even counting Johnston. But I was guessing he wouldn't make that mistake again today. I stepped over to the bodies to have a quick look.

I wanted to know just one thing, first and foremost: Had these people contacted anyone with a report that they were under fire? One by one, I checked and found their com units in their holsters, clipped to their belts. That was a good sign, and I allowed myself to be optimistic. I turned to the Marine who had made his report to Sgt. Alvin.

"Did you see any of them make a report? Any indication they might have started a couple hundred of their mates headed this way, before you tagged them all?"

"I didn't see anything like that, sir. They were shooting, not talking. They were all shooting, rapid fire, but not on automatic, I could tell that much."

Sgt. Alvin made a noise, snorting at the comment, and saying, "Not shooting very well, though." Sgt. Alvin advocated the school of combat shooting that said a troop should fire full automatic, or carefully aimed, single shots. Nothing in between. And there was evidence to support his view that the least effective form of fire, especially from a beam weapon, was rapidly fired single shots. It tended neither to suppress the enemy sufficiently, nor to increase casualties on him.

"Yeah, they must have been pretty surprised," the corporal tacitly agreed. "They didn't take cover or go prone, or anything. Just stood there, shoulder to shoulder, firing their weapons about as fast as they could pull the triggers." He looked past us, down the hall, at the plethora of scorch marks on the walls down there.

While this was going on, someone had seen to Pvt. Butcher, dressing his wound, and then slapping a patch on his vacuum suit, to cover burn hole, and the subsequent tear in the material they had made to facilitate treating his wound. I looked him over from a few feet away. He looked like he was ready and able to get back to work, and I figured it was time for some encouragement, for all these troops.

"Well done, men. Pvt. Butcher, be more careful about stepping into the open. The rest of you, good work. You saved your teammate, and put down four of the enemy. A straight up firefight, with even odds, and you took one casualty, a light wound. That's good work. Now, let's move out. Maybe these guys didn't get a chance to call it in, but we made plenty of noise here. We should get out of the immediate vicinity, ASAP."

A chorus of "Roger that!" and "Yes, sir!" came back, and we stepped out, moving deeper into the ship. I didn't miss the observation that these men all walked a little taller, while still ratcheting up their alert level a notch or two, in my estimation. I saw what any combat soldier will tell you: So long as errors of overconfidence are avoided, victory breeds victory.

And this bunch had just won one. It was good for this point-squad fire team, and just as good for the men following them.

Butcher formed up with his team, limping only very slightly, though I guessed that limp would likely become more pronounced after the anesthetic in the battle-dressing wore off. Still, he and his teammates stepped off sharply, with Butcher back on point. I turned to Sgt. Alvin with a raised eyebrow, and he caught the drift of my thoughts.

"They're good, sir. They got through that firefight with better marksmanship, and better tactics than their opponents. And the private maybe learned a good lesson, there, as well." He started walking, me beside him, as the team moved forward. "It's a good start, Cap."

It was just then that Duvall's voice came over my com, on the command channel that only myself and Company Master Sergeant Alvin would receive.

"Vince . . . they just got Bob Smithson. We've been monitoring with our sensors, and Mark saw the shot. A direct hit; nothing much left. No need to respond to this transmission. I just thought you would want to know. No other activity observed at this time."

Smithson was gone. That last bit of the message, about "no other activity" was Duvall letting me know that Harley hadn't broken cover and tried to run yet. We were still too close to his position, and *StarFire* was still too deadly. Harley was playing possum, waiting for us to improve his odds before he played his hand. Harley would have heard Duvall's report to me, and I realized that, having heard it, Harley was likely leave it to Duvall to find a way to broadcast a message letting him know if we managed to disable something significant on the ship, making it the right time for him to run.

And then, there wasn't any more time to catch up or even think about the situation outside the ship. The hammers-on-iron sound of another fire fight rang down the corridor, and we were all suddenly running in the direction of the noise. Things were heating up.

* * *

Over the next half hour or so, we bumped into a couple more groups of four enemy marines—always four at a time—and our progress slowed as a result. Somewhere along the way, Squad Four had finally reported on the coms they were engaged as well. The terse report by that sergeant fit with what we were seeing: Small groups of *StarFire*'s marines, apparently just patrolling areas they had been assigned to, trying to ferret us out. There was no indication of a really organized response yet, and no indication that they were anticipating our path through the ship. It was almost as though each small group simply headed to wherever we had most recently been engaged, and were a little surprised to discover we had moved a little farther along in between actions.

Alvin caught the pattern first, and coached the point men that we were no longer just trying to move along, getting to the interior corridors which most likely lead to the significant areas of the ship. He had them hunting, assuming that more marines were headed towards us, and if we detected them first, we had a good chance of continuing our streak of good luck and small victories. We had picked up a few more wounded, nothing very serious, and we were still doing far better than we had a right to expect. Alvin had the support crew closed up right on the heels of the point men, and that worked out well for us when we finally crossed paths with a larger group.

We had come onto a large equipment bay, a place where cargo-handling machines were stored and maintained. The high ceiling was crisscrossed with cables and cranes, to facilitate repair work on the machines, while the floor of the large room, perhaps sixty yards by forty yards, was lined along all four sides with stacks of drums, crates, boxes, and tool containers. In the center of the room resided enough cargo handling equipment to operate a small manufacturing facility. Forklifts, self-propelled platforms, even a small cargo truck, what the Navy called a "mule" sat clustered together, idle, but ready for use. The mule was an electric vehicle with minimal payload capacity, but enough torque to pull several trailers at a time. The trailers were there, too.

The point men, hopped up on adrenalin and on their run of good results, still had the good sense to hold up before entering this large, open space, and they stopped at the entrance. As the column closed up on them, Alvin had a quick look through the huge, open cargo access doors, to the interior of the bay. He turned to face the men, all now bunched up near the entrance, except for the security element, which had seen us and stopped, taking positions a bit further out, so as to cover the approaches to our position while we worked out how we were going to go through this space.

One of the men offered an opinion. "Looks empty, Sarge. I don't see anything moving."

Alvin answered him gently, but firmly. "It looks empty, but it ain't really empty until we clear it, Marine." Very quickly, he issued orders, speaking to the squad sergeants, but just loudly enough that most of the men nearby could hear him. "I want two squads, one squad to each side. Move along the wall, advancing by teams; one team covers when the other moves. The third squad goes straight down the middle. For that group, move to cover fast, as a unit, then hold up and wait for the side columns to catch up. The side columns are your covering fire. Each time they are in position, move to the next covered position. Now listen up: If we are engaged, you do not break out of your columns. There's no reason we can't cover each other across the width of this cargo area. Support flows up the columns, on each side, but you stay in your zone and move forward to support, not across. Clear?"

Three squad sergeants all affirmed they understood, and then checked in with their men to make sure each one had gotten the orders. Then, Squad One entered straight on in, taking the middle position, and moved to a large pyramid of barrels, just inside the doors. They took cover behind and around it. The two other squads moved off, one to each side, and half of each squad took cover around whatever was handy, weapons leveled and at the ready, while their mates dashed up to the next batch of decent cover, rapidly, but moving low, and staying close to the walls. In another moment, Squad One rose up together and advanced, up the middle, until they had cover again. In this way, one third of the men advanced, while two thirds were in ready firing positions from cover. Then, when the forward third took cover, the others caught up. Alvin and I remained behind, covering the cargo hatch we came in through, as rear guard, along with one fire team, the security element from Squad One. We were getting ready to move forward, ourselves, as the last men of the side columns were just catching up to the forward group, at the halfway mark. Then the enemy entered the bay from the other side, in one group.

This is where training pays off, if it's going to. We had been working our way through the large bay, not in anticipation of a group coming through from the other side, but simply from being cautious about bumping into personnel that might be on duty in this bay. The enemy, with no need for such concerns, was not working through the way we did, from cover to cover. They essentially just marched into the room, apparently only intending to cross through to some position already behind us. Because of Sgt. Alvin's careful tactics, twenty of my thirty men were already positioned, in cover, weapons ready, when the enemy was spotted. Another six were just arriving at cover, three on each side. And six of us, counting Alvin and myself, were all the way across the room, some sixty yards away. We had taken our cover positions against the possibility of the enemy coming up on us from behind, which left us out in plain sight to anyone coming from the other end of the equipment bay, and they saw us right away. But no quicker than Sgt. Alvin saw them.

"Incoming, take cover!" Alvin yelled out, loosing several shots from his carbine, as he swiveled quickly around the pyramid of barrels we were still using for cover. I didn't see how effective his fire had been, as I was busy making a lunging dive off to one side, myself, in the other direction. As beam fire started lancing down the through the open areas of the floor, the thin metal which made up the barrels we were using for cover made a different sound, not the deep, bass ring of energy beams hitting bulkheads. It was a lighter, popping noise, like sheet metal popping as it is bent into a new shape. More than a few pops sounded in my ears by the time my body hit the floor, and I slid a couple feet further on, before scrambling to crab my way around another stack of supplies. Then the hissing and spitting sound of beam carbines filled the air around me, as my men began returning fire, and looking back, I saw the barrels I had so recently been standing in front of were ruptured and they began to spill a viscous liquid, perhaps some sort of lubricant, which ran rapidly down the stack of barrels and out onto the floor. The sound of hammers rose again, the shots following my men away from the barrels, as my men took cover, and misses no longer impacted the lubricant drums, but slipped past, to strike the walls behind us. Our enemy began to fan out, to bring more guns to bear, and the rate of fire increase even more.

I could no longer see the enemy from my position, and only surmised what was happening at the other end of the room from the rain of beam fire directed at us. It seemed to be double what it was just a few moments ago, and then it doubled again, a few seconds after that. I began to wonder how large a group we had come into contact with, because it seemed impossible that this much fire could be coming from a group even our own size. We were thirty-two, counting Alvin and myself, spread all around this cargo bay. I guessed we had to be facing at least twice that many, from the fire they produced, and I worked my way around to a corner of the stack of crates I was taking cover behind, desperate to see what the situation really was, and wanting to shoot back. If they were starting with twice as many guns as we had, that was going to be a serious problem. We needed every beam carbine to be active, and as soon as possible.

But we had an advantage or two ourselves. We were spread out, and therefore, harder to spot. And we were all, or nearly all, in covered positions, using the materials and machines scattered around the bay. That made us much harder to hit. When I popped my head up for a quick look, I was surprised at what I saw. The enemy was spread out, as I had guessed, but they weren't taking cover of any kind. They were standing in loose ranks, literally lined up across the other end of the bay. And every one of them was firing at the position we had just moved away from. Instead of holding fire, and watching for targets of opportunity, they poured fire at and all around our last known position.

I ducked down again, actually before any of those impressions had worked their way up to my conscious mind. It was a technique designed to minimize exposure time to enemy fire: Pop up, look, and duck, and process what was seen only after getting back into cover again. After reviewing those first impressions, I did some rough estimating, and figured we might be looking at forty hostiles, but probably not much more. Assuming I had seen them all, and there weren't forty or fifty more still outside the hatch, who hadn't entered yet. And assuming that a dozen or two hadn't been smarter than the ones I saw standing in ranks, and ducked behind something when Alvin started firing. I dismissed those thoughts. It was bad enough, without imagining an even bigger problem than I had already seen, but not nearly as bad as it could have been. The volume of fire reflected their hurried trigger fingers, not their total numbers, and they fired at an almost frantic rate. That would reduce their accuracy, I hoped.

I moved a few feet laterally, just in case one of them might have aimed his weapon at the place I had just popped up, waiting for the next time I took a quick look, and ready to fire instantly if I did. When I was four of five feet over, I was at the right-side end of my cover anyway, the end towards the middle of the room. I readied my weapon, extending the collapsible stock, and seating it firmly against my shoulder, and then I popped up again, a little taller, this time.

Looking down the barrel of my beam carbine, the weapon's optical sight presented a small chevron, like an upside-down "V" shape. The beam would impact at the pinnacle, the point of the "V" at the top. It was a holographic sight, and the bright red figure seemed to float a half inch or so above the top of my carbine, and a few feet forward of the end of my weapon. All I had to do was to rest the tip of that "V" on the body of my target, and squeeze the trigger. If I could hold steady while I did that, I could be confident of striking my target. It was an effective, intuitive, "fast-sighting" system, and I was a good marksman with the weapon.

Since I was on the left side of the cargo bay, the enemy was all to the right of me. I started aiming at figures on the far right of the enemy group, those farthest from me, which left me still behind cover relative to most of them. I aligned my sight with the chest of the first man, on the farthest right end. The weapon crackled, a blue glare flashed at the end of my gun, instantly drawing a perfectly straight line directly to my target, and I had already shifted my aim to the next target as my peripheral vision registered that the first man dropped a moment later. I squeezed the trigger again, quickly, and shifted to the next one, moving left. My eyes registered a miss on the second target, as I had let the beam weapon traverse too far, too quickly, before getting the trigger pulled far enough to fire. My training kicked in again, and I calmed myself, taking a shallow breath, and holding it, while I tracked back right, and steadied the sight again on the chest of the man I had just missed. The weapon sizzled and crackled for an instant again, and this time the man went down. Traversing left again, I realized that there were no more of the enemy in my line of sight of from my current position. Hugging my cover closely, my field of view was limited, and I leaned further out to line up the next one. I couldn't find him. I edged farther out, and still, I couldn't see any of them. It took me a long moment to realize that they were all down.

The entire firefight had taken much less than thirty seconds, though I didn't actually realize it at the time. With the adrenalin that came with combat, time was dilated, and perceptions unreliable. But I did know we appeared to have won another engagement. A couple of my men, the ones that figured it out first, rose up and started cheering. The others caught on pretty fast, and everyone was giddy with the victory. Then, a few of the men started moving forward to check on the downed enemy troops we had fought, and others started checking on their buddies, looking for wounds that might require attention. But the cheering was still going on when we discovered that we did have a few light wounds, and also, we had lost two men.

CHAPTER 15

Defense Space Station G-13, 246.163.12

After Action

Linda Tillman had stopped taking notes, at some point. I didn't notice exactly when. And now she sat silent for a moment. I figured this was her, showing respect for the memory of a fighter pilot who had basically volunteered for an incredibly dangerous mission, and lost his life doing it, and for the men who boarded *StarFire* with me, and taken such incredible risks, and executed their orders with such diligence. I looked away, not willing to intrude on her moment of silence.

I looked back in time to catch her looking at the floor, as I had been a moment before. I told her, "So, Lt. Smithson . . . I put him in for a decoration, and wrote the letter to his parents. He was single, no children, so, the letter goes to his parents. It wasn't the first time I had to write one of those letters, but it was a hard one."

"I'm sure they're all hard, Captain Lombard."

There wasn't anything to say to that. Of course, she was right. But still, some are harder than others, and they stay with you longer. I figured Robert Smithson's would be one that stayed with me my whole life. Lt. Tillman went on, after a moment. "Is that what you meant when you said, 'It got worse'? That men started dying?"

I shook my head. "Men dying is a part of combat. My men, the enemy's men. Even with a complete victory, death is a part of the equation. You don't get used to it, but you learn to deal with it. So, yeah, that's bad, but . . ." I paused, gathering my thoughts. "No, what I was talking about things getting worse wasn't about the pressure of combat, or the deaths of the men- ours or *StarFire*'s. It was about the way that combat was shaping up.

"What we should have noticed, and didn't, after that first big fire fight, was that *StarFire*'s marine complement wasn't fighting the way we were taught to fight. They shouldn't have lost four men while only inflicting one light wound on my forces in that first exchange. And no way should they have traded forty lives for the two they cost us, in the fire-fight in the equipment bay. I was just too full of myself, and full of confidence in my

men, to understand right away that something weird was going on. But it
didn't take too long after that before it became pretty obvious."

CHAPTER 16

Alliance Military Ship StarFire

Action

The action seemed to come faster, after that large engagement in the equipment bay. Alvin and I agreed, there were a couple of likely reasons for that; maybe that large group had communicated our position and even an estimate of our strength back to their commanders, or maybe we were just getting much closer to critical areas, now that we were near the center of the ship, and the opposition had simply put more of their firepower near those critical areas. We didn't know, but whatever the cause, we were seeing the enemy more frequently. We also soon noticed they appeared to be more aware, harder to catch off guard. Gradually, it seemed, just as the small engagements were coming faster, each one was also getting harder to win.

The next encounter started like the very first one had. A Marine on point turned a corner and looked straight down the hallway to see enemy combatants headed right for him. He got the first shots off, his teammates jumped into position, and they put the enemy down. It was fast and dirty, and none of the men on that point team were hit, that time. But a just minute later, the security team was engaged. The enemy had caught up from somewhere behind us, and our rear guard found themselves in a firefight.

Several of us were still standing over the bodies of the enemy from the previous, forward engagement when the barrage of hammer blows filled the air in the corridor we had come from. A moment later, the call came over the coms.

"Security element is engaged with multiple targets. We are outnumbered, and require support." The coms were still supposed to be used for emergencies only, but emergencies were becoming more frequent all the time. And maybe it didn't matter. They always seemed to know where we were as soon as one of them made contact, anyway, and as I said, that was getting more frequent.

The support teams heard the call and were already falling back, to cover the security squad, while Alvin shouted orders to the point team which had just been engaged.

"You stay put," he hollered at them, raising his voice over the din of beam fire and misses ringing off the bulkheads. He pointed at each Marine with his finger, to make it clear who he was addressing. "You're forward security now, until we see what we are up against back there. Find some cover, and face the way you were going, not back towards us. You hold this space until we call for you, or we come back through here. Don't let us get pinched between two groups unaware. You see something, even if you think you can handle it, you sing out." Then he was moving back, following behind the support teams. I had already started, while he was coordinating the point men, but he caught up with me in no time.

It was a pretty straightforward operation, one that didn't require much in the way of strategy or original thinking. The four-man security team had been alert, and caught sight of the enemy from positions of decent cover. I learned afterwards that they had opened fire as soon as they saw that the enemy outnumbered them significantly, choosing to engage at whatever distance they could, because they wanted to use direct fire to drive the enemy into cover. Their reasoning was, it would slow the enemy advance and give our support teams time to come back and get into position to reinforce the security squad. It was a pretty good tactical decision by the non-com in charge, and probably exactly what I would have recommended, if he had asked me on the coms before making that decision.

But the enemy did not duck and run for cover. As soon as my men opened up on them, they raised their guns and started shooting, all of them who had a line of fire unobstructed by their comrades, standing in front of them. What my men told me afterwards was strange, though. They said that, of the five or six shooting in the first minute, every single one of them appeared to home in on the same target— that is, the same one of my troops, a private named Baily.

Pvt. Baily had decent cover, having crouched down directly behind a support column that extended about eighteen inches out from the wall at that spot in the corridor. There weren't a lot of these support columns, which was one reason the security element decided to hold at that particular place, to use the columns as cover. Looking at his position afterwards, I estimated that Baily was perhaps twenty-five percent exposed as he fired at the enemy. That made him neither the easiest target, nor the most obvious one. He wasn't the first of his team to fire, nor the most accurate. But he was the closest to them, and he became the target the enemy homed in on. It wasn't proper Corps doctrine, to focus on one position like that, and in fact, it worked in our favor, because none of the other troops were suppressed by the fire on Baily. It wasn't even a particularly effective method for getting Baily, speaking in tactical terms. What struck me, though, was that it was new. They hadn't done that before, and I wondered about that for a moment.

The other troops who witnessed it told me that the fire rained in on Baily's position for a good couple of minutes before they got him, and except for a couple of minor burns to his right arm, on the side he exposed as he engaged the enemy from behind that column, due to the need for leaning out from his position to fire, he lasted a good little while in that position. He finally took a severe and mortal wound, after the enemy fire actually burned through the support column he was hiding behind. A corpsman, after having a look at his body, told me he might have been hit with three or more beams, all at once, when the metal finally gave way. And all of those shots went through a hole perhaps two inches in diameter to strike Baily in the chest. It was uncanny, and hard to make sense of, for a couple of reasons.

This was an Alliance Military ship, and that support column Baily used for cover was one hundred percent durasteel. It should have resisted normal beam fire for quite a while. Because normal fire would have been a little random, and spread the heat out over a larger area. Under normal fire, that column would have lasted long enough for the whole fire-fight to be over, one way or another. So, to accomplish this, not only were all the enemy shooting at Baily, but at some point, or maybe from the first moment, they all started shooting at the same spot on the support column. Most likely, it seemed, just for the purpose of combining their fire, and burning through the cover. Obviously, someone had decided that they were going to get at least one of us, this time, and directed the others to support that effort. The question on my mind as I looked at the evidence was, how did they coordinate that? How do you get the attention of five troops engaged in a firefight, all of them under fire themselves, and pick out one spot on an unmarked support column to concentrate fire on? I could maybe do that with five guys like Company Master Sergeant Alvin, or Platoon Sergeant Simpkins, but they were the very best of my men, and even then, we would have to plan it ahead of time. No way could I count on that kind of level-headed performance from my average Marine. At least, not without drilling the men for a few weeks in advance. But so far, we had seen nothing to suggest these men had ever been drilled in anything. They weren't even in vacsuits, for crying out loud. The only thing we had seen so far that actually looked like Galactic Marine Corps training was that they marched together real well, so long as they weren't under fire. But here they were, executing a crackpot idea someone had, to focus their fire on one enemy in a firefight. It was not a very good idea, but they executed it perfectly. There was no way to get my head around that.

I turned and ran through that train of thought with Sgt. Alvin, explaining why I found it so strange. He listened to me, and then looked the scene over, very carefully. And then promptly pointed out something else to me, after examining the column on the other side of the corridor. Something I had missed. When Pvt. Baily fell, the whole group of shooters had apparently shifted their fire to the support column on the other side of the hallway, where another Marine was shooting from cover. And they focused on that column, in the same way, several of them firing on the same point, it seemed, because that column was very nearly burned through, as well. If we had the time-line right, they had had much less time to work on it before the support teams showed up and started evening the numbers out. That Marine was not hit, but it looked like it was a close run thing. What had saved him, Alvin and I both suspected, was that the support teams had a free hand picking targets out with very little pressure on them, because all the fire was on the support column. No suppression fire was directed at the rest of my men.

We were still talking this over as our men organized some first aid for the wounded. A medic had started working on one of the guys who had taken a light wound. Then, after looking around and finding that no one else needed him on our side, the medic ran a little way down the hall, to where others of my men were checking the enemy bodies. One of them wasn't quite dead yet, so the corpsman set to work on that man, doing what he could to save his life, enemy or not. G-Marine medics are trained to do that, since you never know which enemy soldier might turn out to know something or be important, and because after our own wounded are seen to, it's just humane. But especially because we were fighting G-Marines, whatever the circumstances, our medics were disposed to do what they could for the enemy wounded.

That man, the enemy survivor, was in a bad way. Unconscious, or at least in a stupor, he had one arm nearly burned through, above the elbow, where he caught a beam discharge. And he had severe injuries in both his legs, also beam burns. The medic, working fast, immediately slapped an autotourniquet on the least injured leg, the only one really bleeding, and the only appendage of the three which he could probably save anyway. He activated the self-constricting, adhesive device, and then turned his attention to taking vital signs from his patient, before deciding on the next step. He had gotten as far as checking him for pupil reaction, one of the fastest ways to differentiate a significant head wound from unconsciousness resulting from simple shock, when the enemy marine appeared to come to his senses a little bit. He started squirming, like he was trying to get up.

Holding him down with one hand, and still shining a little light into one of his eyes, the medic tried to keep the man calm.

"Take it easy. I think you'll be alright, buddy. Your left leg is shot through, but the right one isn't so bad, and if we don't find any other problems, I think I can stabilize you until your shipmates find you, and haul your ass down to sickbay. They can fix you up, just fine, there . . ." He was still talking when the enemy troop got his wits gathered up enough to focus on a real response.

It wasn't a verbal response. And he didn't scream or moan with pain, either, as most men would have been doing. He just reached up with his good arm, and after fumbling around for a moment, got a grip on the medic's throat and started doing his best to throttle him, one handed

I was standing right there, talking with Alvin, but watching the whole thing, and when I realized what the injured man was doing, I stepped forward to lend a hand to my medic. I was a half-step too slow. The medic, after a momentary struggle, gripped his beam carbine with one hand, the other being busy trying to pull the patient's hand off his neck, at this point. Then, he used that carbine as a club, and whacked the injured man a good one, right across the top of his head. It was an awkward blow, without much swing behind it, but maybe adrenalin boosted the corpsman's reaction, because it sounded like a solid whacking, like an MP might give a drunk and violent sailor he was dragging away from a bar fight.

It was enough. The injured man collapsed, and his hand came of the medic's throat. The medic went back to what he was doing, checking the wounds and taking vital signs, but he gave up almost immediately.

"Huh. I must have hit him too hard," the medic said, sounding surprised. I looked down at him. I didn't understand for a minute, but then I caught on.

"This one's dead?" I asked.

"Yeah, stone dead. It's weird. He was pretty chewed up, but look; no major organs hit, just these leg and arm wounds, and none of them bleeding bad, after the autotourniquet had a chance to tighten down on the leg. The other wounds were pretty well cauterized by the beam heat."

"So, maybe he lost too much blood before you got to him?" I suggested.

He glanced at the readout on the autotourniquet. "His blood pressure was fine, right up to the end. I mean, not great, but not fatal. He didn't bleed out." Now he used his fingers to probe the scalp wound where he had hit the man with his carbine. "And I don't feel a fracture or anything that should have killed him from that blow to the head."

"So, he had some internal injury we can't see, and won't ever know about, short of a full autopsy."

He sat back for a moment, and looked up at me. "I don't see any reason for him to be dead. Maybe shock?" He said it like he was trying it on for size. "Why did he try to choke me out? I was going to save his life." He gestured to the rest of the men, milling about nearby. "It doesn't make any sense. Even if I didn't whack him on the head, he would have been cut down before he could strangle me. There're guys with carbines all over the place." The medic was truly and entirely bewildered by the whole thing.

"Forget it, son. Whatever he was thinking, we'll never find out from him. You did your best. Above and beyond what's required of you. Nice work." That was what I needed to say to the corpsman, but to be honest, I was as rattled by what I had seen as he was. It didn't fit, like a badly tuned violin that stands out in the orchestra, no matter what the music is. And once you pick that badly tuned instrument out of the chorus, you can hear it, plain as day. In fact, once you notice it, you can't stop hearing it. And the natural reaction is to listen to the other instruments more closely, see if they are all in tune, right? It started me thinking of a number of odd things I had noticed since we began the assault. But I didn't have time to work it all out right now. We needed to move out before the enemy caught up with us again.

"Alvin, we need to move. We've lost time, backtracking, and they are finding us faster all the time. It won't be long before they hit us again."

"Yes sir, Cap. I'm in complete agreement." That was out of character for Sgt. Alvin, so I turned and looked at him, eyebrows raised, wondering what he was getting at.

"Something else you want to say?"

"No sir. Just, I agree with you, they are finding us pretty fast. I wonder which way you would like us to go now, sir?"

So that was it. All those "sirs" were a way of catching my attention, a way to get me to ask him for a suggestion I wasn't asking for. Alvin was not quite openly suggesting that I pick a new and, hopefully, unpredictable direction, and get us off what was apparently becoming a predictable path to our adversaries.

"You want a new path of advance? I'm good with that." I looked around, quickly. We didn't really know where we were going, so one direction was as good as another, as long as we continued to generally head towards the deep core of the ship. I didn't have a preference, and beyond that, I wanted some time to think. "Alvin, you keep us moving deeper into the ship, but do that any way you want, for the time being. If you think it will help to detour a little, I don't see any harm, so long as we don't lose ground. But you handle it, would you? I have something on my mind I need to pay attention to for a minute." And that turned out to be one of my more fortunate decisions, in a couple different ways, turning the operational command over to Sgt. Alvin for a little while.

* * *

Sgt. Alvin changed the direction quite handily, by deciding to ditch the standard question of "left or right?" He cut through that conundrum by choosing "down." But first, just to get us out of the path of anyone headed for the space between our last two engagements, he took us off at an angle perpendicular to our previous path, and after just a few minutes getting some small distance between us and our previous position, he picked out a smaller corridor branching off the main passage we were in. Then, very quickly, he put men to checking out compartments we could enter, but only those we could get into by opening hatches, instead of blowing them.

He wanted to be able to close the hatch behind us, and not leave an obvious trail to follow. We had some luck, and the second compartment the men checked out seemed to serve his purpose. Alvin detailed a few men outside, to keep watch, and then, he had a squad sergeant deploy breeching charges, inside the compartment, preparing to blow a hole in the deck. Sgt. Alvin was going take us to a different level of the ship for the first time since we had boarded. It was good a good tactic, though not really a new idea. We did it from time to time in a number of different exercises. The trick to this sort of thing was in knowing when to use it. It was about timing, guessing when the enemy would be less likely to think of that possibility while they looked for us. It worked best when the enemy got complacent, and had formed a habit of looking on one level, and they had gotten used to thinking two-dimensionally. Alvin had a talent for that sort of thing, out-guessing the competition. It was just like his talent for bluffing on the poker tables, and he decided the time was right. When everything inside the compartment was ready, he pulled his last few men in, and then he pulled out some welding tape, which he unrolled and pressed into the mechanism of the hatch on the inside of this compartment.

When everyone was in place, he had one of the sergeants blow the charges. With the deck opened up sufficiently for the men to move down a level, he sent a few ahead to look it over. One of them came back in just a minute, hollering up through the hole in the floor that it looked good, clear of the enemy, and with promising avenues of access to other areas of the ship. Alvin ordered the rest of the men down to the compartment below, and then turned around to the hatch. Welding tape, once in place, required only activation. In normal use, a torch is held to one end, to ignite the chemical composition, which would melt a metal core in the tape, while chemically and mechanically bonding it to almost any metals it might be used on. In this case, lacking a torch, Sgt. Alvin simply dialed his beam carbine down a little, and discharged it at a section of the tape. It ignited immediately, but for good measure, he put beam discharges into a couple other places, as well. Then, as the tape started its burn from three separate locations, rapidly fusing the mechanism of the hatch cover, the last of us dropped down through the hole in the deck.

We were now off our previous path. Only about twelve feet off it, but with some solid durasteel plate between us and the bulk of the folks looking for us. Additionally, we had left no signs outside that last compartment showing which way we had gone. To cap it off, no one was coming through that access hatch to the compartment above us any time soon to see the hole we used to change levels. Overall, I guessed it was a pretty good disappearing act.

* * *

We took full advantage of the reprieve Alvin had bought for us, and while we still moved carefully, we made good time, and finally approached our goal: We had reached the deepest, central area of the ship. Here, we would find the rooms that housed the major systems. Alliance warship engineers and designers tended, very sensibly, to protect the most critical battle systems by placing them as deeply into the bowels of the vessel as possible. In that sense, all the levels of floors, the less essential storage areas, cargo bays, compartments, living quarters—all of that amounted to layers of armor, a buffer protecting the vital equipment necessary to the function of waging war, which is why a military ship primarily exists. Even personnel were expendable in comparison to the war-making machinery and systems which a battleship served to carry from place to place, and put into use, when called upon.

In addition, by the time we had reached the core of the ship, I had been able to spend a little while thinking of the things I had seen, things that were finally working their way up to my awareness, but which I should have noticed right away, if I had my head in the game from the moment we boarded.

I had been thinking about the way *StarFire*'s marines were approaching each engagement, standing shoulder to shoulder, and not seeking cover when the shooting started. And their sudden shift in tactics, when they decided to focus all their attention on one trooper at a time. About their remarkably poor performance, so far. And about how not a one of them had offered to surrender, even when the last man was standing after his comrades had fallen around him. I spent a lot of time thinking about that wounded marine who had died trying to throttle the medic who was working to save his life. Sure, maybe he felt he had nothing to lose, since, if he was a mutineer he would be executed anyway. There would be those types, the "never surrender" guys. But generally speaking, experience had taught me that proportionally, there were always a lot more of the other kind, the kind who felt like, "if I can just survive this, I'll deal with that whole military court and execution problem later." That was human nature, when staring death in the face. Survive the moment, worry about the rest later. But *StarFire*'s men didn't seem to think that way. Not a one of them.

And finally, I was re-thinking the whole problem of how the enemy was finding us more and more rapidly after each engagement, in spite of the fact that we had not seen any of the enemy use a com device. We hadn't even seen a com dropped on the floor, suggesting it had been in use. They were always found still in their holsters, on the bodies of the marines we killed. Taken in context with the observation that I hadn't heard any verbal orders given by the enemy non-coms during the engagements, it was . . . well, it was troubling. I couldn't remember one example of "Take cover," or "Fire at will!" or even the ubiquitous, "Incoming!" to warn comrades they were under fire. These guys didn't talk to one another at all, so far as I had seen.

It wasn't normal. It wasn't right. I finally turned to Sgt. Alvin and voiced my thoughts to him. I went down the list, and then added a couple more anomalies I thought of while I was speaking to him.

"Alvin, none of this makes sense to me. We're still fighting G-Marines who haven't bothered to put on vacuum suits. They fight as though they haven't had any training whatsoever. We're slaughtering them, and taking very light casualties doing it."

"Yeah, our boys are holding up their end pretty good, I think," he interjected. "Better than I hoped."

"Our boys are doing fine, Alvin. But that's not what's really going on here. Think about it for a minute. It's not at all like we're fighting men who have had the same training we have had. They don't do anything to minimize their losses. They just try to take a couple of us with them each time we engage."

Alvin gave me a sideways glance, as though patiently waiting for me to get it before deciding to speak. He must have gotten impatient, though, because eventually he let me in on his thoughts.

"Yeah, they're not the best bunch of G-Marines I've ever seen. Maybe they're troops some other commanders transferred out because they weren't performing. But ours are as good as we can make them. This is training and discipline, paying off."

"Really, Alvin? You think Fleet Command put the worst performers in the Corps on their flagship? Come on, man. These guys are going down easier than the simulations we faced in boarding exercises a week ago." That got through to Sgt. Alvin. No one had more contempt for the level of competence shown by the simulation programmers than Alvin had. I pressed my point. "Even if all these guys we're up against are cherries who've never seen combat before, we shouldn't do this well. We ran fifteen percent casualties on takedowns with simulated crews of fifty. Here we are, hours into a boarding action, doing more fighting than we have on any single exercise before, and we have, what, four KIA, and a half dozen lightly wounded? And, do you think cherries would stand and fight to the last man, every time? Tell me how that makes sense, Alvin. We don't train our men to fight to the last man, and throw their lives away, once a situation is hopeless. A trained G-Marine who wanted to delay our progress would surrender, knowing that hauling a few prisoners around would slow us down, and require a few troops to guard them, taking them away from future firefights. Hell, a half-dozen prisoners would have removed more guns from our side of each contact than they have managed to kill, so far!"

Alvin took a moment, but after running it through his head, he came to the same conclusion I had already come to, but hadn't said out loud.

"They can't be G-Marines."

I agreed. "Thank you. At least we're on the same track." And now that it had been said, neither one of us wanted to say the next thing that came to both our minds.

G-Marines and Alliance sailors came out here on this ship. They were the only humans in this sector. If these weren't G-Marines, I didn't know what they were, but I knew what they were not. They were not human.

CHAPTER 17

Defense Space Station G-13, 246.163.12

After Action

" And by 'not human,' you mean . . . ?" Linda Tillman had a curious look on her face, like I had said something enigmatic. Maybe she was just trying to draw me out, but really, how many different ways can you take, "Not human"?

I shrugged at her.

"I don't really know. I mean, those folks looked human, and operated human equipment, like the beam carbines, just the same as ours. Hell, they even bled like humans, and my corpsmen didn't notice anything when they were working on them. But they didn't behave like human beings." I had faced the same problem in my written report. What was I going to say that wouldn't sound crazy? Aliens and humans often had some basic similarities, enough that some races adopted human clothes, and even approximated human male and female traits. But none of them would be mistaken for human if someone sat in the same room for a few minutes of conversation with one, or even just looked closely. Much less if they had a good look at their insides, like, if they had been opened up with a beam discharge. But I was telling Lt. Tillman that the troops we faced were wearing Alliance uniforms, on an Alliance ship, and could not be differentiated from humans in any observable way, but were not human. In my written report, I had catalogued the strange behavior, but didn't draw any conclusions from it. I suppose I was hoping some intelligence guy would connect the dots, and have this argument with Fleet Command, so I wouldn't have to. I wanted no part of it, really, because no one was going to like the implications of it. In my experience, it's pretty much axiomatic that the first few people to be the ones saying, "Hey, we have a real problem here. There's a threat on the horizon that might just destroy civilization as we know it," tend to be pretty unpopular.

My interrogator spoke up again, saying, "So . . . you think, what? There's a race out there just like us? A race that we can't tell from human?" Lt. Tillman showed open skepticism, now, so maybe that was a sign of some sort of progress. It meant she was at least engaged in the conversation. Nobody intentionally has "conversation" with a mad man.

"I don't think anything, Lieutenant, except that what we saw on *StarFire* wasn't like any pattern of human behavior I have ever come across before. I'm not a xenobiologist. I'm a combat G-Marine line officer. And I'm saying combat G-Marines are not what we fought against on *StarFire* that day."

Lt. Linda Tillman sat for a while, just looking at me. Maybe she was trying to figure out how to put this into her notes. Or maybe she was just now thinking she wished she hadn't drawn this particular assignment. My guess is the latter.

CHAPTER 18

Alliance Military Ship StarFire

Action

We were in the right area for critical centers of the ship, but we had yet to actually find anything useful to disable. *StarFire* was so incredibly big, it was like trying to find the power plant in a small city, on foot, without a map, with the power cables all run underground, so we couldn't even follow them in one direction or the other. In fact, that would have been easier. We would have had a fifty-fifty chance, doing that.

But on the upside, we seemed to have slipped away from the pursuit. Once I realized we were up against something unusual, I gave orders that changed the rules of engagement. We hadn't been found again, yet, so I thought it was an opportune time to change the game a little, and try some new tactics. Standard boarding doctrine is to assault, and capture or kill whatever members of the target ship's crew are encountered. The goal is to contain the ship's crew and confine any crewmembers who are capable of resistance, which is theoretically all of them, to non-essential areas. That's how ships are captured, and how invading boarding parties get the opportunity to incapacitate enemy warships while sustaining the lowest number of casualties possible. But this situation was different, in that we were assaulting a ship which had the singular feature of crew numbers so overwhelmingly superior that if they ever managed to marshal a sufficient percentage of their crew, even unarmed, they could overrun our entire invading force.

But if the previous hours of this operation told me anything, it was that, while our enemy had some trouble organizing their response, over time they got better at it. And this was going to take some time. For the first time in my experience commanding boarding operations, stealth appeared to be a better option than direct assault. Therefore, instead of assaulting any personnel we came across, the point teams were instructed to advance even more carefully, and back out of any encounter they could avoid without being detected. The point teams would back up, and we would re-route, whenever possible, bypassing any personnel we did not absolutely have to engage.

The men followed their orders, and it was working well. For a while. The point men peeked around corners and signaled back to advance, if the way was clear, or just eased back away from the corner, and set out in a different direction, if it wasn't. But ultimately, a group of thirty is just too big to move through even a ship as large as *StarFire* without being detected once in a while.

Eventually, unavoidably, the ship's marines found us again, and our advantage from the simple expedient of changing levels was lost. It was back to run and gun, and this time, if anything, it was worse. They found us faster, and came at us harder with every passing minute, no doubt in part because in any firefight that lasted more than a few seconds, my own men were calling for support on the coms. Each fight got a little more desperate, as more enemy troops gathered, and their tactics became more effective for combating us. They seemed to be learning very rapidly how to locate us, and even more rapidly, how to handle us. We were taking casualties at a higher rate than before. And gradually, calls of "I'm hit," or "Medic!" sounded on the coms more and more frequently. And that was a real problem.

More than just giving our position away with every com call, it brought home how fast we were taking hits. It was as though our opponents had learned something about beam weapons over the course of the day, and their fire was increasingly effective. They had stopped the rapid-fire, single-shots approach, and adopted the standard small-arms doctrine, what we had been using from the first engagement: Suppression fire from a few weapons on automatic, and precision fire from all the others. It was just like what we did, except their suppression fire was pretty accurate. Better than ours. And while they still weren't using anything in the way of covered positions, they no longer stood straight up in ranks to present volley fire, as they had early on. Now, they advanced through our fire rapidly, some of them moving closer even as men around them were cut down. It was almost like an infantry charge, just slower. I didn't know where they got that idea; it sure as hell wasn't from us.

Anyway, we killed them faster when they did that, but it was very dangerous. Sooner or later, I figured they would hit us with enough numbers to get a few of theirs in among us before we were able to cut them down. A half-dozen of them in our ranks, when that happened, would cut us in half in no time.

And still, we hadn't found what we needed to find. We were running out of time. Alvin caught up with me after one skirmish and suggested we would have to change our tactics.

"Cap, we've got eighteen wounded, but still effective. Three ineffective. We have another eight KIA. That's about one third losses, KIA and ineffective, already. We have to do something if we are going to get Lt. Harley his chance." Alvin was talking fast, almost panting, out of breath from running back and forth between the point men and the security element, along with the support teams.

And he wasn't telling me anything I didn't know. It was like our group had become a magnet, or had a homing beacon on our backs, the way we were drawing the enemy to us. After our respite, earlier, when we changed decks, things had been looking good, but once things started going bad, they went bad in a hurry.

I started reviewing options in my mind. Dropping down another deck wouldn't be likely to work. They would have learned that trick, having found us after the first change. I considered the idea of going up a couple of decks instead, but shelved that idea just as fast. Going up was much harder than going down, took longer to accomplish, and really, how much imagination does it take to figure out that option, once down has been tried? The time it would buy us wouldn't be worth the vulnerable minutes we spent executing the operation. And besides, this level appeared to be right about central; a couple floors up would be moving away from our objective, if my observations were correct.

The only other option I could think of wasn't attractive, but it might give some of us some more time. It was to split up the group. We had started with thirty two in this group, and were down to twenty two effective troops, counting Alvin and myself. But twenty two was still too many to be subtle. Three to five was probably the optimal number for stealthy movement. And in small groups, we could make it harder to focus their strength, make them spend more time tracking us down, if we weren't all in the same place. It was a trade-off. At the expense of being even more severely outnumbered when they did manage to pin any of us down, we could make it take longer to find us, but anybody caught in a pickle would take severe losses, maybe even total losses. Which only meant we couldn't let them pin us down, I told myself. I made another decision.

Implementing my decision was another challenge, but I calculated that they had our current position figured out pretty well anyway, and Duggard had assured me they wouldn't be able to decipher our com signals, except for frequency of communication and position. I had nothing lose by using the com system, and it would save time spreading the men out. I clicked into the company channel, the one that all my men would receive.

"Company, we have to break up into small groups. I want one fire-team and one non-com in a group. Every non-com takes a fire-team, and when you get a chance, peel off as opportunity allows. Pick a direction, and move away from the larger body of men, and continue the mission. Avoid conflicts, and look for systems to damage. Any system. I don't care if it's just plumbing, start tearing it down. We might find something by accident. Move up or down levels at your own prerogative, but keep moving. At the very least, we'll make them cover more than one deck, and that might thin them out a little on this level. That is all. Execute your orders. No acknowledgement necessary." I didn't want them all clicking their coms to tell me they heard me, and giving the enemy an accurate count while they were at it.

Now Alvin and I would have to decide what we would do. We could tag along with one of the fire-teams, or we could strike out on our own. What we couldn't do was stay put. As the men melted off in small groups, we would have fewer and fewer men supporting this position, and this position is where the enemy was most likely organizing to assault us.

"Alvin, come on. Let's get out of here," I decided, figuring that we would take our chances as an independent team. "We can look for something to bugger-up just as well as any of our men can."

"Cap, we need to move, yeah, but you can't just run and gun like these boys can. Sooner or later, you are going to have to make decisions for these teams. That will mean using the com, and then they will have your position. We need to find a place to hole up. We need to pick a place with a couple avenues we can retreat from after you use the coms."

That was Alvin, doing his job, thinking ahead and keeping me out of trouble. He was right. But we didn't have a place to hole up, and I didn't want to spend our time looking for one, instead of getting the mission accomplished.

"Alvin, like you say, if we have to use the coms, they will have a position, and they'll move in on it. We might as well be on the move ourselves."

"No, Cap, that's not right. Moving at least doubles our chances of getting seen, and keeps people on our ass. And you didn't keep anybody back for security. That means we need a hidey-hole, where they can go right past us. And unless your wonder boy, Duggard, can figure out a way to keep your com locator turned off or something, it has to be a hole with three or more avenues of retreat. Can he do that?"

"No, he said he didn't have time to turn off the location pings on the com transmissions, needed another week to do that. All he can do is make up a bunch of ships . . ."

I trailed off, looking at Alvin, and thought about Duggard . . . I hadn't given him more than a passing thought for some time, now. Duggard had been working on a way to spoof the locations of our ships, sure. But hadn't he said that the suit's coms worked about the same way?

"What it is, Cap?" Alvin could see the wheels turning in my head. I ignored him, and clicked my com over to command channel.

"Duvall? Lombard here. You got my tech-type guy on-hand, Duggard? Tell him to click into command channel, would you?" I didn't need the whole company listening to this; they had other things to think about.

Jimmy didn't even respond, which left an empty feeling in my stomach for a moment, wondering if the 'lander might have been over-run. But he must have just been closer to Duggard then he was to the com, because about three more seconds after that thought crossed my mind, Duggard clicked into the command channel.

"Captain Lombard? Captain Duvall said you wanted to talk to me, sir?"

"Yeah, Duggard. Listen, that scheme you had for spoofing the bad guys about ship positions? Would that work with my troops' coms?"

"Yeah, sure. Coms are coms. I can spoof up a bunch of troop positions, easy. All I need is some positions our guys really are in, to work from. It won't fool them if a bunch of guys start appearing where there hasn't been any trouble, too far away from where there has been."

I looked at Alvin, who also listened on the command channel, and whose bright, white, toothy, smile suddenly seemed to absolutely glow.

* * *

"All units, report by groups." I sent the command, asking for what amounted to a roll-call. Meanwhile, Sgt. Alvin had pulled a display pad out of his pack, and muttered into his com, talking to Duggard about how to set it up. We had holed up in some ventilation ducting Alvin had picked out, very near to where we had been when the whole idea had come together. It was a little cramped, but very good cover, a main duct moving fresh air from one part of the ship to another. The ducting ran through the upper half of the structural walls throughout the ship, which was an unusual design in a spacecraft; it required automatic, independently operating seals in between major areas, to allow the isolation of the atmosphere in any section that was breeched or vented. I was surprised when Alvin found it, and supposed it was something made necessary by the immense size of the ship, necessary for moving renewed and refreshed atmosphere from somewhere deep in the ship out to the peripheral areas. Space stations typically had this sort of ventilation, but I had never seen a spacecraft with it. But I had never heard of a ship this big before, either.

A main duct gave us enough room to lay prone, nearly head to head, comfortably. We probably had enough room to sit upright, side by side, if we chose to, but it would have been cramped; knees drawn far up, and heads bent down over our chests. We chose to lie down, and our position gave us an only slightly obstructed view of the corridor, through a vent panel, cross-hatched with horizontal direction vanes. We used ear buds, because our helmets tended to bump on the sides of the vent duct accidentally, if we moved at all, and we spoke in very low tones, even when we couldn't see anyone directly outside. We might have had about enough room to reverse direction, in a pinch, and move away inside the ducting in either direction, if we had to, though turning around would have taken more time than we would have, if we had to move in a hurry. Better to scootch along backwards, if we had to move with any urgency.

The men started reporting in, each group of four troops, plus one non-com, reporting as a unit. They reported with the name and rank of the non-com, plus the number of effective fighting men each group had, like "Corporal Jones, plus four." I noticed a couple of them only had three, and one report was a non-com and only one other man, but it didn't matter, tactically speaking. This was all just to get Duggard locations on each group.

Alvin had the white data pad set up, now, and as each report came in, a red dot appeared on the board, with a unit notation, in black, right under it. These numbers were generated randomly, and they didn't mean much to us. It was just something Duggard had written into the program, to increase confusion in the enemy. There wasn't a map or anything, just red dots, floating on a blank slate of white, above black unit numbers. Almost immediately, the unit designations started changing at random, as well. I figured Duggard wanted the enemy to waste some time trying to decode that information, hoping to mark particular units and follow their movements. I made a mental note to commend Duggard for his attention to that detail. Then, as we watched, each red dot blossomed, with a scattering of similar red dots popping up all around. Some of these were in motion, and some others appeared static, but all of them began to fade as soon as their message was complete and the signal stopped. And then I watched our apparent forces multiply before my eyes, by a factor of eight or ten, as new, false signals were generated. Which gave me another idea.

"Duggard," I spoke into my com, "Can you put enemy com locations on the screen, also?"

"They already are, sir," came the reply.

"Then, how do I know which are ours and which are theirs?"

"Well, sir, the software knows which encryption algorithm is ours, and makes those red. Anything not ours appears as blue. But you aren't seeing that because the enemy is not using coms. They are radio silent."

"How long have they been on radio silence, Duggard?"

"Um . . . all day, sir. I haven't picked up a single enemy or unknown com since we started monitoring, right after you went aboard." Duggard sounded apologetic, like the enemy was getting over on him, somehow, by not using their coms.

It was pretty much what I had been thinking for a while now, but it was nonetheless a little surprising to have Duggard confirming it for me. Alvin didn't get it right away.

"They have to talk sometime, Cap," he said. "I'll let you know when they start showing up on the board."

"No, Alvin. I mean, yeah, let me know if you see something, but I'm saying I don't think you will see them. They aren't using coms, and they aren't using voice, so far as I have seen when we are eyeball to eyeball with them. They communicate some other way."

"What, like . . . sign language? Passing notes?" he asked. I wasn't sure if he was being sarcastic, or actually trying to figure it out.

"Hell, I don't know, Alvin. Maybe they have some different type of com unit we haven't noticed and can't detect electronically. Or maybe they're mind-readers. All I know is, I haven't seen any of them talk all day. I don't think they do, at least, not like we do." Alvin didn't have a response to that, or if he did, it was a facial expression I didn't see. I was still looking at the display pad, and thinking.

"Alvin, they will still gather up in numbers to hit any groups that they locate by making contact with them. But if they are monitoring our com positions, they will have to check out every group to discover which are spoofs and which are troops. They'll break up into smaller groups to do that, now. Tell the men to go as stealthy as possible, and to break contact whenever possible, as fast as possible. Make stealth the number one priority, second only to damaging any systems they find. Get some of them up into these ventilation ducts, like we are, and designate them to see if they can move through the ducting, instead of in the corridors. Use the smaller, under-strength groups for that. Tell them not to fire on any groups that don't see them, unless they have found something worth fighting over. And I want all of them spread out pretty wide, relative to one another." I left Alvin to accomplish that and switched my attention back to Duggard, then.

"Duggard, I want to be sure you keep spawning new spoof targets. I don't want the enemy eliminating the possible targets as they check them out, and figuring out which are real and which aren't. I'm sure their computer can track that."

"No problem, already programed in, sir," he replied. "The program simulates a unit location by generating a false communication signal. It uses coordinates from areas we have already been in, so we know we aren't generating images of units, say, outside the hull or something. The only way they will know one is false is if it generates a signal right where the enemy is standing. We can't control for that, because we don't know where they are." He was on the ball. I was going to have to make sure Duggard got his week on a casino station, after all, I thought . . . if we survived this. I started wondering if there was anything I was overlooking, any other way to take advantage of Duggard's ability, and something popped into my head right away.

"Duggard, one more thing. I see these red dots moving around, and I figure, that makes a map, right? I mean, if we were to start saving the strings of the real position data, and plotting them, wouldn't that give us a sort of rudimentary map of the areas we've been in?"

"What color do you want that in, sir?"

"I don't give a-" I took a breath. "Duggard, I don't care what color. Can you do it?"

"I've been doing it all along, sir. I use grey. Check your board, see how it looks to you."

And sure enough, when I looked, there were gray lines all over the place. Some of them outlined whole compartments, where my men had walked through and made a search. Others were less-completely sketched out, and there were large gaps between sections, because no one had used their coms there. But for the first time, we were organizing data in a way that might take away one of the enemy's real advantages: They knew the layout of the ship, and we didn't. It had never mattered, before, on standard-sized vessels, but on *StarFire*, I figured it could make a real difference. I studied the map for a moment, and realized Duggard had even used two different shades of grey to show the change when we went from one deck to another. Definitely, if I survived this, Duggard was getting a vacation. Maybe even a promotion.

* * *

Everything calmed down rapidly from that point on. Our enemy had, in fact, been using our coms to find us, and now they had a whole lot of extra work to do, if they wanted to continue that method. Our casualty rate dropped down to near zero, and our men moved around much more slowly, taking even greater care to be quiet, except on the odd occasions when they made contact. Even then, the emphasis was on getting away, and breaking contact, not on dropping the enemy troops. But Alvin and I saw the results of all that, as enemy marines started passing by our hidden position more and more frequently. It took me a minute to realize that they were flooding this section of the ship, maybe because they now thought there were a hundred or more of us around here, all the sudden. That was the down side. It hadn't occurred to me that they were doing anything else, before; that they were sending what they thought were enough troops to do the job. I would have sent everything I had from the first minutes.

But with the spoofing going on, there were advantages too. My men were far more free to use the coms, raising their efficiency, and adding more spoof units to the board, each and every time they used them. The map was developing rapidly, from their position reports, and I figured that soon now, we might have enough data to begin making guesses about where to look for the systems we sought.

I remarked on that to Alvin, quietly, as we watched yet another group of about twelve marching by, but my concern about numbers still took priority, in my mind.

"They still know we are in this part of the ship, and they are going to keep sending men here until they have some stationed at every intersection. Then none of us will be able to move without being seen or heard by someone." As I spoke, very quietly, two men from the detail going by dropped off, and posted up as guards, not more than twenty feet in front of us. Alvin raised his hand, unnecessarily suggesting silence. As soon as the tramp of feet from the other ten men in the group had gone on a little ways, silence descended, and we didn't dare even whisper. That didn't stop Alvin from communicating with me, though.

He didn't need to think it over. Having sentries this close wasn't a condition he was going to tolerate, and a slight smile twitched up the corners of his mouth as he held up two fingers. "Two," he signed, pointing to them, and then, "Two," pointing to himself and me. His meaning was clear: One each. Then he eased his beam carbine forward, until it was almost pressed against the vanes of the vent grill, and held the weapon with one hand while motioning to the back of his head with the other. "Shoot them in the head," he was signing.

I help up my hand, quickly. "Wait!" Then I brought up my own carbine, and shouldered the stock. Then, very slowly, gently, I used my left hand to raise the grill. I didn't want to try to shoot through it; I wanted to open it, just far enough to shoot past without risking the split second it would take to burn through the grill, and the noise it would make. I also wanted to have the option of staying in this position, which we would not have if we burned a pair of holes in the grill from the inside. The grill panel was hinged at the top, so I could be sure I wasn't going to drop it accidentally, and it seemed worth the risk of making a small noise or getting seen before we fired, to keep the option of staying put in this spot.

As I worked at raising the grill, Alvin and I both watched our enemy sentries. They stood as still as troops on parade, standing at attention. In fact, they were actually standing at parade rest, but absolutely still, as though they were mannequins displaying a scene of Marines on sentry duty. While I slowly raised the grill, Alvin took a bead on the trooper to his side. I tried to keep the other one in my sights as I worked the grill up.

There was a slight click, as the built-in support-arms that held the grill up for maintenance locked into place. As one, the sentries turned to look back behind them, right at us. Simultaneously, two blue bolts took them, one each, right in the head, about one quarter turn before dead center. They fell as one, too.

Since neither of us missed, there was only the sizzle of beam fire, no telling "BANG" as a bulkhead expanded and popped, or the rattle of burning through the grill. Almost surely, we had been quiet enough that no one had heard us. Alvin took one look, and quickly held a finger up. "One moment!" that finger said. He slithered out of the vent, and ran to the bodies, and dragged them just slightly around the corner of the intersection where they had been posted. I understood immediately, and it was brilliant. He put them in a place where, when they were found, someone would think the one position they could NOT have been shot from was where we were actually sitting. His plan was a big step towards keeping our hidey-hole safe. But he wasn't done.

Arriving back at the vent, he pulled at his pack for a moment, digging something out, before he pushed the pack in and then crawled back into the ductwork behind it. I dropped the vent grill back down, carefully, preventing any but the tiniest of sounds, while Alvin worked on something. And then, when I was done and turned to see what he was doing, he surprised me.

Still remaining silent, he opened his hands, and showed me what he had taken from his pack. It was a pair of breaching charges. Golf ball-sized hemispheres of high explosive. He stuck one to the back of the ventilation shaft, directly behind the grill. The other he anchored to the inside of the grill itself. Then he tied the lanyards together, so they ran like a wire between him and myself, from the back of the vent shaft to the surface of the grill, and he armed them both. I looked at the swaying lanyards, bent into a loose "U" shape by the slack he left in them, maybe eight inches or a little more. Once more, he put his hand up, for "Wait," and then five fingers, so the whole message was, "Let's wait five minutes." I nodded. It didn't take five minutes, though.

In less than one minute, men arrived at the intersection our sentries had been posted at. We heard them coming, both Alvin and I signaling each other, "Listen!" at the same time. They weren't just men headed from one location to another. They came running, like they knew something had happened, and came straight to the intersection in front of us. A little chill ran up my spine, as I found that very curious indeed, wondering how they knew something was wrong here. I determined to watch all the closer to see if I could learn something. Surely, I thought, they would have to discuss things when they found the bodies. But judging from the sounds when they arrived, they didn't spend any time examining the bodies, and didn't discuss a thing. And while we couldn't see them immediately, since the bodies themselves were around the corner from us, it sounded like they didn't take any time looking around for possible ambush sites, either. They didn't even stop at the bodies, but tramped a few more feet down the hallway towards our position and, without pause, turned the corner to face our position, with carbines already raised. Four of them. They looked things over for just a split second, long enough to take aim, and then they started firing, all four of them, simultaneously, right at the grill we hid behind. As if they had already discussed it.

Alvin and I didn't have to discuss it, and didn't waste any time. After a quick glance at each other, we both immediately started scootching back, sliding on the floor of the ductwork, pushing with our hands, in opposite directions, as fast as we could move through the shaft. We didn't even have to worry about noise, with all the gunfire going on. The durasteel that made up the bulkhead walls wasn't nearly as strong or durable as what made up the support columns the enemy had fired through before, but it was enough to require two or three shots on the same spot to make a significant hole. Our enemies weren't wasting time, and I was maybe two feet past it when the first hole appeared in the grill. It helped, though, that our enemy was advancing while they fired; their shots weren't as precise as they could have been, and it took them long enough to make each hole that both Alvin and I, moving separate directions, managed to stay ahead of the shots punching through. Small comfort, I knew that would last only as long as it took them to open the grill and lean in. Then they could fire straight down the ventilation shaft, and we would both get slagged, if they got there before we could turn a corner.

And that's when I realized what Alvin had done, and started scooting even faster. Those troops were going to open that vent grill, and two breeching charges were going explode, simultaneously, right in their faces. One, on the back of the vent wall, and the other, on the backside of the grill itself. I looked up, and could see Alvin, maybe fifteen feet away by now, grinning at me like a schoolboy waiting for a firecracker he has just flushed down a school toilet to go off, as he pushed himself backwards with his hands. I saw the shadow of somebody blacken out the little bit of light leaking through the vent grill, and got a quick impression of Alvin pulling his helmet forward, up over his head. I just put my face down, covering my head with my arms. I opened my mouth, to prevent my eardrums from rupturing when the blast went off, and then . . .

The next thing I knew, I had a high-pitched keening in my ears, and dust obscured my vision. My throat felt like I was breathing chalk, and I generally felt like I was waking up a little punch drunk, the way someone does after they have been cold-cocked in a bar fight. Then, someone grabbed my arms and started trying to pull me to my feet, or pick me up, whichever they could manage. I wondered if I was the one who had been sucker-punched in the bar fight, and if I was, did I get in a few licks of my own on the bastard who hit me?

It was Alvin. He had pulled me out of the ventilation shaft, and was trying to pick me up, to carry me away from the scene. Conscious, now, I shook him off, and rose, painfully, shakily to my feet. Alvin was saying something to me, but I couldn't hear him over the high-pitched siren in my head. I looked around, and saw four men in Alliance G-Marine uniforms laying in awkward positions, blood highlighting various wounds, scorch marks and burned flesh making up most of their faces, heads, and shoulders.

I turned back to Sgt. Alvin, who still seemed to be smiling while he plucked at my vacsuit, urging me to get moving with him. I was still wobbly, but I trusted this man, drunk or sober. If he wanted me to get moving, I would get moving. We stumbled away, down the corridor, Sgt. Alvin holding on to my arm like I couldn't be trusted to keep my eyes on him and my feet moving at the same time. He might have been right about that.

* * *

Things started breaking our way after that. We had a real advantage when we scrambled the coms' location signals with spoof signals, and my men were now able to move through the ship without having to do as much fighting. Alvin and I had found our next hiding place, stumbling into a small tool room, where bench-work maintenance was performed on small instruments and machines. It was a small, out-of-the-way room, and we simply barred the door, figuring it was about as good a spot as we would find quickly, and it was better to get out of sight immediately. There were a series of large, metal storage cabinets, and we each cleared out the contents of one shelf on each side of the room, so we had a quick hiding place if we heard the enemy begin a search on this little side corridor the room was on. Then we huddled together over the data pad, to check on the progress of the men. We hadn't been there long when some of our groups reported in.

First we got the word that the enemy's response to our faster movements was an expedient sealing of all hatches. Alliance ships all had this feature, the ability to close and seal any or all hatches from a remote control system on the bridge. Suddenly, my men were having inordinate difficulty moving about by ordinary means, and found themselves having to use breeching charges any time they wanted to move past the next hatch. No problem, there were plenty of charges available, but they were noisy. As long as we were operating in atmosphere, the enemy could hear a charge go off, and know immediately what direction to move in. It was ironic, but where before we wanted atmosphere so we wouldn't have to rely on the coms to talk, now the same atmosphere we had worked so hard to conserve was working against us, all because the enemy had thrown a switch somewhere up on the control bridge, closing and locking all the interior hatches on the ship.

I was considering what to do about that. One option was to peel away some of the men who were guarding the landing site of the transport/lander, and set them to blowing hatches and venting atmosphere again. That would require the enemy to send troops to different parts of the ship, and might make them unlock at least some of the hatches, to facilitate their own troop movements. But that would be of marginal help, since it was hatches ahead of my men that were causing the problem with movement, not those behind us. I was still thinking about it when another call came in.

"Captain Lombard? This is Squad Sergeant Atkins. Listen, we found . . . well, I don't know if it will help Lt. Harley or anything, but I think we're looking at an environmental control panel here. I mean, a whole room full of environmental panels and equipment."

"Atkins, stand by." I clicked off and spoke to my sergeant. "Alvin, did you get that? Can you think of any reason not to blow that whole room? I'm thinking anything that makes it harder for the enemy helps us out, even if we have to operate under the same conditions, too."

Alvin drawled, "Well, yeah, I agree with that. But mostly I think it will slow down those boneheads that didn't put on vacsuits a whole lot more than it will slow us down."

I hadn't made that connection yet, but he was right. It would take a while, but with environmental systems down, anyone not suited up would gradually find the interior of the ship to be a very uncomfortable place. And after a while longer, it would become a downright hostile environment. StarFire's crew would have to suit-up or hold their breath for a very long time, when the atmosphere started to go bad. I switched back to the company channel.

"Atkins, blow that panel, and whatever else you find in that room. Do a thorough job of it. Everyone else, when you have a chance, check your suit integrity. You're going to need them in a little while. We'll have a little time before the atmosphere gets bad, so don't take any chances, but I don't want to hear about having to check seals when men start passing out. And check your internal oxygen/nitrogen cartridges. Anybody below two-thirds should start looking for emergency vacsuit storage sites on board. And when you find them, pick up spares. We don't know how long we will be here." I clicked off. That was one advantage of boarding an Alliance military ship. They would have plenty of vacsuit supplies perfectly matched to our needs.

"Alvin, how long do you figure before the atmosphere starts to matter?"

"There's no telling," he shrugged. "Depends on how big an area that room controls and supplies, and how many hatches and bulkheads have been breached in the area. We'll know soon enough, though. If it's going matter, we'll either start seeing the enemy in vacsuits, or the men will start finding them passed out or dead of asphyxia. Couple of hours should tell the story."

In the end, it took longer than a couple of hours. Alvin and I spent some time taking reports, and giving the men what support we could over the coms. We used the developing map on the data tablet to give them what guidance we could. We had been locked up in that tool room long enough, I figured, to be pretty sure no one was sending anyone to check it out.

"Alvin, I'll keep an eye on the data tablet. See if you can jimmy that hatch, make it hard to open from the outside, so we still get a little warning if someone tries to come in, but still leaves us able to get out in a hurry when we're ready."

Alvin complied, and while he was looking the hatch mechanism over, figuring the right place to stick a small lever in the works to jam it without damaging it, I brought up our data on the ship's layout, based on the troop movements Duggard was tracking. He had added a feature in the couple of hours since I last looked: With the coms open, he was getting reports from the men on what kinds of spaces they were in, and pasting those labels into the image. It was starting to look like a real schematic. Alvin finished his job, and came to look over my shoulder.

"Cap, if those labels are right, this ship looks pretty symmetrical to me." I was still looking at it, and I could see Alvin was right. It would have been normal for an atmospheric craft to be so symmetrical. They had to worry about gravity, and keeping the ship in trim, and well balanced. Spacecraft tended not to be burdened much by such things, and very asymmetrical ships used computers to balance thrusters and the like, rather than going to the trouble and expense of keeping any kind of trim solutions imposed on the construction and layout. In gravity, a heavy side would tend to make a ship want to turn over, but in space, it just added inertia. Boost the thrust on the heavy side a few percentage points, and you have no problem.

"You think the symmetry will help us find what we need, Alvin?"

"Depends on how far they took it, I guess. But for real symmetry, any kind of installation there's only one of will be in the dead center-line of the ship. Just a question of how far forward or aft they put it. This looks very symmetrical to me."

I knew right away what he was getting at, and I voiced it. "Engine rooms."

"Yep. They might have different control and targeting centers for different batteries of guns, so they could be balanced, and put anywhere. But there's only going to be one engine room, no matter how big this tub is. And nothing on this craft will have the mass to equal the engine room."

"Then, we know how to find it, now."

"Shouldn't be too hard. Some designer left a big weakness here, building a ship that looks pretty on paper, instead of one that hides its secrets in random places." He was right. The engine rooms didn't house the actual thrusters, the way they did in the old ships, when engine rooms were always the farthest aft compartments of the ship. That was just for convenience, even then. The engine room just generated the energy that the thrusters converted into plasma, and all the other energy a ship like this ran on came from the same engine room. That energy was fed to various areas of the ship, according to need. The thrusters got most of it, but it didn't have to be generated right there where the thrusters were physically housed.

Clicking into the company channel, I broadcast a simple message: "Men, we are getting a decent diagram of this ship developed now, and it looks like the engine rooms are going to be dead center in the middle of the ship. It'll be a tall room, probably taking up to half a dozen levels, vertically. It'll take up a lot of floor space horizontally, too. Find that room. Get to the center axis line of the ship, exactly, and move forward or aft, along that line. Contact me when you think you have it found. But don't assault the engine room alone or in a small group. We will want to gather everybody up for that. It will be heavily defended, and we may only get one run at it. Try to stay out of sight, and report the position of that engine room. That is all, execute your orders."

"Cap, if I can make a suggestion, you might want to tell the boys to take atmosphere readings. Or maybe even tell them to just go ahead and seal up. It's been over two hours since that environmental systems room was smoked. You can't count on oxygen-deprived men to notice they are getting dumb."

Alvin was right about that. It's a curious feature of the human body that the reflex to breath is not normally spurred by a need for more oxygen. It's mostly driven by the need to exhale carbon dioxide. In the case of gradual development of hypoxia, or lack of sufficient oxygen, the body will detect it and react with symptoms described as "air hunger," and the like. But in cases of rapid onset hypoxia, the first symptoms of trouble may be changes in levels of alertness or even unconsciousness. That's why asphyxiation by breathing pure nitrogen is a pretty peaceful way to go. No panting, struggling for breath, or panic to get air; just normal, relaxed breathing while you get a little dizzy, and then fade out. Even drowning is supposed to be a pretty calm affair, once you get past that first lung-full of liquid, though that's admittedly a pretty rough hurdle to get over.

But suffocating in a closed environment is pretty harsh, because the immediate problem is a buildup of carbon dioxide, not a lack of oxygen. As carbon dioxide builds up, in the body and in the environment, usually much faster than the minimum oxygen requirements are depleted, people breathe harder and harder, trying to clear the CO2 from their systems. They experience headaches, nausea, and a whole raft of other unpleasant effects. So, if CO2 was building up, my guys would catch that.

That's why emergency systems in everything from submarines to spaceships emphasize carbon dioxide scrubbers as a last-ditch, buy-some-time strategy. The CO2 is the first danger; oxygen depletion comes later. Even then, if oxygen dropped very slowly, over several hours, they would likely notice it. But a sudden drop in oxygen in the environment can be very dangerous, especially to men that had other things on their mind, like not getting shot. That's why Alvin was concerned about the men becoming oxygen-starved, and not knowing it. If there were CO2 scrubbers working in various locations around the ship, but refreshed oxygen levels were interrupted by the damage to the central environmental systems, men could be running along feeling fine, and fall over unconscious, ten seconds later. We were hoping that would happen to the enemy. We wanted to avoid that happening to our own men. I re-opened the channel and passed along the orders. I especially emphasized the need for my men to locate stores of atmosphere canisters to re-supply their vacsuits. We had already been here too long to rely on the primary canisters the suits were equipped with when they were dispensed.

What we didn't think of, though, sitting there in that tool room, watching little red dots float around a white display, was that Alvin and I might also need to resupply our atmosphere canisters.

CHAPTER 19

Defense Space Station G-13, 246.163.12

After Action

"We weren't running around, expending extra oxygen, like my men were. And we didn't want to go outside our tool room, and risk being seen. But the truth is, we just didn't think of it. I didn't think of it. We had other things on our minds," I answered Lt. Tillman, when she asked for clarification on how Alvin and I eventually wound up short of air. "But, if you're wondering if I needlessly endangered my company sergeant, the answer is yes. I should have thought of it, and I didn't."

"Well, it's not the first time a commander thought of his men first, and himself long after, Vince. History is full of examples. I've read that captains of water-born ships, more than a thousand years ago, used to be honor-bound to go down with the ship, rather than take up room in a lifeboat, when there were usually more passengers and sailors on board than seats on the lifeboats to begin with. I don't think the air-supply issue is going to be something the Board of Inquiry wants to hang their hat on."

I just looked at her, and held my peace. She might not think it was a big deal, but it turned out to be a very big deal to Alvin. It was my responsibility, and no one else's. It didn't matter if the Board thought it was a big deal or not, because I did. She resumed a moment later.

"So, this idea you came up with, fiddling the coms' locator functions. On the one hand, it was probably the only thing that allowed your mission to succeed. But on the other hand, you admit that it was absolutely against regulations. Do I have that right?"

I wasn't too worried about this angle, at least insofar as my own welfare. There would be Naval and Galactic Marine commanders on the Board of Inquiry, and none of them liked being bound by regulations when it came to effective measures in combat. If they indicted me on this point, they would set precedent that could be used to convict them, later, if they cut a corner and came up with something that won a battle for them, someday.

"Yeah, sure." I shrugged. "I admit that. It was absolutely against regulations. And entirely my responsibility. Technician Duggard told me the theoretical aspects, and he reminded me that regulations forbid tampering with the security features of the software. And I ordered him to do it anyway, in the field, where he couldn't report me or appeal to higher authority. This falls on my shoulders, entirely." Military commanders were likely to protect me on this, if they could, just to give themselves more latitude if they needed it someday. But they would not protect Duggard. He was enlisted, basically the same rank as a lance corporeal. They would throw him to the wolves and never give it a thought. "Duggard objected to the orders, and asked that his objections be noted in the log. I was going to do that, but things caught up with me, and I never got around to it." An exaggeration, but it should be enough to protect Duggard, I thought.

"You realize he will probably be called to testify about this issue?"

I hadn't realized that. In fact, there was no reason to do that at all, since I had just accepted responsibility for the whole thing. Hell, I accepted responsibility just to prevent that. So, why would Lt. Tillman tell me this? Letting me know that Duggard was on the witness list, and she thought he would be called to testify even though I accepted responsibility? I could only ask.

"Well, actually, no. Why would they call him to the stand? You did hear me say I accept responsibility, right?"

Tillman stared right at my face, and just arched an eyebrow at me, mimicking my own expression of, "don't you get it yet?" And then I did. I wasn't enough for the Navy. They wanted to bring down my men, too. Or at least some of them, whoever they could. It was going to be like Roman Games, in that Board of Inquiry. The Romans didn't throw Christians to the lions because the lions were hungry. They did it because they wanted to get rid of the Christians. And Navy wanted to get rid of anybody and everybody who was any part of the whole *StarFire* fiasco.

CHAPTER 20

Alliance Military Ship StarFire

Action

The air was slowly going bad in the tool room, and Alvin had to pull his wedge out of the hatch mechanism and open it up a little for some circulation. We hadn't lost a single man in the last few hours, and engagements with the enemy were few and far between. But we were starting to despair of ever finding the engine room, or anything else sufficiently critical to serve our needs. There was just too much area to search, and every additional square foot my men explored increased the risk to them, which meant they had to go forward slowly and carefully. As a result, Lt. Harley's fighter was still sitting on his rock, while he watched and waited for his opportunity.

On the upside, we had been on board for several hours, successfully extending our incursion well beyond what I would have dared to hope for, at the outset of the operation. That was at least partially because, so far, there had not been a single attempt to take the transport/lander, either from inside the ship, through our breech point, or from outside, over the hull. Security at the breech point now stood at two complete squads; the 'lander security squad, and Squad Four, the men I had sent forward earlier to vent compartments while the rest of us went aft, and then deeper into the ship.

Squad Four had been chased around for a while, after the enemy began to react to the damage they were doing, but eventually, when Duggard's com locator program went active, they were able to break contact and return to the original breach, the place where we had come aboard. As it stood now, there were more troops still combat-effective back at the entry site than there were with me, in the deep areas of the ship. I was still worried that the crew of *StarFire* might attack the lander, but I authorized one fire-team to come out and recover our non-ambulatory wounded, and the bodies of our comrades who had been killed in action. So long as the recovery detail stayed silent on the coms, they had a good chance of moving around undetected. Especially since Duggard, working from the main cabin in the 'lander, didn't have to stay silent. He directed the recovery detail on paths to our dead and wounded, paths which kept them some distance from the hotspots where the enemy was likely to still be hunting us.

So, with the hatch propped just slightly open, to allow a little air from the corridor to waft in, Alvin and I huddled close by, studying the data tablet, and staying off the coms as much as we could while listening to the reports of our mobile units, and trying to piece together enough information to locate the kind of systems we needed. I was frustrated, out of patience, and struggling to keep myself from feeling desperate. Alvin was more sanguine.

"Look, Cap, we've got most of the aft half of the ship plotted by now. There aren't many more places to look. I think the answer is already in here, we just haven't found it yet."

"Alvin, if we haven't found it, it's not on the map. We've been doing nothing else for hours, now. I could half build this ship myself, I've been looking at the data so long."

"Well, let's just back up a minute. There's lots of data there, I know. But some of that data is likely to be erroneous, right? I mean, it's just made up of what the men reported to Duggard, and what he thinks it means, right? So, the boundaries of the rooms will be right, that's straight mathematical plotting. But if he got the wrong idea from what the men said over the coms, it would be labeled with the wrong information here."

"Maybe so, Alvin. But how are we going to find it? These labels are all we have, so even if we know one or more of them is wrong, that doesn't tell us what really is in that compartment. We'd have to send men back to check it out again, to correct it, and that would slow us down even more." I sighed my exasperation. "We might be better off if we tried to do an end run, find another avenue to attack systems that would do us some good, instead of wondering around blind, and trusting to luck." Just talking about it, I was warming to the idea. "You know, we have two squads back at the 'lander. That group is bigger than we are, right now, and they're rested, fresh. I could authorize them to go over the hull and try to take out the forward batteries from the outside . . ." I mused, trying the plan out in my head, just thinking aloud.

"Yeah, and we might get that desperate in a while. It's not a bad idea, except we don't have anything that can burn through the outside bay doors except the 'lander's thrusters. Do you really want to tell Duvall to hover in front of those guns long enough to burn through those gun bay doors? If the gun bay is shut, the guns can blast right through the doors and slag the 'lander faster than the 'lander's thrusters can burn through from the other side and slag the guns."

Of course, I knew that. I knew it before I even offered the comment. I was just trying on different ideas, hoping something would come to me. Alvin went on for a bit, talking about staying on the course we had already started, while I turned back to the data tablet, tuning him out for the most part. He was winding up his argument while I was looking at a middle-sized room some of my guys had been through an hour or so ago.

It was labeled, "x-tra power mach.s." I assumed "mach.s" was Duggard's shorthand for "machines," but I wasn't even sure of that. In my pique I had a moment to decide to reprimand him for slovenly work, failing to even properly note the limited intelligence we had. By using some made-up shorthand instead of the correct terminology he was delaying us even more. Sure, he had a lot to do, but doing that work in a hurry was no excuse for doing it poorly. Alvin continued to talk while I distracted myself, sorting out Duggard's shorthand.

I started with that example, "extra power mach.s," thinking to myself, hmm . . ."x-tra power, obviously, 'extra power.'" Extra, as in more? Is that "extra power," as in, "machines that have, or require more power"? Or "more machines of the power variety"? Or maybe "extra" is used here as in a synonym for "auxiliary," or maybe "redundant"? Probably auxiliary, I guessed. And "power mach.s," I had already speculated, might be for "power machines." But that made no sense, if "power machines" is like "power tools." All machinery on a starship is "power machinery." The only thing NOT "power" on this ship might be a few wrenches in one of the various mechanical bays. So, not "power machines" as opposed to "manual machines," it had to be . . . what? Machines that make power? Like, generators, maybe? So it's probably . . . Auxiliary Power Generators, I guessed. My eyes widened a little, and I felt my heartbeat speed up a notch.

"Alvin-"

". . . so, we can't get all worked up over it. I'm just saying . . ."

"ALVIN!"

He heard my tone, and he broke off, suddenly all about the business at hand.

"What is it, sir?"

"Auxiliary Power Generators. Look, right here. Duggard wrote 'extra power machines.' What would that be besides power generators?"

Alvin stepped closer to look over my shoulder.

"I can't think of anything else that would be, off the top of my head." And after a moment more, he nodded his head, saying, "I wouldn't have thought of that, but I guess it'll do."

In another moment, I had switched my com to the company channel, and now gave my men the location of that room, and asked who had been in it. A short conversation with those men took another minute or so, and then I had every able body headed in that direction. Including Alvin and myself. And I had Duggard putting up false locations everywhere else, to try and give us a chance of getting there.

* * *

"They are generators, sir, and they are tied in to the ship's systems, through switchable lines," one of the first men arriving at our destination reported. "They're idle, but running, just making minimum revolutions. They have to be the emergency power system, reserve generators in case the main generators get knocked out." The report came over my com, as Sgt. Alvin and I neared the room I had located on the data pad. I didn't acknowledge. I didn't want to draw attention by having more than one com signal located in or near that room come up on the location pings.

Arriving on-site just a few dozen seconds later, I found all my men were set up in tactical layers on the approaches to that room. They were all com-silent, and had all arrived without arousing the enemy, being seen, or otherwise tipping them off to where we were. We were likely to have at least a little bit of time to work. I ducked through the hatch, and found the trooper who had made the report to me.

"Show us what you have, here, Marine." I stayed off the coms and just raised my voice a little above the background hum in the room.

"Yes sir." He waved his hand at a row of four massive generators, which sat facing a row of four more on the other side of the room. Each of them was larger than our transport/lander, and they all hummed and vibrated with power, turning over smoothly and quietly for such huge installations. They were like massive, metal, mechanical dragons, alive but resting, and even at that, we could feel the energy in this room as a prickly sensation on our arms and the back of our necks, if we stood still. Even through our sealed vacsuits, everyone in that room could feel it. These machines were serious equipment.

The Marine I spoke to didn't say another word, after that first, "Yes sir." Just waving in their direction was enough, and I supposed there wasn't anything much to say, after that. Alvin thought of something, though.

"Private, are you familiar with these machines? Do you know how to operate and maintain them? "

"Oh, yeah, Sarge. My dad operated power generators for the off-world mining companies. They haven't changed all that much since then. These aren't even the biggest I've dealt with."

"What's your name, Marine?" Alvin asked next.

"Private First Class Benjamin Holiday."

Alvin looked his next question at me. We hadn't talked about it, but I knew we were on the same page. We had worked together for years, and after all we had been through, there were plenty of times we didn't need words. I just nodded at him. Alvin turned back to Pvt. Holiday.

"Son, I want you to look this system over, and figure out how to take these generators off-line, temporarily. Then I want you to spin them up to maximum power, and when you have the whole chorus here singing just as loud as they can, throw the switch putting them back on-line. All eight of them, at once. Can you do that?"

With a casual glance back at the machines, taking in the wiring around them, Holiday replied, "Sure, Sergeant. No problem doing it. But- a power surge like that- it'll fry every circuit and wire on the whole vessel if we do it that way . . ."

Alvin just smiled at him, and said, "You have your orders, son. Jump to it."

"Just a moment," I interjected. "The enemy is likely to know it when you take these off-line. They'll know where we are, even if they don't guess what we are doing. So you figure it all out in advance, Private. I don't want any surprises, or any delays, once you start. Men will be dying out there, before too long, buying you the time to get the job done. Make sure it's as short a time as possible, will you?"

Holiday came to attention, suddenly much more serious. "Yes sir." And then he saluted me, and as I returned the salute, he turned to get to work.

* * *

When they came for us, they came hard, but just as before, the first groups were small. My men handled those first ones easily. They were the closest small groups, moving fast, and showing up one after another, in series, and we had them outnumbered as they arrived, for a little while. But within just a few minutes, those that came from farther away had more opportunity to bump into each other and join ranks along the way. The groups that hit us started to get bigger, and before long, the men outside were feeling the pressure. We no longer had the advantage of numbers. Alvin, still in the generator room with me, listened to the com reports, and finally turned to me.

"Sir, seems like they could use my help out there. If you're going to stay and keep an eye on Pvt. Holiday, I think I'll go outside and lend a hand, see if I can find something to put a little thermal beam energy into." He patted his beam carbine. I was just starting to answer him when Duvall came on the com, over the command channel.

"Vince, what are you boys up to? The ship is changing course, for the first time since we put down, and it feels like she is trying to speed up, starting some slow acceleration." I had no idea what that was about. It didn't seem related to us. But I needed Duvall to pass on a message for me.

"Jimmy, we found something to work on. You just get on the horn and tell Harley that we're on to something, and he might get a break here in a few more minutes. He should be ready. I'll try to let you know when, and you can pass the word on to him."

"Okay, Vince. Let me know when, and I'll pass it on." Then Duvall was gone, presumably relaying my information to Lt. Harley on the inter-ship frequency, telling him to be ready. I turned around, and Alvin was gone too. Already outside in the fire-fight, I knew. So, with little else to do, I moved over to where Holiday was working. I didn't speak to him, not wanting to slow him down, or distract him. I just waited nearby, in case he needed help, or had a question, or . . . well, for no good reason at all, really. There was nothing I could do to help him. I didn't know much about these machines. But someone had to stay with Holiday, if only because, should something happened to him, we would have to find someone else who could finish the job. In the end, nothing happened to him, he just kept working, and after a bit, the energy in the room started building. In another few moments, it was building big.

It was probably only a few minutes from the time I noticed the power picking up until Holiday was done, but it was a strange feeling. I hadn't ever experienced anything like it. I could feel it in my whole body. My teeth ached with the pent-up power humming through the room. Soon, my peripheral vision began to close in, and the central image of whatever I looked at flattened to two dimensions. Next, it became an effort to remember to inhale again after each breath, as though the energy was interfering with my brain processes. Somewhere along the way Holiday had started a little running commentary, but I missed a good bit of it, before he got my attention, while he finished some task or another.

". . . quite a bit of power, sir. More than I was really expecting. It's probably a little disconcerting, if you've never been around it before . . . Power like this takes a little getting used to, just to work around it and stay functional." I lost the thread, and focused on taking my next breath. But a moment later, Holiday was talking again, and I became aware that this time, he had stopped working and stood there, in front of me, looking at me. I pulled myself together.

"What was that, Holiday?"

"It's ready, sir."

"Great. Let's hit the switch."

"It's that button, sir." Holiday pointed to an ordinary panel button on a large panel of lights, switches, buttons of all kinds. Pvt. Holiday was deferring to me, as the officer in charge, but I wasn't interested in ceremony, and wasn't feeling real sharp anyway. It was almost beyond me just making sense of what he said, much less trying to sort out something like which button he was referring to. I raised my voice just a touch, for emphasis.

"Holiday, TURN IT ON!" I ordered.

He didn't answer. He just pushed the button.

* * *

It was a long second before anything happened at all. Then the machines, turning high revolutions, and humming a high-pitched song of power and potential mayhem, barely restrained, all seemed to lug down, like a tractor pulling a cable taught, and digging in for a long, hard tug-of-war with an immovable object, and more than a little pissed off about it. Their notes dropped a couple half-steps on the scale of power and fury, as energy sluiced through cables, out of those machines and into the power grid of the ship. And then all hell broke loose.

Cables, wires, circuit boards, switches . . . everything connected to the power grid started melting, smoking, sparking, or actually caught fire and burned. And that was literally almost everything on the ship. The paint on the walls and bulkheads started curling, and flaking off. Wisps of smoke spiraled up from invisible seams and joints around the room. Every board in every panel poured an avalanche of sparks out its face and down onto the deck, below it, like great beasts which had been drinking liquid electricity, and were now drooling it down their chins into puddles on the ground. In another moment, smoke began billowed across the ceiling, and visibility began to drop. The whole room seemed to be burning and melting, and I was sure the whole ship was, as well.

All of us, Holiday, myself, and the men out in the corridor, were sealed in our vacsuits, both because of the poor atmosphere, and because we expected the fire and smoke. Instead of relying on the coms, I grabbed Holiday by the shoulders, and slapped my helmet down next to his, making contact.

"Good work Holiday. Now let's get outside and lend a hand in that fight." He was making some kind of reply to that, but I didn't have time to hear it. I clicked on the company channel.

"Men, we've done it. Whatever happens now, we have won the fight. They'll never fix this in time to go after Lt. Harley. They'll never fix it at all, out here in space. So, we fight our way back to the 'lander, and let's see if we can get back home. We're done here."

I switched to the command channel next. "Duvall, tell Harley to lift off. He's as clear as he's going to get. Duggard, you tell the squad sergeants at your location that I want one squad to slip out of there and start blowing hatches open, clearing a path for us back to the 'lander. They've locked down all the hatches we didn't blow on the way out here, and we're headed for your position, as soon as we can break contact. You stay on the coms with that group, and with my sergeants here, and guide them to each other. We will want to link up without any wasted time. We're in a fire fight down here, so there may be deviations, but I want you to keep us headed back to the 'lander on the most direct route possible."

Then I checked my beam carbine's settings, and stepped out the hatch of the generator room. I was as done as I could get, for now, with no more decisions to be made. It was time to join the fight.

* * *

For hours on end, we had been fighting defensive engagements, always trying to break away, always focused on moving further along. This time, we weren't in a position to break away in a random direction. We needed to move back through the enemy position, not evade him and disappear deeper into the ship. Once the enemy realized we were headed out, they would know exactly where we were going anyway, so I figured this would be a long, running fight.

The corridor immediately outside the generator room was crowded with my men, and just about every possible scrap of cover already had a Marine taking cover behind it. I stepped out of the hatch in time to watch four or five bolts of blue energy scream past my head, blazing on down the corridor. I lost little time stepping back into the hatchway, and pushing Holiday back into the other room, since he was close behind me.

Then, with a deep breath, I just leaned out, this time with my carbine shouldered, and started picking targets. I had always been a talented shooter, scoring very well in competitions, in my early days as a young officer. My best days of competitive shooting were already behind me, but I could still shoot. I took my time, firing single shots of carefully aimed fire, and in between shots, I raised Alvin on the coms.

"Alvin, that smoke is going to get real thick in a very short time. Figure out a way to take advantage of that."

"Already working on it, sir. Some of those guys still aren't in vacsuits, so that will work for us. I'll see if I can figure something out for when the visibility gets low, too." Alvin appeared to be in fine humor, at least. I kept shooting.

A few minutes later, the smoke had thickened to the point that every beam shot seemed to leave a swirling trail behind it, as the air reacted to the sudden flash of heat traveling through it. For the first time, it occurred to me that this smoke could render our beam rifles ineffectual. Beam weapons are energy based, but a lot of that energy was in the visible and invisible light spectrum. Smoke is actually very fine particulate material suspended in the air. It doesn't take much particulate matter to interrupt the path of light, and every particle the beam struck on the way to the target soaked up a good bit of the energy, turning it into heat. In thick smoke, those particles were right up next to the rifle, and even inside the thing. The electrical contacts of the beam carbines could melt, or fuse, and rapidly.

Back on the company channel, I shouted, "Single-fire only, men. Don't melt your guns down firing in this smoke!" Alvin added his own instructions, too, knowing that Marines who were designated for rapid-fire previously would have the power settings on their carbines lower than maximum. It was a trade-off, more power meant more heat damage to the weapons, but less meant much less effective range in this kind of environment.

"This smoke will soak up energy, boys. You all dial your rifles up to 'Crispy Critter' on the power settings. We ain't here to help 'em work on their suntans. More power, slower rate of fire."

The pace of firing on this end of the corridor fell off rapidly at the same time visibility fell off, and rather suddenly, at that. It got to where I couldn't see far enough to make out any distinct targets. When it reached that point, occasionally I would see a small spark of blue, as an enemy fired, close enough for his discharge to register through the smoke. Then I would quickly aim for that spot, and toss a bolt right back at him, but I couldn't tell if I was doing any good or not. It was developing into a stalemate, neither side really able to do much damage to the other. But a stalemate would be temporary, because, while we were already outnumbered badly, the enemy had hundreds more troops available to bring to the fight. I calculated we had a small window, right now, where the failure of many of the enemy to don vacuum suits would work to our favor, due to smoke irritating their eyes and interfering with their breathing. But that advantage that would erode rapidly as enemy reinforcements arrived, and enemy troops were able to disengage and finally find the vacsuits they would surely realize they all badly needed to get into, now.

"Alvin, it's not going to get any better. I'm thinking we need to charge through them right now. You want to bunch the men up, and let me know when we're ready?"

"Sir, I think if you'll give me about one more minute, I might have a better option for you."

"I—Alright, Alvin. Fill me in when you're ready." I had to have faith in Alvin. I had said it before. Sgt. Alvin Alvin was the best ground combat Marine I had ever known. I had a policy of always trusting Alvin when he said he had an idea in regard to combat tactics. I would trust him this time.

A minute later, Alvin was back on the coms.

"Cap, if you'll get us some support, I'm ready to give this a try."

I grabbed a couple of men close by, and we formed up on Alvin, just behind him, and to either side. When we were ready, I tapped Alvin on the shoulder, and he started forward, moving in a low duck-walk, keeping his eyes below the level of the worst of the smoke, and moving forward only a few feet at a time, as he peered ahead for some sign of the enemy.

The biggest problem with attacking through smoke is that you can't always get a good estimation of just how far you really are able to see when there is nothing in front of you. Sometimes, you might think you have forty yards of vision until the enemy materializes in front of you suddenly, and you discover that ten yards is your limit. In this case, though, Alvin was apparently able to pick out something that I had not seen, because he suddenly stopped, and after fiddling with something for just a moment, he cocked his right arm back, and I realized what he was doing. I got on the coms while he held that pose for a couple of seconds.

"Men, get low to the ground, or get behind something. I think Sgt. Alvin is planning to blow something up."

The men with us separated, moving close to the corridor walls on each side, and I followed one of them, as Alvin tossed a breaching charge up the hallway. It was gone in a second, and I had no idea how far he had been trying to throw it until it blew up in a sudden flash and a loud "WHUMP!"- a sound slightly different from when these breeching charges are pressed into place on a metal bulkhead.

The response came almost instantly. From very close to where the flash of light seemed to be centered, five or six blue bolts suddenly shot down the corridor. They couldn't see us, but they knew we were here now, and Alvin's improvised grenade hadn't had much effect on them. We retreated rapidly.

"It didn't do much, because we don't have anything for fragmentation. I was hoping it would be at least as good as a concussion grenade, in these close confines. What we need is a crate full of nuts and bolts, or ball-bearings." Alvin was frustrated with the failure of the breeching charges to affect casualties on the enemy. Fragmentation grenades are devastating weapons in situations like this; low visibility allows a close approach to the enemy, and close quarters makes it easy to be sure the grenade lands reasonably close to them. We don't commonly use them in boarding missions because the fragments are lethal for distances between fifteen and thirty yards, depending on the charge, and the density of the fragmentation element. A metal case, a notched wire, tightly wrapped around the charge, or even ball-bearings in a small canister make effective fragmentation missiles. But unless you toss them out from behind cover, using them on a ship usually means that the guy who threw it is as much at risk as whoever he threw it at.

Concussion grenades, on the other hand, don't rely on fragmentation missiles. They kill in a much smaller radius, perhaps two or three yards, on average, just due to the concussive force. They're an excellent weapon for dropping into tunnels, open tank hatches, enclosed gun emplacements, or even two to four-man foxholes and the like; anywhere the enemy is clustered in very close confines. But these shaped breeching charges didn't create as much of an explosion, by themselves, and the corridors of this spacecraft were only narrow in terms of width. They were wide open regarding length. And precisely hitting a two-yard long target zone was asking a lot, with this limited visibility. The breaching charges Alvin had set when we were in the maintenance shaft had worked for two reasons: First, the back wall of the shaft directed more of the force forward, towards the enemy, and second, the ventilation grill acted as a large fragmentation medium. The open deck of the hallway provided neither of those features, directing most of the force straight up, into the air.

"It was worth a try, Alvin. What do you think about putting two charges together, and trying that?"

"That was two charges. And I don't think four would really do much more. We really need fragmentation grenades that would clear, say, five or ten yards of corridor at a time." He looked at me, and asked, "Did you see anything back in the generator room that might work? A bag of screws or something?"

I shook my head. "Nothing like that. Anyway, even if we had screws, we don't have anything to put the projectiles and explosives in, to keep them close to the charges while they go off. We could maybe cut some sections of pipe for containers, if we had a way to seal them." I thought a moment . . . Seal them . . . ?

"Alvin, give me your pack. You still carrying a bunch of sealing gel?"

Alvin looked at me just a moment before he got it, too.

"Sure thing, Cap." He shrugged out of his pack, and turned it upside down. We both felt the pressure of time running out before the enemy would feel they had enough forces gathered to assault us, and we wanted to find a solution and get moving before that happened.

Alvin started grabbing up breeching charges, and pressing them together, two at a time. He set them for lanyard detonation, and put the timers at seven seconds before handing them to me.

Meanwhile, I opened a quart tub of sealing gel and scooped a good handful of it out. As Alvin handed me charges, I pressed a handful of sealing gel into a blob around the charge, and then, gingerly holding it by the detonation mechanism, a square chunk of metal about the size of the end of my thumb, I liberally sprayed hardener all around it. A few seconds later, I could set that one down and work on the next one.

Sealing gel is designed to harden very rapidly, the assumption being that whoever is using it might be losing atmosphere as it is applied. The crystalline structure of the hardened gel was not as dense as the metals used in frag grenades, but that would work in our favor, as we didn't want a large explosive radius. The lighter fragments made of hardened sealing gel would lose momentum and destructive force over a much shorter range than metal fragments would. When we had a dozen made up, I was out of gel, and it was time to give them a try.

This time we needed to gather all the men, and move in force. We had to get out of this corridor either way, and the longer we waited, the greater our enemies' advantage. We were also suddenly very optimistic about our new grenade design, and I didn't want to warn the enemy with a trial run, and give them time to spread out their numbers. It was time for us to move, one way or the other.

I put the word out, and had the sergeants organize the men, designating some of them to help the wounded, and others to function as rapid-support fire-teams. I rigged Alvin's pack as a shoulder bag, and put the little bombs in it, stowing the rest of his gear in my own pack. And finally, I fastened a small strobe on the back of his vacsuit, so my men would be able to see him, and know how far ahead he was, and avoid shooting him in the back as we moved forward.

When we were ready, I clicked into the company channel, and told the men we were moving out. Alvin took the lead, moving low and slow, and I was next, right behind him. With the men strung out behind us, we slinked along the hallway, straining our eyes to catch any movement or blue flash in the space ahead of us.

Alvin must have had great eyes for this environment, or a sixth sense, or something, because after we moved a little ways, he stopped. I was watching for this, and managed to hold up without bumping into him, but I could hear a few shuffling thumps and a muffled "Oof!" or two, coming from the men behind us. Alvin cocked his arm suddenly, and held the pose for a moment, counting seconds off the timer, I presumed, of an already-jerked lanyard. He let the grenade fly, and a moment later the hallway lit up- not with the flash of explosive, but with a string of blue beam discharges, at much closer range than I expected, perhaps ten or twelve yards. The enemy had moved up while we were working.

I shouted "DOWN!" into the com, and simply dropped where I was crouching. Alvin, I could see, was slightly faster than I was, already falling to the deck before my faceplate was pressed to the floor. When the small bomb went off, it was a white flash crossing the deck below me while I dropped, and a sharp "CRACK!" came, the report of an explosive firing from inside a hard container, rather than the duller, open sound, of a charge going off in the air.

Still on the deck, I opened the coms again.

"Anybody hurt?"

No reply, which was good news; either everyone had gotten down, or the fragments hadn't traveled too far. But the best news was, there was no more beam fire for a moment, either. It started up again, in just a few seconds, but from further away. Alvin had taken out every enemy for a good twenty yards in front of us.

* * *

We moved like that, all the way back to the 'lander, with Alvin in front blowing up small bombs, and the men behind, either carbines at the ready, or helping out a wounded teammate. When Alvin ran low on charges, we put the word out on the coms, and someone came forward to provide more charges, and more sealing gel. We had plenty of both.

When we had covered maybe a little less than half the distance, Duggard came on the coms.

"Captain Lombard, you'll be running into Squad Four any time now. Don't shoot them."

"Men, Squad Four is just ahead. No shooting unless we are fired on first. Clear?" A series of acknowledgments came back, and Duggard started estimating positions for both teams, the better to avoid a friendly-fire incident.

Squad Four saw us before we saw them, but not by much. The smoke was still coming, as wiring continued to burn, and visibility got progressively worse. That was to our benefit, since all we wanted now was to avoid contact and get the hell of this ship. We got all the way back without any further conflict, after we hooked up with Squad Four. It took me a little while to realize that it had to be due to the effects of Duggard's program. I clicked over to command to ask him about it.

"Duggard, what are you doing that's keeping them off our asses? We haven't had contact for quite a while now."

"Oh, well, I just took a guess as to where the bridge is likely to be, and when you started home, I started about eight spoof squads towards the bridge. If it's working, they're piled up about neck-deep in defensive positions around the bridge right now."

I wondered if the company budget could afford two weeks of casino station leave for Duggard.

* * *

As we arrived near the corridor just outside the storage room we had made our entrance into the ship, the men of Squad Four told us that the corridor was under pressure, and we wouldn't have vacuum until we unsealed the hatchway into the storage room itself. That meant the smoke we had just come through would be present in that corridor. No problem, except for the difficulty in checking seals and suit integrity for the wounded. The positive pressure of the suits would be working now to keep smoke out of the suit environment, but in vacuum, air needed for breathing would escape very rapidly. It was almost impossible to take a wound without compromising the vacsuit, and anybody with a tear or hole in their suit might have only moments to detect it and ask for help. Depending of the severity of the leak, a man might have no more than eight or ten seconds of consciousness after being exposed to vacuum. The suits would have to be examined before moving them through vacuum, and that would take longer than usual because of the low visibility.

It was, I expected, the last problem we would have to deal with before lifting off of *StarFire* in the 'lander. The wounded would have to be laid out, and their suits examined in detail before the last hatch to vacuum was unsealed. But it would leave us very vulnerable to enemy fire while the procedure was carried out.

The solution wasn't all that difficult to figure out. That long corridor outside the storage room ended, on both ends, with sealed hatches on right-angle turns. A couple of men at this end, acting as a rear guard, and a couple more at the other end, doing the same job, would free up everyone else to examine vacuum suits, and help get the wounded transferred to our waiting spacecraft. Alvin made the assignments, sending two men to the other end of the corridor, and picking one to stay with him at this end, while the wounded were moved to the center of the length, and prepared for vacuum. Except, I wasn't going along with it.

"Forget it, Alvin. I'm staying with you, here. Send the private on in with the others. He can help prepare the wounded." I told him.

"Cap, if it's all the same to you, I think you should-"

"It's not all the same to me, Sergeant. You know my policy. No one gets left behind. Ever. And to be sure of that, I need to be here. I will be the last man to step through that hatch."

"Captain, you know I'll-"

"You have your orders, Alvin." I looked around for a moment. "There's not much cover here, so let's take positions just inside the hatchway. When they're ready to proceed, we'll step out again and seal the hatch before they open the entrance to the storage room. It will limit the venting to the volume of the corridor, and help them get the wounded loaded up that much faster. Tell the team on the other end to do the same."

Alvin stood there for just a moment, wanting to argue with me more, but knowing it not only wouldn't do any good, but would also piss me off, and waste time. We were all tired, worn down from the stress and efforts of combat. And in a hurry. I decided to spur him on a little.

"You're wasting time, Sergeant. Get these men busy making the wounded ready."

"Yes sir." Alvin gave out my instructions, and people started getting things done.

It didn't take as long as it might have, though a couple of troopers did find small repairs to make in the suits of the wounded. In just a few minutes, Alvin and I were stepping back out the hatchway we had taken our positions on the other side of, and we sealed it behind us.

This was the most vulnerable we had been since we left this corridor behind us, coming into the ship. Right now, the enemy had a very good idea exactly where we were, but other than our two carbines, and any grenades Alvin had left, we had no support.

'Toon Simpkins, loading the men, reported on the com as they made progress.

"Captain Lombard, we have everybody in the storage room now. I'll close the hatch here, and you can begin falling back right away, be right outside this room as the last of the wounded are passed up through the breach, into the 'lander."

"Belay that, 'Toon Simpkins. Don't waste time sealing that hatch. We aren't moving yet. We're going to hold here until you folks have everybody on board. I don't want to wind up holding the enemy just forty or fifty feet from the 'lander, if they show up. Just work fast."

Simpkins acknowledged my order, and Alvin and I settled in to wait. In a little while, word came back that the last of the wounded were being loaded. That was also when *StarFire*'s marines caught up with us again.

* * *

In the low visibility, we didn't see them coming, and they didn't know exactly where we were, either. They essentially just marched out of the smoke and right into us. Alvin reacted first, clicking his carbine to automatic fire while I was still standing with wide eyes, trying to make sense of the formless shapes, differentiating smoke shadows from solid bodies, and having a hard time reacting to what I was seeing. Four men fell at a distance of less than fifteen feet with Alvin's first burst of beam fire. I raised my weapon, while at the same time calling the other rear guard team on the com, telling them to fall back to the lander and board. This was exactly what worried me: The 'lander was still very vulnerable as long as it was on the hull of this ship, and all the more so when all the men were aboard, instead of deployed around the landing site in defensive positions. That 'lander wouldn't be safe from a marine assault group until it was back flying under its own power.

Alvin and I both went prone and started firing down the hallway, tossing bolts randomly, assuming there were more troops behind those Alvin had just put down. The beams flashing back towards us confirmed it. We kept firing, taking turns, alternating every few shots to allow the other man's weapon to cool a little between sets of five or six shots, except at times we had actual, visible targets. Then we both opened up. We were grinding away at them when Duvall came on the com.

"Vince, we have everyone aboard. It's time for you to make a break for it. I'll wait long enough to see you back here."

"Jimmy, we can't do that just now, and the other end of the corridor is unsecured. Do you have the 'lander broken free?" I was asking about the magnetic and mechanical mating that the 'lander established when we set down. Magnetic usually wasn't a problem, just a question of flipping a switch, but the mechanical mating involved setting what amounted to big metal hooks into the hull of the target ship, around the area where the thrusters had burned our access way through.

"Roger that, Vince. We are un-locked and broken free. I'm holding her down with a little upward thrust, just waiting for you two guys."

"Maybe have your weapons man train his turret to the rear, if he has an angle. I'll call you before we show up. If you see anyone, and I haven't called you, shoot them, and take off. That'll mean they got by us, and there's no reason to wait for us anymore."

"Fair enough, Vince. Just don't let it come down to that, would you?"

"I'm trying, Jimmy. We're both trying."

Alvin and I continued to fire. We had been catching a few near misses from beams occasionally, but Alvin suddenly put his hand over the sights of my carbine.

"I haven't seen any return fire for a minute, Cap. We might have got them all. Or almost all, anyway. Time to bug-out, I think."

I paused, listening and watching, for just a moment.

"I think you're right, Alvin. Let's go." We both got to our feet, cautiously, and then I turned to the hatchway, moving to open it.

"Brace yourself, Alvin. This will be a big venting, I think."

"Just a second, Cap." I turned to look at him, and Alvin had pulled out one last grenade. "There's one or two more out there. I just heard them moving." I looked, and sure enough, Alvin had the visor on his helmet open a couple of inches, enough to facilitate his hearing in atmosphere. I can't imagine how he had tolerated the smoke he had been breathing to do that, but I supposed it was paying off, if it warned him we weren't actually alone here, right now.

Alvin pulled the lanyard, and held the grenade for a couple of seconds. Before he threw it, a shape materialized right in front of us, and I fired my beam weapon just as Alvin made a very short throw. A second later we felt the concussion of the explosion, before a patter of sealing gel fragments slapped across my vacsuit. And the body of one of *StarFire*'s marines, pushed by the small blast, stumbled forward into the two of us.

We pushed him off, and he fell backwards. As he hit the wall of the corridor, just forward of our position, a series of sparks went up. Alvin had blown off the cover panels of a bulkhead there, when the grenade exploded, and the exposed conduits were tangled, broken, smoking . . . but some of them were still live and sparking. I turned back to the hatchway while that troop screamed as he was electrocuted. There must not have been all that much juice left in the wiring, though, because it was taking him a minute to die, and he kept screaming.

After maybe three for four seconds of that, I stopped what I was doing, and looked back, because something was different now. It just took me a moment to realize it.

This man was screaming.

It was the first time since we had come aboard that I had heard any of *StarFire*'s complement make a vocalization. Before this, I had not heard a word, a moan, not even a sigh. Grievously wounded men had held silent. Not a single enemy sergeant even cursed at us, or at his men. But this man was screaming.

It was only eight or ten steps, but I ran to him. He was wearing a vacuum suit, and I only heard him screaming because his visor had come up about halfway, probably when he bumped into us and we pushed him. But the suit offered an easy way to get him off the wall, so I just hooked his shoulder-loop epaulette with my beam carbine and pulled him off the wires. I caught him as he fell limp in my arms, and I laid him down, carefully. Looking him over, I noticed the rank insignia. He was a captain, same as me. Probably the commander of one of the companies on this ship, I guessed. I glanced at his name tag next. Halverson, it said. I didn't know if his com was on, or what channel it might be set on, so I just pushed his visor further up, and then raised my own.

"Captain Halvorson? Captain?"

His eyelids fluttered for a second, and then he seemed to focus on my face.

"Where . . . ? What's going on? What happened to me?"

"You've been injured, Captain Halvorson. What can you tell me about this ship? What happened here?"

"I don't . . . what ship? What ship is this?" And with that, Captain Halvorson's eyes rolled up, and he fell unconscious again.

It's pretty difficult to take a man's pulse while you're wearing the gloves of a vacuum suit, but I didn't need to. There was an easier way to see if Halverson was alive. I just pulled his visor down again, and watched for the tell-tale fog his breath made on the visor as he exhaled. Satisfied that he was breathing, I flipped my own visor back down, sealing up, and then I wrapped his arm around my shoulder, to pick him up off the deck, and then bent over while I draped him across my shoulder in a fireman's carry. He was heavy, and his weight pressed against the back of my helmet, but I could handle him, bent over, and watching the floor, just ahead of my feet. I got back on the com.

"Alvin, we're taking this one with us."

"A prisoner? But Captain . . ."

"Shut up, Alvin. He goes. He was talking, and I want to know- hell, Fleet Command is going to want to know what happened here, why they went rogue. Here, you take him. You're bigger than I am, and stronger. You get him to the 'lander, I'll cover the rear." All this time I had been hauling Halvorson towards the hatch, where Alvin was standing by. Now, just as I reached him, Alvin was still arguing.

"Captain . . . uh, you take him. You're right, he'll have the answers. That's got to be a priority. I'll just open the hatch, and you take him right through. Don't wait for me."

"What do you mean? Alvin, I can handle a beam carbine, just take . . ."

I trailed off, looking at Sergeant Alvin, now that I had come up next to him, and raised my eyes while we talked.

A beam shot smacked into the bulkhead next to us, but I didn't move, for a moment. I heard another hammer blow, as another one landed, right next to the first one. Some random part of my mind calculated that we had at least two enemies taking pot shots, probably still a little ways away. But mostly I stared at Alvin.

Alvin's visor was cracked. Not just cracked, but a jagged piece about the size of my thumb was missing. It had been hit with fragments from the last grenade he had used. Almost certainly, the fragment had been the metal of the timing/detonation device, because the sealing-gel fragments had not retained enough energy to shred our suits. But the denser metal piece had hit harder, and the unsupported bottom edge, where he had lifted that visor to enhance his hearing had been broken. Alvin immediately saw in my face that I understood his situation. Drawing himself upright, he dropped all pretense, and his face took on a serious cast.

"Captain Lombard, it's been a pleasure serving with you. You've become a fine officer, in the time we've worked together. You take that wounded man to the 'lander, and get off this tub. Get home. Take care of my men."

"Alvin . . . we have to slap a patch on that visor . . ."

"A fiber patch won't stick to the visor, sir. You know that. And my atmosphere supply is almost depleted. I can't just cover this hole with my hand and make it through, leaking what air I have left all the way. If I had a full cartridge, it would be worth a try, but I don't. I'm just about empty. I can't get through the vacuum, no way, no how. So, you take that prisoner, and get on the 'lander. You can write me a commendation, posthumously, if you want, when you get back. Send it to my mom. It'll make her feel better, thinking I went out doing my job."

"Alvin . . ."

Company Sergeant Alvin T. Alvin saluted me, and turned to the sealed hatch. As I reached out with my free hand to stop him, he spun the hatch open, and the sound of wind filled my helmet.

CHAPTER 21

Defense Space Station G-13, 246.163.12

After Action

"That was the basis of your recommendation to decorate Sgt. Alvin?" Lt. Linda Tillman turned to face me. It wasn't the question I expected.

"Absolutely. He opened that hatch because the enemy was approaching again. We were already taking beam fire, and we both knew it was going to get worse. He was trying to get me out of danger, and back to the 'lander before they got so close we couldn't break off contact and make a run for it." I thought for a moment, realizing something else. "You knew that. So, you've already read the recommendation I wrote."

"Of course. I reviewed the whole case file as soon as I got the assignment."

"Well, then, you know how the situation turned out. I don't suppose you know what the higher-ups are doing with that request?"

"I don't think . . ." she hesitated, "I don't think they will make any decisions about those things until your inquiry is concluded." She was dodging something, keeping back something she knew, but I couldn't guess what it was.

"So . . . what? A Marine can't get decorated without actually dying anymore? What Alvin did was heroism, any way you shake it, no matter how it turned out."

"I don't think that's the issue, Captain. In any event, the issue we should be talking about, which will surely come up in the inquiry tomorrow is, how do you justify your decision? Surely you realized that your prisoner, assuming he survived, would have been Fleet Command's priority. They won't be happy you left him there."

"I don't give a rat's ass what their priorities are. Sgt. Alvin opened that hatch. He was willingly sacrificing his own life, in order to give me a chance. You don't leave a man like that behind."

"But with his suit compromised, and you under fire, no chance of repairing it, making some kind of patch, even just enough to get him to the 'lander . . . and Captain-- who was it? Halvorson? His suit was fine. He would have had a very good chance. How do you make a decision like that? One man with almost no chance, and one with every chance of making it through . . . How do you make the choice you made? How did you know what to do?"

I paused before I answered her, and took a breath, then let it out again. Tillman was getting worked up. I had been arguing with her, thinking, how can she not understand this? Until I realized, maybe she did understand. Maybe she was getting worked up because that would get me worked up, and make me a little less deliberate about what I said. I needed to address this carefully, because she had just told me I could expect to be grilled on this very point. I needed to make a full answer, for the record.

"My orders were to find *StarFire*, and either render aid or report home. Nothing in my orders included an assault, or taking prisoners. It was just the situation I found myself in. We assaulted in order to facilitate getting the report home. The prisoner, yeah, he would have made the report more complete. He could, maybe, have answered a lot of questions. But at the time . . . in the moment, sure, I had suspicions that something really strange was going on, but nothing as strong as my opinions were later, after I had time to think it all through, and reflect on what I had seen. At the time, the only question I was faced with was, save one of my men, or save one of the enemy. If I could have saved both, I would have, but that wasn't on the table, so far as I could see. And frankly, I knew the situation was maybe not as hopeless as it looked, regarding getting Alvin through it alive, if you understand how decompression works."

She just raised her eyebrows, so I explained it to her.

"Lt. Tillman, when a person undergoes rapid, severe decompression, they lose consciousness in about ten seconds. It's supposed to be a pretty painless way to go because of that fact. No one stays conscious in vacuum for long, and if they keep their wits and do the right things, like letting their breath escape before they get an air embolism from the over-pressure in their lungs, then by the time the real damage starts they're in la-la land, not feeling a thing. So, after Alvin opened that hatch, I stood there for maybe ten seconds, and watched Sgt. Alvin fall over. It didn't take long for him to pass out. But I knew I had about ninety seconds to get him back into atmospheric pressure before any permanent damage was likely. After that, past the ninety seconds, it's a crap-shoot, and the odds go down fast. Water and vapor embolisms in the bloodstream, bursting capillaries, a host of problems develop quickly, then. But a minute and a half is a long time for a G-Marine to get something done, so I got started.

"I dropped Captain Halvorson like a wet dishrag, and picked up Sgt. Alvin instead. I didn't calculate the odds, or think it through. I just got him into that 'lander as fast as I could. It was a close-run thing, I'm sure, but I did everything I could to increase his chances. I called ahead on the com, had a couple guys meet me at the breach point. And the medics were ready, too. Somebody figured out a make-shift patch for Alvin's visor, using the handiest thing, something I hadn't thought of. They slapped a piece of welding tape on over the missing chunk of his visor. That tape is basically just a slow-burning plastic explosive, so it's malleable, like thick putty. They just used the raw tape, they didn't have to light it or anything. And it only needed to block airflow for a couple of minutes. Then, they re-pressurized him right in his suit. That held down the bloodstream problems while the cabin pressure came up, in maybe two more minutes. And after that, they had him revived in no time. His head hurt all the way home, and I guess they broke a couple ribs pumping his chest before one of them got a defib unit on him, but he made it.

"And it would have been nice if Halvorson had made it, too. And if Alvin or I, either one, had thought of the welding tape trick, we might have pulled it off, and gotten both of them out. But we didn't. So, I can admit, it would have been a great help if we could have gotten some intelligence out of Halvorson. But then, when they were done talking to him, they would have stood him against a wall and shot him for munity. I'll be damned if I will ever let a good man like Sgt. Alvin die just because Fleet Command has some questions they want to ask someone before they kill him anyway. And you can quote me on that, all day, tomorrow, at the Board of Inquiry. I'll say it just that way, myself, if they ask me."

I realized I had turned away, and was looking at the wall as I finished what I was saying. I suddenly turned back to Lt. Tillman. She covered it quickly, but I caught it: She was smiling at me, just a little, while I spoke with my back turned to her. I reviewed it in my mind, wondering how something like that could have come out as humorous. I thought I had Lt. Tillman figured out, until then. Now I wondered if she had been a step ahead of me the whole time. Because the thought crossed my mind that just maybe she had been rehearsing me, and her smile was from satisfaction that I was getting it right.

CHAPTER 22

Military Transport/Lander 246.163-12-02

Action

As the medics worked on Sgt. Alvin, I made my way to the cockpit. Duvall had already started the procedure for lifting off of *StarFire*'s hull while he waited for the last of us to board, and now he wasted no time getting the craft up. But he didn't go far. By staying close to the hull, he made it impossible to shoot at us with the ship's guns, which was a good thing, even if the targeting systems were all fried. He did move us away from the hull breach, where attackers could still come through to the outside and fire on us with handheld weapons. It wasn't likely they would do much damage, but on balance, not getting fired on is generally preferable to taking fire, whether it's a serious threat or a mild one.

"Jimmy, we're set. Did Harley get away?" I asked as soon as I was at the entrance to the cockpit.

"He lifted off a while ago, as soon as we detected the degradation of *StarFire*'s systems. She tossed a few salvos at him, but Mark says he didn't see any hits," Duvall answered me. I looked at Lt. Goddard. He had a somber expression on his face, which worried me for a second, but the news wasn't that bad.

"Yeah, they were shooting, but the shots were all over the place, maybe consistent with manual alignment, from visual observation. There were some that might have been pretty close, maybe even a couple of grazing shots, or too-close-to-call misses, but if he took any damage at all, I couldn't see it on the sensors. His exhaust signature was pretty stable. He ducked out through the asteroid belt, low-speed, high maneuverability, until he was out of sight. We caught just a trace of something, probably Harley, leaving the system altogether from the far side of the belt," Goddard filled me in. My relief was palpable.

"That's great news. Okay, Jimmy, what's our plan? How do we get away without taking a lucky hit from a manually aligned gun, ourselves?"

"We have another problem first, Vince. I told you *StarFire* was changing course, and increasing her thrust?" I remembered hearing something like that, during our push back to the 'lander, though I hadn't paid much attention at the time. "Well, she is still accelerating, but on this new course, she's headed for a human system." Jimmy glanced at me in the reflection of the windshield, gauging my reaction. "It's a high-population system, Vince."

"Jimmy, I don't think they are going to be able to repair her, out here. If they ever get any navigation control back, it will be weeks from now, but I don't think they have weeks. Everything burned when we overloaded the electrical system, and I bet that includes the environmental controls and monitors. It's already pretty bad in there. Toxic."

"Yeah, that's about what I figured, Vince. But here's the thing: That ship will continue to build speed as long as the fuel holds out. That could be weeks, even at constant, full acceleration. She'll be trans-light in a few hours, at this rate, and still have weeks to build speed. Once she passes light-speed, which will be later today, it will be very hard to stop her."

I listened to him, and I still didn't get it. But I responded to what I thought the issue was.

"Jimmy, we don't have anything to stop her with. Nothing we have will make a dent in her drive systems from outside the ship. Cooking off her control systems and computers gives us a chance to get away, but her armor is fully intact. We can't kill her, Jimmy. We have to let her die at her own pace, from internal conditions."

Now Jimmy murmured to Mark to take the controls, and then actually turned in his seat to look directly at me.

"Vince, let's try this again. Listen to me. *StarFire* is a few hours from becoming a giant, trans-light-speed, kinetic missile, aimed right at one of our inhabited systems. They don't need to get nav control back, she's a planet-buster if she hits anything in that system already. And by the time she gets there, she'll be going so fast that, with her mass, nothing will stop her."

Now, finally, I understood. Duvall wasn't saying she could still become a danger. He was saying she already was. A deadly serious threat to a significant human world.

"You think they actually targeted one of our systems? They aren't just going in that direction, they really want to hit something there?" I asked him.

"Who knows what they are thinking? Our best calculation of their course suggests at the least a very near miss of a high-population, industrially developed planet, at speeds that will make her impossible to stop. Even if she misses the planet, at the kind of speed she'll be going, ordinary intra-system traffic won't be able to avoid her. If she just hits a passenger liner, it's bad enough."

"Okay, I follow you," I was nodding, getting a better picture. "So, if we notify the right people, make sure they know she's coming, they can figure something out, right?"

"That's what I'm saying, Vince. I don't think they can figure something out. It's nearly impossible to hit something traveling faster than light with guns."

"Maybe a barrier? A debris field for her to break up on before she gets into atmosphere, or high-traffic areas?"

"No, Vince. *StarFire* is too big, many times the total mass of any other ship we've ever seen. And a debris field takes time to disperse. On top of that, it would have to be really massive, to be sure to intercept *StarFire*, but it would have to be dense to be sure to break her up. So, a really large debris field, but also very dense . . . it's not really feasible, and would take months to clean up and clear the space lanes again, at best. But even if they did it, and managed to break her up, breaking up that much ship into pieces small enough that they won't make it through the atmosphere isn't going to happen. It would just make *StarFire* into a shotgun-pattern instead of a rifle shot. She would take out satellite systems, become a massive risk to any traffic moving in-system, hell, she could take down the whole defensive array of space stations and installations, and even if all that went the best possible way it could, then she would still have a high likelihood of impacting the planet catastrophically."

I absorbed all that, not speaking for a minute. But, like our ingress into this system, it wasn't really within the parameters of my own training. This was pilot and navigation stuff, not combat tactics and strategy. I felt so helpless working through the information, I literally shrugged when I spoke again.

"So . . . what can we do? You want us to take the engines out before she goes trans-light? My men aren't going to be able to get back in and shut down those engines, Jimmy. I mean, even if we tried, even if we lost every man trying, those troops were getting better with every minute we stayed on board. They still outnumber us at least ten or twelve to one. They'll chew us up if we go back, and we still won't get the job done. Hell, we would be starting with half the force we had before! It would be throwing my men's lives away, without any hope of getting the job done and making a difference." I said all of that knowing full well that if there wasn't another option, that's exactly what we would be doing, soon.

"No, not you guys, Vince. I know you can't stop her. But we can. Mark and I, and this 'lander. We can use the thrust of the 'lander to nudge the *StarFire* onto a new course, a course that doesn't threaten anyone. In fact, we can probably point her to a star that will swallow her up inside a couple of weeks or so."

"Okay. So, do that," I offered, feeling relief that he had another plan, but still not sure where Jimmy was going. This was a lot of drama, if the solution was that easy, so I was still waiting for the other shoe to drop.

"It's not so easy, Vince. You'll have to make the decision, but there are problems. Look, I think this 'lander will hold up to the abuse, but, it's not what these things are really designed for, you know? There could be damage. But outside of that, it's going to take a lot of fuel."

"Gotcha. Fuel, and maybe damage. How much fuel?" I asked him.

Jimmy hesitated, just a beat.

"Too much, Vince. We won't get all the way back home on our reserves, if we do this."

So that was it. Already exhausted before I got this information, I sat down on the deck, trying to put it all in order in my mind. Captain Duvall was, properly, deferring this decision to me, as the mission commander, and he was trying to give me a complete picture so I could make it. Clearly, he thought we had a duty to act, or he wouldn't have put it to me this way, so all that remained was for me to draw my conclusions and make a decision. I grasped at straws, for a minute or two, started to speak a couple of times, but my own logical thought process answered my questions and eliminated possibilities as fast as they came up. In the end, it came down to one thing.

The formula for the energy a projectile delivers on the target is $M(V^2)=E$, or "mass times (velocity squared) equals energy." Meaning that velocity is a much bigger factor than size, in calculating the potential damage a given projectile would do to a target, just in terms of the energy released when it hit. StarFire might literally burn up a planet, in a scenario like the one we were talking about, as her kinetic energy was converted into heat, on impact. If she didn't literally burn it to a crisp, at the very least there would be huge atmospheric calamities, resulting in devastating weather anomalies, tidal changes, temperature fluctuations, ranging from extreme heat for a period, perhaps followed by an ice-age, and a thousand other things we couldn't even guess at. Any way you shake it, a planet hit by a trans-light speed projectile the size of StarFire was in for a bad millennia or two, after impact. It would be on the order of the calamity that killed off the dinosaurs on Earth. At least.

Duvall saw that I was thinking, and he left me to it, turning back around to face forward, but I could see he was still watching me in the reflection of the windshield. He knew what he had dumped on me, and that it would take me a little time to come to terms with it. After a moment, he took control of the craft again, and suggested to Lt. Goddard that he let me have his seat for a few minutes. Mark was a good lieutenant, and he didn't question Jimmy. He just said, "Sure," and got up, stepping around me. After a moment, I pulled myself up and fumbled into Goddard's seat.

"Jimmy, I don't even know where to start asking questions about something like this. You've been thinking about it a while, if I know you. Just fill me in on your thoughts, would you?"

"Sure, Vince. I figured it out maybe half an hour or so ago, and I've been thinking about it ever since. It's pretty straightforward. I figure that after I make a long burn to turn StarFire to a new course, I can probably get us back to our sector. Probably. That's key, because if I'm wrong, well, nobody much comes out here, and we're toast. But G-13 has some cargo traffic, and if I can get us into a trade route, we might have a decent chance of getting spotted and catching a ride home."

"How decent a chance?"

"Oh, that's hard to say. It's a good news/ bad news sort of problem."

"So, give it to me."

"Well, the odds of getting picked up are pretty variable, depending on how far we get. The good news is, unless we use all of our fuel turning *StarFire*, which isn't going to happen, once I get us pointed in the right direction, we can coast almost all the way back to G-13, if we have to. Once we break light-speed, it doesn't take a lot of fuel to maintain it. The bad news is we have already vented atmosphere twice, getting you guys on and off the 'lander. We're going to run out in a few days. If we headed home now, we have a good two-day cushion on air supplies, about double what we need, and well within tactical specifications. But if it takes more than four days to get back and get picked up, we're in real trouble."

I digested this for a moment before responding, "So, what if we send a message with our projected course and situation. Surely they could meet us partway, with a resupply, right?"

Duvall nodded. "I've already factored that in. But we don't have a lot of extra capacity in our com system. We can generate a signal that will reach our base, but it'll take us hours to do it. So, we start that in motion as soon as we head out. We can't afford to wait until the signal goes out to do the job on *StarFire* and then head for home. Procedure for this sort of thing is, you never plan to have less than two days cushion on air supply, even on training missions in the neighborhood of your base support. It's a big universe, too many things can go wrong. We're a long way away, and we're already at the two-day limit, even if we leave right now."

"My guys have picked up some extra vacuum suit atmosphere canisters. That should give us a little more cushion. We can rig them to cycle into the general atmosphere, releasing oxygen and scrubbing CO_2, just by attaching them to a suit that's opened up, and turning them on."

"That will help, but don't kid yourself. It's still a gamble. There's no easy answer, here. Say you buy us an extra day, or even two, with those canisters. We might find a big luxury liner floating along as soon as we hit the trade routes, and never even have to worry about air. Or we might wind up sitting along the outside edge of a minor trade route, and have to wait a lot longer, while whoever is bringing our resupply is looking for us, high and low, in all the wrong places. Hell, somebody might find this old bucket a hundred years from now, with a couple of pilots and a company of Marines, all dead, sitting lined up at the portholes, watching for our rescuers. They'll just wonder what we were all looking at when we died." Duvall looked over at me. "I just don't know what else we can do, Vince. It's a big gamble, but you have to make the call. I know you have a duty to those troops, back there. But you also know what your larger duty is or isn't. My view is, I don't see any way we can leave without doing everything we can to turn *StarFire*, and even if I knew it would kill us all, I would make that attempt. But it's better than that. We do have a chance. I just can't tell you how much of a chance. And I wish I didn't have to put it on you to make the decision, but that's how it is."

I was so tired, I was starting to feel like I was already low on oxygen. "Jimmy, you didn't put the responsibility on me. Colonel Parsons did. And if I wasn't willing to make the tough calls, I have no business being an officer." I thought of something else, then, maybe trying to put off the choice I was going to have to make. "Jimmy, are we burning much fuel now, hovering over the hull of this ship? If I take a minute to think about it, am I putting us at greater risk?"

"Not a bit, Vince. You can take a few minutes to think it through. You can even go back and talk to some of your guys about it, if you think it would help. If we stay at this level for half an hour, it won't make a dime's worth of difference in the long haul."

It was a good answer, but it didn't help. I had to decide, and then live with the outcome. I didn't talk to my men, not even Sgt. Alvin. I just spent a few minutes thinking. And in the end, here's what it came down to: If everything went right, we could shift the trajectory of *StarFire*, and make some distant population a lot safer, and we still might get picked up rapidly, and make it home in one piece. Plus, I had to take into account that the military existed exactly for the purpose of protecting populations and developed worlds. Finally, I had to consider the fact that, while we didn't know Lt. Harley's situation exactly, we had every reason to believe he would be making a pretty full report when he got home. He wouldn't be able to say what happened to us, but every box was checked on the mission parameter board, because he would be able to tell Colonel Parsons and Fleet Command what we had found out here, and what we had done about it, and he would have the video evidence to prove it. He might not know *StarFire* was doomed, but he knew she was hurt. That just meant Fleet would send a task force out here to look for *StarFire*, and engage her. They would hurry, hoping to catch her still disabled, but that wouldn't hurt anything. They just wouldn't find her. Ever.

Taking all that into consideration, I finally decided we would play it as if everything was going to break in our favor, and see if we couldn't sweep the board, win it all. It was possible, after all. Everything could go right.

* * *

That hope, that everything could go right, didn't even survive through the first phase of the new operation. Duvall brought his copilot, Mark, back up front, and sent me back out to the main cabin, saying, "Vince, we don't need the distraction of having you here while we do this, and operational standards say we should close this cockpit hatch anyway. You go tell your boys what we're up to, keep them in line, and I'll keep you posted on the coms, okay?"

"Sure, Jimmy." I clapped him on the shoulder, to show support before I slipped out the hatch, and closed it behind me.

I'm sure that while I was in back telling my men what the pilots were doing, Jimmy and Mark had a pretty good conversation weighing the options, and deciding the best way to go about what they were about to attempt. And I'm pretty sure that what eventually happened didn't even come up in that conversation.

Captain James Duvall brought the transport/lander around to the spot he and Mark had picked for their pressure point, and then he announced it to me, on the command channel.

"We're about ready, here, Vince. Maybe you can get your guys to sit down and strap in for this? Could be a little rough, while we make contact with her hull."

I acknowledged, and passed on the order. I also told the men to check their seals, but said they could leave their visors up. I wanted everyone ready to go on vacsuit atmosphere in a second, if worst came to worst. The medics made some last-minute arraignments for some of the wounded, making sure they were ready for seal-up as well, and they designated men to keep track of any wounded who were unconscious. One or two of the worst ones got another dose of painkillers, to make up for any jostling they were about to be subjected to. I clicked back to command channel to tell Jimmy we were strapped in and ready.

There was a rough bump when we made contact, but nothing that seemed like anything to worry about; it was no worse than a lot of combat landings I had experienced. Then Jimmy and Mark spent some time spinning the main thrusters up, very slowly, while they juggled the 'lander's attitude against the bigger ship with the attitude thrusters. Maybe five minutes after the first big bump, Jimmy came on the coms, company channel, this time, so everyone could hear him.

"We have a good contact position, and our attitude is stable. We'll be running the thrusters up slowly, and then holding steady for a long burn. You folks settle in for a bit, and we'll let you know how it's going when we start to see results. It's likely to take at least a couple of hours."

I understood the physics of the situation. Thrusters the size of what we had, meant to work well for moving this little craft around nimbly, were not much when put up against the inertia of something the size of *StarFire*. But "not much" isn't the same as zero. What the massive thrusters on *StarFire* could do, small thrusters could also do. It would just take longer. I listened closely for a few minutes, and finally detected a minute increase in the pitch of the engine noise, and determined that Jimmy was still tickling the throttle a little, trying to get every little bit of thrust he could, without putting too much stress on the 'lander's frame.

* * *

A couple of hours later, Jimmy came back on the command channel for a little private communication.

"Vince, Mark has some numbers to work with, now, and it isn't looking very good."

I didn't like that, but I kept my voice neutral when I replied, "Okay. Fill me in."

"We're moving her, but too slowly. It's barely registering on our equipment. We don't need much at all, in the long run, but if we're going to point her away from that human system, we need more than we're getting."

"I understand. What is it, a fuel problem? We can't stay long enough to get the job done, and still make it into the trade routes?" I asked him.

"That's what it looks like right now, the way we've been trying to do it. The thing is, we can probably get a more efficient ratio of fuel to effect at a higher burn rate. That should solve our effectiveness problem, and use less total fuel to accomplish it. But it means more stress on the space-frame."

I digested this. "You're asking for permission to stress the 'lander's frame a little more, to increase the odds of getting the job done?"

"Yeah, I would say that's it in a nutshell. Mark can go over the math with you, if you want, but the numbers add up on the fuel savings, and we won't need to push past about eight-five percent of the original stress tolerance of the space-frame specifications. But those are specs for a brand-new craft, and this one's seen some use, so eighty-five percent is about as far as I want to go with it. Your call."

"Nope. Jimmy, the mission is mine, but this craft is yours. My orders to you are, do the best job you can, using your best judgment. If you think we can't do it, then stop, and we'll go home. If you think it's likely you'll be successful, do whatever you have to do." This time, the shoe was on the other foot. Duvall wasn't out of line asking me, but I was well within military command guidelines to rely on his expertise and judgment. Not to mention, I trusted him.

"Okay, Vince. Thanks for that. I'll be increasing thrust, as gently and smoothly as I can. It might get noisy, but in this case, the cockpit is sort of a crumple-zone, so any stress should show up here, first. Let me know if we crack a window back there, or something, though. And have some men standing by with sealing gel, just in case."

"We're on it. Get the job done."

I didn't see any reason to get the men worked up, so I just looked around until I got 'Toon Simpkins' attention, and signaled him to come over and talk with me. I had him gather up a couple quarts of sealing gel, hardener, and some plate stock, and we divided it up between the two of us. Then we sauntered over to opposite sides of the ship We each grabbed a couple of not otherwise engaged privates and said we wanted them to stand by and report any signs of stress. We sent them fore and aft, so, including Simpkins and myself, we had three men on each side of the craft, watching and listening. We needn't have bothered, though. When it started to go wrong, everybody knew it at the same time.

Jimmy came on the com, command channel, and said, "Vince, it's working. We're getting real progress with less fuel use. This won't take any time at all . . ." While he was speaking, the hull started creaking and popping. It sounded like a tin can being fed into a shredder, very slowly. Immediately, every trooper in the cabin stopped what they were doing, and listened, some of them wide-eyed and looking around with alarm. Then there was a shuddering in the cabin which built suddenly from slight to severe, and a quick, lurching jolt. It felt like the craft had jumped about three feet forward. But that was impossible, because "forward" was where the craft was nosed-up against *StarFire*. The men all started talking at once, and I slid my visor down. We weren't losing air back here, but I wanted to be able to hear Jimmy if he came on the coms. I figured I would wait for him to call me, though, since it seemed likely he had his hands full. I was sure of it a second later, when the thrusters suddenly stopped.

Defense Space Station G-13, 246.163.12

After Action

"Well, it was worse than having his hands full," I said to Linda Tillman. "The front surfaces had taken damage, coming through the debris field on our approach to *StarFire*. Severe damage none of us were aware of. Jimmy came on the coms in a few minutes and told me what had happened." Lt. Tillman was respectfully quiet, and, of course, I was aware that she already knew what I was about to tell her, from reading my written report. But she was here to get the account directly from me, in greater detail, so I went on, anyway. "When the frame gave way, it was all front-end damage, and in terms of distortion, it wasn't as much as I feared, based on the lurching and bouncing of the craft. But it was more than enough to cause real problems. Durasteel is pretty resilient stuff, so when Jimmy cut the thrust, the frame actually sprang partly back into shape, hard enough to actually push us off the hull where we had been putting pressure on the larger ship.

"But the damage was done. Jimmy informed me that some of the forward duraglass panels had been cracked, and one small panel had blown out completely. They had catastrophic decompression up there, in the cockpit. Worse, Lt. Goddard had been reaching forward when the frame gave in, and his suit had torn when he hit the instrument panel, at the end of that jolt. A long tear, along one arm. He was already gone by the time Duvall got word to me. I rushed to the hatchway, thinking of the ninety seconds that Alvin had survived, but Duvall wouldn't open the hatch.

"He told me that we didn't have the air reserves. If we opened the hatchway, he figured we would vent atmosphere much faster than we could get Goddard out. And in that case, we wouldn't even have enough air to recompress the compartment, once we shut the hatchway again. We would all be on suit canisters, and Mark would still be dead, because we couldn't treat him in a vacuum suit.

"It was lose-lose, he said, and there was nothing we could do, except disengage and head for the trade routes. On the up side, it wasn't a wasted sacrifice. Duvall and Goddard had accomplished the goal, and bent *StarFire*'s course far enough to make her trajectory safe. On the downside, we lost our long-range communications, and couldn't send a message back home with our status and course plot. We also lost our navigation computer, and some of the sensor suite. Jimmy plotted our course by hand, and checked it from time to time against the sensor-readings we had. He calculated how far we could go, and put us on a course that had us entering a pretty popular trade route, and then programmed the autopilot to take over for him, when he ran out of air. Which happened long before we got anywhere we could hope to be spotted. "

I stopped talking then. For me, that was the end of the story. There was more detail, of course. How Jimmy and I had spent the next several hours in conversation, on the coms, while his air ran out. What he had told me about the course he had set. That was pretty ingenious of him, by itself. Jimmy got us started back towards G-13, and then put his mind to optimizing the time we would be closest to heavy trade-traffic patterns. He spent hours calculating it out, the last hours of his life, and then put us on a course, and programed the auto-pilot for regular burns to keep us in the optimal speed/distance equation. And he set it up so that we would enter a trade route and drift through it, at a modest speed, staying close to optimum positioning until several hours after we could even hope to stretch our air supply.

And he did all of this knowing with certainty that he would benefit from none of it. His own vacsuit air would run out long before we got there. He would then switch it out with Mark's unused air, having had the good sense to shut that suit down after it was clear Mark was gone. Much of it had vented, but it would keep him going another very few hours, he thought. But he would not, under any circumstances, allow me to open the cockpit hatch. His own air would run out long before the cabin atmosphere got bad enough to require resorting to the salvaged canisters from *StarFire* my men had grabbed, so any attempt to bring him back to the main cabin would have cut the available air for my men by many hours. Anyway, I couldn't even open the hatch from my side unless he unlocked it on his side. It was a feature designed to prevent enemy combatants from entering the cockpit, if they managed to get on board, and there was no way to override it from my side.

All of this was in my report. I even offered to use the equipment compartment as an airlock, and try to spacewalk forward, to minimize our air loss, and take an extra couple of canisters forward, on the outside of the craft. Jimmy nixed that idea, saying it wasn't worth the risk, and there wasn't any way to get the canister inside up there, anyway. He was right. Anyway, I skipped all that, and cut to the chase, the end of my story about the mission.

"Jimmy got us all set up, and then, when his air ran very low, he told me what he was going to do. He didn't want to sit in that suit and struggle for every breath, as the oxygen got lower and lower. He waited until the dials told him it would be getting uncomfortable very soon, and then he said good-bye. I told him to turn his CO_2 scrubbers all the way up, and turn off his oxygen. He would have just gone to sleep, gently. But he said he was a combat space pilot, and the only way for a combat space pilot to go out was a blast of beam fire, or vacuum. And when he was ready, he opened his visor."

My throat ached, and my voice finally quavered a little, but Tillman was gracious enough to ignore it, and didn't offer me a hanky, or a hug. She kept it business like, though I could tell it was getting to her, too, a little.

She commented, "You brought him home. That was your duty, and all you could do for him. I think Captain Duvall would say it was enough."

"He was a Marine. He knew I would bring him home. We always bring them home. Anyway, it was a couple days later when a freighter caught the distress signal Jimmy had set up on short-range communications, and followed it in to us. We had used every canister of air, saving only about ten minutes' use in each, one for every man aboard, including Jimmy's crew, the two warrant officers, in the back with us. The freighter didn't have the right connections to hook up with us, either to transfer air or fuel, and didn't even have a proper airlock we could mate with. So we had to spacewalk over. While the men were doing that, I went forward, outside the ship, with a beam carbine. Alvin had more or less recovered, by then, though I'm sure his ribs were bothering him, but he insisted on coming with me. We cut out the cracked duraglass, and recovered Jimmy and Mark's bodies. We brought them with us, each of us towing one of them into the freighter's hold, and put them, respectfully, with our own unit's dead."

I paused then, running the personnel list through my head. When I was done, I added one further comment, more for myself than for Tillman, though I had already calculated it out a hundred times in the last couple of days.

"Lt. Smithson's fighter took a direct hit. We know from scans that his body was incinerated, or we would have made an effort to recover it. One way or another. Lt. Harley is the only one we lost, the only one who didn't come back, dead or alive. We don't know what happened to him. But we know his fighter wasn't destroyed outright, so, one day, it might be discovered. He might be brought home, too. That's my hope. That one day, we will have every man who went on that mission back home."

A long silence stretched out for a few minutes. I didn't look at Lt. Tillman. I was looking, in my mind, at faces I would never see in this universe again.

Finally, Lt. Tillman spoke once more

"Thank you, Captain Lombard. I wish you good luck in your Board of Inquiry, tomorrow. My report will be submitted tonight, and I'm sure the relevant people will see it before the Board convenes. I will note on this report that I feel you have given a full and complete account, that you cooperated in every way, and that I am satisfied that the relevant facts are all in evidence, so far as you can provide them."

She stood up, and I stood with her, automatically, rising to my feet as a lady was leaving the room, not staying seated as the senior officer, when a junior officer leaves the room. It was a momentary lapse on my part, I'm sure. Then Lt. Tillman surprised me.

She seemed to hesitate for a moment, as though she felt she was forgetting something, and I waited for a last question or observation. But then, Tillman brought herself to attention, and bent her arm in a crisp salute, holding it for a long few seconds, until I gathered myself enough to remember to return the salute. I understood she wasn't saluting me. She was saluting the heroes who had gone with me to *StarFire*, and accomplished the mission they were given. I didn't give her the casual, acknowledgment salute I could have, but brought myself to attention as well, and returned the respect she was paying my men.

And then, without another word, she left my quarters, and I listened for a last time as her business-like shoes tap-tapped down the hall.

CHAPTER 24

Defense Space Station G-13, 246.163.12

Inquiry

"Administrative Dress" is the uniform called for when Galactic Marine Corps officers are scheduled for major disciplinary proceedings. It is the same uniform as is required for formal daytime ceremonies, including funerals, marriages, major decorations, and change of command ceremonies of any major installation or asset, such as a base, a space station, or a ship. I generally had a reason to bring out my Administrative Dress uniform at least once a month, even serving out here on the frontier. Unlike the even more formal Evening Dress Uniform, which is appropriate for balls, formal state dinners, and the like, Administrative Dress was often called for in the normal course of duties. There was, however, one version of the Administrative Dress Uniform I had never planned, or expected, to wear. For a Board of Inquiry, as for Court-Martial, there is one minor adjustment.

An officer under investigation, or an officer being tried, wears a blood-red blouse through the proceedings. The rest of the uniform is the standard white shirt, regimental tie, blue trousers, and black shoes. Everything is the same, except the jacket. It is the only occasion any service member wears the red jacket, and all branches of Alliance military use it for this purpose. It is theoretically a symbolic reminder to all participants that the officer is relying on a just and fair investigation, because his career, and perhaps even his life, hangs in the balance.

In a similar vein, the officers who comprise the actual Board wear Administrative Dress Whites, if they are Navy, or Greys, if they are G-Marine Corps. The symbolism in that is obvious: Fairness and justice. Everyone else involved, including any witnesses, must wear Blues. I suppose the symbolic meaning of that is that these others, who are neither being investigated, nor standing in judgment, are being reminded that they are simply doing a job, and their duty is to do it diligently. All the other participants in both Boards of Inquiry and Courts-Martial, besides the judges, the accused, and the witnesses, are professionals. Their jobs are to facilitate the dispensation of justice. The prosecutors, bailiffs, investigators, secretaries, court reporters, all of these are people who work in and around the military justice system every day. Only the judges are not a permanent part of the justice system. The military has no professional judges. Senior officers fill that role, and always in panels of three or five. They are expected to know the military code of justice, and to judge their colleagues based on that code, applying it rigorously by the standards that their own experiences and history in the services dictates.

Of course, Blue and Grey Dress uniforms were already a part of my uniform wardrobe. I had to purchase the red tunic just a day before my Inquiry began. The irony of being required to purchase the uniform that sets a man apart as under suspicion of malfeasance is not lost on those officers who have been through the process. Fortunately, modern producer machines allowed the quartermaster to program in my specific measurements and turn out a tailored jacket in a matter of minutes. In fact, this one blouse I put on today fit better than the rest of my wardrobe, having been made to spec based on my measurements taken the day I purchased it.

Looking at it, it was really a very striking color, bold and dramatic. I thought it was too bad that the red had been consigned to this purpose. In a bitter moment I imagined choosing to wear it to some social event the Navy sponsored, if I was acquitted without charges. Of course, that sort of insult to the Navy would be political suicide, and I would never go through with it, but it was a diverting and entertaining thought.

Early on the day of my Inquiry, standing in front of a mirror, I smoothed the lapels of my red uniform jacket and went over my appearance with a critical eye. I could find no flaws, even by exacting military standards. I was as ready as I was going to get, and with that reassurance, I let my mind turn to reviewing the process, still standing in front of the mirror in my quarters, waiting for my escort.

A Board of Inquiry is simply the first of several steps along the progression of major disciplinary proceedings. It was the Board of Inquiry which would prefer charges, if any charges were actually leveled. In fact, in the same way civilian criminal cases were called things like, "The People vs. Lombard," my case, if I went to Court-Martial, would be called, "Board of Inquiry vs. Lombard." In that case, if the Board found charges warranted, I would quickly find myself shipped off to one of the human worlds where the Alliance Navy kept a major base, or just possibly to Galactic Marine Corps headquarters. It would depend, primarily, on available transportation, or on political considerations, if my case was of high enough profile to garner attention. Once there, wherever they sent me, a military tribunal would conduct a formal Court-Martial.

In the event of a conviction resulting from those proceedings, and depending on the charges they upheld, I might or might not have a chance to appeal to a United Government Counsel, a semi-civil authority made up of all three branches of the Alliance Government. If my case qualified for appeal, and they deigned to hear it, I would present arguments to representatives from each of the three branches of government:

Legislative, Administrative, and Military. There, I could only make arguments to the effect that, in my specific case, the interests of the Military were contrary to the interests of one or both of the other branches. In such a case, while the Military found it expedient to punish me for my actions, if the other branches decided they had been well served by my decisions, they could negate or reduce the punishment. The charges would still stand within the military, and in their eyes, I would still be guilty and my career would be over. But the punishment could be mitigated, or commuted entirely. My civilian record could even be expunged of my military service, if they chose, to reflect no finding of criminal actions, thus facilitating my return to civilian life. Or, they could support the military tribunal's findings. Finally, they could simply hear my case and come to no conclusion, choosing not to act at all. Then, my sentence would be carried out, in full.

In that case, I could look forward to transportation to a penal colony for incarceration or execution, whatever the sentence turned out to be. A charge of treason, for example, carried the opportunity of appeal to the United Government, before mandatory execution. On the other hand, a charge of dereliction of duty or incompetence did not rise to the level of potential execution, but those charges were "military standards" charges, and I had no right to appeal them to the United Government authority. I didn't know which was worse.

I realized I had been standing for several minutes now, in front of my mirror, while I cast my thoughts down those convoluted corridors of possible outcomes. I still had some time before I was expecting my escorts to arrive, so I decided try to relax for a bit.

I took off my jacket and hung it up, to avoid wrinkles, before sitting down in my only chair. Leaning back, I tried to let go of some of my tension. I closed my eyes, but soon blinked them open again, glancing towards the clock next to my bunk. For the next quarter hour, I alternately closed my eyes to relax, or watched seconds grow into minutes at a glacial pace, waiting for show-time. Military service teaches patience, but after fifteen minutes of that, I could tolerate it longer. I picked up my com and spent the remaining interlude reviewing legal procedure, in a section of the Uniform Code of Military Conduct Database entitled, "Boards of Inquiry; Criminal Investigations of Officer Misconduct." Specifically, I was reviewing the standards listed in subsection headed, "Egregious Loss of Major Material Combat Assets." This was where the Alliance Uniform Military Code differed for the different services, a set of details which I suspected might bear significantly on my case.

The Alliance Home Guard Army is tasked with the defense of well-established, populated and developed worlds, both human and non-human. These are worlds which are considered major assets in the prosecution of interstellar war. They included all human worlds which supported significant populations, because they are the places where soldiers, sailors and Marines are recruited. In many cases, there were also training facilities on these worlds. Some other, less well-populated human worlds, and certain non-human worlds also fell under this umbrella, due to their manufacturing capacity. The production of ships, guns, bombs and other tools and materials useful in the prosecution of war made them significant. The Army protected these resources with permanent and extensive defensive installations. The key word here is "defensive."

The officers of the Alliance Home Guard Army who operate these installations are typically selected by careful psychometric analysis of their predilection for following orders to the letter, applying standard military defense doctrines, and using equipment and men in officially approved ways. Army commanders are not expected to, and are even virtually prohibited from, using their own assessment of circumstances to justify deviating from approved tactical and strategic doctrine in the defense of their installations and the worlds they are designed and built to protect. Imagination and creativity were not valued in the Alliance Army, and the saying was, "No one ever retires from the Army to become an artist." It wasn't quite literally true, but it summed up the Army's attitude regarding duty.

This doctrine was not unsound. The Alliance Home Guard Army had developed a near-perfect system for generating a force of entirely interchangeable officers and personnel. Lost a unit commander in battle? No problem, we'll have another one in place in twenty-four hours, and there will be no appreciable loss in unit performance while the new commander gets up to speed. Upon arrival at his new post, a replacement commander could actually run a unit the same day, while reading the guidelines for that position from a binder, in real-time, under attack, if necessary. Perhaps some units did not develop their full potential for combat effectiveness under this system; perhaps they were only eighty or ninety percent of what they could be, under a more imaginative commander. But on defense, the key is predictability and planning. The Army could allocate resources and shift personnel according to threat assessment, and rarely be found wanting due to an error on the part of their deployed personnel. If some units functioned twenty percent below their possible potential, that was easily remedied by assigning twenty percent more resources to the job. But if a unit which was functioning at a very high operational effectiveness level acquired a new commander, who was not as effective, then a weakness suddenly existed. A weakness which command might not observe for weeks, months, or even years. And if the weakness was undetected, no remedy of higher resources allocated to bolster that unit would be made. The system was designed to take such considerations out of the equation, and it worked well in that way.

In contrast, a Galactic Marine Corps officer, and by extension, his whole unit, is an offensive weapon. Galactic Marines, along with Naval vessels, made up one hundred percent of expeditionary forces and offensive operations. The G-Marine officer's primary purpose is not to keep his people alive, or conserve resources, but to facilitate the elimination of an enemy's capacity to conduct war. This includes the destruction of enemy assets, and the death or capture of enemy combatants. The G-Marine officer is expected to expend his men and equipment in the accomplishment of these goals.

Over the history of the Galactic Marine Corps, G-Marine officers had been charged and convicted for such offenses as "Failure to Maintain a Sufficiently Aggressive Posture in the Field," and "Neglecting to Pursue High-Risk Opportunities" on the theory that such missed opportunities had the potential to yield very high results. If command felt an officer should have noticed and acted on something, and didn't, he could and would be held accountable. The G-Marine officer's job was to roll the dice and win, or die trying. Either was an acceptable execution of duty, in the eyes of Command. Very few G-Marine officers had ever been charged with failure to adequately safeguard the lives of their men, or for moving too boldly into battle, and therefore sustaining unnecessary losses. Of course, that may be due in part to the very low likelihood of the commander in such incidents actually surviving combat and facing trial, but the principles were clear. And as a G-Marine, that was the standard under which I would be judged . . . or should be judged.

The Alliance Navy had their own standards, as well. There was only one sin Naval commanders had to fear: Rendering a ship unavailable or ineffective in combat. This included moving a ship, without direct orders, to a position where it was too far from battle to be useful, or letting systems or crew run down to the point that the ship was less than a hundred percent effective in combat. Even failing to repair combat damage fast enough was a Court-Martial offense. Beyond that, it could consist of something as mundane as failing to note a sudden increase in fuel consumption by Naval ships in a given area, and therefore allowing a ship to fall into a fuel shortage, preventing movement at a critical time when it is needed. And of course, it included the loss of any ship, whether in combat, due to navigation errors, accidents in equipment maintenance, or anything else. Naval commanders were entrusted with assets that included their ship, equipment, and the lives of their men, but they were judged on-- and liable for-- their use and protection of the ship or ships they commanded.

I expected that the Board I would answer to would be entirely, or nearly so, made up of Naval officers. Men steeped in the tradition that the greatest crime was the loss of a major asset, especially a ship. To them, the issue would be simple: Had I caused or recklessly allowed the loss of a major Naval asset, to wit: AMS *StarFire*? Not just an asset, but the biggest, most important asset the Navy had? That was going to be a problem for me. I had absolutely facilitated the destruction of *StarFire*, and I was about to testify to that fact. Over and over.

And that was my conundrum. I was convinced that I would soon be in the position of presenting a Galactic Marine Corps defense to Alliance Navy senior officers. That worried me.

* * *

I was still sitting, going over these differences in standards for the branches of the military when I heard footsteps in the hall. I stood up and carefully pulled on my red blouse, buttoned it deliberately and properly, and pulled my shirt sleeves down through my jacket's sleeves, and tugged at the bottom hemline, making everything straight and precise. A quick glance in the mirror, ensuring once more that everything was proper. I brought myself to dignified attention and waited for my escort.

There would be four of them. They would be officers of similar rank to my own, not enlisted guards. They would be colleagues unacquainted with me, personally, and therefore, I could assume, all of them would be Naval officers, not G-Marines. They would be gentlemen, behaving as though we were simply attending to another day's typical duties. They would form up around me, and escort me to the Board of Inquiry, and they would be genuinely shocked if I resisted or in any way attempted to avoid attending that inquiry. But they would not introduce themselves, or offer to shake my hand, or touch me in any way. They would keep their distance, socially and physically. There would be no conversation, and certainly none about the events I was answering for, or regarding the proceedings of the Board. They would be self-consciously proper, and unconsciously aloof, finding the whole thing to be uncomfortable, distasteful and threatening. They would not want the stench of suspicion to waft too close to their own careers.

They arrived, and I stepped out, into their midst. None of them met my glance, and instead, when facing me at all, kept their eyes about chest level. I wondered for a moment if they were staring at the red blouse I wore, the almost literal scarlet letter of my profession and circumstances. That thought led me to bring myself up and square my shoulders, to present the confidence and calm expected of a military officer with nothing to be ashamed of, a G-Marine officer in control of himself and his surroundings. As soon as I was in my place among them, we started out walking. Within a few steps, we had unconsciously synchronized our gaits, so that we were marching as precisely in unison as any parade review.

* * *

"This Board of Inquiry is convened. The respondent, Vincent Lombard, Captain, Galactic Marine Corps, is brought before the Board of Inquiry, to answer, for the satisfaction of the officers of the Board, questions in regard to the decisions and actions undertaken as officer in command of a unit assigned to locate and aid an Alliance Military Ship. This ship, AMS *StarFire*, which was listed as Missing In Action in the Fleet Command Log of Naval Assets, as of . . ." The bailiff droned on, but I tuned him out. I already knew this part of the story, and I turned my thoughts instead to the makeup of the Board. We were standing for this part of the proceedings, and I took a moment to look them all over.

Five senior officers stood behind a long table, facing the rest of the room. One G-Marine colonel, named Kershaw, in ill-fitting dress greys, obviously someone passing through the system on route to somewhere else. He had to have been drafted for these proceedings based on availability, simply in order to give the Corps a token representative. I guessed he was a passenger on one of the ships presently docked at the station, which suggested to me that he probably had to borrow the grey jacket, since he wouldn't have had his Administrative Dress greys in his day cabin on the ship. It was undoubtedly buried deep in the storage holds of the ship he traveled on, with everything else he was taking to his new post, but which there was no reason to expect to need before he arrived at his destination. That would explain the poor fit of the uniform, especially if he was pulled in at the last minute, maybe even just this morning. With just one day's notice he could have had a new uniform produced, one that fit better. None of that would likely influence him positively in regard to me. He probably resented the delay in getting on with his job. But at least he was able to borrow the uniform. He might have resented me even more if he had been obligated to purchase a new uniform, simply to sit on the Board investigating me.

I looked him over with a critical eye, perhaps because he alone of the Board officers represented my own service. Even allowing for a borrowed uniform, Colonel Kershaw didn't present much of an image of a combat Marine. Appearing as somewhere around his late sixties, I guessed that colonel was probably his terminal rank, and he would not likely rise higher before retirement. The noticeable paunch around his midsection gave the impression that if he had ever spent much time as a combat Marine, he had left that part of his career behind long ago. He had the rheumy eyes and slightly forward-leaning posture of a man who spent ten or twelve hours a day bent over a desk, doing battle with stacks of paper and government forms, rather than armed enemies. I marked him down as a supply administrator, or perhaps a personnel and recruitment functionary. But at least he was a Galactic Marine. He had the same training and conditioning as I had been through.

The other four were all Navy. Three captains, and one low-level admiral, very recently promoted, judging by the brand new, immaculate condition of his uniform whites. But all of these Navy men looked like ship commanders, to me. They were men who carried the lines of responsibility on their faces, as do captains who have actually held the reins of one of the Navy's interstellar vessels. Even the admiral had the proud posture and bearing of a man who had been fired in the crucible of command. None of them gave the impression of being career military bureaucrats. Even if they did not command combat vessels, they had been through challenges and overcome obstacles in their careers. Commanders of cargo vessels faced problems that desk captains never saw, from dodging pirates to plotting their way through asteroid fields, to handling ship discipline with a tough crew, a few hundred light years away from the closest military authority and support. Those were the sorts of challenges that required captains of interstellar ships to be exceptional men.

I calculated that things could have been a good deal worse.

Now my eyes traveled to the prosecutor's table. Lt. Linda Tillman was standing there, next to the man who would drive these proceedings. The officer's panel would make decisions and ask questions to clarify issues, but Commander Wayne Stafford was the choreographer who produced, directed, and starred in the show about to be presented to those senior officers. He was a career prosecutor, and I knew him, by reputation, as the type of man who wielded the law like a bludgeon. It was a way of exercising power, to him. And the scuttlebutt was that he had political ambitions. Rumor had it that he was well connected in the Navy's Office of Legal Affairs, and that he generally managed to be assigned cases that had some profile to them. In other words, the more the public was likely to hear about a case, the more likely Stafford was to get that assignment. It was curious to me that he was here. I would have thought the last thing Navy wanted around this case was publicity. It made me wonder what angle there might be that I hadn't picked up on yet.

Stafford looked like a recruitment poster, tall and lean, in his Administrative Dress Blues. Navy blues are a few shades darker than my own Corps blues, and his sandy-blond hair and Nordic features were well-complimented by his uniform. I looked him over long enough to notice that Tillman seemed a little overawed by his presence, glancing more often up at his face than at the bailiff who was still reciting the ritual that was the prelude to the inquisition.

I was watching when her gaze flicked over to catch mine, a moment later. I would have given her a slight nod or something, to let her know I saw her, a way of saying hello, if I hadn't been so preoccupied with my own thoughts. But she dropped her eyes immediately, before I reacted, and spent the last minutes of the prelude staring at the floor. I wondered what to make of that, too, for a moment, but the bailiff finished before I came to any conclusions, and it was time to sit down and begin.

The Board took a moment to organize itself, the senior officers speaking quietly to each other as they jockeyed around the table. I gathered that there was some question of seniority that had been confused. But they got it all brushed out, and of course, the only seniority issue that really mattered much was that the ranking man, the rear admiral, took the center seat. He would be Judge Advocate, responsible for governing the proceedings, subject to the suggestions of his fellow panel members, and the regulations. His colleagues, while junior to him, were all equals to each other in this matter, regardless of seniority. At least, theoretically.

When they were ready, without any speech or discussion, the admiral simply nodded to Stafford to begin.

"Sirs," Stafford stood up, nodding to the panel. "We are here to consider the circumstances and any appropriate charges related to the reported loss of AMS *StarFire*. This ship, *StarFire*, a brand-new battleship, of a brand new class of battleship, was on her initial shakedown cruise, tasked to travel to a nearby sector when she fell out of contact with Fleet Command." What followed was the background everyone in the room already knew, much of what the bailiff had just covered, but now cast in the light of my own malfeasance. I tuned it out, and spent my time studying the officers of the board, looking for their reaction to Stafford's interpretation of the events of record. And got nothing for my trouble. They all appeared to be attentive and calm, serious about the task ahead of them. Well, maybe I didn't get nothing, after all. At least it appeared that they were applying themselves, so the verdict wasn't in before we even started.

* * *

After his introductory remarks, Stafford wasted little time before going on the attack. He called me to the witness stand. As an officer, I was not required to take an oath to tell the truth. It was understood that I would tell the truth, and any demonstrated failure to do so would result in further charges being lodged against me, as Conduct Unbecoming an Officer.

"Captain Lombard. Please tell the Board, what was the make-up of the unit you took into Sector G-14, for the mission described earlier?" Stafford stood before me, looking down at me in my seat. He hands were clasped behind his back, as he adopted the innocuous air of a man mildly curious about something.

"One platoon of G-Marines, drawn from my own company. One military transport/lander, piloted by Captain James Duvall, and the accompanying crew of an additional co-pilot and two warrant officers. Two Galactic Marine Corps long-range fighters, piloted by Lieutenants Robert Smithson and John Harley." This was standard stuff, just Stafford warming up, I gathered.

"Very good." I bristled a little at his patronizing tone, as though I was performing well under Stafford's tutelage, but there nothing to be gained by showing that. "Now, Captain, would you please tell the Board, where are these vessels now?"

I blinked, not sure where he was headed. "All of these craft were lost in action, or disabled and abandoned." Stafford was still looking at me, as if my answer was incomplete. So I added, "Except one. Lt. Harley's fighter is missing. I haven't heard anything official, but I expect by now his status is listed as 'presumed lost in action.'" Now Stafford nodded his head.

"Indeed. Lost in action." He turned away and began to pace, a few steps away from me, a few steps back, as he went on. "Tell me, Captain, what mission did you hope to accomplish with one platoon of men and two fighters?" Now he paused, eyebrows raised, the very image of curious contemplation.

"My orders were to locate and assess the situation of AMS *StarFire*, and to return back here with a report, or to render aid, if necessary. That is the mission I hoped to accomplish."

"Oh." Stafford turned his back, as though to resume pacing, but he stopped after one step and turned back around to look at me. "I'm sorry, I don't understand something. What benefit are fifty armed Marines in locating a lost ship?"

So, I thought, he's opening with the theory that I had actually been planning an assault from day one. "The benefit, or lack thereof, was not the issue I considered at the time. I am a G-Marine. We travel in groups. If I was going to take a transport/lander, it made sense to put men in it." This answer bordered on insolence, but stopped just a bit short.

"Really, Captain? Does every shuttle or transport that leaves this station have to be crammed full of Marines?" He waved his hand at me. "Never mind. More to the point, Captain, would it be reasonable to say that a platoon of fifty G-Marines was of no use you could conceive of as you set out on that mission?"

I recalled my thoughts as we sat on that asteroid, waiting to spot *StarFire* a second time. I had considered, then, that I could have left my men at home, and avoided risking their lives.

"It is not only reasonable, but that train of thought actually crossed my mind, at least once, in the early phase of that mission."

Stafford smiled. It was the smile of a carnivore, savoring a small mammal he had caught for his dinner, but which he had not yet killed.

"Oh, good, I see we're on the same page here. So, really, I understand that a couple of fighters allowed you to spread out your search pattern, so that's a sensible decision, to take the fighters. But there was no reason you knew of in advance to take a platoon of G-Marines?"

"I believe I just said that."

"Indeed. Which leaves just one conclusion, I suppose. You took your men with you because you anticipated the possibility of hostile action, yes?" He stood there with open hands, palms up, as if entreating me to acknowledge the sensible conclusion he had drawn. "Your orders were not written to suggest Colonel Parsons expected an assault, but . . . you had an inkling, an intuition. Something in your gut said you had better take some men with you. Is that about it?"

These were deep waters, with subtle currents, and an undertow that could whisk me out to sea before I even knew I was wet. I thought I could see where Stafford might be going. He wanted me to admit to something no officer could be condemned for: planning ahead, and covering my bases. No doubt he intended to maneuver me into something that would make it look like I was already expecting trouble, and when I finally found *StarFire*, he would say I acted without waiting to see if I needed to assault her or not.

I took a breath, ready to deny entirely that I went there looking for trouble. And then I remembered what I had told Lt. Tillman. That I had gone so far as to check into the com systems, in case I found myself engaged with an enemy who had our same hardware. I couldn't deny that I was preparing for trouble, before I even left the station.

"I had no specific information, and no 'inking or intuition' of trouble. I anticipated whatever needs I could conceive of, and addressed them as effectively as I could. That included taking a platoon of men, the largest number I could take, and still keep our profile as low as possible—that is, one 'lander and two fighters. If a transport/lander held a hundred and fifty, I would have taken that many. If it held ten, I would have gone with ten. The number was simply a function of the capacity of the craft, not a factor in my expectations of what I would need."

Stafford was nodding, as if beginning to understand my reasoning. "Oh, I see. Certainly. You had no plan to board a ship which had a complement of three thousand with only fifty men. The number was irrelevant, because you could conceive of no way to assault a target that large, in any case. Do I have it correctly, now?"

I nodded, cautiously. "Yes, I suppose that is essentially correct."

"Because, that would be crazy, wouldn't it? I mean . . . you would have to be under some severe duress to do something like that. It was so crazy, you couldn't take enough men to make it worth considering. Since you couldn't take . . . I don't know, four thousand, five thousand, you might as well just take the fifty that fit easily in the 'lander. Do I have that right? Because, you know, you had no plans to assault this ship, anyway." His tone sounded like he ended with a statement, but his face and raised hands, again, palms up, and a little shrug . . . he was turning it into a question. It was subtle way of coaxing me to agree with him. So, what did he want me to agree to? That I was crazy for doing what I did?

"I'm not sure what the question is, Commander Stafford. Could you clarify for me what you want me to respond to?" His response was a quick grin. I wasn't sure, but for just a moment it seemed like the grin of someone who has you by the balls, but is pretty sure you haven't realized it yet . . . but immediately, it was just a friendly, polite smile again.

"Well, begin with this, Captain Lombard. Clarify this for us, please: Did you, or did you not, order your men to assault AMS StarFire by boarding her?"

And I saw then and there an opportunity, a chance to make clear to these senior Navy men the difference between what I did, and what their tradition painted as the worst crime an officer can be accused of: The loss of an Alliance ship.

I remained perfectly still, to betray no sense of equivocation, and spoke in a clear, calm voice.

"No, I did not."

Every eye in the room turned to me, wide in surprise. Lt. Tillman, particularly dumbfounded by my response, let her mouth drop open. Only one person present didn't seem surprised by my answer. His name was

Commander Wayne Stafford. He just relaxed, and smiled at me, while my stomach clenched, and I wondered what trap I had stepped into, just now.

"Well. Thank you for that forthright reply, Captain." He stepped a little closer to me, and turned his side to me, looking away from the senior officers of the board. I read him as wanting to appear less threatening. "That took courage. Now then, I suppose it would be best if you tell us what really happened out there. To you, and to the other officers who went with you." His voice was natural, calm, even friendly. Just like one man talking to another, giving him advice, like, "We've all strayed in our marriage, at one time or another. It's best just to come clean. Tell your wife, and ask her forgiveness. I'm sure it can all be worked out." That's when I realized what had happened.

Stafford's line of attack was exactly what he thought I had just said; that I had not ever assaulted *StarFire*, and the whole thing was just made up, a way of avoiding a duty that I was afraid to carry out. Maybe even a way of avoiding admitting failure on the first criterion of the mission, finding the ship. I wondered for just a moment if he thought I had murdered the other officers and whatever of my men refused to support me in the lie. But I had no time to think of that now. I had to correct the record. I paid careful attention to keeping my voice just as calm as I had a moment ago, and explained my answer.

"AMS. It means, 'Alliance Military Ship.' You asked if I attacked 'AMS *StarFire*.' When I attacked *StarFire*, she was not an Alliance Military Ship. Her markings were unchanged, and the Alliance flag still showed, painted on her hull, but she fired on an Alliance fighter which was sending identity codes, and with IFF transponder in full operation. I believe it was a reasonable conclusion that she had previously fired on the sloops, *Elysium* and *Archer*, both Alliance ships, whose wreckage we had already observed and catalogued in the system. I assumed *StarFire* had destroyed them, from the evidence on the scene, and from her actions against our fighter. Whoever had taken control of that ship, whether people from her own crew, or someone else, *StarFire*, at the time of our assault was an enemy vessel, captured from Alliance service, and now firing on Alliance forces. So, if you meant to ask, did I assault *StarFire*, the answer is of course, yes, I did. But if you are asking, was she an Alliance ship at that time, the answer is obviously no."

Stafford began a slow boil about the time I finished the first sentence. By the time I was done speaking, he was apoplectic. He thought he had broken me with five minutes of oblique questioning, and now, in his eyes, I was denying my previous admission. But I didn't care about him. As I wound up my answer, I was watching the senior officers, the Board. The rear admiral did not seem impressed, but he didn't appear to be hostile, either. One of the captains seemed to be considering the point. The other two were looking down at some papers in front of them, and I couldn't gauge their reactions. Colonel Kershaw was relaxed, attentive, and sanguine. He seemed to think my answer made perfect sense.

Stafford excused me without further questions, though reserving the right to re-call me at any time. First, though, it seemed he wanted to lay a little foundation work, presumably for his next line of attack. He called Technician Duggard to the stand.

Duggard was an enlisted man, and therefore not presumed to be a gentleman. He was asked to swear to tell the truth, which he willingly did. The questions he was asked were predictable, based on everything in my report, and everything Lt. Tillman had added, from her interview with me.

"Mr. Duggard, did you at any time leave the transport/lander and board any other vessel, prior to spacewalking to the freighter that eventually brought you home?" He had not.

And then, "Mr. Duggard, were you familiar with the vessel, AMS *StarFire* before you set out on this mission? Could you have identified her, say, from a photograph- or better yet, could you have drawn a picture of her, from your own previous experience?" He was not, and could not.

"Are you trained, Mr. Duggard, in ship design or even ship identification?" No.

All of these were attempts to suggest that I might have fooled some of my own men into thinking we were attacking a ship that either didn't really exist, or wasn't really *StarFire*. But then things took a new turn

"Mr. Duggard, do I understand correctly that Captain Lombard ordered you to materially alter the communications software used on close-range and ship-to-ship coms? What did Captain Lombard tell you was the reason for this breach of regulations?" and so on.

This was part of what I had left out of my written report, but which Linda Tillman had uncovered, and maneuvered me into addressing. Well, they had the information, I couldn't change that. The worst of it was, I couldn't even cross-examine Duggard, and paint a better picture out of his answers. This was a Board of Inquiry, not a Court-Martial. It was like the Grand Jury of old times. The prosecution was convincing the Board to prefer charges, not actually trying to convict me. The standard he had to meet was simply to present enough evidence that a crime might have been committed, create enough doubt to justify trying the case.

Duggard knew what was going on, and he did his best for me. I cringed, a time or two, when it became obvious that he didn't want to answer some of the questions, because he thought it would look bad for me. He didn't realize that those efforts made me look more guilty, not less. It made it look like we had something to hide. I would have preferred that he simply answer each question, as simply and directly as possible. Stafford would almost surely have to call me back to the stand and give me the chance to explain my actions and decisions, after they were all brought out by other witnesses. By the time Stafford was done with Duggard, I felt like I had been mugged by proxy, and the only thing that was worse was how bad I felt for Duggard. If he knew how much his evasive answers had damaged me, he would be miserable about it for a long time.

Next, Stafford called the warrant officers from the transport/lander. He kept the questions to them even shorter and simpler, establishing only that they did not ever leave the lander and therefore they had no idea what had really happened on *StarFire*, or perhaps more accurately from the way the questions were asked, whatever ship it was they thought might have been *StarFire*. Those men did know something about ship identification, so Stafford wisely stayed far away from any questions to do with that, choosing simply to imply his own confidence that they might, somehow, have been fooled by me.

It was getting late in the day, now, but the military doesn't run on banker's hours. Stafford called me back to the stand. I was sure he wasn't done with his list of witnesses, but he chose to examine me again, probably because he was about to change the course of the narrative, and thought it best to cement my answers to these witnesses responses before moving into a different area. I was amenable to that. Since I couldn't call witnesses of my own until I was in Court-Martial, I felt like the more time I got on the stand, the better.

Stafford put up a skeleton diagram of *StarFire* on the large screen along one side wall of the room. He asked me to identify the location we had breached the hull, which he then marked. Next he asked me to identify the path we took as we moved into the ship.

It was interesting to me. Of course, I had carefully mapped our path for my original report, so I was well-equipped to do it again for Stafford. I didn't see the advantage he hoped to gain, for a few minutes. Not until he took issue with me on one of my comments.

"You say this was an equipment room? A compartment used for the storage of tools, one that you moved through on your way to . . . let's see . . . to this cargo hold? Is that right?"

"That is my recollection, yes." I was pretty sure I was correct. I had been in that room myself.

"Then why is this room designated as 'maintenance and repairs' on the map Duggard provided for your report?"

I shrugged. "Duggard was making notations as the men called information back to him, reporting what they had found. We were hoping to use the contents of the storage rooms to help us identify any proximity to critical systems, so I had the men report their observations to Duggard. But Duggard, while he is a great technician on coms, has limited experience with ships. He probably wrote down what he thought the men were describing. I expect you will find more errors in Duggard's labeling, but they are errors that can be understood, if you take into account the second-hand nature of Duggard's information." Colonel Kershaw, I noticed, was growing bored with this line of questioning. He saw it as the straw man it was. But Stafford wasn't done.

"I see. Well, that's certainly a reasonable explanation, Captain Lombard. On the other hand, what if Duggard's notes turn out to be more reliable than your own recollections? What would that imply, do you suppose?"

"It would imply, I suppose, that in heat of battle, under a substantial degree of pressure, my recollections might at times be faulty?" I made the answer sound like a question, like I was trying, but couldn't see what Stafford was getting at. It wasn't hard to do; I was trying, and I couldn't see what Stafford was getting at.

"Or, perhaps, Captain, it would imply that Duggard's notes were copied from actual diagrams of StarFire's construction, not from the reports you claim he got from the men on board. And your recollections are less perfect, because they are fabricated."

I'm sure my voice hardened a little at that speculation. "Hmmm . . . . I see your point. I suppose it could look that way, especially to someone who hasn't spent much time on ships." That was a not so subtle reminder to the ship commanders on the board that, like them, I was a combat professional, while Stafford was merely a lawyer. But I wasn't done driving that nail home, yet. "But if you had spent more time actually in space—I mean, as crew, not as a passenger—you would no doubt be aware that crews are prone to carry small items to the tool room to work on them, rather than carrying very heavy tool sets out somewhere else to do repairs. The rule tends to be, anything lighter than a full tool box, you carry to the tool room. Anything heavier than a tool box, or fixed in place, you have to carry the tools to the broken machinery. Every tool room I have ever seen on a starship is a repair room within a few weeks of departing the last port of call." I avoided looking at the board when I said this, but I caught one of them nodding, in my peripheral vision. Stafford must have caught it to, because he was flustered, just then.

He opened his mouth once, and closed it. Then again . . . and closed it. This was a man who wanted to put me in my place, but he was back on his heels, because he had just seen me score points with one of the judges, and he didn't want to alienate that judge. I was sure he couldn't care less about Kershaw, figuring the Marine colonel would back a fellow Marine just on principle, and so the colonel was already a lost cause. But the Navy captains? He would need at least three of them, if he wanted to see this case go farther.

"Do you have more questions, Commander?" This was a voice we had heard little of, in the proceedings so far. It was the admiral. I judged he was getting restless, probably already late for his first cocktail of the evening, and he wanted to move things along.

"I—uh, need a moment, if you please, sir." Stafford didn't want to give this up yet. He had spent some time soliciting information from the other witnesses today, and if he was going to use what they gave him, he needed to do it now, before starting with other witnesses tomorrow. He walked quickly over to his table, where he bent over Lt. Tillman for a moment, and conferred with her. It was easy to imagine that conversation: "Give me something I can use, here, damn it!" And Tillman, it seemed, had an idea, because she scribbled out a note and handed Stafford a piece of paper.

Stafford, reading the note as he walked, approached me again.

"Captain Lombard, Lt. Tillman has just reminded me that you reported taking a prisoner, briefly, while you say you were aboard *StarFire*."

"Yes. Briefly."

"And you . . . it seems the man was injured, and you had considered taking him back to the 'lander, but changed your mind? After speaking with him briefly, and carrying him several feet, you changed your mind about taking him aboard the 'lander?"

Where was he going with this one, I wondered. Did he think he was going to impeach me by implying that I couldn't take the prisoner to the 'lander because he was made up? Never existed? If they ever called Alvin to the stand, he would clear that up, right away. Even if they court-martialed me, I would then have the right to call Alvin to the stand myself. I had nothing to fear from this line of questioning. I didn't even need to explain it. I could just answer his questions and see where he took it, because this one couldn't hurt me, even if I had to go to Court-Martial before I could prove it.

"Commander, that is correct. I had intended to take the man on board the 'lander, but circumstances changed, and I was obliged to leave him behind. It was regrettable, but necessary."

"I see. What was his name and rank, Captain?"

"Name and rank? His insignia was the same as mine, a G-Marine captain. And his name tag said, 'Halverson.'"

"Ah, thank you. Captain Halverson, G-Marines . . . now, let me see . . . ." Stafford walked back to his table and picked up his com unit, tapping the keys. "Halverson . . . Halverson . . ." He looked up at me. "Captain Lombard, I'm afraid I have some bad news for you." I waited, refusing to look flustered by asking what it was. Eventually, Stafford went on. "The list of personnel on board *StarFire* does not list a Captain Halverson. In fact, there isn't a Halverson of any rank in *StarFire*'s personnel files. Would you care to try again?"

Stafford was pretty good. This was damning, coming on the heels of his inconclusive arguments that my testimony was unreliable because it was fabricated. And after fuel and ammunition, perhaps the next highest priority for a ship captain was keeping track of the personnel aboard his vessel. It was the first prerequisite for provisioning the ship with food, water and air. No ship commander would have an outdated personnel table. It was my turn to be speechless. And I was.

Stafford, though, knew a good thing when he saw it. Rather than push further right then, perhaps because he was out of things to push, or perhaps to leave the Board with this impression overnight, before moving on, he turned to the admiral.

"Perhaps this is a good time to recess, sir?"

The admiral wasted no time checking with his colleagues. "Adjourned until oh-seven-hundred, tomorrow." Crack! He banged his gavel.

I didn't stand up right away. I was still sitting in the witness chair, and I wasn't in a hurry to form up with my escort, and try to move through the crowd of people in the room in a squad of five, with me in the center. Besides, I would have to pick up my com unit, which I had been using to take notes during other testimony. It was still sitting at the defense table. And since the Board officers hadn't waited for the bailiff to call everyone to rise, they were already halfway out the door, leaving me no reason to be concerned with appearances. So I sat, and looked over at Linda Tillman, as she gathered her things to leave. I was feeling very much thrown under the bus, just now. I had mentioned Halverson in the written report I had made, but not by name, since he hadn't actually identified himself with it. There was always the chance that someone was using a vacsuit with the wrong nametag. I had given the name to Tillman, in our interview though, and she, or someone, had obviously checked it against the ship's roster. And found the name Halverson wasn't there. If she had simply come back and asked me about it, I wouldn't have stepped into this trap. Or would I?

I had to admit, the truth is I probably would have said the same things. It was one thing to exaggerate to protect Duggard, or any of the other men, but quite another to deviate from what I knew to be true regarding my own actions and decisions. If she had told me Halverson wasn't on the roster, I could have denied paying any attention to the name, or I could have said I wasn't sure about it . . . but that would not be true. I was sure of it. The man's name tag read "Halverson." So, if Stafford had asked me, I suppose I would have said the same thing.

But that didn't make me any happier with knowing that Linda Tillman was the enemy, that the time I had spent with her, and the emotion and sympathy she had shown was nothing more than her doing her job. The trust I had begun to develop for her just meant she had done her job well. Her purpose, as I had suspected and tried to guard against from the beginning, was apparently to get me to say things that could be used against me, and they were.

I wasn't angry about that part, in particular. It was her job, and I suppose she though it was her duty, as well. Certainly, the man she worked for thought it was her duty. In that light, I really didn't mind that she suggested Stafford take this approach. But if she was trying to be fair, I guess she would have taken reasonable measures to sort out any confusion. Maybe, asked me about that name, given me a chance to recall the spelling, or see if I had it just slightly wrong, or something. I remembered it as Halverson, but she couldn't know how sure I was about it. A fair person would have checked; maybe it was Hathcock, or Hepplerson, and I didn't remember it as clearly as I thought. Maybe if I had been shown the ship's roster, I would have had one of those "smack your hand on your forehead" moments, and remembered a slightly different name . . . and she could have given me that chance. If she wasn't just trying to trap me. If she cared about the truth. So, I was just . . . disappointed. In her, sure. But even more so, in myself. For giving a damn about Lt. (JG) Linda Tillman.

CHAPTER 25

Defense Space Station G-13, 246.163.12

Inquiry

I roused myself, finally, getting up and moving to pick up my com unit. Out of the corner of my eye, I spotted Tillman glancing my way. She started over, moving in my direction, but I turned my back to her, and headed for the door, figuring my escort would see me and pick me up before I got that far. I was right, and two of them formed up on me halfway there, the other two waiting ahead, right next to the exit.

I kept a brisk pace, meaning to get out of here, and get to my quarters, where I could put a couple more dents in my brain trying to think all of this through, but when I got to the doors, they were closed, and I had to stop while the officers escorting me got into position before letting me through.

The sudden stop caught someone walking behind me, just as briskly as I was, and I felt a bump suddenly, when I pulled up. I heard a bundle of papers hit the floor.

"Oh, excuse me!"

I knew the voice. Tillman wasn't going to let me ignore her. When I turned around, she was standing there looking all flustered and helpless, the way pretty girls do when they have dropped something and expect a gentleman to pick it up for them.

I was tempted, just for a moment, to put some shoe-prints all over her paperwork, stepping on them while I graciously moved to her side and said something like, "Oh, are you alright?" instead of bending down to retrieve her dropped paperwork. G-Marines learn passive-aggressive tactics as fast as they do combat tactics, I suppose. But I resisted the urge, and simply crouched, in silence, to pick up her things. I didn't know what game she was playing, or why she thought I would be interested in talking to her now, but the Galactic Marine Corps had declared me an officer and a gentleman, and so far they hadn't rescinded that. I would play the role for at least a few more days.

I was picking up paper, and then Tillman was crouched with me, gathering up paper, when suddenly, I saw her furtively push one of them towards me, instead of picking it up. It was from the tablet she had used to write her note to Stafford. I couldn't help looking at it. It had Halverson's name on it. Specifically, it had "Captain Harold Halverson, GMC, #708-998-1535B/N," written in block letters. I picked it up and handed it to her, with the rest of the stuff. And then I turned to leave, without saying a word. No way was I going to give her an "Excuse me," or anything else, when she obviously had bumped into me on purpose.

And then I stopped. On purpose? Why would she do that? I turned back to her.

"I hope that little accident didn't inconvenience you too much."

Lt. Tillman looked up into my eyes, and said, "No, not at all. It was my fault, anyway. I should watch where I am going." And she glanced around her, quickly. But she didn't move away.

So, I glanced around too, and saw nobody near us except my escort, the four Navy officers. And then I got it. Navy officers. Linda had something to say, but not in front of Navy. So I loitered a moment, and then brought up the only thing I could think of that this might be about.

"That thing about Halverson. I have to admit, I didn't see that coming." She didn't glance to the side, or look away, the way we do when we are trying to remember a name, or a face. And she didn't glance down or blink, which suggests an attempt to change the subject.

"Who's that?" she said, looking right at me, directly into my eyes, the way we do when we are saying something we are certain of, not like she was asking a question at all.

I blinked, and then I was looking at her back, watching her walk away.

* * *

As we approached my quarters, none of us had said a word, myself or my four Navy colleagues. But for the first time, I had something I wanted to say to them, a request I wanted to make. I stopped just short of my open door.

"Who's senior, here?"

They knew what I meant, and one of them spoke up, saying, "I'm in charge of the detail. What can I do for you?"

"Please tell Commander Stafford I want a legal consultation, and I won't go forward with the inquiry until I get one." It was within my rights, only because Stafford was calling me as a witness. "I can take care of it tonight, if he'll tell the communications people to let me make some calls with my com unit." Out-bound calls had been disabled on my com since I had been confined to quarters. Inbound calls were restricted to people calling from an approved list. "I'll need to call my C/O, and ask for a referral, and then I will want to call whatever lawyer he suggests to me."

"I'm sure Stafford will provide you will a lawyer from the Legal Affairs Division, and you won't have to pay for the services," he suggested, helpfully.

"Thanks, but that's like asking a head-hunter to give you a haircut. He'll probably give you one, but maybe not the way you were hoping."

The Navy officer barked a laugh. "I'll tell him. Anything else?"

"Yeah. Tell him I have friends in the com group, and he can listen long enough to find out who I am talking to, but if he tries to eavesdrop past that, I'll find out about it, and file a complaint. Remind him this station has been my regular duty station for a while." The guy, warming up a little after my head-hunter joke, bristled at that last remark, trying to decide if my suggestion that Stafford might want to eavesdrop was disparaging to Naval officers in general, or just prosecutors. He must have decided it was an insult to prosecutors, though, because he didn't start a fight over it.

"Anything else?"

"Nope. Thanks for your courtesy. You guys have been pretty decent to me." I went into my room, and for the first time, closed the door behind me.

* * *

An hour and a half later, I got a chime on my com, and a message that said outgoing calls would be accepted, but I would have to get each number cleared before it would be approved. No problem. I called Colonel Parsons first.

"Colonel, I need a favor. I need to consult a lawyer before the inquiry starts again tomorrow. Can you refer me to someone?"

"Yes, happy to. But you know, Navy has the best lawyers for military law They get first pick of the recruits, most of the time, and send some of the best to law school. You might do better going through their offices."

I knew he was right, if I wanted actual legal services. "Well, I'm sort of in a hurry, wanted someone I could get on the coms tonight. And, I was sort of hoping for someone who was, you know, familiar with how G-Marines do things." There was a slight pause, while Colonel Parsons read between the lines.

"I have one name. A retired G-Marine who practices civil law, now. I suppose he would remember quite a bit about military procedure, and might do the trick."

Colonel Parsons was tracking me, and I started to feel a little surge of energy. We were up to something, but no one listening would pick up on that, or guess what this was about if they did. The colonel gave me a com code for a lawyer living in a nearby system, and I thanked him and disconnected.

When I told him I wanted someone who knew how G-Marines do things, I was telling him I wanted a Marine, or a retired Marine, which amounted to the same thing. When he told me he knew a retired Marine that "might do the trick," he was saying this was a reliable man who would do a Marine a favor, if he could. Neither of us was unaware that while any conversation I had with my lawyer was privileged, any conversation I had with my commanding officer was presumed to be military business, and fair game for tapping.

I placed my next call, asking the com station to clear the number and prepare for System-to-System communications. That took a while to set up, requiring time to generate the signal, and co-ordinate it with the destination, so we would have real-time, two-way communication. It would have been very expensive, but since I was in a Board of Inquiry, the government was picking up the tab for the call.

* * *

"Mr. Hoffman, I am Captain Vincent Lombard, GMC. Colonel Rick Parsons gave me your number."

"Ah, Colonel Parsons. Good man. He's well, I trust?"

"Very well, sir. He sends his regards. I'm calling because I'm facing a Board of Inquiry. It's already started, but they've pulled a fast one on me, and I need a little help."

"Hmm. Well, an Inquiry is just the first step. They can't do anything to you there, just refer you for court-martial, where you will get a military lawyer, if you want one. I recommend you accept the lawyer they appoint."

"Sir, I don't need a military lawyer. Not yet, anyway. What I need is . . . First, is there anyway to be sure our conversation isn't being monitored? I'm calling through the FTL system, on base."

"Son, you should hope they ARE listening. Because everything that happens in the FTL com center is logged, and if they violate your privileged communication with a lawyer, not even the military can bring charges after that. The FTL com center is probably the safest way in the universe for us to talk. Safer than if I was sitting a room with you on base."

"Okay. So, let me give you a little background, and tell you what I'm thinking . . ."

We talked for a few more minutes, and then I disconnected and set the com unit down. I needed to get some sleep, if I could. I didn't know how much time I would have, later.

* * *

My com started chiming at oh-four-hundred. It was Mr. Hoffman.

"Captain, your man Duggard just got back to me."

"He didn't use your number, did he?"

"No, I borrowed a com from a neighbor, as we discussed. Anyway, Duggard says the files were buried pretty deep, and he couldn't get a lot of information, but I'm forwarding the report he sent me to you now. He also said another search was recently done on the name you gave me, and he said to tell you he figured you might want that tweaked a little. And then he said something odd."

"What's that?"

"He said, 'Tell him I'm not just a technician.'"

"Got it. Mr. Hoffman, will the file be as confidential as our voice call?"

"Oh, even more so. Because I'm encrypting it."

"What code do I use to decrypt?"

"Duggard gave me the code. He said use the name of his favorite vacation spot."

"Gotcha." It would be some variation of "casino," I knew immediately. The line about "I'm not just a technician" was a reminder of that conversation. "Thanks, Mr. Hoffman. I owe you one."

"Oh, not at all. I'm charging you my office rates for all this. You'll get a bill. Including the System-to-System call charges on my neighbor's com."

"Absolutely, Mr. Hoffman. Can I call you again if I need to?"

"Of course. From what Duggard said, this case is probably all politics. If I can be of help, you call. Any time."

* * *

The file, when it came, was very interesting indeed. I tried a few variations until I hit the decryption code, which turned out to be "Casino Station," and after I opened it, I stayed up quite a while, reading it, re-reading it, and making a strategy to deal with it. At first, I was suspicious, thinking this could be just another trap, carefully laid out for my big feet to step into, because it seemed Stafford had already looked into this. But at the end, Duggard had also put in a personal note, a line that read, "Hoffman told me who tipped you to this, and when I looked, that was who had previously queried these same results. So, I took some initiative and changed the query tag-line, as appended on the report. I figured you needed to know that. Then I covered my tracks, so no one will know anybody else checked the file. I'm pretty sure the data is solid, and the trail is clean. After all, I'm not just a technician. I'm a G-Marine technician."

He sure was. From his note, I knew that Lt. Tillman had been the one who checked this file previously. I looked at the report again, where it listed who had queried this information recently. After Duggard's fiddling, there was only one entry: Commander Wayne Stafford. I smiled, suddenly sure that I had what I needed. This wasn't a trap. It was an investigator, doing her job, and letting someone know what she had found. This time, she was letting me know. It probably didn't matter that Stafford's name sat at the bottom of this query. All that mattered was, it wouldn't come back to bite Tillman, if someone checked on it. If Stafford himself checked on it, he would know someone had done this for me, and it was someone with skills. But he would never know that Linda Tillman ever had the information, and therefore, that she could have tipped me to look into it.

* * *

In the morning, I was a little slow getting ready when my escort showed up. I was in no hurry, wanting the room to be waiting for me when I arrived, if at all possible, so even when we finally left I made excuses for a small detour to pick up a power cell for my com, and then to get a lint-roller for my uniform. I had even gone so far as to sprinkle a few whiskers from my morning shave on my shirt collar, to make it believable, but after that, there was no slowing my escort down. I was their responsibility, and any more than a couple minutes late would have reflected badly on them. I didn't mind, a couple minutes would be enough, and these guys were being decent to me. One of them even helped me, handling the roller on my collar, in the back, so I could present well when we arrived.

Stepping into the room, I could see that I had timed it right. The bailiff had already seated everyone, and the admiral was glancing at the time on his com as I stepped in and walked down the aisle towards the front of the room.

"Captain Lombard has arrived," the admiral said with a slight frown, a little chapped that I would be anything other than ten minutes early for my own Inquiry. "Commander Stafford, how would you like to begin . . ." The admiral broke off as I walked right past the defense table and up to the witness chair.

I murmured a low "Excuse me, I apologize for my tardiness," to the Board officers, and sat down.

The admiral looked little taken aback.

"Captain Lombard, what are you doing?"

"Sir, we recessed after the commander there asked me a question. I have yet to respond."

Stafford, no slouch, could see I was up to something, and would have no part of it. He rose from the table where he was sitting next to Lt. Tillman, and stepped out in front of it to speak. Linda Tillman gave me a neutral look of curiosity, with maybe just the smallest hint of a smile trying to tug at the corners of her mouth, while her boss waved his hands and started talking.

"No sir. I had the answer to the question I asked. I was done with this witness, and I'm ready to move on." The admiral was looking back and forth between the two of us. I spoke up again, then.

"Sir, procedure is that I may only answer questions posed to me by the prosecutor, but that I may answer any question asked, at least, so long as I stick to the question itself. That is my right, as the officer under investigation."

Stafford spoke hurriedly, "But, you answered the question! You said the man you took prisoner was named Halverson, and I finished by pointing out that there was no one named Halverson on the roster! Admiral, this is some kind of effort to disrupt this Inquiry, and I suggest that you-"

The admiral held up his hand, and even Commander Stafford knew it was time to shut up. As soon as it was silent, the admiral turned to the court reporter, and said, "Please read us the last line you recorded before we adjourned."

The reporter glanced at her screen, and said, "Commander Stafford to the witness: Would you like to try again?"

The admiral raised his eyebrows a smidgeon. "It seems Captain Lombard is correct. I take it, Captain, that you would indeed like to try again?" he asked me, but before I answered, he turned to Commander Stafford once more, saying, "I presume the question means, 'would you like to try and identify your prisoner again,' is that correct, Mr. Stafford?" The admiral was going out of his way to let Stafford limit the scope of the question, not knowing what I had in mind.

"I wasn't asking him to try again. It was- it's a saying. It means, you got that one wrong, would you like to . . ." Even Stafford could see he had lost that argument, and he trailed off.

"Thank you sir," I said to the admiral. "I would be happy to try to identify the person in question more precisely, and I thank counsel for pointing out to me that I gave insufficient information in my first answer." I nodded to Stafford, and took a breath, preparing to lie to the Board. What I would say was the truth, couched in misleading information as to where I got some of the data. It was the only way to be sure Tillman wouldn't fall under suspicion.

"I had several moments to talk with this man before he fell unconscious again. During that time he was able to tell me his name and serial number, which he gave as Captain Harold Halverson, GMC, #708-998-1535. I presumed at the time that he was following protocol for a prisoner of war. I did not ask him his role or position on the ship, but I have the idea he was not regular crew, because when he first awoke, he asked where he was. When I answered 'On the ship,' he asked me, 'What ship is this?' Of course, he had just been wounded, and was somewhat . . . confused, I suppose. But most men posted to a ship would know the name of that ship as well as they know their mother's name. So I would guess he was a passenger being transported, before the ship was lost to- to whatever happened." Yeah, it was an embellishment on the truth, but it was the only way to get the information out, and I figured there was no way for anyone to show different.

One of the Board captains turned and nodded to two of the others, apparently agreeing with my assessment that a passenger might be confused as to what ship he was on, but a man posted to that ship would almost certainly not. In fact, it was common for retired sailors and Marines, when they got old enough for senile dementia to set in, to be confused and think they were still on one of the ships they had spent time on. They forgot the names of their wives and girlfriends before they forgot the names of their ships.

Stafford stood mute. I had stopped him in his tracks, it seemed, and he wasn't sure what to do now. Linda Tillman was at the table, behind him, looking down at her pad. The admiral actually gave me a little smile and a nod. It seemed he liked evidence to come out, and didn't care which side it fell on so much as he cared that we were getting closer to resolving the issues. So, I took a chance.

"If someone has a com, and the court would care to learn more, perhaps we could access the military database, instead of the ship's roster, and look for any information on this Captain Halverson. I, for one, would like to know what he was doing on *StarFire*." I looked my question to the admiral, who nodded again, and turned around, looking for someone behind him. It was a habitual gesture; he was looking for his aid, who would usually be standing right there, but who was not, while the admiral functioned as Judge Advocate. It took him only another moment to spot the young ensign, sitting in the spectator seats.

"Charles, look this man up, send the file to all our coms."

Ensign Charles jumped to his feet, to facilitate pulling a com unit out of his pocket, and started typing away. I spelled the name, and then rolled the memorized serial number off, slowly, while the Board officers chatted quietly among themselves. A few minutes later, chimes rang on five com units at once, sitting at the table, and a second later, another one, as Commander Stafford's unit received the file, as well. Mine did not.

I didn't mind. I had already seen a much more detailed report than the one these men were looking at. Duggard had spent a couple of hours digging away in the system to compile that one. I just sat quietly while the other men read, and I waited for the decision I was sure was coming.

"Ah . . . well, then." It was the admiral, as he finished perusing the information. "Commander Stafford, I think we are best served if there are no more questions regarding this Captain Halverson. I think we can stipulate that Captain Lombard has provided us with a satisfactory answer to that question. We, ah . . . we will be forwarding some observations and questions to Fleet Command, and then . . . well, let's get on with it. Commander, what's next?"

"Sir, I don't . . . well, I had some more, er, evidence regarding . . ." Stafford was flummoxed. He had come in with no intention of addressing the Halvorson issue further, but he was confused now, by what he had read, and it was shaking him up. He had left last night thinking he had me cold. It was the second time he had made that mistake. He wasn't going to want to go on until he could piece together what had happened here. "Perhaps a short recess, so I can, um, realign my material to reflect this information?"

The admiral wasted no time. Crack! Went the gavel, and we had an hour to kill before we had to resume.

I just moved from the witness chair to my defense table, keeping my gaze a few inches above everyone's head. I didn't want to give anything away in my expression if I accidentally met someone's gaze, especially Stafford's. But after I sat down, I snuck a look over at Linda Tillman. She was either distracted, or avoiding eye contact, maybe a little tense, waiting for any fallout from what had just happened. She didn't know Duggard had changed the query information on the file, and she might have been worried that if Stafford looked close, he would see only one name attached to the information. I chuckled, inside, thinking about Stafford seeing his own name there, if he checked.

The military database had very little information regarding Captain Halverson. His enlistment dates, promotion dates, and a couple of early postings. And then a posting for "Special Training, Weapons Design and Engineering, Fleet Academy." That lasted for three years before his next notation, "Weapons Design Facility, location redacted," for four more years, which brought us up to his most recent notation: "Killed in Action, location redacted." That notation was dated as effective the same day we took *StarFire*.

Now that was a mystery, even to me. Because it meant that someone had known Halverson was on *StarFire*. And someone had known he was killed there, even though the ship had not been located, so far as I knew, since I left her with my men. And no debris had been found that I knew of. In fact, this Board of Inquiry had so far been discussing whether or not she had been found, or destroyed, or what. *StarFire* was still listed as "Missing in Action" in the Fleet Registry of Ships, and Halverson, if someone knew he was on board at all, should likewise have been listed as "Missing in Action." But the court had just come across some pretty damn strong evidence that someone higher up knew very well what had happened on *StarFire*.

My case was looking very good, right now. I didn't need to point out the dates of the assault on *StarFire* and Captain Halverson's status as KIA were the same. And if I did, it would just make Stafford find a way to say it meant little or nothing. But the officers on the Board wouldn't miss that detail, even without me mentioning it.

* * *

When we reconvened, Stafford had, reluctantly I'm sure, given up on the "You never even found *StarFire*, did you?" approach. He was not at a loss, though, for another angle to take.

His first witness was a G-Marine captain. It was Ben Bowman, one of my colleagues, a company commander from this very station. The one who blamed his poor scores for boarding exercises on too many green men, compared to my high ratio of veterans. Bowman marched in as though the entire purpose of this meeting was to celebrate him, and he took the witness chair as though it were a seat of honor. I wondered what possible purpose Bowman cold serve for Stafford.

"Captain Bowman. You are a company commander here on Station 12, with the defendant, is that right?"

"Yes, sir. That's right."

"And you are familiar with Captain Lombard, correct?"

"Yes, sir."

"How would you characterize him, as an officer?"

Bowman hesitated, looking around the room uneasily. I knew how this happened. In a private interview, Bowman had spouted off, voicing his disdain and dislike for me enthusiastically. But now he was being asked to pass judgment on a fellow officer on the record and in front of his peers, and that was a much different story. What he said now, he would have to live with for quite some time. I suspected that prosecutors ran into this all the time, and were ready to deal with it.

"Ahh . . ." Bowman grasped for something to say that would be consistent with what he had told Stafford, or perhaps Tillman, in private, but wouldn't diminish him with other company commanders on the base, and especially with Colonel Parsons, when the story reached his ears. "Lombard is . . . an effective enough officer." I resisted smiling. Bowman would have to do better than damning me with faint praise, if he was going to help Stafford's case.

Stafford didn't miss a beat, and didn't hound Bowman on the equivocation. He just rephrased, working his way around to an answer he wanted, like a fox, working his way around a henhouse.

"Describe his tactical approach to us, please."

"His tactical approach?" The mark of a man who doesn't want to answer a question is the tendency to repeat the question. It's an unconscious means of buying time to think. "Uhm . . . Well, Lombard is prone to use tricks, uh, to try to find his way around obstacles, instead of fighting through them, like the rest of us."

"I see. Can you give me an example of that?"

"Well . . . we were doing boarding exercises a couple of weeks ago, and Lombard, he kept trying to find ways to cheat the exercise. Like finding loopholes to beat the simulation, instead of fighting his men through to the objective, the way the rest of us do." Bowman was warming up, now, gaining momentum. "Everybody else was clearing compartments, like we are taught to do, but Lombard was just sealing them up, so the computer would score the defenders inside as . . . as captured, or something."

I was curious. How did Stafford figure that painting me as an effective and innovative tactician was going to help his case? Surely even Navy captains preferred effective Marine operations to ineffective ones.

"So, in your experience, Captain Bowman, Captain Lombard is an officer who looks for advantages, who might be willing to cheat? An officer who doesn't follow standard directions?"

Now I understood what Bowman was here for. Stafford wanted to paint me as a loose cannon, a leader who created more problems than he solved. But to what end?

Bowman, his willing lackey, latched onto that description. "I would say . . . yeah, I think you could say that about Lombard. Sure." He was nodding, making a pretense of thinking it over, and reluctantly agreeing that the description was an accurate one.

"Captain Bowman, have you been on any of the ships now docked at the station's concourses?"

Bowman raised his eyebrows, the question taking him by surprise. "I can't say, for sure. I don't know what-all ships are docked just now."

"But you have been on ships docked here before, yes?"

"Yes, sure. Lots of times."

"And in general, do you find the ship's crew to be helpful, or hostile?"

"I don't know what you mean by that." Bowman was as confused as I was.

"Let me ask it this way: When you arrive aboard Alliance military ships, are you ever attacked, or treated with suspicion?"

"No, of course not!"

"Does anybody question you, ask what you are doing on their ship?"

"No, Never."

"Why not? I mean, you don't belong to the ship's crew, you aren't usually known to the men personally, are you? Why aren't they worried about being taken over when you, and some of your men, are on board?"

"Because I'm a G-Marine officer. They know that. They can see it from my uniform."

"So, in your experience, Alliance sailors don't usually get worried just because they see G-Marines on board their ship? Even armed G-Marines?"

Stafford's plan of attack was clear now, and I began to anticipate what he was going to say. It would be that I was only successful in taking down *StarFire* because my men wore the same uniform as their own Marine contingent. That they couldn't tell I didn't belong on the ship, and didn't realize I wasn't a part of their own marines. But it turned out I was wrong. He was going to say something worse than that. Bowman had to answer him, first, though.

"No, sailors don't worry much about seeing me and my men. They have their own Marines on board, and they're used to seeing our uniforms."

"So, a crew that was not hostile, just going about their duties, busily operating the ship, if they saw a bunch of G-Marines moving about on board, they would have no reason to think they were being attacked, is that right? They would not put up a fight, at least not right away, because they would assume that any G-Marines they saw, even if they weren't from their own Marine complement, they would think they were their comrades-in-arms, is that right?"

"Of course." Bowman still didn't get it, but I did now. Stafford was setting the stage for saying that I attacked a ship that didn't have any reason to suspect they were under attack. That I slipped up on an unaware crew, and destroyed them for no reason except that I had assumed they were mutineers, or rebels, or something, without any evidence, and that I was successful because they didn't catch on that I was hostile until it was too late. They weren't expecting trouble because they hadn't done anything to cause them to expect trouble. I leaned back in my chair, a cold knot in my stomach, as Stafford began to fill in the last holes in his argument.

"Captain Bowman, let me ask you a different question. What would you say the odds would be of taking a hostile ship with a complement of three thousand, if you had to attack with, say, one platoon?"

"Well, those are pretty long odds, sir." Bowman grinned, self-consciously, foolishly. As though he didn't realize that this "hypothetical" being put to him was what had, in fact, actually happened. "I mean, I would make that attack if I had orders to, of course, but . . . I wouldn't expect to win."

"What would you expect, Captain Bowman? In ordinary circumstances, attacking a hostile ship like that, what would the outcome be?"

"Well, we would likely be wiped out, sir. In short order."

"Short order? That's an interesting phrase. How short?"

"Sir?"

"How long would you expect until the ship's company counter-attacked? Say they had a thousand G-Marines, or their equivalent? How long until they rallied and counter-attacked with overwhelming numbers? In your experience, please."

Bowman shrugged, trying to figure out how to come up with an answer.

"I guess . . . they tell us in training to expect if we don't have the bridge in fifteen minutes, we should expect organized resistance. So, maybe fifteen minutes?" Bowman looked at Stafford, wanting approval of this answer. It was a ridiculous answer. Most ships we simulated attacks on had theoretical compliments of two hundred or less. Most could be crossed, from stem to stern, even in combat, in less than an hour. *StarFire* was nothing like that. Further, taking the bridge only mattered when the mission was to capture a ship. We hadn't gone anywhere near the bridge of *StarFire*, and never had a thought of capturing her. I could take this argument apart in ten minutes of cross-examination, except of course, I would have no opportunity to do that. Not before charges were preferred and I faced an actual Court-Martial, anyway.

"So, if the G-Marines on *StarFire* did not counter-attack, what would you say is the most likely reason for that?" And even Ben Bowman couldn't miss the answer to that one, after the set-up.

"I- I guess because they didn't know they were being attacked. They saw G-Marines, in G-Marine uniforms, and that was a normal enough thing to see on the ship. Likely they didn't resist at all, until it was too late."

"Thank you, Captain Bowman. I have no further questions for this witness," Stafford pronounced, like a man stepping away from a finished project, satisfied with his work. Bowman looked towards the Board, not sure if he should step down, and the officers there shifted a little in their seats while the admiral held his hand up, staying Bowman from retreating just yet.

"Captain Bowman, let us see if any of these officers have questions for you," he said. And that was where I had to look for salvation. The Board could ask questions of Bowman regarding any of his testimony, or anything else, for that matter, if they thought it would be helpful to them in considering the case. I was hoping for one of the Navy Captains to ask questions about the kind of ships Bowman was referencing in considering his answers regarding boarding operations, but in the end, no one got a chance to ask anything.

The doors in the back of the room opened up, suddenly and a little noisily, and Command Master Sergeant Bart Hastings, Colonel Parsons' personal aid and secretary, walked straight down the center aisle. The Board officers all stopped what they were doing, and looked up at him. Sgt. Hastings marched directly up to the front table and came to attention in front of the admiral. Then he stretched out his arm, and offered the admiral a note. The admiral accepted it with without any fuss, and Hastings simply stood and waited while he read it. Then, to my surprise, the admiral made an announcement.

"There are new developments which may bear on this case. We are adjourned until tomorrow, oh-seven-hundred. Gentlemen," he said, looking around at his fellow board officers, "you will, no doubt, want to accompany me." CRACK! The gavel came down, adjourning the session, and personnel started hustling around, trying to find out what was happening, while the admiral, three Naval captains, and one Marine colonel hustled out of the room, Sgt. Hastings leading them . . . somewhere.

* * *

Two of my escorts, caught by surprise, took a couple of minutes to round the other two of them up. By now everyone else had left the room, so it was me, and just one of my escorts, the other one out looking for the missing two, who I presumed were probably down in the cafeteria, thinking they wouldn't be needed for another couple of hours, at least.

I didn't bother thinking about what might have pulled the admiral out of the room so quickly. I figured I would find out soon enough. I was worried about Stafford's new approach to my case. After the new evidence regarding Captain Halverson, the Board officers seemed willing to accept that I actually had boarded StarFire. So, that was progress. But Stafford was lining up testimony to suggest that I had attacked her, unprovoked, and managed to destroy her because, as we were G-Marines, her crew did not see us as the enemy. And I thought that as a theory it was going to be difficult to put to bed. But beyond getting me charged and into a court-martial, I didn't understand Stafford's purpose behind it. In a court-martial, I would bring my own witnesses, all of my men, the warrant officers from Duvall's 'lander, and Technician Duggard. They would never be able to convict me. It was starting to look like Stafford just wanted me off this base, and tied up for a few months with legal proceedings.

I thought about that all the way back to my room, after my escorts finally arrived to take me there. And once back in my room, I fell into my chair to think some more, and still, I couldn't figure Stafford's game plan for after the Inquiry. I was still thinking when my phone chimed. It was Hoffman, my off-station consulting lawyer.

"Congratulations, son. I hear you have the case beat," Hoffman led off with.

"Is that so? Sounds like you know something I don't. They just adjourned the Inquiry suddenly, but nobody told me why."

"Well, Duggard got a message to me, and said to pass this on, in case they didn't tell you right away. A certain Lieutenant John Harley has turned up, and should arrive on your station pretty soon, if he isn't there already."

That was terrific news, even aside from all the implications it had for my case.

"Harley made it? That's great! Did Duggard tell you anything else? Like where Harley's been all this time, or how he's doing?"

"No, he said he didn't have any more information. If I was guessing, I would lean towards the possibility that Duggard came across the little bit of information he had, um, sort of accidentally. Maybe he accidentally read someone's mail, or accidentally picked up a conversation he wasn't properly supposed to be listening to."

That was easy to imagine. Since we got him involved in tracking down information on Captain Halverson, Duggard had probably spent a good bit of time over the day scouring the 'nets and the station communications files, looking for anything else helpful. One thing about Duggard, once you got him started on something, he took it all the way.

"I think that might be a pretty good guess, Mr. Hoffman. Anything else?"

"No, I was just passing on that message. Duggard told me Harley's fighter will have the data you need to prove your report, so I figured he was right, it was probably important to let you know."

"Thanks, Mr. Hoffman. I'll touch base if I need you, if you don't mind."

"You bet."

I terminated the call, and wondered when I would hear what Harley had brought back, and what he was saying.

CHAPTER 26

Inquiry

In the morning, I went to some effort to hustle my escort along, hoping to get in a few minutes before the Inquiry was called to order. The enforced isolation I had been living under hadn't been much of a hardship up to now, but suddenly, wanting news of Harley's condition and what had happened to him, I was hoping I might pick up some information just by being around where people were talking. In hindsight, I might have had better luck if I had maneuvered my escorts into taking me by the mess hall. But I did get a different sort of message, once we arrived.

Looking around the room, I saw several enlisted men who had been on the *StarFire* mission with me. Duggard was there, although he had already testified once. I recalled Lt. Tillman hinting that he would be on the witness list regarding the communications issue, but that had already been covered, so I wasn't sure why he was here again unless this was off-duty hours for him, and he just wanted to see it play out. A couple of the squad sergeants were there, also, and one of the medics from the platoon. And, though I didn't notice him right away, sitting in the back was the chief warrant officer from Duvall's crew. Several more men from the mission were present, and scattered around the room.

I mulled that over for a while. I had already reached the conclusion that Navy might be looking to punish anyone and everyone who had been involved in the mission, to whatever extent they could, and I could see how Stafford might want to try to implicate Duggard for the software tampering on the com system. But I had no idea what the other men were there for. Nor could I saunter over and ask them. I was allowed no contact with potential witnesses until the Inquiry was over, to prevent tampering with their testimony. That was the primary reason I had been segregated by moving me to Navy quarters, and it still held, in this room.

But most troubling of all, I saw no sign of Lt. Harley. A dozen possibilities ran through my head, including things like, maybe he was hurt, or ill, and couldn't testify. Or maybe Duggard's information was wrong, or Hoffman had misunderstood the message, and Harley hadn't been recovered at all. I even wondered if the misunderstanding might be that Lt.

Harley's dead body had been recovered, instead of him being rescued alive.

When Commander Stafford came rolling in a few moments later, I studied him closely, and Lt. Tillman, tagging along close behind. Stafford was businesslike, staid and professional. There was nothing about him that looked like either victory or defeat, but more like "just another day of business." Tillman, on the other hand, was a little more animated, almost perky.

That was of little help, I discovered, thinking it over. Lt. Tillman was a mystery to me. While the information she had gathered in her interview had been used, as best it could, against me, that was neither positive nor negative. She had to turn in her report, and she did. She also provided Stafford with the question he had tried to use to cast doubt on my testimony that I had ever even set foot on *StarFire*. But then, she had provided me with a lead to get the information I needed to turn that around, when she asked me the seemingly innocent question, "Who's he?" after I mentioned Halverson's name to her.

So today, after the news I had received that Lt. Harley had been recovered, what did it mean that Lt. Linda Tillman was feeling good? Who knew, maybe it just meant that the breakfast selection in the mess hall had been pretty good this morning.

The panel of Board officers filed in, then, and I quit speculating. We all rose, the bailiff called the Inquiry to order, and after the admiral nodded to him, Stafford rose to start the proceedings.

"Judge Advocate," he intoned, as a greeting to the admiral, followed by, "Officers of the Board," nodding to them, "developments have surpassed our presentation of this case. I have presented witnesses, based on my best understanding of the issues under examination at each turn of this case, and twice now, new evidence has come out while testimony was still underway. We are now quite comfortable, in the light of some of the most recent evidence, to stipulate that Captain Lombard's report is accurate and complete. There remains only one issue to be resolved, and that is, was Captain Lombard operating within the boundaries of his orders when he destroyed AMS *StarFire*? Or did that decision exceed his authority, to the detriment of the Alliance military readiness and strength?"

I deduced from this opening that Harley's fighter had come back intact, and that his recordings of the combat with *StarFire* were clear and convincing evidence that, first, she fired on Alliance craft, and second, that I boarded her and caused severe damage to her systems. There must have been substantial indications of the latter for Stafford to cite her as "destroyed." But that wasn't sufficient for him. Now, I gathered, he wanted to have me tried simply for the fact of my victory. I wondered what motivated him to that goal while Stafford went on speaking.

"I will be calling several witnesses today. These are enlisted men and warrant officers who were present when Captain Lombard made his decisions, some of which were clearly in violation of regulations, and others which obviously stretch beyond what would normally be within the purview of a mere Captain of the Galactic Marine Corps."

Colonel Kershaw, who had been the least animated member of the Board over the last two days, suddenly looked up at Commander Stafford. He had a question.

"Why are we taking the testimony of enlisted men before we hear from the officers involved?"

Stafford nodded, as if to confirm the validity of the question before he put it to bed. Then he spread his hands, and said, "Captain Duvall is dead, as is his co-pilot, Lt. Goddard. They were the only officers present on the transport/lander with Captain Lombard."

Kershaw knew a dodge when he saw it though, and a look of annoyance crossed his face. "What about this Lt. Harley? He was present for the combat-planning phase of the operation, according to Lombard's report. I suppose I would expect that he was in communication with both Duvall and Lombard throughout the assault, as well. I, for one, would like to know what he has to say, before I ask subordinate NCO and enlisted men to second-guess their commander in the field!"

Now Kershaw looked around at the board, all of them Navy, and all of them very senior officers. On balance, the Navy is the most segregated, in terms of separating officers and enlisted men. The three captains were all immediately sympathetic to Kershaw's suggestion, and they all looked to the admiral, nodding their heads in agreement. The admiral, for his part, didn't look entirely pleased. I suspect that he simply wanted to keep things going, and saw this as a delay. But before he pronounced a decision, Stafford took another swing at the ball.

"Colonel, I understand your very reasonable point. And I'm sure we will have an opportunity to hear from Lt. Harley, if he has anything useful to offer, just as soon as my investigator has a chance to depose him. But I must point out that he was not involved in the combat aboard *StarFire*. While that took place, he was sitting in his fighter, some distance away. In the meantime . . ."

Kershaw erupted on him. "Commander, isn't that your investigator, sitting right there at that table? Hasn't she been sitting next to you since you came in?" He didn't pause for an answer to either question. "Don't you tell me you are arranging for deposition when as I far as I can see, your investigator is preparing to do her nails! I sat here and listened to you call this man, Captain Lombard, a liar. You were prepared to sell us on the theory that he made this whole story up, and never even set eyes on your ship. When he disposed of that argument, you didn't bat an eye before you started painting him a coward, a man who attacked an Alliance ship before even ascertaining whether it was hostile or not. And from what I understand, we now have incontrovertible evidence that *StarFire* destroyed one of his assets before he took any hostile action, and that he survives today, along with most of his men, because he executed his duties superbly. So, in light of all that, I'm interested in hearing from Lt. Harley before I let you waste another day of my time."

The Navy men on the Board were taken aback, more than just a little bit. It was quite an outburst. But what Kershaw had said was part of the record, now, and they had to take it seriously. The admiral conferred with the captains for a moment, and then when he saw that his four colleagues were all in agreement, he simply conceded.

"Commander Stafford, if the Board prefers to hear from Lt. Harley, then I recommend you bring him to the witness stand. You will have time to bring your other witnesses later, if it still seems necessary and useful to, afterwards."

Stafford looked like he had just found half a worm in his apple.

"I, er . . . we don't know what Lt. Harley's condition is, just now. We haven't spoken to him, and we don't know what testimony he might bring . . ."

Kershaw interrupted him, in a loud voice, saying, "I'm sure that's all right. We can question him ourselves, well enough, I expect. Bring him in. I look forward to hearing his account."

And the admiral concurred, saying, "We will recess for-" he considered a moment, and came to a different decision, "until thirteen hundred hours. That should give Commander Stafford time to locate the Lieutenant, and arrange for his testimony." Crack! The gavel came down.

I made a mental note to put Colonel Kershaw on my Christmas list.

* * *

When we returned that afternoon, I was surprised to observe Colonel Kershaw was late getting back to the room. His seat was empty. The admiral and three captains fidgeted, checking the time, and looking around. I fidgeted, checked the time, and looked around. Lt. Tillman seemed confused by his tardiness, as well, searching the room for the colonel. But Stafford sat calm and relaxed, like a patient man, waiting for the world to catch up with him. I started to get a bad feeling. If anyone knew where the colonel was, it was Stafford, and he was relaxed. That didn't bode well.

Finally, the admiral sent his aid outside, obviously to look into the colonel's whereabouts. When he had been gone for about fifteen minutes, he came back in, and slipped right up to whisper in the admiral's ear. They had a terse exchange for a moment, and then the aid went back to sit down, and the admiral called the Inquiry into session.

"It appears that Colonel Kershaw was unexpectedly called away on an emergency issue. This means that the Board now consists of myself, and the three captains, and because we have no alternate, the Board's final vote could conceivably result in a failure to reach a majority decision on the merits of the case before us. However . . ." he looked around at his colleagues, "I am confident that with clear evidence, we should have no trouble coming to a three to one majority, or even a unanimous decision. Therefore, I move that we continue with the Inquiry, and if at least two of my fellow board officers agree . . . ?"

While my stomach turned over, the captains, caught a little off guard, looked around at each other for a moment, but none of them got to their current rank and responsibilities by being afraid to make decision. After a moment, they all nodded their assent to the proposal. The only thought running through my head was, what could be so important that they would pull all these strings to prevent Colonel Kershaw from asserting himself on this Board? I was sure that getting rid of the Colonel was no great feat of tactics. All they had to do was gin up a little supply depot shortage of some chemical necessary to the function of some equipment or other, or a minor miss-shipment of replacement parts necessary at one of the defense stations. But removing him like this? That action would cast a shadow on the whole proceedings. It was like cutting off a toe to get rid of a hangnail. And the admiral didn't hesitate, he rolled right ahead.

"Very well. Let the record reflect that the motion to continue is carried, unanimously. Commander Stafford?"

"Thank you sir." Stafford rose to face the board once more. I could see the wheels turning in his head, and he glanced at me, momentarily, but gave nothing of his thoughts away as he did. "Then, I would like to re-call Technician Duggard to the stand."

One of the captains, the one who had been sitting closest to the end where Kershaw had sat before, spoke up then. "I thought we had agreed to hear from Lt. Harley? Commander Stafford, you were given directions to produce this man Harley. The fact that Colonel Kershaw is no longer present does not negate instructions you received from the Judge Advocate on that issue." The other two captains nodded their agreement. It seemed they didn't like the air of manipulation in the room, any more than I did.

Stafford looked at the admiral, a silent appeal, but in his role as Judge Advocate, the admiral was not a senior officer. He was simply the most senior man among equal judges. He could not legally overrule all three captains. He could not even bring the weight of his rank into play to decide a tie decision, forcing a two-two decision to shift in his own favor. If that was the result, they could convene another board and start again, or they could drop the issue and let me get back to work. And he was equally stymied in regard to his previous decision to have Harley called to the stand.

"Bring Lt. Harley in, Commander, if you please," the admiral directed Stafford.

With an air of frustration evident in the crisp, jerky motions he used, Commander Stafford pulled his com unit off his belt, turned it on, and spoke into it. A moment later, the doors opened, and Lt. Harley strolled into the room, a little tired looking, and leaner than I remembered him, but stepping out with a jaunty attitude. He was followed by two Military Police sergeants. I suspected that was not the image Stafford had meant everyone to see, when he finally called Harley in, and everyone saw the MP goons he had keeping track of Harley. I wondered if he would pay a price for it later. I was under investigation, but they had officers escorting me. Harley wasn't under investigation, so the obvious question was, what did Stafford think he might do that justified setting MP sergeants on him? To the Navy, especially, that just looked like an insult. But I suspected I knew better. It was Stafford keeping track of Harley, because Navy had it in for everyone involved, as I had begun to suspect before.

Harley looked good, to my eye. Tired perhaps, as was to be expected, but in good health. He walked steadily to the witness chair, and sat down.

Stafford approached him, hands clasped behind his back in a soft, non-threatening pose. "Lt. Harley, I'm pleased to see you safe and sound. Please tell the Board your recent whereabouts since losing contact with Captain Lombard on your mission."

John Harley started speaking, simply explaining that his fighter had, in fact, taken a glancing hit from *StarFire* before becoming sufficiently hidden in the asteroid field to make his escape. The damage was minor, but it took out all his communications, his navigation computer, and some sensors. Further, although it didn't immediately show, his right-side thruster had been damaged slightly, and while it didn't slow him down right away, within a few hours, he had been forced to cut power to that thruster. That reduced his speed significantly, and he took several days to make it back to this base.

As John was testifying, I caught some movement out of the corner of my eye, and looked towards the doors in time to see a man slip in and take an empty seat. I didn't know him, but saw a Galactic Marine Corps officer's uniform.

Stafford was speaking now. "Lt. Harley, Captain Lombard has informed us that his craft was out of air within two days of leaving the scene of the confrontation with *StarFire*. How is it you were out four days after that, and did not run out of air?"

"I was in a long-range fighter." John stopped, as if that explained it, and Stafford had to prompt him to continue.

"Yes? And what does that signify, Lt. Harley?"

I had to hide a grin when I saw Harley's slightly incredulous expression, along with a hint of his own amusement. I realized what he was doing. He was pointing out to the Board that Commander Stafford, though he wore the rank and uniform of the Alliance Navy, was not a traditional military man. He was a lawyer, and didn't understand the things that Harley, and all four of the officers on the Board understood and took for granted.

"A long-range fighter is equipped with things that allow it to go, uh, you know, a long way. Like extra fuel tanks, and larger air reserves. In a pinch, I could fly a long-range fighter for, I dunno, maybe ten days? It depends a little, and the calculation has to take into consideration your exact weight when you start, but my last rating was for nine days. I've lost a little weight since then, though. Probably sweated it off, bringing my horse home on one engine, this time. So, right now, maybe ten days." A small chuckle rippled across the room at the little sarcasm the joke implied, pointing out that Stafford was now questioning a warrior, returned from battle, based on theories Stafford had come up with sitting at a desk. I glanced around the room, and saw men and officers smiling. They liked John Harley.

The commanding captains were not amused, but I figured them for practical men. They wouldn't miss John's point. Looking around, I also saw two more men slip into the back of the room. One Navy and one Marine. It was getting crowded in here, now, and I wondered what was going on, if Harley had made enough of a name for himself getting back so late after being thought lost that they were all coming in just to hear the story.

Stafford, meanwhile, had caught on to Harley's innuendo, and his neck was getting a little red at being set up for that little lecture by this upstart fighter pilot. He couldn't let on, though, so he swallowed his anger, and continued the questioning.

"Lt. Harley, were you present at a planning meeting that took place on the transport/lander which Captain Lombard was using, along with Captain Duvall, his copilot, and Lt. Smithson?"

"Yes I was."

"And can you tell me, what consideration was given, in that planning session, to ideas for capturing *StarFire*?"

John Harley looked surprised. "None, that I was aware of."

Stafford smiled at him. "None? Really?" His mouth was still open, and he was about to go on, but Harley jumped in right then.

"What do you mean, 'really'? Didn't I just say 'none'? What is it, you don't believe my testimony?" He had raised his voice enough to show he took the insult seriously, but not enough to get slapped down for contempt, or disorderly conduct, or insubordination. Stafford, though, was taken off guard, and immediately started to back-pedal. Lt. Harley was pretty close to a hero, and he didn't want to alienate the board officers by picking on him gratuitously.

"No, no, not at all," he said, "I was merely surprised to hear the topic didn't come up, I don't mean to impugn your testimony, Lieutenant."

"Oh." Harley was all fire and ice as he spoke. "Well, I guess that's fine, then. It's just that, what we've been hearing outside of this room, what I've been told since I got back, is that a G-Marine officer in this room is assumed to be lying unless he can prove he's not. So, maybe I jumped to conclusions for a minute there." Harley's inference was clear. He was referring to the way I had been treated, so far.

The admiral couldn't let that statement stand, and he didn't waste any time stepping in. "Lieutenant, let me remind you that while on the witness stand, you are still under military discipline. You cannot be held in contempt for speaking the truth, but you can and will be held in contempt for making scurrilous comments!"

John Harley turned slightly to look straight at the admiral, then.

"Sir, of course I understand that perfectly. But that's not a scurrilous comment. That's exactly what I have been hearing for about twenty hours now, from the moment I got out of sickbay, after the doctors checked me over. And that's not all I heard, either. You might be interested in some of the other things going around the base."

The admiral, not a resident of the base, really couldn't have cared less what problems this hearing was causing among base personnel, but one of the captains spoke up. He wasn't encouraging Lt. Harley, he was warning him. I could have told him not to bother, John Harley was "transmit only" on the intimidation wave-length, but then, as it turned out, it opened things up further.

"What are those other things you have heard, Lt. Harley? Do they bear on this case? Because if not . . ." And Harley jumped in, right there, before the captain could finish saying that if they didn't bear directly on the testimony, he should shut-up about it, already.

"Well, sir, I've heard that after Captain Lombard gets run through the grinder here, that I'm next on the chopping block. I've heard that the reason Commander Stafford set two MP guards to following me around is not so he could summon me to these proceedings. He could do that with a simple com message. It's been suggested to me that those two goons are on my backside, closer than my government-issue underwear, so they can take me into custody next. Which is why, if the captain isn't acquitted with no charges in the next couple of hours, I will be resigning my commission, immediately, and shipping out on the next shuttle or freighter that will transport me."

The captain turned a deep red, properly hearing this as a threat. "Lt. Harley, if you are required to present yourself for a Board of Inquiry, resigning your commission will not stop the proceedings. If you do not return for a hearing, you will be investigated in your absence. Furthermore, I'm sure you know that officers can be recalled at the pleasure of command in any event. So my advice is, don't you go making any rash decisions that will prejudice any case brought against you!"

"Sir, thank you for that advice. Here's how I see it: If I resign my commission and get off this rock, it will take you a couple of weeks to get the paperwork done to recall me, and a couple more to track me down. When you do, if you manage to get a summons to me, I'll answer the summons, as I am required to. And if you recall me to service, I will serve, just like I am now. But you might find it a little tough to accomplish all that, because this defense station will be short a few dozen pilots by that time. The way I hear it, if pilots are going to start being brought up for Boards of Inquiry just because they followed orders, and accomplished their missions, there's a whole lot of pilots who are going to start looking for private work. At least that's the rumor. Sir."

I threw a glance back around the room, taking in all the new arrivals, those who had shown up after Lt. Harley came in. Now that I knew what to look for, it was obvious. They were all pilots. Navy and Marines, fighter pilots, transport/lander pilots, even a bunch of pilots from the larger ships, docked at the station. And they were all officers. Each and every one of them could resign their commission, if they had served out their original commitment, and surely, most or all of them had. And they could all be recalled, but they couldn't be all be punished with bad assignments. The services would still need pilots for the jobs these guys were leaving. They just wouldn't have them for a few weeks, while they got the paperwork done, and then tracked them down and brought them back, one at a time.

What John was talking about was, essentially, a strike. As if the pilots had a union, and had voted to strike if I was brought up on charges, or if John was.

Well, the military had laws against unionizing, and therefore, I was pretty sure no one had actually said anything like, "Let's all threaten to go on strike." I'm sure each communication was well documented, either voice or text, through the com system, where it could be found and examined. They would all be simply one man telling another that he was thinking of resigning, because he felt he could not depend on command to take care of the pilots anymore, and maybe asking for a reference, or a suggestion on who was hiring pilots for freighters and the like. It was beautiful. It was organized, and powerful.

And the admiral saw something else, immediately. He understood in a nanosecond that if this happened as a result of this board of inquiry, word would get around real fast. It would be said that he should have seen this coming, and that there must have been something very funny about that Board of Inquiry, if it inspired a pilots' strike. It could, and very likely would, wreck his career.

Well, the dance was over, all that was left were the final notes of the music. The admiral reigned in Commander Stafford, very quickly, and dismissed Lt. Harley from the witness stand without further testimony. Then he adjourned the Inquiry indefinitely, saying that the Board would confer and decide if any further testimony was needed. I got the idea he was pretty sure it would not be. He banged his gavel, and then stood up, but while everyone else was leaving, he called Commander Stafford over for a quick conference, and whatever he said, it turned Stafford's ears red. Meanwhile, Lt. Tillman cocked her head at me, and gave a little jerk. She wanted me to come over to where she sat waiting for Stafford. I assumed that was because it would be easier to explain than her coming to me. I strolled over.

When I got there, she spoke quickly, and quietly.

"Captain Lombard, you need to understand, this won't end it. Stafford won't be allowed to let it end here. He has orders."

"Thanks. I'm beginning to get that picture. And it looks to me like the admiral is in on that little secret, as well."

Tillman scrunched up her face, as though she was dying to tell me more, but didn't dare to. At least not with so many Navy personnel around. So I took her off the hook.

"Never mind, Lieutenant. I think I understand. I'll be watching my options, and I'll figure something out. Thanks for the warning. And for . . . you know, ah, thanks for everything." She knew I was talking about the tip on Halverson.

"Captain . . . I want to . . . you have to believe . . . I didn't know, when I started this. I wouldn't have been any part of it, if I knew it was something other than an inquiry."

"Thanks. I was already sure of that. Listen, you might want to transfer out of Legal Affairs. You're a good investigator, but whatever is going on here is corrupt. If you stay, after this, and it all comes out later, the stench of it will follow you. You want to be able to point to a transfer and say you got out, at the first sign of something wrong."

"I've already put in for a transfer."

"Military police?" She was an investigator, after all.

"No, Intelligence." She flashed a smile at that, too.

We stood there for a moment longer, and then I smiled at her. "So, maybe you better stand up and tell me to get lost, or something. You know, in case someone is watching." She started to smile back, but then it hit her, I was serious. So she just gathered up her things and stood up.

"Nice to have met you, Captain. Thanks for telling me your story, and the time you spent with me. I wish it was under other circumstances."

"Well, maybe I'll see you again, under other circumstances. You never know."

"That sounds like an invitation." She flashed me a last quick look, and then she left, doing her best to make it look like she was in a huff, like maybe I had asked for her private com codes or something. I chuckled, and shook my head, like "Dames. Who can understand them?" for the benefit of anyone watching. Then I signaled to my escorts that I was ready to go. I wasn't free yet, but I was beginning to think I would be soon. Free of the Board of Inquiry, at least, and most likely, free of the Alliance military. I had not been formally acquitted, and that would not quite be a black mark on my record. More like a question mark. But in the military, record is everything. My career, I suspected, was over.

CHAPTER 27

Defense Space Station G-13, 246.163.12

After Inquiry

The next morning, instead of an escort, Stafford came to my quarters. He was alone, and he came straight to the point. He was very much matter-of-fact about it, and showed not a hint of doubt about what he was telling me.

"Lombard, you're finished as an officer. All that's left is to see how much trouble you want to cause yourself before you resign. You have one chance here to make yourself a good deal. After that, I have been ordered to, and will, personally hound you until we manage to lock you up."

"Yeah? How's that working for you so far, Commander?" That was nothing more than bravado, on my part. I knew that the military is no place to try to fight uphill battles against authority. But I didn't like being threatened.

A Navy commander is actually one rank above a Marine captain, and Stafford didn't miss that I omitted the "sir" when I spoke to him. That told him what he really wanted to know; I was ready to make a deal and get out. It was a strangely characteristic trait, like a tell, that someone was fed up, done with the military hierarchy, when they could no longer bring themselves to offer that note of respect.

"So. Let's get to business. My office requires that you resign your commission, effective immediately, today. You will receive a general discharge, and your background record will be amended to show that you are ineligible to re-enlist at any time, in any Alliance military service. Your service record will be classified. You will agree to sign secrecy documents that prohibit any discussion or disclosure of the *StarFire* mission, under the Military Secrets Act. And you will present for examination of compliance to this agreement twice in the next year, and every two years thereafter, for as long as we require you to." That meant, basically, that they wanted me to turn up at a military post for a lie-detector, twice this year, and every two years afterwards. It also meant that I would never be able to prove I had spent all these years in the service, because of the classified records. It would be like I had been unemployed, and had gained no skills or training in the service, so far as getting a job outside the service would go. Without a record, that would eliminate most of the companies that contracted with the military.

I sat down, in the only chair available, and crossed my legs, and then crossed my arms over my chest. Stafford stood there for a moment, waiting, before he lost his patience.

"Well? What do you have to say?"

I picked my teeth for a moment before answering. "Nothing."

"Nothing? Fine. I'll have the paperwork sent down within the hour."

"That will be a waste of paper, commander."

"What then? If you have something to say, spit it out, man!"

"Why? Why do you want me out so bad? And why would I resign, when you and I both know that I did my duty to the absolute best of my ability?" My anger was coming up, more and more, the longer I spoke, so I stopped before I got too escalated and said something I might regret.

"I don't know why they want you out. I don't even care. I was told to get you sent off for court-martial when I took this assignment, but they didn't give me a reason."

"Oh, so you're a happy little mercenary. Justice doesn't enter the equation anywhere?" I thought his answer was despicable. He worked for a military court, but it was still a court of law. Supposedly. And theoretically, as an officer of the court, justice was his first duty. Stafford disabused me of that notion, immediately.

"Lombard, I follow orders, the same as you do. I don't always get told the reasons behind those orders, just as you aren't always told the reasons behind your orders, and you don't always tell your men the reasons you give them orders. But as it happens, I do think you are guilty of something, and that's enough for me." Stafford, still standing, leaned back against the wall, behind him, suddenly looking a little worn out, like explaining this to me was above and beyond the call of ordinary duty. But in a moment, he had gathered his thoughts and went on.

"If I take your report at face value—and I'm not saying I do—but if I did, one thing stands out to me: You seem to think that something strange was happening on that ship, *StarFire*. You went to great lengths to persuade my investigator, Lt. Tillman, that something odd had happened there. Maybe something very dangerous. And you had the answer, right in your hands, with that prisoner you took. A live body, without any obvious life-threatening injuries, whom you could have taken to your 'lander and brought back for questioning. But you decided not to. It was inconvenient for you to do that."

"Inconvenient?" My rising blood pressure was evident in my voice. "I had to choose between my sergeant, who is also my friend, a man who has saved my life more times that I can count, and a mutineer! That is not a question of convenience. And, my orders didn't say anything about bringing back prisoners for questioning!"

Stafford just shrugged at me. "True. I've read your orders. They didn't address prisoners at all, that's correct. But you were given the task to find out what happened to *StarFire*. And you could have. But you didn't. Your duty was to expend the lives of your men to accomplish the mission command gave you. Saving your sergeant the way you did makes you a hero to your men, but it was dereliction of duty. In the eyes of the military, you chose to save one man, at the expense of successfully accomplishing your mission. And for that, I will require your commission to be resigned."

I was silent, because he was right. He knew it, and to be honest, I knew it. I had known it all along. Given the chance to do it over, I would have made the same decision, but when I chose Sgt. Alvin over Captain Halverson, I was throwing away the answers I had been sent to get. Not all of them; we knew *StarFire* was hostile, and where she was, and now, that she was no longer a threat in any remote way. But I hadn't answered the big question, which was, what happened to AMS *StarFire*?

We both stayed silent for a long minute, but eventually, Stafford got back to the duty at hand. "So? What's it going to be? You still don't have anything to say?"

I took a breath before answering him, swallowed hard, and then got realistic, and prepared for the inevitable.

"I'm just waiting for you to get serious. Tell me your real offer. I'm not going to waste my time responding to one that you and I both know I'm not going to take. I can drag this out for months, if I refuse to resign." I started inspecting my fingernails.

"If do you not resign, we will not only ruin you, but we will ruin each and every man who serves under you." Stafford had done his homework. He knew I could never allow that. But I wondered if he knew I played poker, and had spent the last few years learning the art of the bluff from the best teacher in this end of the galaxy?

"I can live with that. They're big boys. G-Marines. They can take a little hassling by the brass. Besides, only the sergeants are really career men, and they're good sergeants. Break them, and anyone who gets them will make them sergeants again as soon as they see their potential." My nails were fine. I wondered if I was going to have to resort to shining my shoes, in a minute.

Stafford stood there, looking at me, glowering down, almost salivating, he was so mad. But in the end, he persuaded himself I was serious. He calmed himself, and figuratively came back to the table.

"Fine. What do you want? I'm telling you right now, I can't give you much."

We hammered it out, from that point. My resignation, effective tomorrow, not today. Immediate release from confinement to quarters, and the freedom of the base my position allowed, for the remainder of the day. That was so I could say goodbye to my men, and thank John Harley, as well as a couple of other folks. In addition, my record would not be sealed, but the details of the *StarFire* mission could be redacted. My men's records would have the mission redacted, and a unit citation issued "for classified action." That kind of unit citation was a real badge of honor, and it was likely to get the boys into some interesting work, the kind of thing all gung-ho soldiers craved.

Stafford hated that part, but I was adamant. My men had performed heroically. They deserved honors for that. This way their record would show they had done something outstanding, but random Navy personnel would not know what it was related to.

In addition, if Navy wanted me out without the possibility of re-enlisting, I was fine with that. I was as done with Fleet Command as they were with me. But they would also have to release me from the possibility of recall. That was critical, because without that, they would be able to hound me at every turn, unless I left human space entirely. Stafford finally agreed. He couldn't see what the harm in that was, since Navy had told him explicitly that they didn't want me back, ever. In the end, after we had everything worked out, I decided to ask the question that had been bothering again.

"Commander, I still want to know, what's the big deal? Why is Fleet so upset about all this? I know, you said they didn't tell you, but I'm not asking for the official version. I just want to know what you think."

To his credit, Stafford gave me what I think was an honest answer. "I don't really know, Lombard. But . . . off the record?" I nodded. "I think some heads have to roll. I mean, you took down their flagship with fifty guys. That makes it look like the big ship was a mistake. Somebody is in deep, over this. So, they're starting with you. It'll work its way up, no doubt, but somebody is hoping that by bleeding you, and getting you out of here, they are laying down a smoke screen, maybe even putting in the foundation of a firewall, to prevent the damage from reaching too high." He shrugged. "Like I said, when I got tapped for this, I was told to make sure you got a court-martial out of it. I looked at the case, and told them I couldn't guarantee a conviction of any kind, but I could probably get you sent out for trial. They said not to worry about the rest, they just wanted you transported home for the court-martial. That tells me they just wanted you to be quiet about the whole thing for a while, buy them some time to start spinning their answers." He stopped for a moment, before adding his last comment.

"You know, you didn't do my career any good, beating me on this thing."

I nodded, considering the man before I spoke. He was a real prick, yeah, but I saw some honor there, some belief that he was doing harsh, but necessary and justifiable things. So I gave him an honest answer, too.

"Yeah, well, I'm all broken up about that. Tell you what, if they fire you, look me up. I'll have a head start on a career in civilian life, by then. I'll make you this promise: If this scotches your career too, you find me, and let me know you're out of the service. I'll kick your ass six ways from Sunday, and then, when we can let bygones be bygones, then I'll do what I can to get you a job. Deal?"

He just laughed at me, and left, the signed paperwork constituting our deal in hand. I wasn't sure, but I thought I had earned a little respect from Commander Wayne Stafford, somewhere along the way. And I didn't want to kick his ass six ways from Sunday anymore. Well, not as much as I did earlier, anyway.

* * *

A little while later, I packed up most of my things, and sent them out to the docks. I kept out my Administrative Blues for tomorrow, with the blue blouse instead of the red, then put on Battle Dress for today, and headed out to make some visits.

No one in my company had heard about the deal I had made yet, though I was sure Colonel Parsons had been informed by now. They were obligated to tell him, so he could request a replacement as soon as the paperwork was signed. So I informed my lieutenants, and gave them some pointers for keeping the men busy while they waited for my replacement, which would come in the next few days or weeks. Then I spent a little time with the men, making the rounds, and shaking hands before moving on.

Sgt. Alvin was still in medical, recovering from broken ribs. I stopped in to see him next.

"Still goldbricking, sergeant?" I announced myself, asking the question from the doorway to his room.

"Cap, good to see you, sir! I got the word they dropped the Inquiry. Congratulations, sir." Sgt. Alvin beamed a chipper smile at me.

"Well, that's not exactly all there is to it. I resigned, Alvin. It was the only way to protect the men from guilt by association."

Alvin got very serious then. "It doesn't surprise me, sir."

"Alvin, I don't think you've ever called me 'sir' this many times in one conversation before. I'm going to start believing that resigning is the best thing an officer can do to increase discipline among the ranks."

Alvin sat up a little in his hospital bed. "Cap, when I retire, I'll look you up. Until then, you will always be referred to as 'sir' in any unit I am running, whenever your name comes up. And with the story of this last mission making the rounds, that will be often, I think."

We talked for a while. Somewhere along the way, I handed Alvin an envelope, sealed and taped. It contained my suggestions for the new commander regarding the different men I had seen performing above standard over the months, and especially from the platoon I had run the last mission with. The new captain might chuck them all, but it was something I could do to help the company out, so I gave it a try. There was also quite a long section about Sgt. Alvin in there, including how the new commander could trust this man with his life, if he did his best and earned a little of Alvin's respect. I didn't mention that part to Alvin, but I figured if he cared, he would figure it out. So I just asked him to give it to the new man, when he showed up.

With that done, we talked a little more, and Alvin asked when I was leaving.

"I still have today as an officer. My resignation takes effect tomorrow, at oh-nine-hundred hours, which is when my transport is scheduled to depart."

"Well, if I can get cleared by the doctors, I'll see you off. You probably plan to be in Colonel Parsons' office at, what, oh-seven hundred?"

"Sounds about right, though I haven't spoken to him yet. But don't trouble yourself, Alvin. You're injured, and . . ."

"Like you said, sir, enough goldbricking, already."

* * *

There were some other people I wanted to see, and I got to them all. Duggard, to whom I owed a special debt of gratitude, for his work on the Halverson issue, as well as his work on the mission. I didn't tell him, but I had already made arraignments with my lieutenants to make sure he got his casino station vacation. I paid for it myself, because I didn't want the lieutenants to have to explain it without me there to take any heat. I had also signed paperwork recommending Duggard for a "Combat Technician" rating, which would increase his pay and prestige, though without actually promoting him in rank. I figured he would enjoy it all the more, getting those two surprises back to back, but I insisted he get the rating before he left on vacation. He had earned the right to wear a combat rating, and I wanted him to get to brag on it a little before the newness wore off.

My last stop was Lt. Harley, who greeted me like a brother, and when I thanked him for what he had done in the Inquiry, he looked at me like I had two heads.

"Really, sir? You're going to thank me for that? I just told the truth. Anyway, what other officer would have attacked *StarFire* with fifty men, just to give me a chance to get away? I owe thanks to YOU, sir. And let me tell you, I played it in court like the other pilots were worried about me being brought up for charges, but every man there was there for one reason: They know most company commanders would have sacrificed the fighters right up front, and made their own run for it. These men won't forget you, sir, and they'll be holding up other officers to the standards you set on that mission." Really, he was so effusive, it would have been embarrassing, except that two men who have been in the trenches together really can't be embarrassed in front of each other after that. Or so it is for me, anyway. I spent a long time talking with John Harley, and we went to dinner together, and then went and had drinks, in memory of the men we lost on the mission. It was late when I finally headed back to my quarters.

When I got there, I found I had one more person to spend a little time with, before it all ended in the morning. Lt. Linda Tillman was waiting in the hallway, outside my door.

"Ms. Tillman. Ah . . . is there something . . . I mean, is this official?"

"No, Captain Lombard. My transfer was approved today, as soon as the Inquiry was dismissed, so I don't care if I'm seen talking with you anymore. Besides, whatever's going on, I don't think Stafford is the kind of man who concerns himself with grudges and such, after the job is done."

"Well, then. Ah, come in, come in," I said, opening the door.

As I said before, my own quarters were quite a bit more cramped than my temporary quarters in the Navy Officer's wing had been. We had to sit on the bunk to sit down at all, but Tillman didn't seem to mind.

We talked for a long time, and she was a little obscure about anything that could be used against her, like the tip off about Halverson. No slow learner, this Lt. Tillman. But she did hint around at a few things, and winked at me when she denied the Halverson tip-off. I actually think it was that wink that got to me, finally slipping past my guard, and Lt. Tillman, now just Linda to me, stayed a long time.

When I woke in the morning, I found a note.

> *Vince,*
> *I'll see you before you leave. There are a couple of things I have to take care of. I hope you don't mind, I checked your com, and saw your note that you'll be at Colonel Parsons' office at 07:00. See you there, if you don't mind having me around (I can wait outside and walk you to your transport.)*
> *Linda*

It was written in lovely, feminine script, and I shouldn't have been surprised to find a note on paper, instead of just a text on my com, like anyone else would have done. I folded up the note, and after dressing, put it in my pocket.

It would be the last time I wore my uniform, and I took my time. If I looked sharp for my Inquiry, today I was immaculate. A Marine's Marine. I cleared the last of my things in the room, and what little I still had around, past what I had already packed up and sent to the docks, fit nicely in a day-bag. It was just enough to travel on. At oh-six-forty-five, I stepped out of my last military quarters, and started walking to the Colonel's office.

Along the way, I bumped into a lot of base personnel, both Corps and Navy. Everyone I saw stopped and saluted. I don't mean, they tossed off a salute as they passed. They stopped. Came to attention. Saluted. It took me ten extra minutes to get to the Colonel's office, because I had to come to attention to return the salutes, as a matter of appreciation for the respect they were showing me. It was a little moving, actually, and I started to hate Navy a little less for it, each time a sailor saluted me in that way, in addition to the Marines who did.

Finally, I arrived, though just on time, rather than the customary few minutes early. I looked for Linda, but didn't see her anywhere around.

Command Master Sergeant Hastings, as was apparently becoming customary around the base that day, also stood to attention and saluted me. I returned the favor, saying, "Sergeant, it was worth all those years of service to receive a salute like that from a man like you. Thank you."

"Thank you, sir. The colonel said to send you right in." Hastings opened the door for me.

I marched in, while Colonel Parsons rose to greet me. He stopped my salute by shaking my hand, as he had once before.

"Vince. Good to see you. Damned shame, the way they railroaded you. Criminal, really. I'm sorry about that."

"Well, sir, you warned me when I took the job, as I recall. You said it was the kind of mission that ruins careers," I reminded him.

"Yes, I did. But that doesn't make it right."

"No sir." By reflex, and for the last time, it echoed in my head: "A Marine can't go far wrong agreeing with his commanding officer." I almost grinned at the habit.

"So, Vince, we have a couple of things to do, I guess."

"Well, I just need your signature on the separation papers, to make it official, I think, sir."

"Oh, I think there's a little more to it than that." He turned to call outside the office. "Sergeant? You have a messenger out there with the materials I requested?"

"Yes sir, he just arrived." the call came back.

"Send him in."

I turned to the door, and saw Sgt. Alvin T. Alvin, in Administrative Dress Blues, coming through the door. And if he was still hurting from his injuries, he didn't show it, with his crisp military bearing.

"Alvin, what are you all dressed up for? I thought . . ."

I fell silent as Alvin came to attention, saluted the colonel, and stood mute. Something is up, I thought. Hastings came in behind him, and Parsons' came out from behind the desk.

"Captain Lombard, in recognition of your years of service, excellent performance of your duties, and the standard of excellence in leadership you have set for your men, it is my great pleasure and honor to promote you to the rank of major." He turned to Sgt. Alvin and held out his hand, while Alvin placed the gold oak leaf insignia in it. Colonel Parsons then executed a parade turn to stand facing me again, and he reached up and removed my captain's bars, and pinned the major's rank on my uniform. He then stepped back to receive the first, and perhaps the only salute from Major Vince Lombard, Galactic Marine Corps, which he returned smartly. Then he put his hand out to shake mine again.

While he shook my hand, he said, "Major, we don't have a lot of time, but I require your attention to one more duty before you are discharged from this service.

"Yes, sir," I replied, wondering what he had in mind.

Sgt. Hastings withdrew from the office while Parsons' grabbed his briefcase, and a moment later he requested that Sgt. Alvin and I follow him. When we got outside the office, Hastings was gone, but Linda was there. She fell in without a word, walking beside me in Administrative Dress Blues herself. So, whatever it was, I figured she was in on it. I leaned over and stage whispered, "You know, I think I like you better in Administrative Whites."

She smiled, but otherwise didn't respond. I gathered she was keeping a secret, and didn't dare speak.

The route took us to the parade grounds, which isn't quite as impressive as it sounds on an asteroid-based defense station. Still, it was the biggest open area on the base, but it was inside the rock, and had atmosphere.

And it was packed. Virtually every off duty person on the base had to be present, and a good number who could slip away from their duty stations for a few minutes. It was easy to tell the difference; they were the ones not in Administrative Dress uniform.

Colonel Parsons looked around quickly, found the platform and lead me up, Linda and Alvin with me, though they stayed one step back from me. As the colonel mounted the steps, the word went out, and the crowd fell into formation, almost silently.

The colonel gave a speech, which I didn't catch most of. Something about answering the call of duty, and setting the standards for the Corps. It was only near the end that I realized he was talking about me being the example of all those things. Then he turned to me, and Linda nudged me, and I got the idea. I stepped forward, next to the podium, and the colonel started speaking again, to me, but next to the microphone, so his words would be picked up.

"Major Vincent Lombard, Galactic Marine Corps, you are hereby invested with the Galactic Heroism Cross, with Fleet and Planetary clusters." I turned to look at him, not sure I heard right, and saw him raise the ribbon above my head, to be draped over my neck. I ducked my head just in time, and after he had hung it there, Parsons turned to the microphone again. He had to wait until the applause died down, but then he went on.

"This decoration is awarded with two clusters. The Fleet cluster is awarded in recognition of gallantry and heroism in the action against the ship StarFire, wherein you successfully assaulted a force not less than twenty times your own unit's numbers, and destroyed an enemy ship clearly superior to any yet seen in this galaxy, further acting on multiple occasions to save the lives of various of your men, at great personal risk of injury or death." Applause, again, but he wasn't done.

"The Planetary cluster is awarded in recognition that, after your successful action against the ship StarFire, it was observed that the wreckage presented a clear danger to a human-inhabited system. At great personal risk, you and Captain Duvall, who is also to be awarded the

Galactic Heroism Cross, with Planetary cluster, posthumously, in a later ceremony . . . the two of you immediately set out to alter the course of the wreckage of *StarFire*, and succeeded in doing so, though it reduced the odds of your successful return dramatically." Applause and cheers drowned out the rest of his speech. Nobody cared, this was a party now, and the ranks fell out and swarmed forward.

By and large, service men and women love to see these sorts of decorations awarded. They see honor reflected on the service, and public recognition of the value of the sacrifices so often made by those who serve. A decoration that is earned is cause for celebration across the military.

I shook hands until my hand ached, and I got my back slapped until I was bruised, and started to worry I might bleed right through the fabric of my uniform. But I watched the time, and in a while, I slipped over to the Colonel. It was nearly time for me to go, but I wanted to speak to him.

"Colonel, is this on the level?"

"Absolutely, Vince. I got it approved by the Commandant himself, about oh-four-hundred this morning. And all the decorations and promotions you recommended are approved for your men, too. I just wish I could have worked it out to let you award those yourself, but at least they'll get the awards." He leaned forward to speak in my ear, not wanting this part overheard. "I think the high command doesn't like Navy screwing with our men. They weren't happy that you took the deal to resign, though they understand that decision. They get it, it was the only way to take care of your troops. Some of them admire you for it. Even though they would rather have fought Navy over the whole thing, some of them realize that the Corps can't fight Navy, politically, and win. Anyway, this is their way of making sure no one doubts their opinion of you, and your performance. And besides, you earned it all, the medals and the promotion." The promotion was particularly significant, because the rank of major is "field grade." The pay takes a big jump there, and the retirement I would be getting soon would be calculated based on my last active rank. This rank, thanks to Colonel Parsons, would be active for one day, enough to make it my "last earned rank," and increase my monthly check a good bit.

"Thank you, sir. For everything. Even for the opportunity to serve on the *StarFire* mission, for your faith in me. We were very lucky, and the outcome could have been much worse in many ways." I started to leave, turned back around. "What about Bowman? Captain Bowman? Colonel, you have to know, he's going to have some trouble with his men, after throwing me under the bus yesterday. His fellow captains aren't going to trust him."

"Yeah, and if he thinks that's rough, wait until he finds out what I do to officers who throw other officers under the bus. Vince, Bowman isn't a great commander anyway. He's brave enough, but lacks imagination, and he shouldn't be leading a ground company. He might serve well in a ship's complement, with a Navy captain looking over his shoulder. I wouldn't get rid of him just for being a bore, but I think his fellow officers will probably start working towards getting him to transfer. We'll see."

I nodded, understanding he wouldn't want to be real specific about the pressures Bowman was about to find himself working under.

"I'd best get going now." I started to salute, but the colonel stopped me. He shook my hand a last time, one hand on my shoulder, and his firm grip doing the talking for him.

I turned and grabbed Alvin and Linda by the arms. "I have to go to the docks. It's almost time."

We walked out together, unobserved in the crowd, and made our way to the civilian transport docks. This time I didn't have to salute anyone, because everyone not busy was at the parade grounds.

When we got there, Alvin took a moment, first.

"Major, I think I've said this before. It's been my honor working with you. You are a fine officer, and a leader of men. I hope I see you again, maybe in a couple of years, when I take my retirement. In the meantime, here's something to keep you sharp." Alvin handed me a small package, wrapped in plain paper. When I opened it up, it was a deck of cards. Instead of plastic, they were fine, particle-paper stock made from real wood, with a slick wax finish. They were antiques, though brand new, un-opened, and probably very expensive. "My daddy gave me those, when I left home to join the G-Marines, eighteen years ago. I was going to open them for my first game when I got out, see if I could make a living as a card player. You're going to have some time, I guess, on a bunch of different transports until you decide where you're going. Cap- I mean, Major, you are the finest card player I have ever been up against and, if you want to, you can land wherever you're going with some money in your pocket. I hope you will use this deck of cards first."

"Alvin . . . thanks. I'm honored." I was honored, and more than a little touched by the gesture. "But you know, for such a fine card player, and all, well, I don't recall ever beating you once!"

Alvin just looked at me like I was talking gibberish. "Sir . . . you had me beat regularly. That's why I always cheated when you were in the game. You would have quite trying so hard, if you knew you could beat me, wouldn't have learned half as much." He held that pose, and that expression, until we both burst out laughing. I would wonder later how much of that was joke, and how much was truth. We shook hands again, a last time, and he left me standing there with Linda.

We talked a little while. What we said is nobody's business. And then I grabbed my day-bag, and started on the ramp to my transport. Linda walked me up, and we waited until the last second, so that I lifted my foot on the station ramp as a Major, Galactic Marine Corps, and set it down on the transport, a civilian.

THE END

THANK YOU

Thanks for reading *StarFire*. Please consider taking a moment to review this book in your favorite forum or site. Thoughtful and sincere reviews help others find the books they enjoy. If you review any Mike Lee books, the author invites you to forward your thoughts directly to him, at the email provided below. If you request it, you will be placed on a promotions list, making you eligible to receive promotional coupons for other Mike Lee books and news regarding new publications as they become available. Email address lists are never sold or distributed, to anyone, and are only used to notify fans of new publications.

The author is always happy to hear from readers, and can be reached at MikeLeeStories@gmail.com. The author is also attentive to requests from fans. If you would like to see other published Vince Lombard stories, please be sure to let your retailer know.

ABOUT THE AUTHOR

Mike Lee lives and writes in Denver, Colorado. He started writing letters to the editor in local newspapers shortly after graduate school, and was pleasantly surprised when they occasionally were run as guest columns. When he worked as a psychotherapist, Mike was solicited to write articles on psychology for a woman's magazine in Bulgaria. He began writing fiction in 2007, published his first novel in 2010. His first book was successful in the e-book market, and is now available in paperback. Mike now writes fiction full time. He can be reached at MikeLeeStories@gmail.com, and is always happy to hear from readers. His dog, Dotty, is his good friend and constant companion.

OTHER TITLES BY MIKE LEE

FEY

The first Vince Lombard story written, *Fey* comes after *StarFire*, chronologically. After leaving the Galactic Marine Corps, Vince is headed home when he finds himself in the center of an espionage adventure, and comes up against the Alliance Navy once again as well as the local police. Although written as a stand-alone novel, readers wrote to request the story of the *StarFire*, which was then written as a prequel. The *Fey* series is now planned as a four book series, of which *StarFire* is the first, though there may be other Vince Lombard stories to tell from his G-Marine days, available in future.

HORKER'S LAW

Book I in *The Six Books of Magic* is the story of Spivver MacAnders. Mike Lee's debut novel has enjoyed significant success.

HORKER'S GOLD

Book II in *The Six Books of Magic*. (Coming soon!)